Maryann Bosah is a British-born author of Nigerian descent. She currently resides in London, where she works as a banker and is an active member of her community, where she volunteers as Choir Director, President of St. Vincent De Paul Society, and Treasurer for the APF Catholic Church mission for St. Wilfred's Parish.

Maryann acclaims that her greatest accomplishment is writing Never Too Late, Anthology of poems, Sid and Lucy meet Etta and Inspirational Christian poems. She is also the mother of four strong and educated children, in addition to being blessed with a love for literature, especially in adventure and crime fiction. She channels her extensive interest in crime mystery and action and has been inspired by writers such as James Patterson, John Wood, Tess Gerristen, Michael Connolly, Martina Cole, and Ian Rankin in writing *Never Too Late*.

Dedication

In the loving memory of my wonderful mother, Patricia Okolo.

Maryann Bosah

Never Too Late

A CIP catalogue record for this title is available from the British Library.

ISBN 9798681233800 (Paperback)

Acknowledgments

I wish to acknowledge my thanks to Peter Standish Evans, who encouraged me to start this journey.

My sincerest thoughts and appreciation go to my husband, family, Chioma Onwere and my special team for their invaluable support while writing and publishing this book.

Finally, I give tribute to the Almighty God for unlocking this literary part in me.

NEVER TOO LATE

"Vengeance, retaliation, retribution, and revenge are deceitful brothers—vile, beguiling demons promising justifiable compensation to a pained soul for his losses. Yet in truth, they craftily fester away all else of worth remaining."

Richelle E. Goodrich, *The Tarishe Curse*

Tonight was the night. His body tingled in anticipation. The hour had finally come. He had watched and waited patiently for this moment. He climbed through the open window and carefully made his way up the stairs. His feet moved to a silent symphony, propelling him to the opening scene of his fantasy.

The breeze tapped fiercely at the window, and the raven-black haired girl hastily got up to close it. Her eyes fell upon the scenery. *Wow! It's nearly Christmas,* she thought as she looked at the neon sign of the Hotel Meridian across the road that shone brightly. The sign looked old and hung precariously on a hinge. The old building stood dejected amongst the high-rise structures that hemmed it in a neighborhood, eerily quiet and decrepit with age.

Snow rained down in large droplets, submerging the entire area under a white blanket and leaving the air cold and fresh. She leaned out of the window and took a deep breath as she drowned out the cacophony of cars in the distance, drifting faintly in the night. Relieved, soon she would be free from this humbug existence.

The fleeting memory of her sister's death triggered a submerged feeling of loneliness; a low purr rolled in her throat as her thoughts travelled back in time to an era and place she once treasured.

Her only sister had died from Leukemia a few years earlier, and the death had taken a deep toll on her parents. They became distant, trapped in their own world. They spoke to her sparingly. Their eyes lost their mirth. The zest for life was gone. The music that usually played in the house was also gone. The music reminded them painfully of Ellen. She could see, as she reflected in her mind, that Ellen was probably loved more by her parents than she would ever be.

Silence had enveloped the house and engulfed its inhabitants; she had lost her parents a long time ago. The accident only moved to accentuate the black hole of despair and sorrow that lay in her heart. She felt so alone. After the tragedies of the last year, she thought that there was no hope for her. She had lost her parents in a ghastly motor accident on Freeway 10 on the 7th of November 1992.

But that was all in the past. Fate had given her a new lease of life when she met Richard. He was the love of her life; her knight in shining armor.

9

Three weeks after the funeral of her parents, she booked a flight to Denver. It was there that she met Richard.

She remembered how she looked after their first encounter. Her long silky hair riding gently on her shoulders, accentuating the beautiful brown eyes that twinkled vivaciously as she smiled. Her small slim nose was nicely crafted and centered firmly in her face. Her cheeks were rosy, silky soft and without blemish. She looked 25 rather than the 38 years she actually was. Love had colored her cheeks, which tingled with pinkness and life. She felt alive. Her face glowed in anticipation of meeting Richard again.

She heard the sound again, the noise abruptly bringing her out of her reverie. She looked around the room as she lay back in her bed. She moved her head slightly and furtively surveyed the dark shadows in the room. The curtain swayed delicately, and a prickling feeling made its way slowly up her back. Was she imagining things? Sitting ramrod straight in bed, she strained her ears, listening for something out of place. There was none. Everywhere was still. But the silence did nothing to quell the quickening pace of her heart.

She turned over and sighed, willing herself to go back to sleep. Burrowing her head deeper into her pillow, she drifted off into a troubled sleep. Startled by the unexpected shift in room temperature and a murmur of soft breathing, a tingling sensation brought her sharply to her senses. A dark shape materialized and stood ominously close to her bed. Her eyes opened in terror as she felt a sudden intrusion. The figure loomed luminously by her bedside, and in one swift movement, a hand shot out and covered her mouth, cutting off the scream rising in her throat. She feebly tried to fight off her attacker, trying desperately to stave off the escalating panic lodged within her heart. Starved of oxygen, her body jerked to an ethereal tune as she felt herself slipping into unconsciousness, long before her body acknowledged the excruciating pain in her brain as it imploded into oblivion. The smothered scream rambled within her trapped throat as life drained slowly out of her.

Chapter 1

Ralph Feldon looked at his watch. The time was 9.04 a.m. The doors swung open and he took his first steps to freedom. For fifteen years he had waited for this moment.

The police warden gave him a violent shove, crash landing him back to the present.

"Move it 732406. You've done your time."

"Get going Feldon," he said gruffly. "I don't want to see your ugly face here again. Got it?"

"Yeah, right. I don't want to enjoy another fifteen years of your lousy hospitality," replied Ralph.

"Well, guys like you can't seem to keep away. Your kind never stay out of trouble for long. Get out."

The iron grill door clanged shut behind him, and before him lay an expanse of open land. He did not look back till he had walked about a hundred yards. He gave a surreptitious nod of satisfaction as he took one last look at what had been his home for the last fifteen years. It was definitely a hellhole. Waldron prison was a notoriously known prison and was regarded as the worst prison in the state. It was rivaled only by Long Island Prison for its subhuman conditions and violent caliber of prisoners. The locals called it 'death row hall'.

The inmates were as hard as nails. It had the highest death rate of prisoners in the county, most of which was attributed to the harsh environment rather than the bloodthirsty nature of the inmates.

Ralph flicked off the speck of dust on the lapel of his grey rumpled suit, adjusted his hat, and walked quickly to the waiting black Lincoln that drew up to the curb. Matthew, his brother, sat at the steering wheel. His fedora hat slouched lazily on the top of his head. His skin was sallow, wrinkles etched deep lines around the eyes, a crooked nose skewed in the center of his face, which was complemented with an angular chin, set as if it had just been carved out of the wall of the Grand Canyon.

Matthew narrowed his eyes to slits as Ralph firmly clasped the handle of the door and yanked it open. He sidled into the car and turned to face his brother.

"Well, little brother, don't I get a warm welcome?" teased Ralph as he watched Matthew, whose lips pursed into a cynic smile.

"Nice to see you," he replied as his eyes shifted and focused on the rear mirror.

He started the engine and put the car into gear, maneuvering the black Lincoln expertly around the corner and onto the highway, constantly staring warily at the rear mirror, searching for any suspicious movement. In his line of business, being cautious was vital for survival.

Ralph leaned back into the car seat, lapping up the softness and luxury of a well-padded seat. Relief filled his mind. The sun radiated its brilliance, and Ralph once again felt exhilarated at the thought that he had made it out of prison alive. He made a silent resolve that he would never go back to there again. He would definitely make sure that it remained that way.

Chapter 2

Angie's Bar was buzzing with activity. It was a Saturday night, and the bar was full. The music played resonantly in the background and the lights were set to emit low flashes of colored lights, creating a romantic setting.

The bar was renowned for its clientele and respectability. Catherine knew that this was the place to be. Money spenders breezing through town frequented the bar. They paid handsomely and did not require much to please. It sure was easy money.

She surveyed the bar for a potential customer. Seated at a table in the far corner of the bar was a young man. He seemed to be about 30 years old. She stood to get a better look. He had dark brown hair casually combed backwards. She could sense that he had broad shoulders under his expensive tweed suit. His eyes roved lazily, sweeping up all the movements in the bar. His gaze lingered invitingly on her as the corners of his lips curved up to reveal his captivating smile.

She moved gracefully towards his table, sauntering seductively in the half cut skirt that accentuated her shapely thighs in response. She stopped short of his table and glided gently into the vacant seat directly opposite the dark-haired man. A shadow of a smile flitted across his face as he viewed Catherine's delectable arrival. His eyes glimmered brightly in the semi-lit bar, giving way to a perfect set of teeth that had formed into a welcoming grin. It showed character, but held a tinge of reminiscence.

"Are you waiting for somebody?" she asked seductively.

"No, I've just met the woman of my dreams," he replied wryly.

She fluttered her eyelids, blushing vividly in response to his comment. *The night could amount to something meaningful,* she thought as she held out her hand.

"My name is Catherine Baxter. I'm here attending a dental convention at Mild Lily Hotel on Fourth Street."

"Steve," he replied modestly. His voice sounded soft, like melting butter. "It's my pleasure to meet somebody as ravishing as you. I certainly did not think that I was going to have such an interesting evening."

He signaled to the waiter as he spoke. The waiter materialized at his side. He looked expectantly at Catherine.

"A Bloody Mary," he answered in acknowledgment of the unspoken question.

"And I'll have a Scotch, please."

The waiter returned almost immediately with the drinks and the menu. They ordered the Chinese dish, which was the bar's special for the day.

Throughout the meal they ate in silence, casting glances at each other in the comfortable silence. Their eyes were laden with desire, and there was an undercurrent charged with electricity. Catherine's heart throbbed to a fluttering tune within her bosom. He was a handsome catch, she surmised. Just the kind of man she had always dreamed of. He seemed so calm and easy to talk to. His voice was so reassuringly soft, like a psychiatrist's. His hands looked well-tended, nails clipped short and the cuticles well cared for. She longed for his touch. The night wore on, and after several rounds of drinks, Steve looked at his watch and said, "Catherine, I was wondering if you would like to come to my room for a nightcap. It's at Mild Flower Hotel, not far from here." His fingers caressed hers as he spoke.

"Would you like the night to go on? I've a conference to go to at 9 a.m. and I need some sleep."

"That would be lovely," she said as she rose unsteadily from the table. Steve's strong arms came up behind her to support her and help her with her coat.

They walked out of the bar together, arm in arm, like two lovers on an obvious mission. Steve flagged down a moving taxi, gave the driver the address of his hotel, and guided an ecstatic Catherine into the back of the cab.

The desk clerk was engrossed in the latest edition of 'Hello' magazine and barely acknowledged the entrance of Steve and his date. Steve steered Catherine to the lifts, led her into the elevator and punched the fourth floor button.

On the fourth floor, he brought out his door key to room 407 and inserted the key into the lock. The door opened to offer a small, crammed room with a double-sized bed placed in the center of the room. Discolored wallpapers, yellowed with stains, lined the squalid room. The carpet was threadbare and looked dusty as the overhead light cast dark shadows on the wall. From where Catherine stood, she could see the outline of the bathroom. The toilet seat was dirty brown, and the walls were encased in tiles chipped and soiled with long use.

Catherine's mind whirled in confusion. What was Steve doing in a dump like this? His clothes and manners conveyed wealth, taste, and elegance. Her eyes flittered around the room and settled on Steve's face with a hint of uncertainty.

His face was expressionless, devoid of the warmth and gentleness that had been there a moment ago. He watched her with keen interest, savoring her distaste, tension and the tinge of primal fear of an animal being caged that he loved most.

Catherine's shoes pierced the silence as she walked shakily to the wicker chair scathed with cigarette marks and sat down. Her eyes roved once more to the bed. The green, flowered bed sheet did nothing to brighten the room, despite the fact that it was freshly washed and ironed.

She gave him a cautious smile. "Well, how about that drink you promised me?" she asked, holding his gaze momentarily before averting her eyes.

She certainly felt uncomfortable, he thought as he filled the two glasses with ice and Teacher's Scotch whisky. He handed her the glass. Their fingers touched, and for an instance, the exhilarating feeling of lust took over. He sipped his Scotch, took off his jacket and dropped it invitingly to the floor. Then casually strolling over to Catherine, he cupped her face in his hands and kissed her gently on the lips, on the cheeks, on the eyes, and then on her neck with urgency.

Catherine's tension slowly dissipated as Steve's amorous advances rose in crescendo, accentuating her senses and ardent desire for the stranger. He smothered her neck with an avalanche of tender kisses that aroused her. In response, she hurriedly stripped off her clothes, delighted that Steve's eyes mirrored lust and appreciation of her well-formed body. A sound caught up in his throat as he ravished her with his eyes. He lapped up the beautiful breasts, well sculpted, round and high, complemented by a slim waist and long tapered legs. *She was the most beautiful yet*, he mused. *Better than all the rest*, he thought with sadness as he went through the final throes of love, the foreplay that would usher in the death of this remarkably stunning woman.

Seven minutes later, she lay there satisfied, her body drenched with sweat after the extraordinary bout of sex. She felt refreshed within. She had yielded herself without any inhibition, with complete abandonment. Her eyes closed, dreamily reliving every moment. Within seconds, her joy turned to terror as she struggled for air. She tried to open her eyes. Her breath became shallow. What was happening to her? Her brain fumbled for an answer, unable to register the searing pain as she foggily fought off death. Moments later, death came thankfully to her rescue.

The next morning, an irate hotel concierge was displeased with the man in room 407. It was 12.25 p.m and he had not checked out. His boss was due to come in at 1 p.m. to check up on the boarding arrangements. He needed to set the records straight. Rising from the reception desk, he hastily made his way up to room 407.

His mind was preoccupied as he fumbled with the keys for the room 407. He knocked lightly on the door. There was no reply. He rapped a second time before inserting the master key into the lock. An eerie silence greeted him and his distracted mind became focused on the need to quickly eject the lodger in the room. He scrabbled with the key, steadied his nerves, and opened the door. A thick musty smell assailed his nose. It was unfamiliar to him. He clambered into the semi dark room as he shirked off a feeling of foreboding. He walked over to the windows in an attempt to open the curtains, a sense of trepidation freezing his constricting heart as he went. The hairs on the back of his neck felt bristly and his heart thumped dangerously on the border of explosion. He drew back the curtain and looked at the bed. He was briefly paralyzed and unable to speak. The terror of what had assaulted his faculties left him numb.

With great effort, he willed his body to move. He took a step towards the door. Horror had gripped him in a wrestling vice. The blood splatter told an unclear but violent story. It displayed what could only be described as a maniacal attack.

The body laid sprawled across the sheets, contorted in death with fatal wounds that had released a steady trickle of now congealed blood. A rancid smell of burnt flesh coupled with the smell of stale blood was so pungent that he threw up. It left a bitter, acrid taste in his mouth.

He pondered fleetingly on what the inexplicable scent could be. The green bed sheet had been stained with multiple splatters of blood distributed unevenly across the floor, bed and walls. The burns appeared to be fresh and extensive.

The clock was ticking. He took a deep breath. This was the first time he had ever had any trouble in the hotel. He knew that it was a rundown place set in a broken-down neighborhood. It was known for its sleazy clientele, ranging from hookers, ex-cons and shady dealers. The price was right if you were just passing through or simply desperate for a room. It was convenient, no questions asked.

In the past, Mild Flower had had its fair share of trouble, but never of this magnitude. There had always been the brawls, busting of prostitutes by the police for stealing from their clients, but never a murder. He was perplexed. His brain sped on in panic, contemplating what the tabloids would say. It would simply destroy the business. Things were already bad. He did not need a killing to put him out of business. He needed an immediate solution.

The police would eat him and his boss raw. He thought about possible closure throughout the investigation, plus the negative publicity. It would certainly wipe them out. There had to be an alternative.

Bold drops of sweat fell freely from his knitted brow. Although the room was relatively cold, he felt the fetid smell of the room build a cloak of confusion and despair in his bones. His brain sought a quick resolution.

There was only one person who could get him out of this mess. Deroni was the answer. He retrieved his steps and closed the door quietly behind him. "Sleep on, pretty one," he mumbled under his breath as he dialed Deroni's number.

After a few rings, a gruff voice came on line.

"Yeah, who is it?"

"I've a situation in room 407," whined the concierge.

"I'll send my boys to clear it up, but you owe me one."

Ten minutes later, the cavalry arrived and the clean-up crew swung into action, clearing all traces of the crime.

Chapter 3

It was 8.30 a.m. when Ralph walked out from the motel room into the morning sunlight. He was going to pay Johnny Deroni a visit and collect in full.

He needed to make plans and catch up on things around him. He had phoned Deroni, and an 11 o'clock meeting had been arranged. He had time to kill and asked Matthew to drop him off at the corner of James Street and drove to meet up with some of his old crew members.

Ralph strolled into Lance's Breakfast Café that was congested with workers on the go. He positioned himself at the last table at the end of the bar, where he could get a good view of people who came and went out of the café. He scanned every face in the room searching for anomalies and faces that stood out. His manner was of feigned nonchalance and covert scrutiny.

He decided to relax a little when his radar failed to pick up any threats. Pretending to be a customer, he ordered toast, scrambled eggs, a rasher of bacon, and a cup of tea. Immediately after the waitress had taken his order, he walked silently towards the rear of the café, where the telephones were lined against the peeling chestnut-colored wall, degraded by cigarette stains, smoke, and mottled splays of what could either be tea or coffee.

His fingers nimbly punched in the number he wanted, and he placed his ear close to the receiver, waiting for the connection to go through. A click was followed by the sound of a young woman's voice, who said:

"Good morning, you are through to King Holdings, who would you like to speak to?"

Ralph hesitated, suddenly unsure of what to say.

"I'd like to speak to Mr. Thomson, please."

More clicking in the background. A ten-second silence, before a baritone voice came on the line:

"I'm sorry; Mr. Thompson is unavailable at the moment. Would you like to leave a message?"

A man with a slight limp brushed against Ralph before he had a chance to respond. Ralph's mind instinctively veered him to the right, dropping the receiver onto the cradle in one singular motion. The man carried on nonplussed, limping towards the men's toilet without a backward glance. Ralph, on the other hand, was suddenly uneasy as he watched the limping man disappear as the toilet door closed. The strangers limp triggered a feint memory that made his stomach churn like curdled butter.

He walked back to his table to discover that his breakfast was now cold. He signaled to the waitress, who replaced the barely touched coffee and turned away with a sultry look on her face.

He ate his breakfast in silence, constantly re-surveying the café for anything out of place.

Five minutes later, two cars pulled up in front of the café, a large black SUV and a black Mercedes jeep with tinted glasses. A third car, a BMW drove past the café and disappeared at the next intersection. A tingling sensation engulfed Ralph as he watched three men alight from the SUV. The guy in front was a brisk, energetic man with wide shoulders and the narrow hips of an athlete. His dark grey flannel suit was worn loosely to hide the slight bulge of his semi-automatic pistol strapped under his left arm.

The second thug walked with precision. His raven-black hair looked oily slick and was combed back to reveal an unobtrusively large skull. His face had a beetroot glow, while his eyes reflected a depth of darkness that instilled fear. The third figure to slip out of the SUV kept his face down. His broad poncho hat protected his face from recognition. He walked with a stoop, conveying the impression of a body ravaged by age.

The three men walked across the street and straight into the head office of Deroni Enterprise. Four other men spilled out of the black Mercedes, blended in with the stream of pedestrians, and were soon lost in the flow. Ralph abandoned his coffee as he watched with rapt attention. He dropped a few $1 bills and left the café. His heart felt constricted within his chest and the vein in his head pulsated dangerously. He realized that things were not going as planned. He struggled to maintain his composure while his eyes raked the milling flow of people.

Sure enough, about fifty yards away, his trained eyes spotted the four men strategically spread out in formation, covering both the entrances and exit to the Deroni complex. Without moving his head, he directed his gaze northwards, ensuring that his eyes did not unveil his surveillance of the situation. He fumbled with his mobile phone, but kept his eyes on the quarry.

"Matthew, I need you. Pick me up at the corner of Garner. Trouble's brewing, and I don't want to be a part of it."

From behind, he felt the muzzle of a gun wedge into his back. The man with the limp was right behind him. Ralph was conscious of the fact that people passing by were oblivious of his situation. The man held an arm on his shoulder and guided him down the street.

"Walk slowly, and don't try anything, do you understand?" he said.

Ralph was puzzled, but his apprehension numbed his senses. He was distraught. A cold sweat creased his brow as he walked before his assailant. He rummaged through the crevices of his mind in search for a plan.

Moments later, he saw the three thugs reappear onto the street and drive off. The BMW sped up, and its doors opened to swallow its passengers. A blast from the thirteenth floor of the Deroni Complex ricocheted in the air, and screams reverberated all around. Bricks and shards of glass rained down onto the street, setting off a panic. Ralph stood rooted to the spot as he watched the stricken faces of people swirling around and scampering for cover as they watched in horror. It was like re-living an enactment of the falling twin towers of September 11. The distraction created momentary reprieve. Ralph stepped back, and quick swung an elbow at the unknown aggressor, following it up with a sharp side kick and knocking the assailant off-balance as he keeled over in pain.

Ralph was on the run long before he heard Matthew's distinct voice zooming in on him. "Hurry up, get in," he said in an urgent and disquieted voice.

With a leap, Ralph scaled the sidewalk and was into the waiting haven which was Matthew's car.

In the rear mirror, he witnessed the attacker muster his dignity and bark orders at the men in the BMW as they scrambled to depart from an already chaotic scene.

Chapter 4

The night was cold and cloudless. A few stars twinkled distantly in the sky. He waited patiently in his black BMW convertible for his prey.

He was oblivious to the people who were running to catch the night bus with his thoughts centered on the kill.

For three weeks he had studied his prey. He knew her routine, and relished the fact that she was a private person. She had very few friends, and kept a 10–4 p.m. shift job at Delaware's casino.

Anne Marie Cummings was born in New Hampshire. After twenty-two boring years at home, she decided to strike out and make a life for herself. She was tired of village life. The bright lights and curiosity of urban life intrigued her. Many of her friends had come up to the Big Apple and made it. She was determined to do so too.

. What was she going to do? She pondered her problem, unaware of the man in the black BMW convertible watching her from afar.

The streets were quiet as she ruminated on her problem. At the intersection of Holly and Down Street, she looked to ensure that there were no moving cars passing in either direction before crossing the road.

Midway across the street, she heard the purring of a car engine come to life. She paused in her strides, craning her neck to get a better view of the oncoming vehicle, while debating furiously within herself. Unexpectedly, she was hit by the speeding car. The force of the hit left her slumped sideways on the cool concrete road. She struggled painfully to her feet as she heard the car come to an abrupt stop. A man quickly alighted from the car, his face shielded away from direct light. He rushed to her side.

"I'm terribly sorry. I wasn't looking. I only bent down to pick up my cell phone, and em…" his voice trailed off. "Please, let me help you," he said, pausing lamely as Anne Marie surveyed her wounds.

"Let me get you to a hospital."

She looked up at him. He looked a little flustered. The ache in her ribs made her cry out. It felt excruciating. She swooned. The young man expertly grabbed her, breaking the fall, then gently steered her towards the open door of his BMW convertible. She lay back into the soft décor of the car seat as the stranger got in beside her and started up the car. Anne Marie pursed her lips and ran her tongue over her chaffed lips. She felt a sudden prick in her arm and fainted. She heard him whisper, "Rest now, for you will soon find peace."

Her eyes struggled to stay open but they felt incredibly heavy. A shadow of a smile flickered across his face as he watched her slip into the darkness of the damned. *The night had been satisfyingly successful*, he thought as he sped along the highway, whistling a song under his breath, having successfully achieved two kills in one week.

The phone rang at 2.15 a.m., Michael stirred lazily from his sleep. His hands moved instinctively to the phone.

"Michael, there's something you better come down and see," barked Tony, his partner.

"Can't it wait?" Michael asked groggily as he sat up in bed.

"No, I'm afraid it won't keep. A young girl's body was found close to Upton Park," Tony added icily.

"I'll be there in ten minutes," he said as he pulled back the duvet, he picked up his clothes draped over the chair and stumbled woozily down the flight of stairs to his SUV parked outside the front of his semi-detached house.

He cut across Rose Boulevard and the Intersection of 43rd before grinding to a halt in front of the main entrance of Upton Park. The smell of burning rubber and screeching tires announced Michael's arrival.

Tony stood peering over the body, taking snapshots of the dead girl who had been wrapped up in a blue blanket frayed and spotted with flecks of oil and blood splatters.

"So, what have we got here?" Michael asked.

"I'm not sure. It seems to be a young Caucasian woman between 20–30 years. There are strangulation marks and severe burns on her forearms and abdomen. She's really messed up. Just look at the trauma to the head. This was definitely the work of a madman," Tony concluded.

The ambulance siren blared loudly as it came to a halt. Two paramedics smartly appeared from the ambulance, stretcher in tow, moving with professional expertise. The paramedics rushed through the maze of flocking people, conveying the urgency of their mission. They gently placed the corpse onto the stretcher, and whisked it away in direct consonance with the clicking cameras.

A reporter from ABC cable news moved surreptitiously near to Michael, dragging her microphone and trail of camera men behind her.

"Detective Michael, can you tell us what happened here tonight?"

"Heh! Get the goddamn microphone out of my face. This is an ongoing murder investigation, that's all you need to know."

Michael stylishly ducked under the yellow tape and made it to his SUV closely parked near the curb. Tony slid into the driver's seat and started the car.

"I think we'd better follow up at the morgue. It's certainly going to be a long night," said Michael.

"Well, what's left of it," Tony retorted as he sped away from the scene.

Chapter 5

Father Murphy moved with purposeful strides down the corridor on his way to the rectory as his black cloak hung loosely around him in billowing folds. He felt agitated at having to conduct the morning confession rather than participate in the seminar on spiritual enlistment starting in the vestry.

The church bell rang, serving as a reminder that he was already five minutes late for confession. He brushed past the heavy curtain that draped the side door leading out onto the altar and hurried down the aisle. He greeted a scanty cluster of parishioners who were anxiously waiting for penance. His face was flushed, and he wiped his brow with his spotted handkerchief. He rubbed his temples and took a deep breath. His breathing slowed and returned to a steady beat.

The housekeeper was the first into the confessional box. Her black, laced scarf was tied tightly around her head.. Strands of her raven-black hair tinted with grey streaks, reflecting the onset of age and her fading beauty. Her head remained slightly bent as she cupped her callused hands in the mode of prayer.

In low monotones, she started to recite the confessional litany, "Forgive me, Father, for I have sinned. It has been two weeks since my last confession…" her voice droned on as she poured out her heart. Father Murphy waited till she had finished, and gave her absolution. Two Hail Mary's, one Our Father and a Glory be to God ended his verdict.

Within twenty minutes he had cleared the confessional area, and about to get up when he heard harried breathing from the stall. He looked through the vent to see a young man sat there in the semi-dark stall. His body radiated tension as cold sweats formed all over his face. His knees bobbed up and down as his eyes flickered from left to right in reaction to any sound.

Father Murphy asked,

"What troubles you my child?"

The Father was met with absolute silence but noticed the agitated movements persisted from the individual occupying the stall.

Minutes passed until the breathing of the two occupants pierced the stillness of the church.

Father Murphy had other responsibilities to attend but did not want to be dismissive. Sitting up right and taking a deep breathe, he decided to try again before leaving.

"I don't know where to start. I keep having these recurring dreams. It's like I'm really there, committing these… I feel like I'm trapped in some sort of semi-reality, Father."

The man's voice sounded vaguely familiar but devoid of emotion and troubled. His words did not match his tone and it was hard to concentrate with the heel of what seems to be a hard-sole shoe still tapping off the stall's wooden floors.

The strangers sudden disclosure surprised father Murphy who was still unsettled by his nervous movements and thoughts of getting back to his other responsibilities. Trying his best to regain composure, he pushed through with a crack in his voice,

"Yes, my son, go on."
And without hesitation the man continued.

"I wake up from these nightmares very confused. Each time I wake up, I'm covered in blood. I don't know where I am or where I've been to. I see these girls everywhere I go. They always remain in my visions."

"Can you describe any of the girls?" Father Murphy probed gently.

"Oh God! There are many faces. So many voices. They are not safe" sobbed the young man

"You are in God's house my son; you are safe here. He has sent you to me so that I can help"

Suddenly, the man's sobbing ceased and there was a brief moment of silence.

"is everything ok" asked Father Murphy. "Should I call .."

A voice much deeper and confident than the one he had grown used to emerged from the young man's confessional box cutting him off to ask

"Then it must be destiny, right? They all came to me because it was their destiny like it is mine to be here with you, right?".

Father Murphy feeling troubled instinctively chimed in

"Our destiny is the path that God has laid out for us based on our actions, hence why he said in Jeremiah 17:10,
I the Lord search the heart and examine the mind to reward each person according to their conduct, according to what they deserve."

Father Murphy heard the man rise to his feet, "Thank you father, I will follow God's will"

Then the scuttling of feet followed as the young man stumbled out of the confessional.

Father Murphy rose and shouted, "Don't go. Let me help you."

It was too late, the young man had already left the church. The boy's retreating back was all Father Murphy saw when the church door slammed shut with finality.

Chapter 6

Blaine walked for hours mumbling to himself. He wrestled with the idea that the priest would tell the police and if he should go back to the church.

The rising sun fell warmly onto his back, and he felt comforted. He pulled the sunglasses closer to the bridge of his nose, shielding his face from further recognition. Then he raised the top collar of his jacket to mask the tattoo of a giant cross on his neck.

He wandered aimlessly, absorbing the hustle and bustle of morning traffic while he tried to figure out what he should do. He doubled back to where he had started, and cautiously hid in an archway opposite the church from where he could watch the entrance. His stomach raged within, and his face was plastered with indecision.

How much had he divulged to the priest?

Could the priest be trusted?

Was the priest on the phone to the police?

Would the priest be able to identify his voice?

A cold sweat broke out on his brow as he brooded on what to do.

His mind raced back to a time when he was an altar boy. *How times had changed*, he thought to himself. He had not been to church in years. His voice had also changed. The priest would not remember it, of that he was sure.

His worry persisted, so he continued his surveillance of the church till late evening. His stakeout yielded no dividend. No one had gone in or come out the church all day. The time was now 5.45 p.m., and hunger pangs stabbed mercilessly into his side. His eyes and legs were also tired of standing for such a long time. He felt that it was time to move on.

He left his sheltered alcove and walked away, blending in with the evening rush hour with Father Murphy stapled to his mind.

Chapter 7

Father Murphy was perplexed by the last morning confession. Activities in the church had occupied his mind till 10 p. m. that night. In the silence of the old church, the thoughts resurfaced, wrestling with his conscious. Should he break his priestly vow?

He didn't have enough information to pass on to the police. Besides, the young man did not openly admit that he committed any crime. He was torn by the fact that he was also under oath not to disclose information that could be used against the stranger. For the time being, it was better to keep quiet and pray. Hopefully, the young man would have the courage to confess or turn himself to the police. Either way, Father Murphy was filled with great sadness and frustration. He knew that the young man was heavily riddled with guilt. He posed a serious threat to society. He felt powerless to this predicament. Plagued by these troubled reflections, he slept a light, delirious sleep, distracted by roaming thoughts of death.

In the weeks that ensued, Father Murphy tried to continue a life of normalcy by trying to push the nagging, obtrusive thoughts to the back of his mind. He was torn between steering the police in the right direction and his priestly vow to keep the act of confession secret.

The shocking discovery of a young woman's brutalized corpse at Lincoln Park haunted him, catapulting his meditation into oblivion. He was racked with guilt. His refusal to disclose the confession of the young man earlier may have resulted in the death of an innocent victim. He could no longer finish his meals and struggled to sleep. He had applied for a transfer to Brentwood Abbey in attempt to diffuse the battle between his conscience and oath.

He knelt and prostrated before the altar in prayer. He prayed in a guilt -ridden tone while fighting to hold back his tears. He asked,

"My Father, whom art in heaven, you said that 'Whoever pursues righteousness and kindness will find life, righteousness and honor. But is there any honor or righteousness in betraying the oath I have taken to serve you? Please send your light and guide my life back to your path"

A feeling of rushing air suddenly enveloped him as he heard a whooshing sound. The candelabra from the altar struck ruthlessly on the exposed part of his neck. His blood splayed in tiny splatters across the altar, carpet, and the high, carved wooden seat reserved for the priest.

Father Murphy lay face down on the red carpet. A growing pool of blood, mirrored a slow flowing river as life drained out of him.

The young man looked down at Father Murphy as he wriggled and slowly stooped moving; conflicting thoughts of regret mixed fascination and euphoria from the kill trose to the surface.

The parish clock chimed. The time was 10 p.m., and the housekeeper looked fleetingly at the clock. It was one hour past the end of her shift. Father Murphy was supposed to collect the keys to the vestry before she left for the day. She had waited patiently for over an hour, and her patience was now running thin. She put her head around the door and peeped into the church. *Strange*, she thought, *there were no parishioners in the church*. Her eyes scanned the arches to determine whether Father Murphy was engaged in changing the flowers at the mini statues of Jesus, Mary, and St. Jude.

The stillness in the semi-lit church was unsettling. The inner sanctum was relatively cold, and the petite housekeeper shuddered involuntarily. She drew her worn cardigan closer to her as she scoured the empty church. It was eerily quiet. Her shoes made a soft clacking noise as she made her way towards the central aisle. *Might as well lock the place before Father Murphy decided to show up*, she thought to herself.

Fifty yards down the aisle, her steps halted. She was transfixed by the pool of blood her eyes were trying hard to comprehend. Her hands came up instinctively to cut off the soul-wrenching cry that escaped from her lips. She sobbed uncontrollably and ran out of the church and into the presbytery where the parish phone was located.

In a tremulous voice, she reported the crime with as much control as she could muster. Within minutes, a police car had been dispatched.

The sounds of blaring sirens thundered in the distance, wrecking the already frayed nerves of the distressed housekeeper. Distinct shouts followed as Michael shouted out orders to the policemen in uniform that had arrived with him. The flurry of footsteps confirmed the arrival of the police, who were flocking to the religious corner like a swarm of bees.

Michael and Tony looked on in dismay. The macabre act staged before them resembled a scene out of the Manson family archives. The county coroner brushed past them and stooped over the body. After a few minutes' examination of the body, he beckoned the two detectives over, ready to give his preliminary prognosis. His initial assessment was that the priest had been bludgeoned to death with a blunt object. He pointed to the trail of blood indicating that the body had been moved from its original position and turned over. The trail of blood left an unsavory pattern of visible rage not disassociated with a maniacal attack.

"He's been dead for about two hours," concluded the coroner. "Even if we had found him earlier, I doubt that he would have survived the trauma. Look here, there's internal hemorrhaging in the left side of the brain. It's certainly depressed with a comminuted left parietal fracture. I will get a better look at him back at the morgue."

Detectives Michael and Tony took pictures, made notes, and watched the forensic technicians extract pertinent clues to be analyzed at the lab.

Later on, they both decided to interview the housekeeper, who was now relatively calm and ready to co-operate. She sniffed on her handkerchief, and her face was clearly distorted with bulging, puffy eyes and a reddened nose enlarged from excessive crying. Her eyes flickered from Michael to Tony and brimmed over with more droplets of tears. Her mouth quivered slightly, but she answered the questions asked in rapid succession.

After forty-five minutes of intense questioning, the strain on the poor woman's face was evident. She looked devastated. Pityingly, they let her go and drove back to the precinct to compile their notes. A long night lay ahead of them, surmised Tony as Michael watched Tony plunk a pot of coffee on his table and recline into his easy chair, ready for work.

The joys of police work, Michael thought as he surveyed the bulging file on his desk.

Chapter 8

Ralph fumed in rage. He had been forced into hiding for over two months. There had been a failed attempt to kill Deroni, and he did not know if he was in line to be killed too. He is an associate of Deroni's but also had a few enemies of his own who were organized enough to make such a bold move in search for him.

The stress and boredom of being holed up in a sleazy hotel was also weighing heavily on his frayed nerves. He had desperately tried to put a mental pin on his frustrations but his patience was edging threateningly close to becoming undone like the pin on a grenade. Anger was clouding his better judgment.

He had to leave his coop. Matthew had asked around. Things seemed to have simmered down. The mob hit had failed. Deroni was said to be at Palm Springs Hotel, a remote place situated two hundred and forty miles away from the Corona wasteland. A formidable place to go to, dried desert land devoid of traffic and passersby. It was a parched, forlorn area of land, sparsely littered with withering plants and little cover. You could be seen approaching from miles away, making it an ideal hideaway for anyone on the run.

Ralph was almost broke, but he was determined to track down Deroni. He did not go to prison for fifteen years for nothing. Deroni owed him a share of the $12 million for keeping his mouth shut. He left the hotel, committed to finding Deroni and making him pay.

Matthew pulled into a nondescript petrol station to ask for directions. A young man working the pumps ambled over to Matthew's Taurus. His eyes looked as desolate as his surroundings. He wore a blue beret, which was bleached white by the scorching sun, to shield his sand colored hair and faded blue dungarees that were worn and torn around the knees from constant wear.

"What you need today, Sir?" he asked.

"Directions to Palm Springs Hotel and a full tank," replied Matthew.

Whizzing around in his seat, he said to Ralph,

"Need to take a leak. I'll be back in a minute." The young man simply tapped on the window and pointed to the back of the office.

"There's a toilet out back if you want to use it," he drawled and resumed filling the petrol tank.

Ralph observed Matthew as he walked away and cornered the office building. The building's windows were mottled with dust. The door to the office sagged from its rotting beams and was discolored from too much sunlight. *Not much work was going on in that office*, thought Matthew. It probably wouldn't be safe to go into the toilet either. He might as well relieve himself outside. No one is watching anyway. Ten yards to the toilet, he looked around. It appeared to be safe.

He pulled down his zipper and relieved himself. He turned to make sure that he had not been seen, and then took a few steps back the way he came. His eyes caught sight of a poster pasted at the side of the toilet wall. Out of curiosity he drew closer.

He was struck dumb by the obituary of Anne Marie Cummings, who had been brutally murdered and found in a dumpster somewhere in Blue County in March. He ripped off the poster from the wall and stuffed it hurriedly into his breast pocket.

Ralph threw Matthew a quizzical look when he returned to the car. He sensed that something was wrong, but did not say anything. Matthew sidled into his seat and reached into his wallet, withdrew a handful of bills, and forced it into the young man's hands, averting his eyes as he did so.

They left the petrol station with a quake of dust trailing behind, leaving a puzzled petrol attendant behind them.

"What happened back there? Did someone peek and see how small it is?" Ralph asked playfully.

Matthew said nothing. His eyes firmly fixed on the road before him.

"What's going on? You certainly left that place in hurry." Silently, Matthew withdrew the crumpled poster from his pocket and handed it to Ralph with an exasperated sigh.

Ralph's face lost its color turning ghostly white with a look of dismay set on his face. The old picture in the obituary was their half-sister. Her body had been found in an alley in Blue County.

Anyone with information on her brutal murder was to contact homicide detective Michael on 045-321-6270.

"Well, Matthew, it seems like we've got unfinished business in Blue County. Let's go see Deroni, get our money, and pay this Detective Michael a visit. We must find Anne Marie's killer."

For the rest of the trip, Ralph and Matthew drove in silence. Both lost in their thoughts on how to exact revenge on Anne Marie's killer.

Shortly before 4.20 p.m., they arrived in Corona. They asked the friendly bar owner for directions to Palm Springs Hotel. The bar owner warned that it was not often travelers ventured into that area for dangerous reasons but the two were unphased by his warning.

Ten minutes later, they parked in front of the hotel. It was a dead, isolated place. The stillness was punctuated by the buzzing of mosquitoes and flies in flight. The brothers travelled light. They carried only one valise case crammed with a few shirts, underwear, toiletries and two pairs of trousers. Their arsenal completed the load.

The bellboy looked up as they walked into the hotel, but made no move to assist them. A bored look was pinned on his face. The tingling bell that had announced their arrival alerted the receptionist, who hastily appeared from the inner room re-adjusting his tie.

"Good evening, gentlemen, Welcome to the Palm Hotel, how may I be of assistance?" he said in a smooth voice untainted by the southern drawl Ralph had expected.

"A room with two single beds would do fine," Ralph replied.

"Certainly, sir. That will be $75 for the night. How long do you intend to stay?

"Not sure yet" Replied Ralph.

"Room 216, Bill. Take their luggage up."

The bell boy hovered instantly by their side and picked up the case. Without a word, he led the way to the elevators and to room 216. At the door, Matthew dismissed the bell boy and carried in the case. Ralph followed thereafter.

"Deroni is in room 351. I think I'll pay him a little visit. He's signed under the name John Berotti. I did a little digging earlier. All it took was a $50 bill. Let's go"

Outside Deroni's room stood three of his deadliest assassins. Two flanked the outer corridor, while the third placed himself between the stairs and the elevator. All three men were bulky and moved with stealth.

Two minutes later, Ralph stood face to face with Deroni. Deroni's personal bodyguard patted him down and directed him to a cane chair placed in the furthermost part of the room. Ralph walked slowly, weighing all his options. He knew that he was in a delicate position, but he was not scared. He had insurance.

Deroni looked tired. His eyes had taken on a gaunt, hollow look. He watched Ralph with wary, distrusting eyes that mirrored his doubt. Ralph, on the other hand, lapped up with private satisfaction the shrunken cheeks and deep stress lines etched into the hermetic face of Johnny Deroni. *He definitely looked dour*, thought Ralph. He decided to keep the meeting brief. The meeting was over before it started. Deroni handed Ralph a check for $2.6 million and waved a hand in dismissal.

Ralph left the room, quite relieved that everything had gone on well. With the cheque, he could take care of Matthew without engaging in criminal activities. They both could make a clean break away from a life of crime. Set up a car-mart business selling cars. Neither he nor Matthew had managed to get an education. He knew that Matthew was an excellent mechanic. He, on the other hand, made sure that he taught himself to read and write in prison. He had been a voracious reader of literature, history, and politics. He also made sure that he learned enough law to keep him permanently out of prison.

He felt good about it too. But first he needed to stamp out the ugly thirst for revenge that was pervading his thoughts.

Chapter 9

Michael woke up with an excruciating headache. His head hammered from lack of sleep. The horrific images from the previous night still vividly replaying in his mind. "What a mess" he whispered in disappointment. First the young women and now a priest. Both murders could be the act of two different killers but if it was carried out by the same person, are they still evolving in their choice of victims, or was it situational? If it was situational then under what circumstances?

Was the killer's chances of staying hidden compromised? did they have a history with the priest or the church? Maybe they saw an opportunity and took it? Michael was paralyzed by thought and barely moved from his resting position since waking.

The recent string of murders strongly pointed towards a serial killer but last night's murder did not match the killer's M.O. He worried that the simple-hearted folk of Blue County were now exposed to a violent invasion of the community's sense of security.

The town's only university, Blue County University, had recently been nominated to hold the world conference on genetic engineering, and a lot of scientific geniuses were expected to fly in within the next four days.

It was to be an international event. Delegates and professionals from different countries were expected to attend.

The FBI was sidelining the local police because of the recent spate of killings in the area. It was rumored that Peter McClaren, a decorated FBI expert, would execute the final security arrangement in conjunction with Agent Cory Raines. Agent McClaren was a sharp dresser. He had been unruffled by the pressure, long man hours, and few clues associated with several high -profile cases that he successfully solved. The last was the Sock Killer, who used the method of lobotomy to take the lives of twelve victims before he was finally caught.

McClaren, Raines, and the Chief of Operations were in Blue County two days early to ensure that there were no surprises lurking in this once sleepy town. McClaren was determined that nothing was going to interfere with the international conference.

Chapter 10

The boys screeched with laughter. It was not often that they were allowed to play in Haverlock Park. The park had been closed for two weeks after the rape incident. A woman had been raped by a trio who had followed her through the park one Sunday morning as she did her daily morning jogging exercise before preparing for work.

Alan kicked the ball pretty hard; it went sailing through the air and landed with a heavy thud in a bush of brambles and wild flowers, about a hundred yards away.

The boys stopped laughing and pointed to Alan with serious eyes. "Well," they chirped in unison. "You kicked it down there, now go and get it." Alan's face turned pink from embarrassment as the boys continued to taunt him.

He walked with false bravado towards the bushes. The overhang from the fir tree cast dark shadows. This part of the park was eerily quiet and obscure. A putrid stench assailed his nostrils through the thicket as he searched for the ball. A moment later, his eyes locked onto the ball that was wedged precariously close to the fettered fence that was rotten by age. Next to the ball were the decaying remains of a body that lay sprawled upside down while the worms feasted hungrily on their host.

A shrill cry ensued as he scampered up the embankment. His eyes filled with terror as he panted in short breaths, fleeing the horrifying scene. His bewildered friends huddled together in consternation, waiting for Alan to explain himself.

"Call the police. There's somebody dead down there," Alan said as he gagged and vomited in quick succession while tears streamed down his reddened cheeks.

The boys stood shivering. Their faces streaked with worry as they heard the blaring sirens draw steadily closer. The strobes of lights converged on what could only be construed to be a two-mile radius.

Michael and Tony flashed their badges and were let past the crime tape. The coroner nodded grimly in the direction of the other crime scene detectives. The detectives interviewed Alan and his friends to determine how much they had actually seen. The woman had been dead for a while. Rigor mortis had worn off. The woman's lifeless arm hung flaccidly on the gurney as the paramedics whisked the body away.

From across the street, the killer viewed the setting with interest. He savored the fact that he had again made news. For most of his life, he had been relegated to the background. His mind spun back to the rush he experienced killing Sally Jane.

He had been a young boy and was constantly beaten by his father, a regressive drunkard. He was an only child who could not be protected by his mother. His mother had died when he was nine years old, having been subjected to the same domestic abuse from his father for many years.

Steven Blaine had taken care of his old man when he was fourteen. But that, perhaps, was not soon enough. At the age of eleven, he made his first kill. He had been disturbed the night he killed Sally Jane, a new girl at Princeton High. The surge of excitement he received from watching Sally Jane die was erotic. He watched Sally Jane squirm in her own blood. Like a villain in a bad dream, mesmerized by the power of taking a life.

. He felt light headed, enthralled by flashbacks of Sally's helplessness that was demonstrated in her flailing and thrashing. He was intrigued by the spasms that shook her body as life dissipated from it. He stood paralyzed by the adrenaline rushing through his veins as he recollected the night and the thrill of hiding her body in his private hideout.

Sally's parents had notified the police and a local search was organized. As weeks turned into months, her family knew that the chances of recovering her body was bleak. Sally's case was retired to missing persons and finally to unsolved crimes.

Her death had disturbed Steven for a while. But with time, his addiction to killing grew, and, eventually, surpassed any atom of conscience that had remained in the crevices of his mind. The thrill of power to execute death at will was indescribable, and superseded the thought of being caught. Rather, he experienced an insatiable craving to inflict death.

Chapter 11

The drive to Blue County had been tedious. Their car had been stopped at the checkpoint. They had been delayed and had to wait endlessly as the security guard scrutinized their driving license and travel documents. Far more embarrassing was the fact that Ralph and Matthew were made to stand conspicuously at the guard stand while a security guard made a show of patting them down.

They felt humiliated at being manhandled under the pretext of a routine security check. The chief security officer crosschecked the number plates on the blue Chevy for the umpteenth time. He was disappointed that the driving license came back clean, and tossed it back recklessly, clearly showing how disgruntled he was. It was obvious that strangers were not welcomed in Blue County.

Thirty minutes later, Matthew and Ralph pulled up in front of Blue County Central, a small motel located four miles away from the town center. They checked in and retired to their room, exhausted by the long journey and harassment by the local law enforcement. Ralph was irritable and steamed about the way they were disrespected.

Around 8 o'clock, the first pang of hunger had set in. They stopped at Angie's Bar and grabbed a quick meal of French fries, double cheese burger, a strawberry sundae, and two beers.

They sat back and watched the locals' troop in and out of the bar. The tempo and blast of the juke box contributed to the ascending level of noise that competed closely with the crescendo of voices speaking at the same time.

Ralph marveled at the racket created in such a small space. Studying local life was boring. Cruising and succumbing to the inviting lights of the west side of Blue County was a more exciting prospect. Matthew and Ralph toured the various bars hoping that they would be able to pick up snippets of gossip and idle conversation about Anne Marie's murder.

By 3 a.m., they were both disillusioned by the futility of their night cruise, and decided to go back to the motel for a well-earned rest. Throughout the night, both brothers tossed and turned, harried by the thought that the killer might escape judgment. Ralph resolved vehemently that he would get to the bottom of things. Anne Marie's death had to be avenged. With this deluge of agonizing notions, he fell asleep.

Chapter 12

2.30 a.m.

The phone rang. Hamilton woke up with a quick jolt. His fingers gripped the receiver as the caller relayed his message. It was time to move the plan into action.

He grunted in acknowledgment and dropped the receiver. He reached for the side lamp and pressed the button, immediately filling the right side of the room with a dim, surreal light. Within moments, his fingers artfully dialed 05-4321-25431. The rendezvous point, Lienkhang Airport at 0600 hours.

His thoughts were on how to mobilize Avery within the time constraints. Avery was a known assassin, presently on assignment in Berlin, Germany. He had been ordered to take out an elitist stock broker, Rudolph Kornmayer, who wanted to divulge the financial trading secrets of OXYZOM Corporation, the sole producer of a recently invented substitute for weaponized anthrax, to the French government for a whopping $4 billion. The American and British governments feared that the exposure of OXYZOM Corporation—a privately-funded organization working in conjunction with both governments—would be at risk of public scrutiny.

Kornmayer had to be eliminated immediately, the safety of the world depended on it.

Avery picked up on the third ring. He had been watching the target for the past one week, committing Kornmayer's schedule to heart. The stakeout had involved gathering information on access points into Kornmayer's impenetrable house, security codes, number of security men, the behavior and timetable of his immediate family.

Avery went over every detail by rote, closely timing every member of the house's activities and noting all deviations. His planned execution was scheduled for 2.45 a.m. By then, Kornmayer would have been asleep for at least two hours. He rarely woke up before 6.15 a.m.

Avery made his way stealthily across the west side of the compound. The regal mansion's back was protected by the plush greenery of Acacia and Palm trees. He scaled the walls with ease, and waited. The patter of dogs' feet followed by the barks of the three German Shepherds alerted Avery of their presence. He lowered his special prize of raw steaks heavily laced with barbiturates and dangled them seductively. Minutes after the deadly bites, the three German Shepherds lay in a comatose state. Avery waited, accustoming his senses to the night sounds before using the shadows cascading off the trees as a protective cloak to approach the main house.

The static noise of the walkie-talkie chirped into life, indicating that the two guards on duty at the east side of the house were awake. He crept up behind the first guard, who was relieving himself of the six cans of beer that he had consumed earlier that evening. Avery wrapped his arm around the guard's neck, drawing his hunting knife and plunging it into the guard's temple and twisting it.

The guard slumped noiselessly to the ground, and Avery dumped the body in a secluded spot camouflaged by wild thorns and berries. He spotted the second guard leaning on the outer wall to the house smoking a cigarette. Decisively, he snuck up behind as he pulled a garrote from his jacket, threw it around the unsuspecting guard's neck and choked him until he stopped squirming. He then disposed of his body amidst the beautifully trimmed rosebush. Silently, Avery disabled the alarm with the assistance of his sophisticated electronic device within thirty seconds. He recalled the blueprint in his mind, climbing the stairs noiselessly on ten toes. He stopped on the first-floor landing absorbing the night sounds. The fridge hummed softly in the background as he made his final ascent to the second floor, where his target's bedroom was located.

The snoring noises of Kornmayer could be heard coming from the bedroom. Avery eased back the handle, put in place the plastic key to secure the lock, and pushed the door slightly ajar. He slipped into the palatial bedroom. The room was massive, crammed with expensive furniture, and littered with the latest novels by James Patterson, Mary Higgins Clark, Robert Ludlum, Martina Cole, Frederick Forsyth, and Jack Higgins. A row of mahogany shelves laden with educational books occupied the left side of the room, along with a well-crafted dressing table engraved in solid gold. A fashionable standing mirror with a golden frame was placed on the opposite side of the room, it was adorned by an array of floral lights that accentuated the magnified effect of the mirror in the lavishly decorated room.

Avery smirked at the arrogant display of affluence exhibited by the criminal he was about to kill. He relished the idea of watching the insufferable pig die.

Kornmayer stirred in his sleep, scared of the relentless demons terrorizing him in his dreams. His eyes fluttered opened, trying to orient himself to the environment. His wife's warm body nestled closer, and he felt comforted. He turned over and drifted back to sleep. Avery saw his opportunity and took it.

Expertly tightening the silken cord around Kornmayer's throat, his prey was dead in seconds while his wife lay beside him in a drug induced sleep, impervious to the fact that her husband was fighting for his life.

Three hours later, Avery was dressed, like a European, in a clean-cut suit with a blue silk shirt opened at the collar and an expensive pair of soft leather shoes to complete the wardrobe change. He had applied brown powder to darken his face and used a pair of contact lenses to alter the color of his eyes.

He walked through customs without being stopped. After a brief delay, he boarded a Singapore Airways flight that was flying to JFK airport. From JFK, he was expected to hire a car and make his way to Boston. A bus would get him to Blue County from there. He knew it would be a grueling fourteen-hour journey. But it would also give him ample time to get six hours' worth of sleep and then get to work.

On Avery's arrival, he made a brief stop at the Blue County Terminus overnight locker to retrieve the 9mm Sig Sauer and a miniature weaponized bomb, hidden in the black attaché case, that he needed to carry out his next assignment.

The instructions he was given were clear. Eliminate Professor Khan. Professor Khan was a renowned microbiologist, and one of the two chosen to sabotage the conference on genetic modification taking place at the Blue County conference in two days. Avery was there to make sure that did not happen.

Chapter 13

Daybreak had not come soon enough. Ralph lay in the RockHard motel bed, beads of sweat rolling off his back as the sheets clung in a limp embrace. He looked at his watch. The time was 7.15 a.m., Matthew was still asleep in his own bed. He reached over and gave him a gentle nudge.

"Hey! Let's get some food and then head over to the police station. I want a word with that detective, what's his name?"

Matthew sat up groggily. He tried focusing on the question, but sleep threatened to suffuse him once more.

"Hey! Matt, did you hear what I said?" Ralph asked, his voice now a notch harsher than before. "It's time to get some breakfast then head over to the station. I want some answers, and we won't get them lying around."

Matthew reluctantly climbed out of bed. He ran a comb through his hair and slapped some water over his face to wake him up fully. *Boy*, he thought, *Ralph sure drove a hard bargain*. His head still buzzed from the amount of liquor he had guzzled the night before. His head threatened to explode from the pounding headache which was shortly accompanied by nausea. One look at his brother assured him that Ralph was not going to take any excuses from him.

Fifteen minutes later, Ralph and Matthew ambled over to the motel's dining room. Breakfast was being served. Three long tables had been set with pretty checkered tablecloths distinctly decorated with yellow flowers. A wide range of fruits, cereals, bread, milk, and fruit juices lined the tables. Ralph and Matthew settled down to a sumptuous breakfast before heading off to Blue County's north precinct.

There they parked the blue Chevy in a parking lot opposite the police station. They collected the parking ticket and walked into the station together.

Michael was sitting at his table, apparently stumped by the events that unfolded in the past six months. It seemed like a lifetime ago that Blue County was a peaceful, crime-free community. Endless hours had been devoted to solving the string of murders.

They did not need the FBI meddling in their case and taking the glory.

His partner Tony had compiled a profile of similar killings that occurred over the last five years in Boston, Texas, New York, Blue County, Nevada, and California. The only interesting feature was that all of the victims were women within the range of 25–36 years old. Father Murphy's death was the only exception. It had brought additional heat because of his position in the area. The forensic reports were inconclusive, offering no clues.

A matching set of results were faxed to McClaren. Hopefully, he might be able to throw more light on the case. McClaren was also a good profiler. His accurate profiling in the Sock Killer case had initiated the national man hunt for the killer, which had led to his eventual capture.

The two partners were interrupted by a knock on the door. The desk sergeant announced the arrival of Matthew and Ralph, who were interested in the Cummings case.

"OK, send him into interrogation room 4. We'll see him in there," Michael replied with a grunt. Five minutes later, Matthew was ushered into the interrogation room. It was a dingy room, no larger than a 6 x 6 cell, and had grey, clouded walls. The grey paint on the walls gave the room a bland look. Matthew sat down in one of the wooden chairs, ill at ease and uncomfortable, while his mind catapulted him briefly to his arrest years ago in a similar precinct. He suddenly felt claustrophobic, boxed in, and eager to escape the restricted walls he was confined within. His thoughts churned within his chest as he looked up at the overhead lamp that hung limply from the ceiling rose, casting a crepuscular view of the room.

Meanwhile, Michael and Tony were watching Matthew squirm in his seat from behind the one-way mirror. Matthew, on the other hand, drummed his fingers on the cracked wooden table. He kept his composure, making sure that his eyes were steadily averted from the one-way mirror.

Michael and Tony assessed the visitor. Matthew was a scrawny looking man with at least four days' worth of stubble masking the knife scar on his left cheek. His blue eyes appeared intent and lucid. His brown hair was greased back. It was apparent to Michael and Tony that their visitor had made an effort to make himself appear neat. Although not quite achieving the desired effect.

They waited a few more minutes before walking into the interrogation room. Tony reached out and gave Matthew a warm, friendly handshake. His smile was disarming, and Matthew felt another pang of discomfort, which he tried to hide behind his faltering smile. He did not like cops. He had, for the most part of his life, walked on the wrong side of the law. Cops could smell villains a mile away. His eyes were fixed on the floor, trying desperately to hide his distrust of cops as well as the anxiety he felt.

Michael cleared his throat, "Well, what we can do for you Mr. Cummings?"

"I'm here to find out about my sister Anne Marie Cummings' murder," he stuttered.

"Are you sure that you are ready for this? The pictures are quite disturbing. I'll go and get the file," Michael said as he walked out of the room, not bothering to wait for an answer. He returned a few minutes later with a slim file under his arm.

"We'll need you to identify the body. Come with me, please." Tony gave Michael a quick glance while Matthew and Ralph nodded in mutual consent and followed them out of the interview room. They took the lift down to the underground room where the morgue was located, and were made to wait another half hour while the medical examiner finished his examination of an accident victim.

After a brief introduction, they were directed to lab 2, which was being used as a screening room. The morgue attendant wheeled in the corpse on a gurney. Matthew tensed involuntarily while Ralph shuddered inwardly. The air around them became charged as the stuffy room emitted its sickly smell of decay and antiseptic. Matthew's mouth was dry and he hastily licked his lips. He was totally transfixed in his tracks; his eyes strayed to the gurney that tantalized them with its rotting possession. Ralph's eyes mirrored the fear he felt as he tried hard to fight back the flow of tears threatening to escape.

The attendant repositioned the body so that the two brothers could get a better view. It was unmistakably Anne Marie. Matthew gagged, reeling towards the nearest sink. He retched twice, relieving his bowels and exposing his partially digested breakfast. He wiped back the spittle that dribbled down the side of his face and kept his eyes focused on the floor.

Ralph, who was trying to show as much bravery as possible, gave a feeble nod confirming her identity. A quick flash of empathy flashed across the faces of Michael and Tony, as they lead the brothers back to their office in a blanket veil of silence. Anne Marie's file lay unopened on the table when they returned. Slowly, the two detectives unfolded the facts of the case as gently as they could, preferring to leave photographs of the scene until the end. Anne Marie's body had been discovered at Haverlock Park. Close-up photos of the body showed the bruises, scratch marks and lacerations found on her body.

There were no current leads and no suspects. Matthew was disheartened by the police's inertia. He left his contact number with Tony, unsettled by the realization that the case had been open for nearly a month and the police had no significant clues to solving the case.

The brothers left the precinct pale and visibly shaken, unable to quell the chilling emotions swirling around in their heads. Their inconsolable grief would give way to a consuming rage. They just needed time to grieve and come up with a plan.

There will be answers, Ralph thought as they drove away from the parking lot.

Chapter 14

The gentle tick of the timer hummed undetected in the busy Euston station. The second hand moved perilously close to the detonation time. The black sports bag lay inconspicuously under the passenger seat, seemingly unnoticed by the throng of commuters jostling for space in the overcrowded coach. The early morning rush hour engrossed the passengers of the Piccadilly Line on their way to work, unaware of the imminent danger they were in.

Professor Gray eyed his watch anxiously. He was already late for his meeting with Dr. Klein. He had boarded the train at Kings Cross Station, hoping to reach his Bayswater apartment and complete his packing within the hour. A light olive-skinned man brushed pass him, catching his attention momentarily. The dark, piercing eyes held a maniacal gleam that sent shivers up Professor Gray's back.

There was a sudden explosion around the tunnel. The left side of the carriage burst open on impact, and Professor Gray found himself sailing through the confined space and landing near a billboard. Smoke enveloped the train in a thick blanket, choking out the little oxygen available. The air became pungent, and the lights in the carriage flickered on and off. The billowing tendrils of smoke hung like a filthy rag, reducing visibility as the passenger swarmed towards the exit created by the gaping hole in the carriage. A blast of orange flames ignited the clothes of some of the passengers fleeing the scene. Limbs were strewn in the wake of the explosion.

Professor Gray was swept along in the pandemonium and escorted safely out of the station for observation. He felt disoriented and overwhelmed by the emotions that gripped his gut. His mind clouded over in confusion. His cool veneer disguised the inner turmoil gripping his body. He walked shakily to a street bench and sat down.

Minutes slipped into an hour, yet Professor Gray sat on the bench, swept up in the forage of destruction, panic, despair, and forced assembling of orderliness imposed on the distressed and petrified crowd, unfortunate to share in these dire circumstances.

His journey back to his flat was filled with gruesome pictures from the day's events. The answering machine relayed a message from Dr. Klein, who was worried because he had not heard from the professor. Grappling with the horror of the last four hours, Professor Gray felt shell-shocked but his heart was warmed by the thought that someone cared about him. He phoned Dr. Klein, who answered on the second ring.

"Hello, who is it?"

"It's me. I must apologize for not calling earlier. I witnessed a catastrophic and traumatic event at Kings Cross," Professor Gray said, trying very hard not to reveal the desperation and sadness that laced his voice.

"You don't sound alright. Should I come over?" Dr. Klein asked lightly, trying to mask his mounting concern.

"No. I'll be fine. I'll see you at the airport at seven. I've arranged for a taxi to pick me up. See you later."

"I hope to see you soon," replied Dr. Klein, then the line went dead.

It was definitely a very dismal day, which reflected his sour mood. His secretary had failed to pack his notes on the cloning effect on designer babies produced through In vitro fertilization. His recent research into cloning had been pioneered by his associate, Dr. Jeffrey Daniels, and was on the verge of a major breakthrough. It could have been an excellent opportunity for him to propound this new theory and demonstrate his findings through his experiment.

About one hour later, the sound of a car horn honking brought him out of his exhausted nap. Looking out of the window, he could see the black taxi parked idly by the curb waiting for him to get in. The dark clouds held an untold promise of a further assault of sleet and the potential rumbling of thunders. Professor Gray set out from his Bayswater home hugging his brown leather brief case and a small travelling bag. The rain drummed down relentlessly on his unprotected head, off his back, and onto his stylish Italian shoes. Dragging his suitcase down the steps, he peered into the taxi, hoping that the driver would be courteous enough to help him with his luggage. The driver quickly rushed over to the back of the taxi and opened the boot but made no effort to help with the luggage. Professor Gray ambled into the taxi and sat silently huddled in the corner of the cab. He shivered involuntarily, peeved by the driver's attitude. He bit back a negative thought and said, "Heathrow Terminal Two," instead.

With an imperceptible nod, the taxi driver pressed the meter and put the gear in motion. The cab pulled away slowly from the pavement right into evening traffic. He was already running twenty minutes late; would he be able to make it to the airport in time?

One look at his rumpled suit, now drenched by the downpour, left the professor feeling more forlorn. His eyes strayed to the rear-view mirror to determine whether the driver was watching him check out his appearance. Content that the driver was engrossed in weaving in and out of traffic, he nestled deeper into the leather seat, wrestling for warmth.

The heater soon permeated the inside of the taxi and sent a warm glow within. Professor Gray relaxed, comforted instinctively by the sounds of other cars speeding by, and tired by the day's events. He tapped on the partition, indicating that he wanted to speak to the driver. Unfortunately, he observed that the taciturn driver was unresponsive, so he simply sat back in the seat.

The professor caught a maleficent smell of spicy lavender filling the partitioned enclosure. Very soothing, he thought to himself as he reached for his phone to check his travel schedule before suddenly feeling confined. He felt an irritation forming in his throat and coughed a few times in an attempt to clear it.

He wanted to ask the driver to regulate the overpowering scent which was attacking his sense. As he slid his phone back into his pocket the professor's felt his muscles relaxing as his thoughts struggled to follow a logical sequence. It seemed that his mind was dancing to an ethereal song. His hands weighed like a ton of bricks. He could not speak. His tongue had thickened and his eyes smarted under the pernicious attack of the suffocating smell that had penetrated his body.

He slumped forward from as his joints stiffened before landing on his side and experiencing what felt like he was falling through the car seat, immobilized and unable to speak. His eyes glazed over as his consciousness faded.

Chapter 15

A female voice announced the departure of Virgin Atlantic Flight 427 heading to JFK airport at 0000 hours. Professor Gray raced up the moving escalator to the first floor. He scanned the information board and ran to the loading gate, arriving with a minute to spare. Breathlessly, he waved his British passport at the flight attendant, who coquettishly compared the passport photo with the handsome dark-haired man whose face registered his impatience at being stalled. His congenial smile held her captive, and she blushed. Hurriedly, she stamped his passport, allowing him access to the aisle and to the waiting plane.

Onboard the plane, he was shown to a first-class seat. A flight hostess appeared by his side, ensured that he was comfortable, and left him to strap down the safety belt, ready for takeoff. Within minutes, the Captain's voice floated over the announcement system welcoming the passengers aboard. The engines started up, and the plane was engaged into takeoff mode. Professor Gray looked down at the retreating buildings in the distance and heaved a sigh of relief. He had scaled the first hurdle.

Chapter 16

The unsymmetrical outline of the distant shores came into sight as the captain turned the steering wheel towards land. The ship was forty minutes away from berthing. A hoot floated across the ship's tannoy system, attracting a cluster of speculating passengers scattered on top of the upper deck.

The buzz of excited conversation filled the air; passengers gesticulated with their arms, pointing out the captivating landmarks that always mesmerized and lured millions of tourists to the shores of Kuala Bay every year.

Kudirat slipped amongst the passengers on the upper deck. Her trained eyes scanned the gathering of people and latched onto Mohammed's. His eyes conveyed his silent acknowledgment that it was time to go. He detached himself from the party of travellers and climbed down the stairs to his cabin to ready for the rendezvous.

The leather briefcase on the bed held the detonator that was carefully dismantled and concealed behind a false panel. The case itself was fortified with a synthetic plate designed to camouflage its contents. Gently, he crosschecked the bomb, assembled the rest of his belongings into a totem bag, and left the cabin.

He was dressed in a floral shirt and casual shorts, with a digital camera slung over his neck, synonymous with the appearance of a tourist. A blue duffel bag held his travel documents and the leather briefcase. He made his way down the gangplank onto the pier swarmed with dock workers and passengers disembarking from the ship. He made sure that the totem bag was carried in front of him, screening the duffel bag from close scrutiny.

Kudirat followed shortly behind, seemingly engaged in an absorbing conversation with an Alabama stewardess who had won a small fortune in the lottery in her hometown. Kudirat feigned interest in the stewardess's boring tale while steering her past the custom officials who were randomly going through the travelling papers of people who struck them as suspicious.

Mohammed lingered for a brief moment, pretending to ask for directions from a dockhand, assessing the level of security. The young Hawaiian dockhand sputtered out directions in his heavily accented English and then turned brusquely to continue loading wooden crates. Kudirat glanced at Mohammed, stopped to check her watch, and continued by him without breaking her stride. They had 36 hours to rendezvous. Mohammed and Kudirat were aware that McClaren and some security agents were covering the event. If reputation was anything to go by, their job had become dangerous. Time and precision were essential if they were to complete the assignment and effect a successful extraction from Blue County

Mohammed synchronized his watch. The countdown had begun.

Chapter 17

Matthew and Ralph had stayed on in Blue County, carefully trying to extract information pertaining to Anne Marie's demise. They had nowhere else to go. They were $2.6 million richer anyway, and could afford to spend a few more days in Blue County to see what the fuss was about. The town was gradually transforming into a tourist center, buzzing with excitement with an influx of visitors from all over the world.

From across the road, Matthew and Ralph watched the bustling activities of news reporters and cameramen shifting equipment and the local police giving out orders and directions. The crashing of a carton full of equipment and swearing from one of the crewmen caught Ralph's attention. The clumsy worker bent over to retrieve the coil of wire and connections.

"Look at what you've done, you silly oaf. That's $150,000 worth of equipment you're messing around with. Give it to me and quit playing around. Leave it and go pick up the other box. I'll do this myself," a CNN reporter retorted.

Matthew and Ralph did not wait around to see the man's reaction; getting into their car, they drove off, heading back to their motel. A black Cherokee jeep passed them by and pulled up in the spot that Matthew's car had just vacated. An olive-skinned man with average build opened the door and walked straight into the Luna Restaurant. He exchanged a perfunctory handshake with another Caucasian seated at table six.

A few minutes later, he stood up and left. He got back into the jeep and drove one block to the Hilton. The usher opened the door and the man got out of the jeep. He went around to the boot of the car where the bell boy struggled to retrieve his large suitcase.

Without a backward glance, the man walked up to the front desk and announced his arrival, "I am Professor Khan. I made a reservation from New York. Is my room ready?"

"Yes, sir. Your room is 302. It comes with a beautiful view of Blue County's Sports Facility from your bedroom window. It is one of the best rooms," the desk clerk said as he handed him the door keys.

McClaren stood a few feet away, scanning a shelf of glossy magazines while observing Professor Khan and his unusually large suitcase. *Why did Professor Khan need such a large suitcase for a two-day conference?* he wondered.

Moments later, Mohammed left the Luna Restaurant by the side door. A black Buick drew up alongside him and he got in. The car sped away. Ralph saw the worker in the back of the restaurant engaged in a heated argument with a woman. Trouble was brewing, he could sense it. He had been in Blue County for over a week, and there was still nothing for him to work on. Detective Michael and his partner had left him and his brother out in the cold. There was no new report. He was not giving up; he would find his stepsister's murderer, no matter how long it took.

Chapter 18

The two moving forms walked side by side down the dark alley. Their shadows morphed into different shapes in the flickering light. The young man's hand drew closer to the woman, gently fondling her breast. His heart thudded with ardent desire. The voluptuous breast spilled willingly into warm embrace as he unbuttoned her skimpy blouse. The musky smell of cheap perfume assailed his nostril, heightening his senses.

The hooker leaned lightly on him while her practiced hands moved sensually to an alluring tune. The man let out an appreciative moan of delight, arching his body in consonance with the rhythm of the hooker's body. His manhood responded and his mind tingled in anticipation of what was to follow.

She tantalized his senses, masterfully guiding him. He felt her exhale sharply as he held her closely; their bodies were intertwined in a lustful embrace until they reached their peak together.

Moments later, the prostitute re-arranged her clothes, a little embarrassed by the fact that she had come with this stranger. In their profession, each act was merely a job, done without feeling. This one was different; she felt a sudden connection with this man. There was no point in dreaming. She smacked on some lipstick, picked up her shoes, and looked at the man expectantly. She wiped off a smudge of lipstick on her lower lip and clipped her mirror shut with a bored look on her face.

"A hundred dollars, soldier. I haven't got all night."

The man reached into his wallet, pulled out a series of bills, and silently placed them into the woman's outstretched hand. A curious look lingered on the man's face as he observed her through half-shut eyelids. The silence thickened like the night sky, and the woman suddenly felt uncomfortable. She started to walk back in the general direction they had come from, unsure of what had changed. The air felt electrified. After a few faltering steps, she looked back to see if the man was walking back with her; to her horror, the man was directly behind her. The look on his face was an indiscernible mask of hate. Her eyes widened in terror as she caught his hand move sharply past her. There was a short pause as she looked down to examine a burning sensation forming over her stomach where her client's hands had just brushed past. She felt the hot blood oozing out of the wound long before she saw the hunting knife gleaming in the faltering light.

Realizing what was going on and finally registering that she had been stabbed, she screamed out in pain and lost control of her cognitive sense as her legs refused to move despite the overwhelming urge to flee. Ignoring the hooker's screams, the man stabbed the hooker's body repeatedly in methodical precision until she became motionless.

He bent down to feel for a pulse. Happy that he had confirmed that the body was lifeless, he climbed over it, wiped the blood off the blade, and walked away in absolute satisfaction at the colorful display of death he was leaving behind. He admired the scene with sadistic delight, and left the alley humming, "Don't cry for me Argentina."

Chapter 19

"Mike, wake up. There's a 911 call on the radio. Listen, a 187 has been called at Lover's Alley, reported three minutes ago. This stakeout duty is boring, and we're only two blocks away. What do you think? Let's check it out," Tony said excitedly.

"All right, call it in. Darcy and Malone are at the other end of the street. They can cover surveillance in the interim," responded Michael, driving the black sedan out of the parking space.

They made their way over to Lover's Alley, where a small crowd of people had already gathered. A bewildered street cop attempted fruitlessly to stave off the prying eyes of the inquisitive public. Lover's Alley was an area in disrepute, known specifically for its nefarious activities, ranging from drug pushers, prostitutes, gang wars, and illegal gambling. It definitely was not a place decent people travelled through.

Michael's viewed the crowd with disdain. A group of bikers had parked by the entrance to the alley, they were represented by their tattoos, a motley collection of leather jackets, pierced skin that glared out like neon lights advertising rejected products, and the inscription 'red devil' painted clearly on their black leather jackets.

Michael and Tony cocked their guns in readiness of hostile action. Fortunately, the crowd, engaged in rather low-keyed whispers, made room for them to pass through. The alley was flanked by two decrepit buildings that sagged uneasily, allowing slivers of lights to pierce the pitch darkness that enveloped the alley. Up ahead, light from the west side of the building threw a cascade of dim light onto the alley, creating a halo effect.

With torches in hand, Michael and Tony progressed down the alley, carefully weaving past the piles of garbage strewn haphazardly. Twenty yards from where the body lay, the alley cleared out to reveal a neater row of dumpsters.

The sounds of sirens punctuated the night sky, followed by the traffic of policemen bustling about trying to secure the crime scene. The coroner and his forensic crew came soon after. Michael and Tony spoke to the first eyewitness on the scene, taking down notes on what they saw.

The coroner called them over to show them a piece of evidence.

"Look at this," he said intensely. "There's skin under her fingernails. Whoever she was, she fought for her life."

"Was she, you know…?" asked Michael.

"We won't know until we've done a preliminary examination down at the forensic lab. I'll let you know later," he replied.

Turning to his team, he said, "Let's wrap this up and get the stuff back to the morgue, guys."

The body was wrapped up in a body bag and whisked off in the waiting hearse. Michael and Tony followed, observing the dispersing crowd. After all, it had been noted that 40% of the time, the killer always returned to the scene of the perpetrated crime.

They scanned the crowd, but nobody stood out.

"Let's get back to the station and compare notes," Tony quipped, opening the door to his unmarked sedan.

Chapter 20

The killer watched from a distance, lapping up the attention his killing spree had attracted. He waited. The first officers on the scene were the two self-important officers from the 67th Precinct. He walked away, careful not to be seen. He kept his head low and the cap on his head tilted, shielding his face from onlookers.

Ralph and Matthew watched the sandy-haired man cut across the street. They kept their distance, following carefully, so that it was not too obvious. The young man stopped by the ATM machine and withdrew some cash. He then went into Angie's Bar and sat facing the window. The place was practically empty. In a few minutes, the den would be swarming with people. The man quickly ordered a plate of steak, cheese, tomatoes, and fries, downed these with a large coke, and was out of the joint before the first of the evening crew arrived. He paid the stewardess by the door, and stumbled out into the warm humid air, not even waiting for his $12 change. He paused outside the bar to light a cigarette and snubbed out his match before walking on.

His hand hurt. The bitch had ripped out a piece of flesh, and it felt raw to the touch. He stopped over at the local pharmacy and picked up some cleansing lotion and a first aid kit. He made sure that he kept the injured hand deep inside his pocket for the entire time he was at the pharmacy.

He walked hurriedly, trying to block out the pulsating pain from his hand, which felt clammy. Maybe it was bleeding again. He needed to clean it up before passersby noticed. A reflection of a stocky man caught his attention, triggering alarm bells in his head. Did someone see him leave the alley?

He needed to get away. Bagging the first aid kit, he walked past the grocery store on Maine Street and took the intersection on Paramour and Lenny Street and doubled back. His brief impression of the stocky man left him unsure. Was he an undercover policeman? He certainly did not look like one. His clothes were a bit tacky and he did not look like an FBI agent either. They were too suave. *Is this an illusion or am I deluded?* he thought to himself. His pangs of paranoia had been suppressed for so long. *Am I losing it?* he thought again to himself.

At the end of Paramour Street, he saw the second shadow. Now, he was convinced that he was being followed. The second operative was smoother. A tall man, about 6 ft. 2. He was a better tracker than the first man, and far more cautious too.

Calmly, he cut across Flap Street and walked straight into the Rodeo Night Club. The place was packed with clubbers dancing away to the blaring music. In grim satisfaction, he went into the gents' and at the last possible moment opened the side door leading out to the back alley.

Moments later, he ran down the alley and jumped over a garden wall. This was his territory, no one could catch him here because he knew the area like the back of his hand, which was now throbbing terribly. He heard the tall man shout out, "Damn it, we've lost him. Get the car around the front, I'll wait and see if he'll come out this way."

"OK," replied Matthew, disappointed by the loss.

Ralph sucked the end of the cigarette, then dragged profusely on it while he waited for Matthew to bring the car around. He seethed inwardly for not being able to catch the man he'd seen running away. There was a possibility that the man could be Anne Marie's killer as well. At least he was on to him. He'll track him down sooner or later. After all, how big was Blue County?

Chapter 21

The conference was due to start in 12 hours, and Hamilton had still not heard from Avery. He tapped his pen on the table in agitation. Martin Lecter had arrived, according to schedule, at the Blue County Hilton under the guise of Professor Gray. The switch in London had been necessary. Avery was an independent operator who rarely disclosed what he was doing. He needed someone to keep him informed. Lecter, on the other hand, complied with the manual and maintained constant contact with HQ.

Sighing, he knew that it was time to put the next phase of the plan into action. He dialed Mohammed's cell number, which was picked up immediately.

"Hello, it's Uncle Charlie. I'll be with you in 12 hours. I'll wire you when I get there. I can't wait for the house-warming party."

"It'll be my pleasure, Uncle. Hope to see you soon, bye."

Kudirat watched Mohammed replace the cradle in its crock looking thoughtful.

"Let's go out for a walk," he said.

"You mean right now?"

"Yes, now," he said with finality, grabbing his coat as he headed out the door, Kudirat at his heels.

Outside, the night was warm. People passed by in bustling numbers. They both walked in silence, hands thrust deep in their pockets with their heads bent downwards.

At the edge of the forest, Mohammed stopped. Everywhere seemed deserted. Cautiously, he scanned the nearby bushes and surrounding area. Convinced that they had not been followed, he turned to face Kudirat.

"The room's been bugged, but we'll proceed according to plan. We'll pull out immediately thereafter," Mohammed said.

"Do you think that they are on to us?" asked Kudirat, inquisitively.

"No, I think it's just the FBI's way of playing it safe. They must have bugged the entire hotel in light of the conference."

"Where did you keep the Semtex?"

"I left it in the trunk of the rental," responded Kudirat.

"We'll keep it there till we need it," Mohammed replied, pensively in acknowledgment of Kudirat's thoroughness.

"Let's get back to the hotel. We'll start at 4.30 a.m. Understood?"

"Yes," Kudirat replied.

Chapter 22

Avery's rental van was parked a few feet away from the Blue County Mail Office. His surveillance camera zoomed in on the bustling activities taking place in the usually desolate mail room. Two poorly disguised agents hung around, turning constantly in different directions while taking stock of the traffic of people engrossed in their mundane lives.

He sat back in his adjustable seat and flicked once more through the contents of the file. He pondered over the pictures of Mohammed and Kudirat, etching their facial features into his memory. He continued reading the thick file. A picture of Martin Lecter posing as Professor Gray lay attached to the first page of the dossier. The inherent similarities were striking. No wonder they chose him. He could easily pass off as Professor Gray, even without makeup or disguise. Unfortunately, his orders were to eliminate all three after the bombing.

Being an exterminator was not always a happy chore, but he relished the excitement and euphoria he got from the hunting and killing of his targets. What made this case so interesting was that he was going to come up against a formidable opponent: another ruthless killer, a man highly trained by the CIA before he was recruited as a professional mercenary. His female companion, Abu Ahmed, alias Kudirat, was a recent addition to the mercenary profession who had become a pitiless executioner within just two years. She worshipped her mentor Mohammed. Avery surmised that she was the weak link, and would hence be a softer target.

Lurking in the shadows, protected by the tenebrous mantle of night, he watched Mohammed and Kudirat leave their hotel room by the service entrance and evanesce into the night. He had planted listening devices in the bathroom and adjoining room and had picked up snippets of their conversation. But his gathered intel did not tell him when they were set to move. He was satisfied that he had put the bugs where he could get the clearest reception. All he needed to do was wait.

Forty-five minutes later, they returned. The air had taken on a charge that had not been there before. Both Mohammed and Kudirat appeared determined and spurring for action. Mobilization time was close. The corresponding vibes were unmistakable. A killing spree was about to erupt, and he was going to be there for the closing scene, Avery chuckled to himself, snuggling further into his haven. Count down had begun.

Chapter 23

The Hamilton residence lay in partial darkness, as the members of the household slept. At 3.43 a.m., the phone rang. Sleepily, Hamilton stretched over his wife, careful not to disturb her, and reached for the phone. The voice filtered through, clear as day, "It's time."

Sitting up quickly, Hamilton replaced the receiver and got out of bed. He dressed in a pair of black slacks and an equally dark colored cashmere sweater. Hamilton left his wife's bedside and headed for the door, carrying his sneakers with him. Outside, a Hummer jeep, with its lights off, was waiting for him in the driveway. Within minutes, the jeep, now carrying its new passenger, made its way out of the compound and sped to its rendezvous.

Senator Lee was waiting for him at the landing bay of the private airfield.

"Send in the sleeper to neutralize Avery. The intelligence report shows that Avery cannot be managed. I don't want a sticky situation. This job needs to be done right. Got it? I will not tolerate a foul up. Is that clear?" hissed Senator Lee. "I'm expecting a feedback at 1200 hours. Now, get going."

Hamilton's teeth were set on edge. "David, you need to keep a lid on things. Everything is going according to plan, I assure you. There's no need to panic. Besides, there's nothing connecting us to the event, so calm down," responded Hamilton testily.

Senator Lee got back into his unmarked car, and drove off without a response. Hamilton gloated over the fact that Senator Lee was on edge. Snapping open his cell phone, he placed a long-distance call to Washington.

"Avery, SL needs to be eliminated."

Yes, Hamilton thought to himself as he drove back to the house. The show had just begun.

Chapter 24

Senator Lee sat pensively in the back seat of his black limo. Doubt riddled his mind. Hamilton was a smart cookie who donated generously to the present cause. Senator Lee regarded him as a formidable ally, one who could evidently be a potentially dangerous foe. He needed to be controlled. But not yet; maybe he would think more clearly about this tomorrow, after the conference center had been blown up.

The black limo stopped at the traffic light as it turned red. A young man on a Tuono motorbike drew up alongside Senator Lee's car.

Out of curiosity, Lee looked out the tinted window at the motorbike and its rider, before turning his attention to the latest edition of the *New York Herald* lying on the seat. He hardly had time to absorb the black ankle leather boots, goggles, brown leather gloves, and serpent helmet before the deafening sound and rain of bullets splayed inside the limo, hitting the Senator.

The traffic lights turned green and other cars scrambled out of harm's way. The assassin sped off at neck breaking speed, leaving in his wake a state of confusion as cars careened into each other and screeching tires and shattered glass sprayed indiscriminately into the busy street, cutting the stunned pedestrians.

Ten black and white police cars chased the biker down the bridge. Two squad cars collided unceremoniously with the balustrade, sending a cloud of billowing smoke into the morning sky. Unperturbed by the carnage he left in his wake, the biker guided his bike up a ramp into the awaiting truck. Instantly, the back of the truck closed, concealing its cargo.

Smugly, the rider descended from his bike, satisfied that he was now completely hidden from the policemen in pursuit. He listened to the sounds of blaring sirens echoing further and further into the distance, before making his appearance in the rear of the van.

Silently, with a smile, he stripped off the black gear he was wearing and took his position in the front seat beside the truck driver.

"Is it done?" asked the driver.

"Yes. Drop me off at Hubbard Street."

The driver hummed in tune with the music on the radio. He reached over to the dashboard and retrieved a package. He dropped the parcel into the assassin's lap.

"Count it. It should be $50,000. That was the amount agreed on, wasn't it?"

Eagerly, the young biker ripped open the package and started counting the tightly rolled up notes. He licked his fingers in awe. Sweat seeped out of his shirt, while his eyes took on a lustful look upon handling so much money. Swiftly, the driver aimed his magnum and fired. A spatter of blood stained the windscreen, clouding the driver's view temporarily.

He parked by the side road, salvaged the blood-tinted envelope, placed the gear in neutral, and shut the door. He opened a can of petrol and poured it, liberally, all over the white van.

He gave the truck a slight shove to get it rolling down the precipice, and threw a burning lighter into the air. Within seconds, the truck was alight. The killer walked away with a self-satisfied look on his face. Mission one accomplished.

Chapter 25

Martin Lecter left the hotel room hurriedly. Panic-stricken by the telephone conversation he had just had with Hamilton. His wiry muscles twitched and his heart pumped in electrified bursts. The unidentified body of Professor Gray had been discovered at a farm in Cheltenham. His mind broiled in turmoil, and, suddenly, he felt giddy. He had left his room without his suitcase or his belongings. He did, however, conceal his passport and wad of notes in the lining of his faded overcoat. He looked furtively outside the hotel. Everybody seemed engrossed in their usual humdrum of activities, and took no notice of the tall, slender, regal stranger.

Yet, dread gripped him in a savage claw. He knew it was just a matter of time before the local police would descend on the hotel. He didn't even have time to dispose of the master plan properly. Fragments of the burnt pieces of the plan littered the bathroom floor. If Hamilton found out that he had slipped up, he would have Martin's head on a platter. There was no time to think. Escape was the foremost objective on his mind. He needed to get as far away as possible.

He stopped to clean his furrowed brow, which was covered by a thick layer of sweat, trying desperately to collect his thoughts. He froze rigid in his tracks. Was it a figment of his imagination, or did he see someone he vaguely recognized in the shop entrance across the road? Huge dollops of sweat dropped on to his feet, and he clutched his coat more protectively around his frame.

He needed shelter. Looking around desperately, he saw a dowdy dressed man and fell in step with him. The young man appeared bewildered, but walked on hugging his groceries tightly while maintaining a safe distance from the stranger. Martin tried a stab of false camaraderie, engaging the young man in light conversation, afraid that anything more would make the youth scurry away like a frightened kitten. The young man eyed him with veiled suspicion;

his replies were stilted and short. Martin's eyes patrolled the parameter speedily as he went, searching for a crevice or opening through which he could retreat. Exasperated by the intrusion into his pathetic little world, the young man ducked into the hardware store mumbling incoherently under his breath.

Feeling stripped and exposed, the feeling of trepidation gripped Martin again. His eyes locked onto a diner two doors away and he quickened his steps. Fragments of shattered glass exploded around him as a series of gunshots smashed the shop window. Instinct made him throw his weight automatically to the ground. Shards of glass sprayed across the back of his neck. Wails from inside the diner confirmed Martin's fears. A bullet had found a victim, piercing the forehead of the waitress through and through. Within seconds, all hell broke loose. People spilled out of the diner; Martin mingled with the terrified crowd and made his way through the diner to the back entrance and into a disused alley. He raced forward blindly, turning and winding through the maze of adjoining alleyways. He was fueled by raw energy. A sense of self-preservation took over, and he moved on relentlessly, breathing in quick, shallow breaths as he labored on, looking for safe shelter.

He ran, for what seemed like another ten minutes, before he stopped at an intersection. Up ahead, a long alley let through a cascade of light. *Hopefully, it would lead to a main road*, Martin thought. Doggedly, he ran on cautiously until he reached the entrance of the alley. Luckily, across the street a taxi cab was parked idly, its light was on. He made a dash for the cab and climbed in hastily.

"Blue County Central, on the double," he said in a shrill voice.

"Yes, sir," replied the taxi driver as he pulled away from the sidewalk.

Martin's mind went blank. A wave of relief replaced the apprehension he had earlier felt. A ray of surreal contentment filled his being as the signpost of the Blue County Central station loomed vividly in his sights. He was almost there. He had enough money to start life somewhere else. But first things first. He had to get the bus to Vegas, after that, everything should be easier. He rummaged through his wallet; there was enough money to make a clean get away. He paid off the taxi driver and bought a ticket for Vegas. He waited for the last call for boarding before embarking. The killer lurked in the alcoves, waiting for the perfect shot. Martin ascended the stairs to the bus, and as he turned, the killer fired.

Martin's mind registered the bullet, and he lurched forward into a nearby seat. In the next fraction of a second, his mind became clearer as his body wrestled with the burning sensation of the bullet that had nicked his side. The bus was finally on its way. He looked behind him, but there was no car in pursuit. Perhaps the killer thought that he had successfully taken out the target. A sprout of crimson tainted his shirt, and he hugged the overcoat tighter over his body. The accuracy of the silencer had nearly hit its intended target; but it went unnoticed by the other passengers. Danger loomed ahead. But, for now, he needed rest.

Chapter 26

Baltimore, 4 a.m.

"Sir, I think we should abort. Lecter just got away," J.K.'s panicked voice floated over the line.

Disgusted by J. K.'s incompetence, the V.P. gritted his teeth. He collected his thoughts and calmly, but brusquely, issued his order, "Mobilize Hamilton immediately."

Breathlessly, J.K. murmured his assent into the phone as the distinct click of the phone going dead sounded in his ears. Hamilton was bad news. He was a mercenary for hire; a ruthless professional who left little to chance. His reputation preceded him. The thought alone sent a sudden chill leaping crazily down his spine. He suddenly felt exposed. He stared mutely at the phone that hung loosely in his hands. His eyes momentarily lost focus while his mind churned. The cogs of his brain shuddered at the realization that things had spiraled out of control. J.K. summoned courage and left the phone booth, unaware of his observer.

The cool autumn air blew softly in this dusty community. The complexity of the situation lay precariously on his shoulders. With his hair plastered to his head and his eyebrows furrowed in a worried expression, he walked on hesitantly, aware that he had to make that call. He gulped the fresh air as he furtively considered his options. Should he simply run while he still had a chance?

He unlocked the door to the rental car and bent down to open it, when a soft whooshing sound that ended in a plop whizzed past his ears. He turned tentatively, unsure of what had just happened. The second shot reverberated off the roof of the car and imbedded itself deeply into his skull. Instantaneously, his body convulsed to an unearthly tune. The impact released a splay of blood that splashed across the windscreen.

His body writhed and slithered to the ground. The spasmodic movement ceased, as life drained from the writhing body of the man called J.K, once known as Jack Kelman.

Hamilton circled the car, inspected his handiwork, and carefully left the scene as unobtrusively as he had entered it.

Chapter 27

The V.P. pondered over the substantial number of deaths that had taken place in recent weeks and heaved a resigned sigh. However, his regrets were subdued by his overwhelming sense of self-preservation and his need to execute the overall plan. He had invested too much to back out now.

Hesitantly, he buzzed for his secretary.

"Rosie, please get Senator Lee on the line."

"Yes, sir," said the V.P.'s secretary, a little puzzled by the digression from the usual routine. What could possibly be so wrong that needed Senator Lee's attention?

Breathing a deep sigh, she dialed Senator Lee's private number. After the usual protocol, she was linked up to the senator.

"The V.P. is on line 2, Sir."

Senator Lee instinctively leaned into his seat to cushion the blow he expected was coming.

"Is Avery in place? I've had to eliminate J.K. and send in Hamilton."

Senator Lee was taken aback. Hamilton was known as a loose cannon in intelligence circles.

"It is imperative that everything goes according to plan. There's too much at stake," continued the V.P.

The senator was tongue-tied and alarmed at the prospect of Hamilton and Avery working the same turf. There were signs of imminent danger ahead, a head-on collision by these two assassins was probable, and there was nothing he could do to avert it. He'd just have to assume that they would at least show enough professionalism to complete the mission before addressing their personal vendetta, which dated back to the Hanover assignment in 2006.

Hamilton said "And, by the way, Lecter got away. He's heading for New York. I've dispatched a local to take care of it."

"Better ensure that Kolinsky comes up with the money. I have facilitated count down. It's show time. Senator Lee replied."

Senator Lee dropped the phone on its cradle, cleared his desk, and left the office in a hurry. Pensively, he made his way to the rendezvous. The clock was ticking, and he needed to cement the deal quickly and quietly. Things were taking an unpredictable turn, and he needed to mobilize his backup plan.

From his palatial surroundings, Simeon Kolinsky, the Russian crime lord, picked up a pink Turkish delight and twirled it in his large hands. Senator Lee was ten minutes late. He threw one of the sweets savagely into his mouth and gave a gratifying belch. This temporary distraction did nothing to curb his mounting rage. His mind simmered over Senator Lee's audacious delay. Simeon disliked him. He found Americans loud and bigoted. Senator Lee was a typical example. Due to his circumstances, he preferred to remain in the shadows. Life had dealt him a sadistic blow. He remained a social recluse, granting audience to a handful of trusted people, people who would never divulge the content of their meetings or his description to anyone else. He made sure of that.

This meeting was unavoidable and very important to Simeon Kolinsky. It entailed money, a lot of money, money beyond his wildest expectations. It was his chance at becoming a world player in politics. It furthered his cause; besides that, it was a grand opportunity to destabilize America. Perhaps it was payback. The thought left a soft, scintillating, tingling sensation running through his veins. Yes, it was time to punish America for abandoning his father.

For the past twenty-six years, he had nursed this hatred. A hatred borne out of betrayal and the fact that he had been forced to live in seclusion. He was stripped of a social life, compelled to live as a hermit, estranged from friends, his love, and… His eyes brimmed over momentarily with tears.

Anyway, it was time to unleash his wrath on the USA. His stomach churned with bitterness that germinated from the gross injustice he had suffered in his homeland, Mother Russia.

The Russian Secret Police—the Ministry for State Security known as the MGB—carted off his father, Dr. Victor Kolinsky in the summer of 1952. In the time of political correctness—where oppression and suppression of personal ideals were dominant—fear, poverty, and communism permeated the fabric of the Russian society. Repression left the people quaking with apprehension. The people were subjected to an obscure, non-descript life, afraid of reproach from the MGB that operated ruthlessly and unbounded under the brusque hand of Stalin.

Simeon's father was a doctor who rejected a life of abject poverty and misery. His ideals did not include guaranteeing the safety of his family. Tactlessly, he had lashed out at the idiosyncrasies of the existing government, speaking out boldly at a state function.

Within the hour, the family home at Leninski Boulevard was invaded by a squad of belligerent MGB men who tore the house down and whisked away the indignant doctor. Bewildered, Simeon held his scared younger brother Aleksei's left hand, all the while clinging protectively to his mother's waist.

His father's abduction left little to imagination. Dr. Victor Kolinsky never returned, nor heard of again. The family he left behind lived in dread. Confused and insecure, Simeon was expected to fill his father's shoes. At the age of fourteen, inexperienced and partly schooled, his resolve to take care of his family brought with it profound hardship. His mother Katrina carried on as usual, but her eyes spoke of her unspeakable sorrow and undisguised pain. He admired her strength. Unfortunately, it did not last long. She was in for another unexpected shock, because two days later, the MGB came and took him away. His mother broke down and sobbed, while their neighbors looked on helplessly. Simeon was forced into an old Skoda. His legs felt confined in the interior of the car. Sandwiched between two hefty MGB men, he reflected in utter puzzlement, dreading to think why he was being separated from his family. He looked into the emotionless eyes of the men next to him and a spasm of fear gripped him. He cringed further into his seat and ran his tongue rapidly over his chapped lips.

After hours of driving, they arrived at a remote old building. He was bundled out of the car and shoved towards a side entrance. Before he had time to catch his breath, he was dragged down a flight of stairs. Simeon heard the sounds of leaking pipes, dripping droplets of water in tune to an unseen orchestra. He strained his eyes to see where they were taking him, trying desperately to commit each twist and turn to memory, in case of an escape. The corridor was damp and dimly lit. Simeon fought off a feeling of trepidation as he walked within the unfamiliar confines of the narrow corridor. Adrenaline coursed through his veins.

From somewhere ahead, a piercing cry of pain rang out, sending a stream of shockwaves straight to his brain. His blood curdled at the sense of impending danger and his knees buckled instantly. Perspiration soaked his shirt. He felt faint, but willed his body to go on. Faltering at this point would certainly draw repercussions. Instead, he tried focusing on his problem, shifting his troubled mind to anything and anywhere, but not on where they were going. Who were these people and why did they take him away from the family he loved and cherished? Were they taking him to see his father? Or was his father already dead? Hot tears sprang to his eyes and he felt very alone and afraid.

When they reached the last door, one of his abductors rapped thrice to a designated signal before the door swung open. The room was brightly lit, in contrast to the dimly corridor that they were stepping in from. It was a cavernous room, with low ceiling and was sparsely furnished. An interrogator was bending over a man who was hunched precariously on a wicker chair. His face was puffy and indescribably marked with scars. Part of his head had been bashed in. Blood had caked around the wound, and the smell of scorched flesh hung heavily in the spacious space. The man on the seat was barely conscious. Deep groans of pain rumbled from within his throat; he was oblivious to the intrusion of the young man and the two MGB men who had entered the room.

The interrogator's raucous voice sliced the tense, humid air. "Who are you working for? Are you an American spy? What was your involvement with Slava?" Simeon's face turned into a mask of horror at the realization that the man being tortured was his father. A cry of anguish left his lips and the man in the chair turned his head imperceptibly to the unknown intrusion. It was followed by a sharp intake of breath. The interrogator, Vladimir Lewinsky, acknowledged with satisfaction the effect the young man was having. Vladimir, otherwise known as the butcher, relished the thought that he had found a chink in the old man's armor.

The butcher's eyes glinted with fiendish delight. He flayed Dr. Kolinsky relentlessly, bombarding him with more questions till he passed out. A bucket of water was thrown forcibly over the helpless man sprawled unsteadily on the rotting wicker chair. Simeon's lower lip trembled and he tried hard to be brave.

He drew nearer to get a clearer view of his father. His father's eyes were bloodshot and tired, but retained acuity and a high degree of intelligence. His voice sounded hoarse but was still tinged with defiance.

"I've nothing to tell. I'm just a simple doctor."

"I don't believe you," snapped the butcher. "This is your last chance. Speak now, or you'll regret it. Who are you working for?"

Dr. Kolinsky shifted his weight uneasily in the chair and looked at the butcher through puffy eyes, stretching the pregnant silence. Disgusted by the doctor's nerve, he turned abruptly towards the boy.

"Bring the boy here," he said, gutturally, through clenched lips. "It's time to teach daddy's boy a new lesson."

Simeon was thrust forward by his captors and landed unceremoniously into the waiting paws of the butcher. He brandished the gleaming scalpel before the quivering boy. A gurgling noise erupted from the doctor's throat as he struggled to lose his bonds. Powerless to stop the cataclysm of pain about to be inflicted on Simeon, he watched the butcher slash the boy's face incisively in three swift movements. Blood gushed freely from the wound, and Simeon reeled uninhibitedly, clutching the wound in shock. In horror, he watched the blood trickle down the front of his shirt. His eyes were affixed on his father, whose eyes showed the burden of pain and perhaps a hint of fear. From within him, a swell of hatred against his abductors soared to his head, filling him with rage. A searing sensation coursed through his body. He let out a vociferous cry and shuddered. In an instant, Simeon crumpled to the ground in excruciating pain.

This diversion was all his father needed. By the time the butcher looked back at Dr. Kolinsky, he was writhing in a series of body wracking spasms. A stream of spittle dribbled from the side of his mouth. In shock, the butcher shook the doctor violently, willing the writhing body to stop jerking out of control. Within seconds, the spasm seized and Dr. Kolinsky was pronounced dead.

From a distance, Simeon stared on in confusion. Spent and weakened by the pain, he lay immobile on the hard floor. The catastrophic effect of his father death's left him drained. He cried silently to himself. In annoyance, the butcher stormed out of the room, his face an emotionless mask of hatred and disappointment. Bewildered, the other captors followed suit, leaving Simeon alone to wallow in his sorrow.

Hours passed by in unpunctuated silence, and sometime during the day, the doctor's lifeless corpse had been hauled out, leaving him lonelier than before. Disorientated, Simeon floated in and out of his delirious sleep without recollection of day or night. He awakened in a chilly room, confused and feeling cold. The sound of footsteps approaching the outer door made him stir. Struggling to focus, he pulled himself up and stared warily at the door. Apprehensively, he waited for the footsteps to retreat before he slithered closer to the door. A rusty plate filled with stale bread and a cruse of mushy soup lay uninvitingly on the grubby floor.

Pangs of hunger stirred within him, but he'd prefer to go hungry than ingest the fusty, poisonous food. His resolve melted as soon as it dawned on him that the only way to survive was to replenish his body's fuel. Resignedly, he dipped the parched bread into the soup and stuffed it into his mouth. *I will live to avenge my father*, Simeon promised himself. *Maybe not today, but I'll bide my time,* he thought with unwavering resolve.

For weeks on end, he floated into a world of surrealism. He was interrogated at odd hours, made to endure numerous ordeals, and drifted in and out of fathomless dreams. His only hold on sanity was the last scene he remembered before he was wrenched away from his family. He prayed that he would wake up from this nightmare. This was not to be. He was subjected to degrading sexual acts, interrogations, and never-ending jibes that left him consumed with a bitterness and revulsion that burned deeply inside him.

His face had begun to release a repulsive, odorous fluid that made him squeal in pain. His skin had taken on a sallow color, tinged with blue. All of a sudden, Simeon felt himself falling, losing touch with reality. A fever raged within him, and the pain in his face suddenly became excruciating. Voices seemed to echo from a long tunnel as the world spun around him; the hushed whispers of the guards were the last thing he heard before he was catapulted into oblivion.

Simeon woke up three days later in a hospital ward, perplexed. The doctors had frantically tried to salvage his face that had been festered by the onset of gangrene. They had desperately tried to save his contused face by arresting the infection and performing surgery.

Throughout the nightmare, he held onto the thought that he had suffered all those months because his father had been an American agent. Where were the Americans when the doctor and his family needed them? Nowhere near, that was for sure.

Well, he was about to make them suffer like he did. He was about to rob the American people of Blue County of a normal life. Payback for all the years he lost. And who better to do it? Yes, with the assistance of Senator Lee, he would be able to execute his plan. Senator Lee was a greedy, ambitious politician who was unaware that he was merely a pawn being used by Kolinsky to bring the full arm of his wrath on the American people. It was amazing what people could do for the right compensation.

The words of Ashly Lorenzana played in his mind:

'There is nothing wrong with revenge. The wrong has already been done, or there would be no need to even the score.'

Ha, ha, ha, he laughed. He had waited nearly twenty-seven years to exact his revenge and, by Jove, he was going to carry it out. The sound of Senator Lee's car brought him back from his torturous thoughts. "Enough," he murmured to himself. "It's show time."

Chapter 28

Scientists gathered together in clusters in the Blue County Hotel's conference, discussing various research projects. Noticeably absent was Martin Lecter. The concierge, Joe, was a little worried that the lodger had not been spotted since yesterday afternoon. Martin had somehow dodged the FBI agent assigned to him. His main concern was who was going to settle the bill.

Joe's staff had been subjected to three grueling hours of interrogation. He was sure that nothing significant had been obtained. Tired and despondent at having his regular routine transformed into a circus show, he decided to have a tea break earlier than usual. He needed to give his frayed nerves a rest. Joe walked through the cafeteria and navigated his way down to the boiler room, where he normally hung out to smoke. The first floor was a non-smoking area, and he did not want the smoke trail to permeate the air.

Relaxed on an old wooden crate, he lit his cigar and puffed deeply, inhaling the rich, aromatic smell of the expensive cigar. His mind wandered off to how he was going to spend the evening with his wonderful Erica. Their meeting had been a chance encounter that had blossomed into a beautiful relationship. His mind reflected on their last intimate evening together. It was simply heavenly. Joe could not believe that he could find happiness so late in life.

His pager buzzed by his side and he was pulled back to the present. Grudgingly, he looked at the pager. Apparently, it was time to serve lunch. He had to cover the reception area while Rocco supervised the lunch deliveries. Acquiescently, he snuffed out his cigar and headed for the stairs. He reached out for the railing and hauled his frame up the first set of steps. His palms rubbed against something warm and sticky. He looked at his hands and saw that the sticky substance was blood. Perplexed by the discovery, he probed further. Aghast by what he had unearthed, he clambered up the stairs and alerted security.

Within minutes, the Blue County Hotel's lobby was swamped with cops. Guests watched with their mouths agape, unsure of what the commotion was all about. Joe was taken into the smallest conference room and questioned by Tony and Michael when they arrived to take charge.

Tony and Michael left the conference room and surveyed the crime scene, taking down notes as they went. A quick search revealed that two of the guests were unaccounted for.

Martin Lecter and Richard Burke, a travelling salesman, were both seen talking in the bar two nights ago. The strident baying of the dogs spiked up Tony and Michael's attention, and they walked hurriedly to the north side of the hotel, where the dogs' insistent barks were rising in swift crescendo and their handlers struggled to maintain control of the leashes. They were beaten to the scene by the swarm of feasting flies that hovered hungrily over the body of Richard Burke. Blood was splattered all over the service elevator, leaving a gory scene in its wake. His body lay in a crumpled heap like a discarded doll, his neck sliced open and his eyes distended like they were about to fall out of their sockets. The handlers were finally able to quieten the dogs, and dragged them off while the crime scene investigators settled down to work.

"Well, one down and one to go," said Tony as his eyes took in the grotesque act of savagery. "Let's get a look at the CCTV footage. It might tell us more," he said wearily.

Chapter 29

Darkness enveloped Blaine's thoughts as he travelled through his nightmare. It was always the same dream over and over again. He'd see the girls begging for their lives, covered in glaring garments of blood. Their deaths appeared to be so symbolic, beautifully arranged in different ways. Well, he had to show his artistic talent, didn't he? His mother never allowed him to play with his colors, or anything else for that matter. But he loved her. Or did he? His nightmare seemed to distort his memory. Yes, he needed to be loved. It was his right to be loved. Anyway, he'd shown them all. He was powerful. None could withstand him. He made all the sluts pay for what they had done to him. Rejection was unacceptable. Yet deep within, the macabre of his revolting exhibition burned deeply into his mind, and he broke out in a cold sweat.

Where could he go to? He had no friends and no family. He had always been a loner. Besides, who would want him? Especially if they knew what he had done. For now, he was free, and intended to stay that way. Dig it. Yeah, he laughed out loud. Free indeed.

Steven Blaine, that's who they say I am, the polite and helpful garbage man who'd been downtrodden all his life. Only his mother understood him. She treated him right. Not like all the others who ignored him. Why did his dad have to beat her to death? She was all he had. That was why he made him pay. The beating had to stop.

He needed to get out of town. He felt claustrophobic. The walls were closing in on him. The place was crawling with feds. He yearned to reach out for newer, unexplored pastures. He'd gotten a fat wad of cash when his father died. It'd start him up in a new town. Anywhere would be better than Blue County right now. There was too much going on. The murder trail might lead the police to his doorstep. *And we couldn't have that, could we?* he thought. It's time to leave. Although he had been very careful, the nosy cop might have gotten a glimpse of his face.

It was now or never. Picking up the few precious things he possessed, he packed a valise and headed for the door. Stopping momentarily, he looked back nostalgically at his home of thirty-five years, probably for the last time. He knew that he could never return again. Sighing regretfully, he opened the door.

His mind froze. He was caught in slow motion. It was totally unbelievable. Tony and Michael were standing on his porch waiting for him, or was it his imagination? All he heard was 'Steven Blaine, you are under arrest for the murder of…'

Like in a bad cop movie, his hands were thrust behind his back and the Miranda rights were read out loud as he was herded into an unmarked police car parked close-by.

This was a different kind of nightmare.

Chapter 30

Senator Lee left Kolinsky's presence with a sense of unease. Simeon was really a ruthless, vindictive man on the border of paranoia. He questioned his state of mind, but that was not what he was thinking about. The sum of $100 million had already been transferred to his Zurich account, and things seemed to be moving well. A thought gnawed at his gut, though. What if Mohammed and Kudirat failed? What would happen to him? The fleeting thought of failure sent a jolt of fear through him. The repercussions would be severe. Where would he run to? The arms of the law were extensive, but they were definitely more palatable than the idea of retribution at the hands of Kolinsky. Even his amassed wealth couldn't protect him. It's been years since he trained vigorously. Besides, acquiring money beyond Senator Lee's wildest dreams had left him weak in his resolve to suffer high level brutality.

Cold perspiration trickled down his hands and his skin suddenly felt clammy. The recent attempt on his life left him jittery. His mind whirled with various exit strategies if things went south. The vibrating cell phone brought him back to the present with a thud. He paused for ten seconds to gather his thoughts before looking at the caller ID display. He listened silently without interjecting, then shut the phone with a click.

It was too late to have pangs of conscience. The show had started. There was no going back.

Chapter 31

Seth Jones woke up with a start, his body tingled with anticipation. The sun has risen in the sky as the wren chirped happily outside his bay window. 'D' day was at hand, and it was nearly time to put things into motion.

He was a professor of biotechnology from Stamford University of Technology, an avid reader and researcher into hematopoietic cancer and stem cell evolution until his life fell apart. Ruefully, he reminisced a beautiful time in his life, when his girlfriend Sheena was still alive. A time of romance, when life was perfect, and time stood still. His heart felt warm with the tender memories, banter, and desire to see the world together.

They shared the same dreams. But that was a lifetime ago. Bitterness rose to the surface, leaving bile in his throat as he contemplated the fact that it was all a lie. His love, his darling, was nothing more than a terrorist who had played on his emotions, manipulated him, and wormed her way into his social circle. An amazingly beautiful and articulate woman with a sharp mind, who later became a terrorist. *Or was that before?* he thought. She must have been a plant. She knew him better than anybody else. Tears streamed silently down his face.

What did it matter now? The history books couldn't be re-written. He had lost everything: his girlfriend, job, and social status. Even his closest friend, Noel, regarded him as a leper and politely avoided further interaction. He became a pariah, a social outcast in the community. His psychological state deteriorated as a result. So many questions remained unanswered.

Why me? he thought. Eighteen months of bliss, climaxing into the blowing up of Bus 101, killing twenty-eight people, twelve of whom were children on their way to school. The newspaper headlines 'Professor's *Suicide bomber claims lives'* shattered his world. Sadly, he could remember vividly what transpired that morning. Going back in time to the event, his mind tumbled and reeled at the gravity of the event that catastrophically changed his life forever.

Yes, he could remember booking a table for two the night before at Fargo's. It was going to be a surprise to celebrate Sheena's thirtieth birthday. Why not a double celebration? He had bought an expensive engagement ring that had a sapphire stone setting. Something special that would go nicely with Sheena's fiery grey eyes. He was anxious; he wanted to pop the question at the right time in the perfect setting, oblivious of the fact that things were not right. Sheena seemed a bit distant too, but he was too preoccupied to notice.

The fateful day began with the sun rising from the east, and a soft westerly breeze. Sheena seemed subdued and wanted to wear the new Samia wool and silk scarf from Jimmy Choo. Seth did not want to argue; after all, it was her birthday. He would be as accommodating as possible, if it meant he'd spend his lifetime with this beautiful creature. Besides, the scarf complemented her fabulous shape. Happily, arm in arm, they left their apartment together. She briefly rested her head gently on his shoulder as they walked, a promise of future intimacy lacing its way through her soothing fingers made Seth tingle in expectation.

Admiringly, his eyes locked onto hers as they walked. As they drew nearer to the bus stop, Sheena's face grew more serious. She stopped hesitantly and looked deeply into his eyes, perhaps looking for an answer. *Nothing was going to mess things up*, Seth thought. His heart was so light with joy at his plan for the evening that he failed to comprehend the apprehension lurking deep within Sheena's stare. She held on to him a trifle bit longer than usual and gave him a lingering kiss. With a palm to her lips, she blew him a final kiss and stepped onto the bus.

He walked a few steps before turning to give her a final wave. He stopped instinctively in his tracks. His mind whirred back to earlier that morning. Her handbag was new and unusually large. He had forgotten to ask her where she had bought it from. Helplessly, Seth stood there dumbfounded as he watched Sheena take off her coat and expose the device strapped to her chest. The scarf was obscuring part of her face. But he knew what was about to happen. Within seconds, he heard a rumble as the bomb detonated and the force of the impact knocked him off his feet and crashed him into the post-box, leaving him stunned and shell-shocked.

Pandemonium stirred all around him while he lay mortified at what had just happened. He struggled to sit upright as all hell broke loose. Sirens wailed in the distance and cries of help punctuated the morning as cars collided into each other in the confusion. This was like a scene out of a movie script, unbelievably surreal. Smoke billowed all around, creating a curtain of deep smog, pervasively shrouding the area and reducing visibility to just a few feet in either direction. Panic gripped him as he lay there. He intuitively knew that this would be the beginning of his waking nightmare.

He wasn't disappointed. Shunned and despised, he bore the oppressive mark of loneliness and despair. Six years on, however, he was ready to leave an indelible mark. Everybody was going to remember the pain and suffering he endured by the emasculation and rejection caused by Sheena's betrayal and the disruption of his life.

Anyway, tomorrow was the anniversary of the bombing. It was going to be a blast. He'd make sure of it. *Blue County would definitely find its place on the map*, he thought as he loaded his luggage and special cargo into his tired, beaten up old Taurus.

Chapter 32

Steven Blaine sat back in a rickety chair in a stuffy interview room, unperturbed that he was being observed through the one-way mirror. He mused sardonically that it had taken the police this long to catch him. He had been very careful. He always wore gloves, and made sure that he left no witnesses. They didn't have a hold on him, he surmised. If things got hairy, he could plead the Fifth Amendment or call in the cavalry. Any lawyer would do. He was, after all, entitled to a lawyer, wasn't he? It seemed to work in the law and order series, why wouldn't it work for him?

He looked at the clock. He had been seated for four hours. He was patient. Time was irrelevant in the hunt. The prize made it worth it. He was ready. He'd wait it out. There was nowhere else to go anyway.

Meanwhile, behind the mirror, Tony and Michael planned their strategy after reviewing the DNA evidence from the lab report. The state attorney watched as they deliberated on how much they would share with the young sub. The horrific photos displayed with candor the sadistic and frenzied attack on each victim. Yet, by appearance, Steven Blaine looked like the man next door. Who would suppose otherwise?

Carrying three cups of coffee in paper cups, Tony and Michael made their entrance into the stifling hot room labelled Interview Room 3. The drab surroundings housed a wobbly wooden table and a broken ceiling rose that cast deep shadows in the corners of the dated interrogation room.

Michael straddled the seat opposite Blaine and pushed a cup in his direction, all the while watching the subject intently. Blaine made no move, just looked on dispassionately, waiting for the next move. Tony leaned off the wall and casually opened the file on the table. Michael placed the pictures systematically in front of Blaine.

"Care to admire your work, Mr. Blaine?" asked Michael.

"What work are we talking about?" replied Blaine. "I'm just a garbage man. I pick up garbage, not drop it, officer," he said laughing.

Michael nettled at the humorless joke.

"Do you find it funny that these eight girls were killed?" Michael's voice rose a notch. "Look at Anne Marie Cummings, murdered in her prime with a deep cut to the throat, severing the windpipe and the root of the tongue, cutting almost through to the vertebrae. Is this your handiwork? Or perhaps Sheila Braxton? Who you butchered with a double-edged knife, covered her face and arms with bruises, and left battered like a broken toy?" anger inflating his pitch.

Blaine eyed the policeman with cynicism in his eyes. "You'll have to do better than that," he retorted. Michael's frayed nerves had reached breaking point. He sprang over the table in an attempt to vent his fury on the scumbag. Tony held on to his partner's arm, preventing him from lashing out at the suspect and literally forced him out of the interrogation room.

Michael returned moments later, ignored the sneer on Blaine's face and resumed the interrogation. After several hours of grilling, he was nowhere nearer to a confession than when they had started. Frustrated, he slouched back in the chair trying to look as menacing as possible while he pondered on what to do next. A sudden sharp knock on the door brought him to attention and the Chief of police put his head into the room and signaled for the duo to come outside.

Leaving Blaine in the hands of the new rookie who was witnessing his first interrogation interview, Michael and Tony ambled out of the room. The Chief's face looked pallid, his sagging chin, stubble beard, and spidery wrinkles interwove a picture of fatigue, age, and pressure. This was highlighted by the way his eyes flittered from Tony to Michael in seconds, emitting a sign of desperation. His slouched shoulders gave credence to his feeling of resignation towards the volatile situation he found himself in.

"Have you found out anything from the suspect? We need to close this case down. I really don't need the FBI breathing down our necks, sticking their nose where it doesn't belong, do you understand? Meanwhile, there's a witness sitting down the hall who might have some information that maybe pertinent to your case," said the chief.

Not waiting for a reply, he said, "Get a move on. You haven't got all day." He bit down on his cigar and abruptly stormed into his office, slamming the door shut.

The witness was sitting close to the vending machine, clutching her bag in a vice-like grip. Her nervousness dripped like a fridge thawing out. For a woman who was normally a very confident, vibrant person, who always made her presence felt, came across as agitated and subdued. She was working at the local grocery store for the last twenty-six years and knew practically everybody there was to know in Blue County. They ushered her over to Michael's desk, which was less cluttered and had some leg space to sit down at. It also offered privacy from the curious, prying ears and eyes of their fellow cops hanging around in the squad room. They offered her the precinct's best coffee, which could only be considered as colored sewer water, before delicately probing why she had come to the station.

With a little encouragement, a stream of words came stuttering out of her in between shallow breaths. She recounted how she had seen Blaine on two separate occasions: on the night when Angela Gomez was killed and on the night of Ann Marie Cummings' murder. She also relayed significant information that related to the timeline of Catherine Baxter's death that placed him in the area. Excited, they asked Mrs. Carson whether she could identify the killer from a line-up. She was adamant that she could. Tony left to arrange the line-up, while Michael went through the mug shot profile with the eyewitness. Forty-five minutes later, she identified Blaine and confirmed from the line-up that he was the man she had seen. It was a slam dunk.

Meanwhile, Blaine knew that he had to confess. Without further persuasion, he gave a breakdown of all the girls he killed. The only place left for him now was prison, where nobody would miss him. Tony and Michael, on the other hand, were happy with the day's result and decided to call it a night. They'd catch up on the paperwork in the morning. Upbeat, they left the precinct together, had a few drinks at Angie's Bar, and headed off home.

Tomorrow was another day, one case closed, one less thing to worry about, Tony thought as he drifted off to sleep. How incredibly naïve was that?

Chapter 33

The incessant rain released a torrent flow of hailstones that tapped in tune with the whistling wind. The gale force billowed and wrapped itself around the trees in an unseemly embrace as the trees danced in cadence to the relentless pounding rain. The thunderstorm darkened the skies and the pregnant clouds stretched to blacken out the shimmer of sunlight struggling to break through.

Under the deepening shadows of dusk, Kudirat and Mohammed alighted from the bus and stepped in line behind a streaming flock of tourists who was making its way to the Blue County Sheraton Hotel and The Concorde, which was situated right next to it. At the last possible moment, they left the group, veered right, and made their way into an alley littered with garbage bags and refuse stacked up neatly against the west wall. They scaled the north wall and slipped into a cul-de-sac where the back door to a two-story wooden house lay open, awaiting their entrance.

Seated in plush, burgundy leather armchairs were Professor Gray, Professor Jones, and Professor Khan, who arose to welcome the pair. After a brief introduction, Professor Gray laid out the schematics to the Conference Room of the Sheraton where the summit was going to be held. He also gave each person in the room a specially coded microchip with specific instructions for each member of the group.

Twenty minutes later, the party dispersed, leaving Kudirat and Mohammed behind. The pair made their way to the top floor, where food and provisions were laid out. They foraged through the supplies and began to assemble the materials for the bomb. They were under strict orders to set off the bomb and obliterate all evidence leading back to their handler. They were under no illusion that a cleaner was also nearby to clean up any potential mess they created, or to act if they failed. 'In war, take no prisoners,' was Mohammed's motto. There were always casualties in war. He just needed to make sure that he wasn't one… Kudirat could take care of herself. She took first watch as he fell into a light sleep.

Forty-five miles away, in an abandoned cornfield, a small Cessna plane landed, earlier under the guise of night, to let off the newest arrival to Blue County, Avery. A ghost in the night, he moved stealthily with purpose, intent on executing his part of the master plan. The only person who knew of his arrival was Martin Lecter who was already on the run.

Chapter 34

The rainstorm had disrupted Ralph and Matthew's plan. The velocity of the swirling wind pounded ceaselessly around the car, rocking the vehicle to and fro in an unsteady rhythm; leaves clung protectively to the windscreen in a tight embrace, strewn recklessly by the blustering wind, limiting their visibility to less than ten yards.

They were, thankfully, on the verge of leaving Blue County, before the front tire deflated. It seemed like an invisible force was compelling them to make an inevitable stop. One more day wouldn't hurt. Anne Marie's real killer had respite for another day; yes, another day before Senator Lee met his Maker, if he was truly responsible for Ann Marie's death. One of Ralph's buddies helped dig up the information. Blaine had emphatically denied killing Anne Marie in his statement. But had stalked her with the intention of killing her.

Discreet enquiries revealed that Anne Marie had been having an affair with Senator Lee and before she died, she had started avoiding Senator Lee. Ralph and Matthew were determined to find Senator Lee as soon as possible. Meanwhile, resigned to the fact that the elements were in control, they found solace at the Blue County Club's bar. Sitting on bar stools with glasses of Bourbon in their hands, basking in the warmth of the log fire in the reception, they contemplated where they could find a room for the night.

Strolling the streets later that night, they stumbled on a box room at The Salon, a three-star hotel situated in a nondescript side street off the town's main road.

This was as good a place as any to hole up for a while. Patience was a virtue they would tap into. It was a waiting game, and they were willing to endure. Revenge, after all, was better served cold.

Chapter 35

The concierge woke up refreshed and totally invigorated after ten hours of sleep. The sun shone brightly, showing signs of a promising day. It was the day of the conference; it was going to have international coverage. If he could pull it off, he was going to put it on his CV. It would be a stepping stone to bigger things, better places. It would finally end his long boring stay at Blue County Concorde hotel as a concierge.

He hurriedly ate his breakfast of oatmeal and toast, looked at the clock on the mantelpiece, and headed for the door. He was cutting it fine. He had thirty minutes to get to work and put the final touches to the seating arrangements of the Harvard conference room. He grabbed his coat and made his way to the front door. The front door bell rang insistently, stopping him momentarily in his tracks. Cursing inwardly, he jerked open the door, taking in the UPS uniform of the man and the package held in his right hand. Bemused, he looked up into the eyes of the young man blocking his doorway. A pair of piercing blue eyes stared back at him. A cold chill tingled along his spine; it was like looking into a mirror. The same height, face, and body mass. The concierge and the man looked identical. He could certainly pass as a twin. In shock, he stared on in stupefying amazement. His mouth opened inadvertently, like a fish out of water.

The blow struck him instantaneously, temporarily blinding him. He was not about to go down. He shook his head, cleared his vision, and was on his opponent in minutes. He grappled with the killer, hands and feet entwined in battle. They thrashed about, upturning chairs and the dining table as they wrestled around the room. The assassin unsheathed his hunting knife and buried the knife deep into the concierge's stomach, moving the knife in an upward slicing motion, piercing the right ventricle. The concierge convulsed, and then lay still as his body succumbed to the final throes of life.

Avery checked for vital signs, making sure that he was dead. He went into the bathroom, changed into a similar uniform as the concierge's, wrapped his blood-stained clothes in a garbage bag, and wiped down the bathroom sink after applying additional makeup to camouflage the scrapes to his face. Methodically, he went through the rooms to ensure that he had not left behind anything incriminating, he retrieved the UPS package and left the house clinking the dead man's Subaru car keys in his hands. He got into the Subaru and drove off.

Avery pulled into the parking lot with seconds to spare. Acting naturally, he locked the car and made his way through the staff entrance, through the kitchen, and into the main lobby. He was stopped by the special agents who were screening the area for any threatening devices. They patted him down and let him proceed down the hall to the Harvard conference room.

The owner of the hotel obstructed the entrance to the room, appearing hot and sweaty, even though the air conditioner was on full blast. A harried look etched lines of worry, leaving contour lines on his forehead. Spider web lines surrounded his tired eyes, revealing the strain he was currently under. He probably had a lot riding on this event. He could not afford for anything going wrong. His skin crawled at the thought that if something untoward was to happen, what it would mean for his business. It would cripple him. It was bad enough that he was already over-extended on his bank loan, and he had re-mortgaged the house to pay alimony to wife number 4, who had made sure that she had cleaned out the rest of his bank accounts.

"What time do you call this?" he asked as his lower lip trembled in outrage. "You were supposed to come in early to finalize the seating arrangements."

Avery smiled sardonically and replied, "Stop worrying, everything is under control. I told Thelma to bring in the flowers, and the seating arrangement for all the delegates have been positioned accordingly. Look, the names are on each table."

With eyes averted and in a lower tone, the owner re-joined by saying, "I'll hold you personally responsible if anything goes wrong, got it? Besides, make yourself presentable. You look like hell," he added, and stomped off arrogantly.

McClaren looked up from the list of attendees fleetingly, before resuming his scan of the register. The slight tilting of his head and sudden shift to his right to get a better look, without appearing to do so, left Avery uncomfortable in under thirty seconds. Making sure that he appeared unruffled by the comment, he smiled congenially to the back of the owner and said in a modulated voice, "That makes two of us," laughing lightly. He moved in between tables checking out the cutlery, napkins, and glasses to ensure that they were laid out properly. Painstakingly, he performed his role like the real concierge would have done. Satisfied that everything was in place, he ambled off, slowly making his way back to the kitchen to check up on the menu. He stopped briefly to reel off a barrage of instructions to the chef, before proceeding to the toilet. Hesitating briefly, he did a reconnaissance of the toilet area. It seemed empty. Everything seemed to be going to plan.

He methodically shifted the ceiling board and lowered his gym bag. Within seconds, he assembled his Sig Sauer gun and replaced the bag and its contents in a secret place in preparation for what was to come. Moments later, the toilet door swung open and McClaren strolled in, narrowly catching Avery replacing the ceiling board. His face was inscrutable. Leaning against the door jamb, he casually observed Avery as he walked over to the sink and went through the motions of washing his hands. In turn, Avery ignored him, dried his hands, and wordlessly walked out of the toilet without a second glance at McClaren, struggling internally to maintain his semblance of calm. Meanwhile, under his armpits an explosion of sweat patches soaked his shirt even as he tried to maintain a facade of normalcy.

A drop of sweat that escaped and rolled down the side of Avery did not go unnoticed, however. McClaren was determined to keep an eye on this fellow. Nothing could go wrong. It would have international ramifications and would look bad on his resume. He had a gut feeling that something was going to happen, but he was not going to roll over and let it happen on his turf. After all, this was his show, wasn't it?

Chapter 36

Professor Gray and his colleagues sat huddled together discussing the latest edition of the *American Medical Journal*— a medical discovery on the advancement of stem re-generation—while other renowned world scientists milled around in groups, talking in low excited monotones about the latest breakthroughs published in different magazines on the subject.

The buzz in the room was electrifying; slowly building up to a crescendo. The exhilarating undercurrent of something amazing that was about to happen left the room charged in anticipation. The intense energy lit up the room, leaving a flow of raw excitement that was palpable on the faces of expectant experts gathered together in the plush drawing room. The feeling was contagious and evident in the animated eyes of the scientists who were eagerly waiting for Professor Gray to offload his recent miraculous findings. The medical discovery had, in fact, only served to wet the hungry appetites of curious scientists who were impatiently waiting for the conference to begin.

Moments later, the hotel concierge appeared and ushered them into the conference hall that had been modestly decorated to portray the sentiments of an academic event. Professor Gray, Dr. Braithwaite, and three other guest speakers were introduced and seated at the high table in preparation of their speeches. Professor Gray's hands trembled under the table. The time for martyrdom had arrived, and his mouth suddenly went dry. Did he have the courage to set off the bomb? All he had to do was press the detonator on his phone, but was he ready to die?

Looking at the sea of faces expectantly focused on hearing what the guest speakers had to say left him chilled to the bone. They were unprepared to die, ignorant of the fate that awaited them. Yes, the arrogant bastards would not know what hit them. *That would serve them right*, he thought. It was too late to back down now, a lot was riding on his singular action. It was the catalyst for what was in store for the American public. His cause was a just one, killing the infidels in the name of Allah. His family would be proud of him when they discovered that he was part of the plot that killed innumerable Americans on their home soil.

Shaking off the bleak thoughts, he stared unfocusedly at his watch as the seconds rolled away, and his heart beat throbbed violently within his chest. Instinctively, he knew it was time, but something held him back. The unexpected rush of uncertainty and conflicting emotions threatened to derail his mission. Droplets of sweat broke out on his brow, and he hurriedly wiped them away while he scanned the room for the second bomber. His eyes inspected the room and settled on the olive-skinned man that was seated in the back row, silently observing and waiting for Professor Gray to act. Professor Gray's beady eyes were uncomfortably fixated on his subject and on his left hand hidden under the jacket he wore.

Even from that distance, Professor Gray knew that the man was an idealist willing to die at a moment's notice. He was someone determined to complete the mission, with or without him. This realization strengthened his resolve to escape. He stood up and ambled slowly out of the room and headed towards the toilet.

Seth Jones took out his mobile phone as he saw Professor Gray leave then stood up and pressed the trigger. The world around him seemed to stop still, the shocked, bewildered look of the horror-struck scientists lingered for a few seconds before the explosion shook the building, propelling him into the afterlife.

Chapter 37

Moments Earlier

The pathologist Mark Richardson looked up at the slides one more time. His heart plummeted at the realization that his friend Professor Gray was really dead. His friend's body had been repatriated from the United Kingdom. The brilliant mind of a scientist now reduced to a carnage of flesh and bones. Now, he was only a corpse on a slab in the cold, clinically sterilized environment of Tennessee's county morgue. He felt sick to his stomach. The forensic evidence had proved inconclusive initially, maybe because he did not want to believe it. However, his skepticism could not outweigh his drive for the truth and, in total submission to his professional judgment, he inevitably returned to the drop site, gathered more forensic evidence and fast tracked it through his friend at Quantico.

The body was obliterated by the elements and feasting rats. Remnants of skin and a few teeth were the only things recovered from the decayed mass of flesh. But it was enough to confirm the deceased's DNA. Resignedly, with a sigh, he made the call. Within minutes, copies of the report lay on the Head of National Security's desk. Seated opposite him were the Head of Homeland Security and Nick Parker, the FBI director. Their faces blanched at the implication of an impersonator infiltrating the conference, despite the high level of security at the conference site. This could only mean political suicide. The United States of America was renowned for its excellent security level and an international incident on such a large scale was both inconceivable and unacceptable.

Nick Parker excused himself to make the call. On the third ring, McClaren took out his cell and thumbed the speaker button. He listened in rapt attention and signaled to another burly FBI agent to follow him. A quick survey of the conference hall showed that Professor Gray impersonator was not among the throng of attendees gathered in pocket groups discussing in hushed tones. They hurried out of the swinging doors to the north entrance, scanning the corridors and vacant rooms on the first floor. Two other FBI agents had already done a sweep of the upper rooms, without results. Their hearts throbbed with bursts of electric currents, their feet moving in agitated swiftness, intent on uncovering the infiltrator, the uncanny mole who had permeated their impenetrable armor of security. Time was of the essence. He needed to be stopped. Did he have other accomplices? McClaren thought as he broke out in a cold sweat. He gave orders as they frantically combed the hotel looking for traces of the missing scientists.

A flashing warning on his cellphone minutes earlier alerted Fake Professor Gray that he had been made. He slunk away to the toilet on the top floor and discarded his mask, clothes, wig and the custom-made shoes that had added two inches to his height. He reappeared, dressed in hotel garbs, smartly dressed as a hotel valet. It had only taken him three minutes to alter his appearance. Nobody would recognize him now. He looked at least forty pounds heavier in his uniform, padded with false shoulder pads and additional material made to create an impressive girth around his midriff. His new masked face made him look closer to sixty, with wrinkle lines dispersed like spidery legs around the eyes. His hair had been covered and replaced with a silver tinged mane of brown hair.

Taking a final look at himself in the mirror and satisfied by his reflection, he stealthily exited the toilets and disposed of the holdall through the hotel laundry chute and made his way down to the third floor to where he had left the hotel cart. With slow decisive steps, he made his way down to the lobby, pushing his cart, maneuvering it carefully to the side entrance of the hotel, close to the cleaning cupboards. To the untrained eye, he was just another employee carrying out his usual function amid the beehive of activities. The hotel was on lockdown, so there was no hope of escaping. He only needed to keep calm and blend in with the other staff for the moment.

Across the street, Mohammed sat at the Blue County Café sipping on his cup of cappuccino, totally bemused. He watched with hooded eyes while he thought about how to extricate himself from this situation. From the start, he sensed things would go wrong. The advance crew had been incompetent from the get go. How could they leave Professor Gray's body where it could be easily found? It was totally unacceptable. This early discovery had inadvertently triggered a set of events that he had no control over. The chemical bomb was supposed to go off at precisely two o'clock, when the vice president was to make his surprise appearance on behalf of the president. This well-concealed fact was unknown even to McClaren. Well, that was not to be, Mohammed had intercepted the call to the Chief of police, where it was relayed that the vice president was being flown back to Washington.

Six months of meticulous planning, now down the drain. He hated failure. Someone was going to pay for the slip up. It was bad for business. His client would not take this error lightly. There were going to be reprisals, unless he could salvage the situation. There was no way he could retrieve the bomb. The hotel would be an impregnable fort with security oozing from every available pore. No, Mohammed mused, Blue County would still make headlines, but the news would have to be radically changed. A pre-emptive strike to the infidels on their home soil should do it. Resolute with purpose, content that this would be a blow to their overrated reputation of security, Mohammed left the café and lingered with the growing crowd milling around the front of the hotel, puzzled by what was going on inside the hotel. *Clueless lot,* he laughed within, *you will soon find out*.

Meanwhile, McClaren's head buzzed. It was a catastrophe. Professor Gray was nowhere to be found. How could he have eluded security? He had expediently locked down the hotel. The remaining attendees were still huddled in the conference room and were being interviewed by his men. While the employees and guests were being rounded up and secured in the Roosevelt Hall, documents and passes were being scrutinized by the security forces. He couldn't have got away. McClaren was determined to ferret out the culprit. He may have changed his appearance, but he'd be smoked out.

Suddenly, there was a commotion. McClaren signaled to two security guards to hold the door while he grabbed Agent Raines and they rushed out to investigate. As he neared the door, the grandfather clock in the lobby chimed two o'clock. Instinctively, he ducked as the building shook in reaction to the deafening explosion. Pandemonium broke out. The ceiling of the lobby caved in, crushing four security agents and two civilians. Debris littered the lobby as a dust cloud settled like a blanket over the foyer, obscuring visibility.

The FBI agents went into rapid response mode, trying desperately to distil the feeling of panic and confusion which was heightened by the blaring sounds of fire alarms going off simultaneously. All hell had broken loose.

Chapter 38

The Joint Committee was ten minutes late in starting. To add insult to injury, the Head of National Security was droning on and on about the late completion of the latest warship, the 'USS Commando', that his men urgently needed to dispatch to the Strait of Hormuz. Senator Lee felt a headache coming on. It was only 10 a.m., but he felt like he had been wrung through a dryer and spat out. He sat upright in his chair and feigned interest in what was going on around him. His stomach churned like fruits in a blender, whipped and whirled about. He definitely felt queasy. The Senator's hands were clammy and he tried to hide his hands under the table to stop them from shaking. His lips also felt dry, and he kept squirming in his chair to the consternation of the Head of National Security, who gave Senator Lee a withering look that summarized his disdain for him.

Senator Lee, on the other hand, was trying to gather his wits about him, when his phone started vibrating in his pocket. Swiftly, he took it out of his pocket and looked at the caller ID. He left the room unceremoniously, leaving a few eyebrows raised at his rapid departure. His throat felt constricted as he fumbled to press the answer button. Kolinsky's voice boomed back over the line, delivering the bad news. It could only mean one thing. He stood to lose everything he had worked for. He had put his and his family's lives in jeopardy by this one singular act of insanity. It wasn't the money. What was it then? Ah yes, a chance to be the next Vice President of America. His burning ambition to be the second most influential man in America was now out of his grasp. He could have wielded more power around the world. He'd imagined his name in the history books as the Vice President of the United States of America, which was now a distant dream. He needed to get out of there before he was detained.

He never called his wife during a meeting. It was an unspoken rule that they had followed for over seventeen years of marriage. Today was different on so many levels. Penny would appreciate the essence of what he needed to do right away.

He dialed her number while he made his way down the elevator and straight into his waiting car that was parked in front of the Hoover building.

She picked up on the second ring.

"Hi Penny, are you alright?" he said

Penny sounded flustered, "What's wrong, you never call this early? Are you OK, Steve?"

"Just listen darling. Don't go home. I need you to go get Bobby from school and head for T. A.," he said in a rush of words.

"Where are you?" she asked again. Imperceptibly, he released an exasperated sigh.

"Penny, just do as I ask; I'll explain later."

He terminated the call and made another call to an old ally, a defector from the old Odessa, his mentor, and the man who had introduced him to Kolinsky in another lifetime. The phone purred to life as it went through a cycle of technical clicks, and then a faint ringing sound followed by a deep resonating voice answered. This was a secure line, specifically given to him for emergencies.

The Russian Bear, as he was known, guffawed a hello. Senator Lee listened intently, and ended the call with a sigh of relief that his friend would have a private plane waiting for Bobby and Penny at the airport. Now, all he had to do was grab his passport from his apartment and meet up with his family at the airport. Money was no object. He had stashed money away under the pseudonym Matt Brent in the Caymans and in Switzerland amounting to $750 million.

Feeling a bit more confident than he had felt previously, he sank back into the comfort of the Escalade's soft upholstery while his childhood friend and bodyguard, Malcolm Frost, weaved through traffic to his apartment registered under another alias, Fred Banning.

Ten minutes later, cutting through side roads to avoid the onslaught of early lunch hour, Frost drove the Escalade skillfully within traffic limits to masterfully bring them within a block of his boss's hideaway. Anxiously, through chapped lips, he dialed Penny to confirm her arrival at the rendezvous point. She picked up on the first ring; her voice pitched an octave higher, as she struggled to maintain her cool.

"I've got Bobby; we are five minutes out. Hurry, darl—" she added desperately. Lee squirmed in his seat trying to catch the last bit of the sentence as a series of static waves punctuated by an explosion of bullets and shattered glass ensued.

A feeling of devastation swept over him, as it dawned on him that Penny and Bobby had been ripped out of this world. It was his fault; he should have protected them better. The phone slid from his hands as grief overtook him. He had always been strong, but this was different. The tears broke through and slid uncontrollably down his cheek. His heart welled up with the inconsolable loss of having lost the most precious things in his life.

Brushing back the tears, he vigorously tried to clear his head and focus on his exit plan. He'd have time to grieve later. Now, escaping this nightmare was imperative. He could not go to the private airport, because they knew he would be heading that way. Mulling over what he needed to do, he failed to notice the 100-ton lorry that had quickly changed lanes and was bearing down on them.

Frost quickly swerved the escalade with a sharp swerving motion into the central lane, jolting Senator Lee back to the present. The lorry increased speed, grazing two other cars in its wake. Screeching tires and the force of the collision sent the two cars into the line of oncoming traffic. Chaos erupted as the lorry increased speed and hit the trunk of the Escalade.

The sudden impact catapulted the vehicle over the balustrade onto the highway below, it flew in mid-air and landed on top of a grey sedan heading northwards. Other cars frantically swerved to avert the accident, while a blue Subaru, unable to steady the car on contact from the spinning grey sedan, spun out of control and hit the guardrail, and burst into flames.

Drivers stopped and abandoned their cars, scurrying away on foot, watching from a distance. Frost removed his seat belt and whirled around to check on Senator Lee. His military training kicked in. He surveyed the crowd, looking for any signs of danger. Satisfied that he had temporary reprieve, he gathered his wits about him and retrieved his gun from the glove compartment. A few brave spectators rallied around to help Frost extract the unconscious body of Senator Lee that was wedged between the backseat and the mangled backdoor. The backdoor did not budge. This was apparently a job for the emergency services.

Within minutes, sirens, commingled with the cacophony of noise, invaded the scene. The firemen worked speedily with precision; they efficiently prized out the roof of the car and extricated Senator Lee. Meanwhile, Frost kept a watchful eye on the crowd while shielding Senator Lee's body from further harm. He moved in cadence with the paramedics as they carried Senator Lee into the waiting ambulance. Following close behind, Frost swiftly jumped into the ambulance and shut the door, making a hasty retreat amidst the commotion.

For an instant, his eyes locked onto the lorry driver, who observed from the upper level of the highway, and a slight tremor ran down his spine.

The lorry driver watched from a distance, disgusted by the fact that they were both still alive. He called it in and dropped the disposable phone amid a pile of litter that lay by the side of the road. He had made sure that the damaged lorry, which, incidentally, had been stolen at a truck stop three nights ago in Colorado, had been wiped clean before abandoning it.

It would be virtually impossible to link the lorry back to him. Or so he thought.

Chapter 39

Before the explosion, two scientists excused themselves from the cluster of academicians, requesting a toilet break, jokingly blaming it on the strong, rich macchiato they had been drinking. Leaving the conference room, they headed quickly in the direction of the toilet. With subtle nods of acknowledgment, the two stationery FBI agents made way for them to pass by, before reassuming their positions scanning the hallway for potential threats.

Locking the toilet doors carefully behind them, they changed into police uniforms hidden discreetly in waterproof bags stashed in the engine of the toilet and synchronized their watches, ears peeled for the explosion that was to come. They were not disappointed; within seconds, the vibration of the bomb ripped the toilet door off its hinges, flinging it against the bathroom window, shattering it to pieces on impact. The commotion geared them into action, as smoke reduced visibility to just yards. Purposefully, they helped some of the guests leave the building, even supporting a young blonde guest who had been hit by shrapnel—from a broken chair or table—that had made contact with her hand.

Safely outside, the two scientists observed the carnage, and waited for the right moment to disentangle themselves from the situation before the real policemen arrived. Vengeance, masterminded by Simeon Kolinsky, was really happening in Blue County. Unobtrusively, they mingled with the crowd and slipped away in the same direction as Mohammed. Passersby stood transfixed to the spot as they watched the drama unfold. They watched in horror as people spilled onto the street, running in different directions, trying to get away from the entrance of the hotel. Blood was splattered all over the place. Emergency services were desperately trying to put a lid on the carnage. Men in suits were shouting out orders, while the policemen on the scene scampered around like headless chicken.

In all the years the spectators had spent in Blue County, they had never seen anything as gripping or as captivating. Excitedly, a young boy took out his cell phone and clicked off some pictures. This was certainly cool. He'd have shots to show at school. It could also earn him a few dollars too. He certainly felt like an extra in an action-packed movie that had numerous police cars, ambulances, and two fire trucks, all at the scene, as bolstering forces of men in suits speaking into their earpieces and directing the flow of pedestrian gave a surreal feel.

Chapter 40

The two scientists, Mohammed and Kudirat, had made a timely exodus from Blue County using a police patrol car and an unlicensed bureau car. They eluded the check point perimeter by seconds, putting as many miles between them and Blue County as possible. They stopped at an abandoned shack ten miles up the road, ditched the cars, changed clothes, and drove off in a blue minivan parked there three weeks ago.

Driving through the night, the scientists, Mohammed and Kudirat, arrived at the Southern Motel at 4 a.m., one hour ahead of schedule, moving silently like silhouettes of ghosts in a Friday night horror movie. Under the guise of darkness, they gathered together in one room to discuss their next strategy and wait for further instructions.

Kudirat felt drained. She needed a wash. A hot shower would sluice away the sweat and grime from the bomb scene. The plan had gone to pot. That is the problem when you have professionals working with people without specialist training. The TV was on full blast, and she could hear snippets from the breaking news bulletin. The reports were filled with speculations and assessments of the collateral damage. There was no mention of how many people were confirmed dead.

She lingered a few moments longer than necessary in the bath. She did not relish the thought of sharing the small motel room with a bunch of strangers who were, in fact, a liability to her and Mohammed. She sensed Mohammed's frustration on the drive over. He was set in his ways. He had an inherent dislike for infidels and believed that he was fighting a just war. Her motives were totally different, but Mohammed had never asked, and she wasn't telling.

Twenty minutes later, she was dressed in a black tee shirt, black leather jacket, and charcoal trousers fitted with an inner compartment where she had stashed her passport, some money, and a hunting knife. She put on her holster and slid her .22 automatic in the top part of her boots. She tied her hair back into a ponytail and surveyed her image in the mirror. She could see the tired eyes alertly and intelligently looking back at her. They still had that feral quality that she had inherited from her father. Her father was a story to be told another day. Extricating herself from this mess would be her first step.

She leaned forward, hand on the doorknob, when she heard the rustle of feet, followed by the intrusion of gunshots as the front door was kicked in. A cry rang out, and the loud thud of a body crashing to the floor propelled her into action. Uncoiling, like a snake about to attack, she slithered lightly on her feet to the bathroom window. She peered outside to see moving shadows merging with the morning dawn. Curling into a ball, she climbed out of the window and rolled into an outgrowth of grass set out in clumps at irregular intervals. Moving deftly on her stomach, she glided soundlessly behind the next motel room. Kneeling on all fours, she crouched close to the wall, ensuring that her body was concealed by the outline of a tuft of sagebrush. She strained her ears to listen for any unusual sounds. Her ears struggled to distinguish the early morning's noises from the attackers'.

She lay still when she heard the soft crunch of boot soles not far from her. Leaving her body in a limber position, willing herself not to breathe, she waited, poised for action if necessary, her gun close to her side. Minutes ticked by, and, with a sigh of relief, she finally heard the footsteps recede, moving in another direction.

In the distance, she heard car doors slam shut and the screeching of tires as two cars made a speedy retreat from the motel. Counting inaudibly in her head, time stood still for Kudirat. Her mind was in turmoil. What had happened to Mohammed? Did he make it?

Tears threatened to flow, but she kept them in check. Quickly scanning the area, she moved stealthily towards the back wall and elevated her body over it, landing lightly on her feet. She squatted down, as if to pick up something that she had dropped, while she scrutinized the area. Nothing seemed out of the ordinary. She progressed slowly, constantly checking out the area for potential threats. Her heart pounded in her chest like a rollercoaster leaving its bay. Walking at a steady pace, she made her way to the bus stop and boarded the bus that would take her all the way to New York.

There, among the moving mass of people, she could finally be another figure in the crowd.

Chapter 41

It was time for payback. Ralph had gotten a call confirming that Anne Marie was probably killed by Senator Lee. The fingerprint profile and the tie pin had mysteriously gone missing from the evidence locker of Precinct 13. The inside man knew that more incriminating evidence was being suppressed. After all, Senator Lee was one of America's most influential men. He was tipped to be the next Vice President of America, or was he? Ralph mused. Well, not if he could help it.

He'd destroyed his sister's life, and now he was going to feel all the pent-up rage Ralph felt, first-hand. Ralph made a few calls and got Senator's Lee address. For two days, they had staked out the joint, waiting for the right time to strike.

Mrs. Lee's schedule was basically the same. Apparently, she was a creature of habit. 8.15 a.m., drive Bobby to school, back by 9.15 a.m. She tottered around the house until 2.45 p.m., and then back to Bobby's school. A brief stopover for ice-cream, then back home by 4.00 p.m. Bobby went to bed at 7.30 p.m., and Mrs. Lee sat up waiting for her husband until well into the night. She didn't even bother closing the curtains.

It was surprising how little security they had in the neighborhood, or around Senator Lee's family. The estate had perhaps always been regarded as secure, or perhaps Senator Lee had all the security, because he was the important one. Just to be sure, they continued the surveillance from a safe distance, as unobtrusively as possible.

Today seemed different. Penny was not on her usual schedule. She was leaving the house in the middle of the day. She looked agitated, pumped with unusual spurts of energy. Ralph and Matthew sat huddled in their old 1974 Oldsmobile Buick, noting the early departure of Mrs. Lee. They started up their engine and followed her without being obvious.

She gripped the steering wheel in rapt concentration, lost in thought, unaware that she was being followed. The roads were relatively clear, so she made her way back to the school in twenty minutes flat. Bobby's teacher was concerned that she hadn't called ahead to let her know, but did not want to make a fuss. These rich women could be vindictive, better not ruin her career by crossing the senator's wife. She did note that Mrs. Lee did look distracted and her eyes kept flitting to the door and the window. Something was definitely not right with the woman, but that wasn't her concern, was it?

Penny grabbed Bobby's stuff and led him gently into the car, keeping a tight smile on her face, trying desperately to maintain a calm she didn't feel right then. Bobby was already upset at the disruption to his usual timetable. *Well*, she thought, *I'll make it up to him once we're airborne.* There were more important things to think about, like survival.

Thirty-five minutes later, they were home. She told Bobby to stay in the car with the window up and made a dash for the house. She stopped short of the doorway and looked around the street uneasily, before inserting the key into the lock. She looked in their direction, but the Buick was obscured by an elm tree. Satisfied, she went into the house and came out moments later with a large holdall and two suitcases. She put them in the boot, closed it, and went back to reset the alarm system before returning to the car.

It was now or never. Ralph and Matthew alighted from their car, crossed the street, and walked up to the car. With keys in the ignition, about to drive away, with her cell phone in her hand, she said, "I've got Bobby, we are five minutes out. Hurry, darl—" Instinctively, she turned as she felt the intrusion, just before a rain of bullets shattered the glass. Protectively, she reached out to shield Bobby. Ten bullets riddled her body and she slumped back. Her eyes lay open and vacant as her fleeting breath dissipated from her body.

The sounds of two cars approaching at terrific speed spurred Ralph and Matthew into action. They quickly returned to the car, slowly pulled off the curb, and turned in the opposite direction. They were long gone by the time two government cars pulled up in front Senator Lee's house. Agents arrived two minutes later to recover the bodies of Penny and Bobby Lee.

Chapter 42

Kudirat's wait at the terminal had been nerve-wracking. She knew that she could be spotted and dealt with at any moment. She had even less confidence in the bus that she was going to board. The company bus parked in the terminal did nothing to assuage her fears; it really did not look like it would pass a routine inspection. However, that was the least of her problems. She needed to put in as much distance as possible between herself and her pursuers.

She clutched the bus ticket tightly in her clammy hands, and found a position that afforded her the opportunity to get a good look at everybody approaching the bus she intended to get on. People milled around searching for the right bus, and she felt safe submerged in the throng of people bustling about. Not enough to let her guard down, after all, professional killers with long-range rifles were formidable and did not care about casualties.

Finally, it was time to board. Yet, she waited. She examined the trickle of passengers boarding the dilapidated bus. It was open seating, and she had no intention of snuggling up with a total stranger. She looked for a place away from the rest. Most of the people had knapsacks, large shopping bags, small suitcases, and bags and pillows. She, on the other hand, had nothing but her ripped jacket that was smudged by caked dirt from when she fell; a few dollars in her pocket; an American Express card she had taken from an unsuspecting traveler at the terminal while queuing for a bus ticket; and her Glock, which she cleverly concealed under her coat.

Once aboard the bus, Kudirat did a nosedive to the back seat near the toilet. She was sure that nobody would dispute her for the chance to sit so close to the smelly toilet that was releasing a steady stream of defecating odor. And she was right. Counting the number of seats being filled, she relaxed a little when the driver, impatient to set off on the grueling journey, engaged the grinding gears, closed the door, screeched on the rusted brakes, and set the bus in motion, even though the bus was not full. Seven hours was a long time, and Kudirat's body yearned for some rest. Within minutes, she drifted off into a restless sleep as her body acclimated to the bumpy ride.

The bus grounded to a final stop, and Kudirat woke up. They had arrived at the Big Apple. Although the trip had been very uncomfortable, leaving her aching from top to bottom, she was thankful that there were no nasty incidents to contend with. Alighting from the bus at the depot, she made her way to the nearest shopping mall to explore the best that New York had to offer.

Thirty minutes later, emerging from the mall from its west side entrance, cradling two shopping bags filled with a new set of clothes, boots, handbags, disposable phones, and toiletries, she headed for a three-star motel. She spent the next forty-five minutes completing her disguise and strategizing where to go to make the call. Leaving the motel fifteen minutes later, with a plan crystallizing in her head, she made off to the Café Boulud for a meal. She placed her order of Wild Arugula salad, heirloom tomatoes, goat cheese, crispy shallots, and champagne vinaigrette. The 2010 Chianti seemed like a good option to chase down the meal with, so she added it to the list of things she wanted. With the order out of the way, she slipped away from her table and went to the Surrey Hotel, which was adjacent to the restaurant, and made her call.

She wasted no time, her fingers deftly punching in the emergency number she had committed to the recesses of her memory. Her handler picked up on the second ring. No questions asked, he rattled off a list of instructions and terminated the conversation.

She returned to her seat in time for her meal. She relished the food; it was quite outstanding. Within herself, she knew she would perhaps never get such an opportunity again. The clock was ticking, and she had to get to the Buffalo Niagara International Airport by 23:00 hours, where a private cargo plane would pick her up. Her handler was specific: if she did not get a call by 21:00, she should abandon the arrangement and make alternative plans. The Buffalo Niagara International Airport was a mid-sized airport used as a gateway by those visiting Niagara Falls. It also served the purpose of being isolated.

She rose from her seat after fifteen minutes, fully sated by the scrumptious meal, and made her way out of the restaurant. She did a quick survey of the sidewalk before stepping out and mingling with the few pedestrians who were pre-occupied with reaching their destinations. The sun was warmly sitting overhead, and it cast a tingling glow over the street. She paused momentarily to look at her reflection in the shop window, admiring her transformation. Instinctively, she ducked to the left as she saw the reflection of a laser light from a sniper's rifle, followed by the plonk of a bullet as it hit the shop window, which shattered on impact. Her shoulder caromed into the sidewalk as she went down. The rain of bullets lasted forty seconds and then stopped. Kudirat was up in an instant running for cover. She caught a fleeting glimpse of a MP-5 being pulled back into a black SUV that made a hasty retreat from the scene. She did not get the number plates, not that it mattered, the car was probably stolen or the number plate was fake. Straightening up, she looked around to assess the damage.

Kudirat looked back at the restaurant. People were slowly getting to their feet. Thankfully, the restaurant had not been very busy, as people were still making their way in for lunch. The casualties were few. From her quick sweep, it seemed apparent that there was only one person down. She did not wait for the police or the emergency services to arrive. She did not want to get embroiled in giving a statement. The message was clear. The bullets were meant for her.

She had to keep on moving. Making it to the rendezvous point was becoming increasingly difficult, but her life depended on it. Kudirat had never backed down on any assignment, and she was not backing down, not now, when it meant life or death. But that did nothing to pacify the bitter taste of bile making its way up from her stomach, or erode the feeling of being so hopelessly alone. Where was Mohammed? She missed him.

Meanwhile, she had five hours and twenty-seven minutes to get to Buffalo International. She just had to find a way to get there. The question was, would she make it?

Chapter 43

Reverberating sounds jangled in his head and a pounding went on mercilessly. McClaren's eyes flitted under his eyelids in confusion. In response, the monitor shrieked, emitting a screeching alarm that announced McClaren's return to earth. He tried to sit up, but was restricted by the tubes snaking out of his body.

A cacophony of sound erupted round him, and he felt people bobbing all around. Two nurses struggled to stop the noise and control the number of security personnel that flooded the room. His brain did little to absorb the concerned faces as he drifted off to sleep once more. Several hours later, McClaren opened his eyes to see the twinkling blue eyes of the matron looking down at him as she checked his vitals. Her radiant smile held him captivated momentarily as his brain geared into action. The realization hit home. He was in the hospital. Why was he here? He vehemently struggled against the restraints, but was gently pushed back by the smiling nurse.

Falling back into the softness of the hospital pillow, the recollection of the past 24 hours came flooding back. The explosion at the hotel had triggered a chain of events that he was unable to control. He could still feel the heat of the blast, the bodies littered around, and the scenery that was punctuated by piercing screams and people sobbing.

He remembered instructing two FBI agents, Jerry and Finelli, to help the survivors while he went further into the back of the hotel in search of other victims and potential terrorists. Dark rivulets of blood flowed in a steady trickle across the hotel lobby floor. His ears picked up the groan of someone in the last room, and he hurried on without caution to assist.

Kneeling down on one knee, he could hear the groaning of someone buried under the wreckage. His hands moved briskly, disposing the trail of broken furniture littering the way, until he saw the face of one of the scientists breathing shallowly. He was in bad shape. McClaren hoped that he was in time to save the scientist. With renewed vigor, he hacked away at the pile of rubble, only to stop short when he saw the device the scientist was holding in his right hand. Dumbstruck, he looked disbelievingly at the scientist, whose eyes were lit by a maniacal glint, he bared his teeth, looked menacingly at McClaren, for the last time, before his eyes lolled back, discharging his hand-gripped cargo. McClaren fell back scampering for cover as the device detonated, lifting McClaren off the ground and into unconsciousness.

The nurse gently readjusted his pillow, and he snapped out of his reverie. He remembered everything clearly. McClaren began to recognize the people buzzing about him, and gingerly worked his way into a sitting position, unaided. The tubes had been removed, and the feeling of vertigo washed over him fleetingly. Two agents stood beside the bed like two Labradors, relief lighting up their faces, while McClaren's boss stood on the other side speaking earnestly with the doctor. Apparently, he was being discharged. A ride downtown to the regional office was on the cards.

Silently, he got up and got dressed. This was an international incident with far reaching consequences. Terrorism on American soil could create national hysteria. He needed to put the pieces together and fast. Why had the Blue County Conference been targeted? It was just a meeting of intellectuals on the verge of scientific discovery, or was it? Intel gathered so far was frustratingly limited, but he had an angle that he could tap into. The deluded scientist he had tried to save was a destructive tool. Why was he chosen to explode the unusual device that almost took his life? Well, that's what he was about to find out.

Fully dressed and motivated, McClaren accompanied his colleagues to the regional headquarters for debriefing. Perhaps an answer to the puzzle was in sight.

Either way, the case had his full attention. Deep within him, the nagging awareness that they had been hit with the aid of home-grown terrorists left a sickening feeling in the pit of his stomach. Seth Jones had been a well-respected scientist, philanthropist, and family man who had recently been nominated to run for the Senate just two weeks ago. Who else was involved in the saga, and how much should he disclose to his boss before checking things out first?

There was definitely more than what met the eye. Morosely lost in thought, he kept his notions to himself as they made their way to headquarters; dread clawing its way slowly into his gut.

Chapter 44

Just as McClaren had predicted, the grim report presented during the briefing and the stacks of insurmountable paperwork set the agents' teeth on edge. The grisly account triggered a seething rage that was barely contained by the participants, who dispersed from the meeting feeling more determined to bring the culprits to justice in any way possible.

McClaren took the copious report into his cubicle, sat down by his desk, and immersed himself in the information gathered so far. He doggedly worked through lunch to late evening, examining each detail with meticulous attention. Seven hours later, with his head reaching splitting point, he was no closer than when he started. A breath of fresh air was what he needed to clear his head. Resignedly, he decided that the answer might come on a full stomach.

Fifteen minutes later, he was seated behind a table at the local Chinese restaurant—Foy Little Tokyo—refreshed by the blast of cold air that had followed him during his power walk to the restaurant. The smell of a tantalizing mix of spices assailed his nostrils, and his stomach growled in acknowledgement. He placed his order and silently reviewed the facts that he had sifted through all day. What nagged at the back of his mind was what had made the scientist participate in this dastardly act of terror. Dr. Jones had had political aspirations. He was an upstanding citizen in his community. His records had been clean. So, what motivated him?

Picking up this train of thought, he phoned Raines and asked him to check it out. He focused on his dinner for the next twenty minutes and washed it down with a cup of coffee. He was still on strong antibiotics, so there simply was no room for alcohol. Paying his bill, he stepped out on to the sidewalk, when his cellphone jingled in his pocket, announcing an incoming call. Raines related his findings over the phone. Excited, McClaren made it back to HQ in seven minutes, exhilarated by the breakthrough. He was hyperventilating, but not because of the brisk walk back, adrenaline coursed through his veins as he scanned through the contents of the wallet and satchel. Two driving licenses that belonged to Dr. Jones and Professor Gray, along with two bus tickets and reservations for room 406 and 409 at Southern Motel, were recovered from the bag. Raines had already found the location and notified law enforcement in the area to set up roadblocks leading to the motel. McClaren dispatched two agents to carry out a clean sweep. He was in no shape to travel by road. He would work from HQ while the agents would perform the heavy lifting. His body needed rest. Maybe a few hours' sleep would relieve his aching ribs and pounding headache. Stretching out on the makeshift camp bed that was set to one side of his office, he drifted off to sleep.

Four hours later, the insistent ringing of his cell phone brought him out of his sleep. They had hit pay dirt. Raines and his replacement partner had got to the Southern Motel too late. Three bodies had been recovered from the motel room and transported to the morgue. The conference tags of the two scientists were found in their pockets. McClaren asked them to stay put and gather as much evidence as they could, while he got on the company chopper and headed for the Kansas Morgue for an inspection of the bodies deposited with the county coroner.

McClaren had worked with the coroner in a previous case in Oklahoma. He was a thoroughbred scientist, articulate, with an uncanny sense of perception, and an eye for detail, always dressed in his brown shirt, green chinos, and a pair of moccasins. McClaren knew he was the best man for the job. He needed answers, and God had just thrown him a bone to work with. The bomb in Blue County was only a chapter in the unsavory saga. The rest of the story was being written, and McClaren prayed that he and his team were on the course to stopping it. First of all, he had to figure it all out. The trail of crumbs was leading him to the three bodies at the morgue. He just hoped that he could figure it out in time, or there would be devastating consequences. McClaren shuddered at the thought, as the macabre vision of the Blue County Hotel scene sought to invade his thoughts.

McClaren found the coroner engrossed in his autopsy when he arrived. He gave no indication that he had seen McClaren enter the morgue lab, speaking slowly and clearly into the microphone as his assistant hovered nearby, handling pieces of surgical equipment as he progressed in the autopsy. McClaren watched intently. The first body under the knife was about 6 feet 3, a white Caucasian about 45 years old, with brown hair and brown eyes. His midriff was riddled with bullet holes. It reminded McClaren of a sieve. Sullenly, he looked down at the lifeless form of Professor Wimple. It was difficult to match the smiling man with the sharp, vivacious, and intelligent eyes from the photo in the FBI file to the cloudy deadpan of the stiff laid out on the cold autopsy table.

Twenty minutes later, after taking full inventory of the body parts, scrapes from under the fingernails, and particles from the corpse's hair, the coroner peered over his glasses and extended his gloved hands stained with blood to McClaren, followed by his winning smile. McClaren was used to the sight of blood, but had no intention of sharing a handshake with someone who had just carved up a body like a butcher cleaving beef. He kept his hands by his sides. Smiling, the coroner peeled off his soiled gloves and washed his hands. Taking on a more serious persona, he walked McClaren through his observations, and promised to send a fax on the three bodies when he had completed the autopsies.

McClaren headed over to the motel to get a first-hand perspective of how things went down. The three bodies were hit many times with more than one kind of gun, clearly indicating that there was more than one marksman. The coroner had been able to retrieve a .38 lodged in Wimple's chest and a locket in a pocket of the third body. No identification papers or money were found on their persons. He had taken a swab of their fingerprints and pictures on his phone that he forwarded to HQ for an ID search in their database.

All he could do now was to wait for the results. The clock was ticking, and he needed to figure it out quickly. Heading back to HQ and going over the files again might help, but he was not entirely optimistic that it would be fruitful. He had to do something meanwhile, didn't he? Struggling within, trying to stave off the wave of apprehension that washed over him, he drove away, destination: HQ.

Chapter 45

The Russian Bear, Alexei Krivov, pulled over five miles away from the highway. He braced himself for what was to come. Kolinsky did not tolerate failure. Admitting the escape of Senator Lee from the crash scene could mean death.

His fingers lingered momentarily on the phone pad, before he punched in the numbers he knew by rote. Seconds later, the sonorous voice of Kolinsky floated over the line. Swallowing quickly, the Russian bear spat out his message, knowing that a barrage of expletives would follow. Holding the ear piece a few inches away, he waited for Kolinsky to calm down. He was ordered to fly back to Oslo immediately. The Russian bear pondered on what punishment would be meted out for his failure. Kolinsky wasn't a forgiving man. Making a hash of his assignment was never tolerated. He had never seen any man survive such royal ineptitude. He was under no illusion that Kolinsky would go any easier on him, even though he was his son. Yes, he cradled that knowledge carefully, he only became aware of the fact four months ago.

Going back to Oslo would be good, if he made it there alive. His mother lived there. It might be a chance to see his mother again. Reminiscing, it had already been six years since he last saw her. Right about the time he was recruited into Kolinsky's secret organization.

Alexei had always had a checkered past. By the time he was seven, he could pack a mean punch. He was a head taller than the second tallest boy in his class. The teachers at the Bergen Public School called him the gentle giant, until Yuri Primakov decided it was alright to taunt him because his clothes were a little too tight on him. Or maybe it was the fact that his shoes were tattered and in need of replacement. He never complained. His mother was a peasant who made her living working on a farm. She worked hard to provide for him, and deprived herself of the dainty clothes the other women wore, just to keep him clothed and put food on the table. How dare Yuri make a mockery of him?

Alexei was determined to teach him a lesson he would never forget. 4th of July 1992 was going to be a day to be remembered by Yuri, he would make sure of that. Alexei waited a full week to put his plan into action. Even at that age, he could be fortitudinous. The day started off like any normal school day. Lesson went right through to 11 o'clock, when it was time for break. Unsuspecting, Yuri was leaning against the wall in the playground talking to Galina, a girl whom Alexei admired, but never had the courage to speak to. Maybe that was why he resented Yuri so much. Cockily, Yuri started to whisper something in her ear while they were both looking at him. Alexei's blood rose to boiling point. In seconds, he was upon Yuri and a fight ensued. He hammered Yuri with the hidden stones that were stuffed in an old sock he could no longer wear. The fight was quite memorable, it left Yuri paralyzed and in a wheelchair for life.

It also changed Alexei's life forever. The fight marked the end of schooling at school. But it brought about the birth of the incredible hulk, which he was called by his schoolmates, and the Russian bear, which he was called by the teachers, behind closed doors. He was now known in the community as a formidable boy, one not to be messed with.

Back to the present, news from America was unpalatable. The Senator was still alive. Why did he pay bungling idiots to do a man's job? Kolinsky wondered to himself. There was only one person he could rely on now. The Chameleon, who had infiltrated the American system years ago and learnt their ways. Most people regarded him as an American. Ha! Ha! Simeon laughed to himself. He was a Russian through and through, and had so far shown unyielding allegiance to the homeland and to his personal crusade.

Picking up the phone, he made the call. Seconds later, he ended the call, satisfied that the matter of the co-conspirator, The Undersecretary was over. All he needed to do now was wait.

Chapter 46

Blue County General had never seen so many patients in A & E at one time. The nurses and fleets of doctors ran between patients evaluating the seriousness of their injuries, then moving on to the next. The stream of victims seemed endless, and loved ones, friends and family members, added tension and stress to the already overworked staff. The Undersecretary of State, James Collingwood, had been discreetly transferred to a private ward on arrival, away from prying eyes. Nobody was to know that the Under Secretary of State was cooped up in a small-time hospital. It would raise questions. What exactly was he doing in Blue County in the first place?

Unaware of the whirlwind of activities happening below, the wounded Undersecretary of State laid, almost cataleptically, under wraps in the new wing on the top floor of Blue County General, away from public view and press vultures taking pictures. Three federal agents watched from their sentry positions on the top floor for any potential threats. Surveillance cameras were also installed to beef up security and to ward off inquisitive eyes.

Four shifts later, the Undersecretary's monitor was still beating like a part of a symphony at an American pop concert. An undercover agent, dressed as a nurse, checked on the Undersecretary, monitoring his progress. He seemed to be responding to treatment. *It might be safe to move him home if he continues to improve*, the agent thought. Stepping outside the room for a minute, he noticed that the other agent was at his designated post; waving to show that he was going out for a smoke, he made his way out through the exit door and down two flights of stairs. The walk down would help his aching legs.

Avery—dressed in grey overalls with grease smeared over all of his face, moustache, hands, and clothes—walked past the agent, holding his arm as if he had broken it. He went to the front desk and asked to see the doctor. He was given forms to fill, asked for a copy of some ID, and if he had medical insurance. Seated, he observed what was going on at the reception. The nurse was being harassed by an irate patient who was tired of waiting. Sneakily, he made his way past the occupied nurse and headed for the lifts. He knew that the Undersecretary was on the third floor. The lift was capped at floor two, but he had help waiting just above. The Second floor nurse, Nancy, had been paid to assist him.

The lift stopped on the second floor and he made his way to Room 42. Opening the door, he saw the nurse, who handed him a badge, white overalls, a vial of potassium chloride mixed with cyanide, and a sheet of paper. Avery viewed the positions of the agents in the schematics of the hospital chart and made his way through the exit door leading to the third floor. Nancy was busy distracting the agent at the end of the corridor, while Avery slipped into the room.

Break time was over, and it was now time to get back to work, the agent told himself as he headed up the stairs, wondering why his supervisor always gave him the babysitting jobs. The boredom was killing him. He had asked for a field job, but his assignments were keeping people secure in safe houses who were about to trade in their old lives for a new ones at the expense of Uncle Sam. After this mission, he was going to ask for a move to Washington, anything was better than babysitting criminals turning state evidence.

Pushing open the exit door on the third floor, the agent looked across to where Marty was supposed to be positioned. Marty was laid out on the ground. The Agent's heart started pounding in his chest as he whipped out his gun and flung the hospital door open; ducking on one knee, he aimed at the intruder standing by the Undersecretary's bed who was attempting to inject something into the tube under the Undersecretary's nose. His bullet shattered the vial, obliterating it into tiny pieces. In one swift motion, Avery spun round, throwing the monitor he had ripped out before the agent squeezed off a second shot. The monitor threw the agent's aim off; the bullet pinged off the wall and imbedded itself into the cabinet. Avery did not wait for the agent to fire off a third shot. He jumped out of the window, whisking the bale of rope and metal clasp onto a tree as he dived out and down.

Pulling out his walkie-talkie, the agent spoke harshly, ordering the other two agents to pursue the runaway assassin. Avery hit the ground, nimbly running as fast as he could, aware that the two agents were bearing down on him. A warning shot and a shout telling him to stop made him halt in his tracks.

"Drop your gun and turn around." He obliged, after all, what else could he do? The two men came up to him, panting. They patted him down and took away the cyanide capsule.

Leading him away to the car, Avery dipped his hand into the lining of his hospital overall and retrieved a miniature object and palmed it in-between his large hands. Looking right and left furtively, the agents ran to deposit their precious cargo in the car and drive to HQ. Opening the back door, the first agent made way for Avery to get in. In two fluid movements, Avery disarmed and shot the agent. The second agent whirled around, trying to draw out his gun from his holster. He was rewarded with a bullet to the head, slumping unceremoniously onto the hard tarmac. Instantly, screams pierced the air. Avery ran to his car, got in, and started it up. In the approaching distance, he could hear the sounds of a police siren en route to the hospital. They were closing in. He knew where he needed to be: miles away. But first of all, he had to swap cars. He drove off, burning rubber, destination – the shopping mall to change his car.

Chapter 47

The FBI agent rubbed his eyes for the fifth time. The grainy pictures were all they had to go on. Seventeen hours of man hours had yielded little so far. The hard-backed recliner looked really inviting given the current situation. Running on caffeine and his depleted stock of cigarettes, he thought that it would be a good idea if he had a break right around now. He had run this CCTV through the new system again, and his eyes were threatening to close, big time.

The face recognition software clicked loudly in the background as he looked at his watch for the umpteenth time. McClaren and Raines made their entrance with fresh coffee and doughnuts to pacify the exhausted agent. He could see himself in his mind's eye holding up a white flag of surrender because of the fatigue. Settling down to take over the screening of the CCTV, a plop announcing a confirmed result from the facial recognition machine spurred McClaren into motion. Moving some discarded cartons of pizza, he made space and sat down. Groaning and releasing a long list of profanities, the tired agent jumped up as a rap sheet unfurled from the printer. Avery's photo sprang to life, filling the whole screen. They all scanned the two-page document, it was grim reading. Avery was a professional with more than forty assassinations under his belt. Wanted in five different countries and known to be proficient with guns, knives, jujitsu, and bomb making.

McClaren called it in, streaming the photo to the airport security team, bus station, train station security teams, and the local police station. Picking up conversation regarding the attempted murder of the Undersecretary of State over the police radio band propelled the trio into action. Referring to CODIS, using the all-known alias, they alerted all parastatals involved in the manhunt. Avery was a professional, boxed in, but resourceful. McClaren wondered if the local police had covered their bases. The county was a small stretch of land, but a lot of it was undeveloped territory. Avery's army records showed that he could be a resident Rambo if the need arose. He would not use the usual modes of transport, which would be too easy, this meant that he had a backup plan.

Liaising with the local sheriff and his deputy, they scoured the maps and different ways out of Blue County. McClaren delved through the paperwork, acquainting himself with the information gathered so far, re-assembling the dossier in a way that outlined Avery's travel arrangements over the past year. The bulky file held incriminating evidence pointing at him as the perpetrator of multiple crimes in four different countries. He was an assassin: illusive and deadly. This was a trained killer who was wanted by Interpol and in three specific European countries for different acts of violence including bombing events. He was an apparition, a ghost who was prolifically good at his job, rarely sighted, until now. What were the chances of catching the illusory hit man who had defied capture for over a decade?

McClaren combed through the slim classified file with the writing 'FOR YOUR EYES ONLY' boldly written on it, searching for pertinent clues that could unlock the secrets behind the phantom. The last sighting had been at Grand Central Station five hours ago. He had characteristically disappeared again.

Another disappointing fact he had yet to concede to. What had he come to New York to do? The agency was already overstretched as it was, and did not need the additional aggravation of looking out for another dangerous killer let loose in the city. This was not the time or place, not now, not ever, McClaren seethed silently.

Chapter 48

In London, Senator Lee's other co-conspirator; David Fox was waiting for the good news. News reports about the Blue County bombing had finally made it into the news, which meant that their plan was underway.

Deputy Prime Minister, David Fox started the day as any normal day. A cup of latte, a slice of toast, and a sliver of marmalade to complete his breakfast, and he was hurrying out the door to his official car parked out front. His wife performed her daily inspection, patted him lightly on the shoulder, and gave him a tantalizing kiss filled with promise of what was to come later. He stopped momentarily in his tracks to savor the kiss before opening the house's door and ruffling the hair of his two-year old son. He waved a goodbye and got into the car.

Life was good as Britain's no. 2. He had a voluptuous wife, a handsome boy, and a wonderful job. He was a mover and shaker in British politics, and very soon he would wield a similar amount of influence across the seas. Sooner rather than later, he mused as he sat comfortably relaxed in his office in a recliner surrounded by the plush Victorian furniture designed by Chippendale and a desk from Sheraton. *Yes, this was the life*, he thought to himself.

The persistent ringing of the phone jarred his senses and brought him out of his reverie. In annoyance, he grabbed the phone. Who dared interrupt his quiet time? It was not from Number 10, or it would have come through the special phone. Reluctantly, he reached forward to pick up the phone, silently resenting the intrusion. Lifting the receiver to his ears, he issued a gruff hello and waited for a response. Senator Lee's agitated tone pervaded the room with a sense of urgency, leaving Fox tingling all over. He gripped his seat as Senator Lee relayed the unravelling of the plot.

In a flash, his world came crashing down, a need for self-preservation kicked in. The Deputy Prime Minister felt physically sick. His stomach did flip flops when he heard the news. His face blanched, and large droplets of sweat stained his immaculately tailored suit. He wringed his podgy hands in exasperation. It was time to get out before the net closed in on him. His desire to unseat the Prime Minister had been so strong that he had already thrown caution to the wind. How could he have been so terribly stupid? They had promised so much and delivered so little.

He would have been the next Prime Minister, after all, he deserved it more than the incumbent bumbling idiot who had only increased the budget deficit and created more hardship with the retrenchment of key officials in Whitehall while the fat cats sat around drinking tea. What was that all about?

Maybe he would not be the next PM, but, by jolly, he would do everything in his power to ensure that he discredited the current administration as much as possible, or was it going to be the other way round? Either way, he had to get away and rebuild his life. The scheme had taken months to formulate, and now he had to accelerate his exit strategy; exposure would only mean jail time. Where was the fun in that? His colleagues would ensure that he got a fair trial. Well—considering what he had embarked upon, a crime amounting to treason—ten years would be getting away with it lightly. A cold shudder wracked his body, jolting him back to reality. Time was of the essence. He had to move now before the dominoes started falling around him.

Lifting his briefcase onto the desk, he hastily shoveled the contents of his desk into it and headed for the door. A flurry of voices on the other side of the door stopped him in his tracks. He could hear the indignant tone of his secretary and the scrapping of her chair as she pushed it back hurriedly. His fear became amplified by the thud that followed, and his parched lips quivered. Collecting his thoughts, he locked the adjoining door and raced through the outer chamber leading to the PM's personal office and slipped out the side entrance. From a distance, he could hear raised voices and hammering against his office door.

David smiled to himself as he ran. Who would have thought that the door he had changed just two weeks ago would be his saving grace? From all indications, it was proving to be an infallible block of resistance. No matter how impregnable it seemed, it had bought him a temporary reprieve.

Avery had arrived via Heathrow Airport three hours ago. He used the satnav to get him to his destination and arrived with ten minutes to spare. Avery found a spot where he could watch without being detected. He noticed that that all eyes were riveted on the entrance, where the authorities anticipated the overweight, perspiring David Fox would come through. He, on the other hand, had other ideas. Biding his time, fully concealed behind the curtain of the main window in the upper conference room, he observed the scene below through his hi-tech modified Remington sniper rifle and waited. His body tingled all over in anticipation of the kill.

Unaware that death was looming closer, David strolled quickly over to his secretary's car and got in. He placed the spare car keys he had in the ignition and looked up. Streaming out of the building were five security men closing in on the car, and a fresh wave of panic sprang to the surface, throwing him into full blown hysteria. He rapidly started the car as the men closed in on the car, trying to block his escape. He swerved the Austin Mini, narrowly missing one of the security men, and veered left onto the parking ramp. Avery saw his opening and released his bull's-eye shot. The bullet went through the windscreen with the velocity of a cannonball from hell and hit its mark, embedding itself dead center in David's forehead. The car spiraled out of control and rammed into three parked cars before somersaulting and igniting into a fireball. Dismantling the rifle, he stopped momentarily to admire his work, and then slithered away with a gratifying sigh. Mission accomplished.

Meanwhile, pandemonium broke loose. The security men set up a parameter, cordoning off the area as the sirens of fire engines and ambulances fought for supremacy. Emergency personnel converged on the area like drones of bees attracted to the queen, battling relentlessly to bring the fire under control.

What had started as a mere investigation, a routine call to bring the deputy PM David Fox in for questioning, had turned into a fiasco. There was a media circus trying to break into No. 10, and the Prime Minister had been whisked away to an undisclosed location while the Head of Security tried to figure out what the hell was going on.

Avery got into his hired Ford Fiesta and made the call. Next stop was Heathrow Airport for his outbound flight to Rio de Janeiro.

He did not want to be late for his next assignment, did he? After all, it was not his place to tidy up the mess for the British, was it?

Chapter 49

Frost had a few moments of reprieve, pondering on what to do, where to go. Senator Lee was out for the count. He needed to take action now, their life depended on it. The killers would be waiting for them at the hospital; that was for certain. He stepped on the breathing tube supplying oxygen to Senator Lee, and the monitor sounded its distress signal, summoning the paramedic to Senator Lee's side.

The paramedic expertly worked on tracing the reason for the beeping sounds. In less than thirty seconds, the paramedic lay face down, temporarily incapacitated by Frost, who knew that he had to make a move if there was any chance of escaping their attackers. Luckily, two blocks of roadwork ahead had created a bottleneck, and the ambulance slowed to 8 m/h. Presented with the opportunity, Frost opened the ambulance door and forced out the stretcher, jumping onto it at the last possible moment to break his momentum. Cars behind the ambulance slammed on their brakes simultaneously, averting a near collision with the trolley.

At gunpoint, Frost commandeered the driver of the first car to help him lift Senator Lee into his car. Flashing his badge, Frost promised the driver with the return of his car as soon as possible and drove off to his last resort, Maryland, where his friend Paul Gwyn, a master forger, resided.

Twelve hours after ditching the car at a drive-thru and stealing another one, they arrived at Maryland. Parking discreetly at the back of a car park, Frost found a young Latino boy of twelve years, a runner by all means, ready to make a few bucks. He gave the boy an address and a note to give the occupant. Like a shot, the boy was gone. Within seven minutes, the boy re-appeared with a grin on his face. $100 for seven minutes' work was simply great. Frost read the note and told the boy to come back in an hour for more work.

Pleased, the boy rode off on his bike. It was his lucky day. Frost did a quick survey of the car and went off to find a chemist and food, after making himself look presentable. He picked a new shirt from the valise in the back seat and dumped his jacket, which was speckled with blood from Senator Lee and a cut from his own forehead.

With a brown, dotted cap obscuring face, he bought first-aid items, some food from a local eatery, and stashed both things in the back of the car. He then re-traced his way to the back of an apartment block that housed his friend's apartment. The alley seemed deserted. He pried open the lock and went in through a back corridor to the foyer where the letterboxes were situated. Carefully opening the letterbox, he took the passports and wad of cash. He deftly retreated the way he came, scanning each doorway as he went.

Picking up his pace, he made it back to the car with four minutes to spare. On cue, the boy came back, took the note, and went off like a bee out of a bonnet. Firing up the engine, Frost made his exit from the front and parked near enough to see the boy go up to the apartment. Viewing from his side mirror, he saw sudden movement. It was like he was looking in slow motion as the scene took on a surreal feeling. The bomb blast confirmed his suspicions. Debris littered the street. People scampered about searching for cover. All the while, a cloud of billowing smoke swirled around, sucking up the clean air, sending people into racking coughs from the condensed smoke.

Frost did not wait; using the disorder as a weapon, he drove off, knowing instinctively where to go.

Chapter 50

Michael walked in with two cups of coffee and handed them over to Tony, who had just pulled a 36-hour shift. His red-rimmed eyes and grim expression said it all. The sensitive nature of Anne Marie's job had brought up invisible barriers that seemed insurmountable. People were uncooperative and unwilling to give them a peek into Anne Marie's work life. As for maintaining a work-life balance, that remained to be seen. Anne Marie was a career animal whose prime function was her attachment solely to her job.

Both Tony and Michael found it strange that such a beautiful, educated, elegant woman had no male partner hanging on her arm or in the background. They had searched her house and come up empty. There were no diaries, letters, or documents that revealed the other side of Anne Marie. Her colleagues were tight-lipped and nobody seemed to know who Anne Marie really was. Whether that was a ploy or was done intentionally to stall their investigation was anyone's guess. The clock was ticking, and their boss wanted them to focus on a new case involving the murder of a shop owner, a robbery gone wrong.

Flicking through the mass of paper spewing out of the folder, Michael grabbed a few of the photos and shuffled them around as he meticulously took in the postures, looks, and background in each shot. He did it a second and then a third time, before dropping the photos in Tony's lap and pointing at two specific snapshots of Anne Marie caught looking absorbed in Senator Lee's conversation with a third man. Despite Senator Lee's pose of seeming indifference, his eyes hid a smoldering look of desire that was totally focused on Anne Marie, while his body was partially turned to include the third man in the conversation.

Two of the people in the photograph were obviously unavailable. They needed to track down the third person, which was easy enough. The third man was a Congressman. The only problem was that no one met such a high profile politician without an appointment. They had wasted enough time as it stood, and new cases were clamoring for attention on their desk. Knowing their boss's modus operands for actual evidence and a justification for man hours spent, if they did not come up with something today, they would be told to close the case in no uncertain terms.

Tony knew a few people in Congress. Picking up his cellphone, he made a call to a young admirer working for the Congressman and within minutes knew how to get a chance meeting. Grabbing their coats, Tony and Michael left their closeted office to track down the one man who was the only viable lead they had. Twenty-five minutes later, the two bedraggled cops pulled up to the diner where the politician Mark Vaughn was eating lunch comprising of a hot Panini sandwich, Cobb salad, and a glass of organic, freshly squeezed orange juice. Vaughn gave both men an annoyed stare, unmistakably relaying his protest to the intrusion, as they sat down at his table and hurriedly introduced themselves. Vaughn was a regular at the diner, and knew that the owner kept a shotgun under the shelf in case things went awry. Besides, the two tired looking men with their rumpled suits could only be underpaid public servants who were there for a different reason apart from killing him in broad daylight. Ignoring them, he tucked in and finished his meal.

Ten minutes later, Tony and Michael left the diner convinced that the link between Anne Marie and Senator Lee surpassed just that of work colleagues. It was about time they stopped by Senator Lee's house and found proof that would substantiate their theory. Everything was riding on the search. The only trouble was getting a search warrant.

Chapter 51

Avery seethed in silent frustration. He had just narrowly missed killing James Collingwood the first time. It was an easy enough operation. Get in, fill the drip line with the poison, and walk away. It just did not go down like that. The second time around would be different. He was a man unaccustomed to failure. There was no room for sloppiness. It was a dent on his impeccable record. In all his thirty years, and he meant thirty years in this line of work, he had never failed a mission. It was not a question of the money; it was a question of professional pride. He was not ready to retire just yet.

A welcome home party was being organized for the Undersecretary after the harrowing experience at Blue County Hotel and the attempt on his life at the hospital. This time, James Collingwood was not going to elude the clutches of death; Avery was going to make sure of that.

After all, the Undersecretary deserved what was coming to him. He was a traitor. How could he set up a clandestine meeting at the Blue County Hotel to sell out his country? It was totally unacceptable. He knew nothing about politics and paid no allegiance to the country of his birth, but Avery hated what Collingwood stood for. Collingwood was a greedy, adulterous, and narcissistic man whose primary focus was living a luxuriant life. The chemical weapon he was planning on selling would have had devastating consequences around the world. The prototype was unstable at best, compounded by the fact that it might have already been unintentionally released on the unsuspecting public of Blue County.

There was nothing he could do about that. Eliminating the Undersecretary James Collingwood was what his employer wanted. With a new resolve, Avery made his way up the hospital steps, intent on completing his mission without incident. Dressed in his white overalls, he studiously focused on the charts he held in hands as he casually strolled through the reception on his way to the third floor. He knew he had just bare minutes to accomplish the killing of Collingwood. There would be no lapse in the Undersecretary's security details this time. They would have security detail on every floor, inside and outside his room as well.

Avery slipped into a toilet cubicle and retrieved the umbrella and discarded the white overalls he was wearing. Putting on a pair of thick rimmed glasses and a moustache, he left the cubicle carrying the umbrella and a small medical bag, looking like a typical patient being discharged from the ward. The hospital was a beehive of activities. Secret Service personnel were shooing away the common patients while they bustled around the VIP who had been stashed away on the third floor. People lingered around on the hospital floor, waiting to catch a glimpse of the special person who was posing a great inconvenience to the rest of the hospital and its patients.

A hushed silence followed as people watched in amazement when the security detail wheeled Collingwood down the ramp to a waiting government vehicle. The Undersecretary, flanked by his security men, made his way steadily to the car parked at the end of the ramp, feeling relieved that he was finally leaving the hospital. His spirits lifted. He was tired of being cooped up in the small hospital room. He yearned for the comfort of his home.

Suddenly, the heavens opened, and within moments the infamous Blue County downpour unleashed its abundant stock of rain. Avery moved in swiftly to offer a quick shelter from the rain before any of the security men could react. A burly security man moved swiftly to block the stranger, while two other security men provided Collingwood umbrella cover till he got to the car. Seconds later, Collingwood was whisked away.

Avery walked away in the direction of the car park and waited. A black sedan with tinted windows and no number plate pulled up and Avery got in. Five miles up the road, they saw the government vehicle parked by the side of the road and security men speaking frantically into their phones. The wail of the ambulance blared in the background. Avery smiled to himself, Collingwood had been terminated. The untraceable lethal poison on the umbrella that he had pricked Collingwood with had had the desired effect. There would be no respite for the Undersecretary, who had quickly slipped into the realm of the dead.

Chapter 52

Moving on had to be an option. The pile up on the highway had cleared, and it was time to track down Senator Lee. It was time for his comeuppance. Ralph and Matthew had been reliably informed by Deroni's informant that Senator Lee had escaped from the bridge in an ambulance, which meant that he was still alive.

Ralph made a call to an old cellmate whose sister-in-law worked at Carl Davidson & Co, which handles the CCTV footage of the highway network in the area. Within twenty minutes, he got a call back. Senator Lee did not get into the ambulance. A bulky looking commando type guy had overpowered a bystander in a navy blue Explorer and transferred Senator Lee's immobile body into the car and drove away. He rattled off the make, number plate, and last sighting of the car, then hung up.

Matthew scanned the map thinking of the possible locations they could search to find the Senator. The man who took the Senator knew he was a wanted man. Where would he take him to, maybe a hospital? No, Senator Lee had a few connections. He could easily avoid a hospital. After all, he had friends of the medical kind residing in the Halifax area who would help him. Leafing through the file they had compiled, one name stood out. Dr. Hendricks was Senator Lee's brother-in-law. That would be the obvious choice. Firing up the internet on their Apple tablet, they obtained the address of Dr. Hendricks' practice. Dr. Hendricks was Senator Lee's brother-in-law, and probably his best option of getting medical help.

Senator Lee and his aide, Frost, may have had half a day's head start on them, but Ralph and Matthew were determined that they would inevitably catch up with them. What they did not have with speed, they would match with vengeance. They set off on their quest with only one bathroom stop. They bought some junk food, topped up the car with gas, took turns driving throughout the night, and made it to Halifax before dawn with an hour to spare. How was that for driving an old Jalopy?

Referring to the Google map, Matthew and Ralph made their way to Dr. Hendricks' house. Morning was breaking, and the usual activities were taking place inside. There were two cars parked outside. Neither looked like any of the get-away cars. A quick sweep of the vehicles showed that they were both registered to Dr. Hendricks. That was disappointing, but not utterly futile. Hidden under the front seat were a bloody swab and some medical supplies. It was a good sign that Senator Lee had been there. There was no plan. How were they going to extract the information from Dr. Hendricks? Would the respectable doctor be stupid enough to stash his brother-in-law in the house? Either way, they were not planning on waiting to find out.

Without further contemplation, they opened their car doors with the intent of stomping the house. Surprisingly, the front door opened and a young man with sandy blonde hair, dressed simply in a pair of tweed trousers and light blue shirt with matching tie, emerged from the house carrying his medical bag. He seemed to be in a hurry. Unaware of their presence, he climbed hastily into his car and fired up. Minutes later, he drove off in the direction of the town at breakneck speed. Matthew and Ralph started the car in pursuit. Dr. Hendricks car was a sports car with far more horsepower, but that did not deter them. There was only one logical place he could be heading to, and that was back to town. Putting their manual gear into overdrive, they speed towards town.

Moments earlier, Dr. Hendricks had seen the two men loitering in the car from his bedroom window. He made a call to Frost to get ready to move Senator Lee. Luckily, Frost had enough medical supplies in his car to keep them going for the next days. Panicking, Dr. Hendricks looked into his rear view mirror to see if the men were close behind. How could he have been so stupid as to get himself involved in this mess? His sister was dead, and it was all Senator Lee's fault. All he needed to do was to give Frost the supplies so they could get out of his life. He needed to think of his family now. That was all he had left. He shuddered at how selfish it sounded to him, but he could not help himself. If what happened to Penny was anything to go by, the people Senator Lee was mixed up with were a nasty piece of work. The sooner the Senator was gone, the better.

142

Pulling up behind the surgery, he hurried across to the waiting car and palmed off the supplies. He then got into his car, made over to the library complex, and parked his car out front. Glancing quickly at his watch, he made his way up the stairs to the annex where his patient was due her regular insulin shot. He administered the injection around the same time every day, which would feed nicely into today's arrangement. He climbed the stairs with a youthful vigor he had not felt for days. He was, in fact, running on adrenalin spurred by fear. Composing himself the best he could, he took a deep breath, rapped lightly on her door, and waited as she shuffled around. Perspiration pockmarked his impeccable shirt as he waited for about a minute that seemed to last interminably longer.

He heard screeching tires and pebbles hitting the asphalt as the chasing car pulled to a dramatic stop in front of the library. The two men jumped out and scanned the area. His heart pumped wildly in his chest and he licked his lips a second time. *I'd make a lousy spy*, he thought to himself. The adrenalin rush was definitely not for him. The shuffling feet came inches from the door, followed by a pause as the old woman peered through the spyhole. Satisfied, she swung the door open with her arthritic hands, letting Dr. Hendricks into her safe haven.

One look at the doctor left her slightly mystified. She had never seen him so flustered. Maybe he had been on call all night, or maybe it was a fight with the missus. Either way, she did not care, he was here now for her. Being an introvert, she did not have many visitors, and she looked forward to his visits, like a seductive vixen waiting for her lover. *Well, maybe if I had been a few years younger*, she said to herself, dismissing the thought. At nearly eighty who would have amorous thoughts towards her?

Distractedly, she made her way to her favorite chair and sat down, rolling up her sleeves for the usual rush of the insulin. Normally, Dr. Hendricks was nimble in administering the shot; today, however, he was dithering, stealing fleeting looks at the window, as if he was agitated by something outside. There really was no way out. He could not get Mrs. Camberley involved. The best thing was to face up to the hoodlums outside. After all, they would not shoot in broad daylight in front of a host of people moving about in the early morning rush hour, would they? Temporarily comforted by the idea, he carried out the perfunctory duty of performing the insulin injection, checking her blood pressure and sugar level, and dropping off her drug prescription for the next two weeks.

Now it was time to go. His patient felt his hesitation, but moving as deftly as she could to the window, she moved back the curtain slightly to observe what was going on downstairs. Committing the number plate of the beat up car to memory, she turned around with a withering smile.

"Tell me Doctor Hendricks, are those two undesirable men from out of town bothering you? I could call the Chief Nolan to send down some black and whites to take them in," she said.

"No thanks, Mrs. Camberley. I'll handle it myself. I'm sure it will be all right. I'll see you same time tomorrow, OK?" he said, opening the door to let himself out. Dr. Hendricks took a deep breath and made his way downstairs to face the pursuers. Walking over to his car, he tried to appear as calm as possible, while inside he was quivering in fear, unsure of what to expect. A dark shadow blocked the light from behind him, and he felt the nozzle of a gun in the middle of his back. The taller of the men spoke quietly in a low baritone voice laced with venom, "Make any sudden movements, and you're dead. Where is he?"

"Where is who?" asked Dr. Hendricks, feigning incredulity in his voice.

"Stop playing games, Dr. Hendricks. I'm not a very patient man. Where is Senator Lee?"

"Is that what this's all about? Seriously, you're asking me about my brother-in-law, the man who let my sister die?" he replied with forceful bravado.

"Look, mister. I have had it with you. Stop stalling. I checked your car earlier and found bloody swabs with Senator Lee's blood all over them. I'm giving you one last chance, or you'll be sorry."

Swallowing awkwardly, Dr. Hendricks considered long and hard about his options. From where he was standing, he really had no choice. Senator Lee had at least thirty minutes' head start. There were two roads leading out of here. He would give Lee as much time as he could possibly give him by redirecting these sour-looking men. Quelling the storm raging within and putting on a cowering expression, resignedly, with his head down in a stooping position, he said, "He left town last night. His aide brought him to me and I treated him and sent them on their way. I want no part of it. Besides, my sister is dead, I owe him no loyalty."

144

Frustrated, Ralph rammed his pistol into Dr. Hendricks' back. "You better be telling the truth. Because if I find out that you're lying, I'll come back and gut you like a fish in front of your family. Got that? Which way were they heading?"

"I'm not sure. They could be making their way to Fort Lauderdale. Jeremy has an old army friend, General Fox, staying up there. He lives just outside army base. That's all I know."

Matthew looked at the map he carried. It sounded plausible. Senator Lee would be looking for extra protection against whoever was chasing him. Where else would you go if you wanted additional fire power? Reluctant to leave Dr. Hendricks without a parting remark, he got into the car and said, "Dr. Hendricks, we know where you live, remember that."

Dr. Hendricks stood numbed and petrified at what had just happened. He watched the men drive off, and mopped his brow profusely as beads of sweat trickled down his face. He had just escaped a date with death. Now would be as good a time as any to take his family on a much needed vacation. Canada would be lovely this time of the year. He was not going to wait around for those two clowns to pay him another visit. It was now or never.

Getting quickly into his car, he hurried home to tell his wife of his new formed plan, praying that she would be just as spontaneous and eager to travel. Meanwhile, old Mrs. Camberley, who had been observing from her bay window, pulled the curtain over the window and tried to contemplate what kind of trouble the good doctor was in.

Chapter 53

It was a miserable Sunday morning. A deluge of rain darkened the sky, promising to release another torrent of rain, further dampening the President's mood. Silently, the President was seething after having a row with the missus. He was supposed to attend a Thanksgiving service for his godson, but that was not going to happen. The news of the chemical bomb explosion in Blue County that was affecting people all over the USA was more troubling than a minor tiff with his wife. Nothing a few flowers could not put right. He had better tell his personal assistant to arrange for the flowers, meanwhile, back to the matter at hand.

Huddled around the table in the Oval Office were his Vice President, the Environmental Secretary, the FBI Director and the Director of Homeland Security, just to name a few, who were all looking as miserable as the President. The briefing took less than ten frustrating minutes. All of them were speaking all at once in agitation, the President waded in by raising his hand to silence them. Turning to the Head of Homeland Security, he said, "What are your boys doing about it?"

Justin Hamilton had just become the Head of Homeland Security only four months ago. At 47 years old, he had served in the 1st Battalion. He also served in the Special Forces for three years and had carried out clandestine activities on behalf of his government in Kuwait, Afghanistan, Iraq, and Mexico, before being re-assigned to Washington after he was involved in a minor skirmish that took the lives of three other fellow servicemen travelling in the same convoy with him in Kabul.

His weathered face, shadowed with worry lines, and voice inflected the uncertainty he felt. He outlined preventative steps taken and passed on the briefing to the FBI Director to fill in the gaps in the evidence recovered from the debris from Blue County Hotel after the conference.

Strategies to carry out a pre-emptive strike were discussed and the positioning of collaborative efforts was mapped out before the meeting was dissolved. The President assigned media control to his Press Secretary to keep a lid on things. His Press Secretary hurried out of the room to manage this momentous task and ensure that effective damage control was carried out. The rest of the participants filed out, but he placed a restraining hand on the shoulders of Hamilton, indicating that he would like a word with him in private. Waiting a few minutes after the room emptied out, he put his trained eyes on Hamilton and watched for a few seconds while Hamilton stewed in his own thoughts, worry lines wrinkling his tanned brown skin.

Without looking at him, the president said harshly, "When were you going to mention that the composition of the bomb at Blue County had the same components as the one that killed members of your battalion?" Hamilton's lip quivered for a second, but he held his ground. He searched his mind for a plausible explanation, but came up with nothing.

He blurted out, "I didn't know what it was. It's still undergoing analysis. The results have not been given to me yet."

"Well, that's why I'm the President of the United States of America. I expected answers, yesterday. If you're not up to the job, step down. Kilpatrick can fill your shoes. Do you understand? You've got 24 hours. Better make them count. Now, get out."

Hamilton walked out of the room, rage simmering below the surface and afraid to admit that there had to be a mole in his office. He had just got the intelligence at 6.45 a.m. that morning. How had the President known? Answers posed more questions. What he needed to do was get to the bottom of this case and then find out who was leaking information to the White House without his approval. He would not be surprised if it was not Kilpatrick. The dirty hyena had other ideas to make Hamilton seem incompetent.

At the moment, he certainly felt Kilpatrick's efforts were working. Pushing the thoughts of doubt from his mind, he hurried down the plush corridor, preoccupied and unable to appreciate the lush paintings and adornments lining the walls. Work beckoned; after all, there was no rest for the wicked, was there?

Chapter 54

Professors milled around in the laboratory in their starched white overalls and latex gloves. The pristine white-washed walls and glaring bright lights provided amazing illumination in the small sterilized room. In hushed tones, they peered over in wonderment at the exhibits laid out meticulously on the steel table. The silence of the room was pierced by the opening of the titanium door that was encased in bulletproof glass, and all heads turned to acknowledge the intrusion.

Hamilton walked in, draped in a white lab coat, booties, cap, and a pair of surgical glasses dangling in his hands. The lab supervisor introduced Dr. Klein, Dr. Barnes, Dr. Heinz, Dr. Mary Schneider and Professor Khan to Hamilton and then left. Hamilton looked around the lavishly fitted lab and marveled at the amount of money Uncle Sam invested in technology. Without a second glance, the scientists got back to work, inquisitively poring over the fragmented pieces recovered from Blue County Hotel.

On the nearby work table lay the body of a bomb victim. The corpse was pretty much intact, except for a missing part of the back of the head, and white particles were imbedded in the dress she wore. *She must have been an attractive girl once upon a time*, Hamilton thought sadly to himself. Dr. Mary Schneider busied herself by taking samples from the body, clothes, skin, and hair for analysis. The male scientists unwittingly left her the task of uncovering the mystery of the particles on the corpse's body and clothes, perhaps in an attempt to preserve her modesty, or simply out of respect for the victim. Either way, Dr. Mary had gotten the short straw. The body had already been ravaged by the bomb and impact of foreign substances. The male scientists were not interested in the carnal pleasure of ogling a pin-up girl, but rather in scientific discovery.

Hamilton watched the scientists at work, totally out of his depth. Answers to the riddle would come, but like with all things scientific, maybe not immediately. All he could do was observe these geniuses and hope that they came up with the goods. Identifying and breaking down the chemical compositions would be a good start. Finding an antidote was imperative if they were going to contain the outbreak and keep it out of the press. Somebody somewhere was bound to talk sooner or later; later, if he could help it.

The little hairs on his neck bristled as his thoughts catapulted him back to his last assignment with the 1st Battalion. His platoon was assigned to recover a colonel who had been captured during a patrol mission in Kabul. Did he mention it before? Yes, it was a covert mission, his team had to simply extract and fly the colonel back to base, where another team was to debrief him. Colonel Nicholas Shaw, unbeknown to Hamilton, was a spy who had infiltrated a secret Russian facility in Islamabad and had stolen vials of a chemical substance that was yet to be analyzed.

Everything seemed to be going to plan; when they were intercepted by a group of insurgents who surprised the convoy by destabilizing and blowing up the first truck with the aid of a missile launcher, followed by throwing hand grenades on the second truck, which dislodged him on impact. The force of the explosion threw him and Sergeant Vickery out of the vehicle. The first two trucks had been obliterated, and the scream of someone howling in pain rung out.

Colonel Shaw had his hand on the package and was pulling it towards him, before a rebel fired at him, killing him instantly. In rage, Hamilton shot down the Taliban and checked Shaw for a pulse. There was no pulse. Scanning the scene, he made out Private Desmond and two other men from his platoon, seriously injured, but was returning fire. He turned towards the direction of the shots and let rip a magazine of fire in response, killing five other insurgents. Apart from the moaning of the American soldier a few feet away, there were no more shots fired. Salvaging the package, he helped Vickery to his feet, and with the two surviving other soldiers made it back to base.

His Commanding Officer gratefully received the package and forwarded it to the Washington base. Well, that was the last he had heard of it, until now. Funny how the past seems to creep up on you when you least expect it. Seven years later, he could now understand that the death of Vickery on American soil was due to his exposure to this chemical cocktail. Ironic, don't you think that he did not die from the bullet shell lodged in his leg when he was rescued, but rather from some unfathomable sickness induced by exposure to the effects of a chemical bomb. Sadly, Hamilton knew that Vickery's death must have been excruciating. The sores, sunken eyes, hair loss, and scabbed skin were the visible signs; God knows what was happening underneath. No wonder they wanted to hush things up. Thinking hard about it now, two other soldiers had died of the same symptoms, but it was all put down to the fact that they had all served in the same area at the time.

This time, he'd make sure that innocent people did not die on his watch. Everything was riding on these scientists finding the answers they needed and coming up with an antidote. Needless to say, the clock was ticking, and all he could do was wait. How uncomfortable was that?

Chapter 55

McClaren was slouched over his desk poring over the copious notes sticking out of the bulging file. Despondent at the man hours dedicated to tracking down the suspects, all without results. The motel fiasco left no witnesses. He could not track down the girl who was seen fleeing the scene. CCTV coverage was grainy, at best. The FBI tech was trying to clean it up so that a clearer picture could be circulated. But it was likely that by the time that was done, the female suspect would be long gone.

They had the bus stations, trains, and airports covered. Border patrols were on the lookout for any suspicious activity, which was a joke anyway. What constituted suspicious activity? The question should have been: when was Lady Luck going to cut him a break?

His partner Raines walked over, sat on the edge of his table, and extended a sheet of paper with a manifest of names from an American Airlines flight dated 20th March. His eyes drifted to the underlined names and he smiled. Finally, there was something to work with. Swiveling in his chair, he fired up the computer and cross referenced the names with the passenger list of a flight that had passed through Schiphol airport four days ago. He pulled up the surveillance tape for the date and there it was. Time stamped 12.41 a.m.; Mohammed and Kudirat were waved through immigration. Kudirat's hijab obscured her facial features. They both kept their head down, away from the surveillance cameras in circulation, as if they knew where the cameras were. McClaren filed that bit of information in the recesses of his brain and pulled up their travel log. After scrutinizing their travel arrangements, he took a picture of the two travelers and told Clarke to circulate a blown-up version of the extracted picture of Kudirat. Mohammed was already in custody, on the coroner's slab.

There were too many outlets to cover, but it had to be done. Three of the purported sightings had proved to be nothing but a waste of time. The mystery woman seemed to have disappeared into thin air; which was not surprising. They had very little to go on. Meanwhile, the only lead they had was of the scientist caught on CCTV meeting Mohammed at a coffee shop before the Blue County incident. Fortunately, Professor Gray was apprehended while being smuggled across the Mexican border and had been detained by the Mexican authorities. Gray had been transported to the New York field office questioning despite his severe injuries.

Driving up to the New York field office, they met with a field agent, who gave them the information that had been gathered so far. The imposter had been a willing witness, detailing other members involved in the plot and their last known destinations. He had folded like a pack of cards. It made McClaren wonder why he was so willing to share. The interrogation tactics used may have been a clue, but McClaren was not interested in delving into the method of extracting information; all he cared about was rounding up the other people implicated in the plot that had killed over 57 people and put 200 in the hospital.

The most shocking revelation was the involvement of Russian baron, Simeon Kolinsky. McClaren made a few calls, the first of which was to the FBI Director to get the necessary clearance he needed. He then called his friend, David Banks, who worked at Interpol and gave him an update of what was happening. Within minutes, an international arrest warrant was issued for the capture and arrest of Simeon Kolinsky. *One down, and one to go*, thought McClaren. The bureau had no clue what the woman would do next. The intriguing enigma of catching the illusive woman once more gripped his attention. Right now, it was like searching for a needle in a haystack.

All he needed was a lucky break, an observant bystander, a credible witness, or an event that would flush her out. *Anything short of a miracle would do it*, he thought to himself. Hell, how likely was that?

Chapter 56

The putrid smell of rotting teeth and feces assaulted his nostrils, evoking an involuntary retching reaction. The temporary holding cell was devoid of any fixtures, except for the deflated mattresses and some threadbare blankets. The overflowing toilet was caked in vomit and urine, which trickled down the side of the bowl, leaving dark blotches running down to the back wall of the cell. The two other occupants of the cell moved around incessantly swatting the army of cockroaches and the oversized rats making their pedestrian crossing on the tray of food being passed around in the 2 x 4 cell, a place that would not qualify as a store room or a cubby hole.

The police man opened the cell door and Blaine froze, the odors of a lack of showers and fear-induced perspiration were palpable. A persuasive thrust on the back sent him sprawling headlong to the dirty floor at the feet of the large ominous man whose tattered trousers and scuffed shoes would not be seen displayed even in the back of a charity shop. The dark greasy floor bore the battle stains of blood and secretions of mucus that had seeped into the splintered crevices of the uneven floor and shades of white deposited on it by other victims unlucky enough to have shared the cell before him.

A sense of foreboding chilled his muscles as the large brute brought him roughly to his feet. He came face to face with the loutish features of a small-time gang enforcer who was being arraigned in the morning for having killed an Australian tourist in a Kentucky bar. Blaine wondered if he would ever see daylight again. With a grunt and a head-butting motion, the brute sent him flying across the cell, caroming into the defenseless second occupant, a wiry British tourist caught with 50 kilos of heroine, who raised his hands to deflect the impact.

The blond-haired stranger picked himself up, accentuating his 6 ft. 4 in height, and eyed up his opponent. If he was to survive the night, he needed his wits about him. The enforcer stood an imposing 6 ft. 8 tall, all muscle. He flexed his muscles to show the rip effect, a raging bull getting ready to attack.

Blaine did not feel intimidated. Before the night was out, there would only be one person standing, and it had to be him. Fearfully, the timid British man fled to the furthest part of the cell, putting as much distance as possible between the three men in the small space. He watched apprehensively, waiting for the curtain to fall. Blaine paced around, using his eyes to sweep the sparsely furnished cell, looking for a potential weapon that could help him take down the menacing creature trapped in the cell with him. Like a panther pouncing on its prey, the thug came at him at full steam. With rapid speed, Blaine partially deflected the incoming blow that landed sloppily at the side of his cheek. Two of his back teeth shuddered on contact, the refraction destabilizing him for a second as he tried to clear his head.

Relishing his achievement at temporarily disorienting Blaine, the thug stepped up to dish out another thunderbolt punch to the gut. Blaine was prepared, anticipating the enforcer's move; he sidestepped in time for the thug to go crashing into the bars of the cell. A rumbling sound of pure rage escaped the giant's lips as he turned to emasculate the mere boy who was showing him up. From behind, Blaine poleaxed the big man's legs with a karate kick that sent him to his knees. In swift, precise movements, Blaine raised his elbow and hammered down on the big man's head. A spurt of blood came gushing out. The blow was not enough to knock the enforcer out. Incensed by the venom in this retaliation, the enforcer held onto Blaine with all his strength.

The first policeman hurried in to find out what the commotion was all about, but made no move to stop the fight, content to watch the big man strangle Blaine to death, possibly. Blaine frantically searched for air with the unyielding grip of the man-beast towering over him. Desperately clawing at the hand that held onto his throat in a vice-like grip, he sent a vicious kick into the big man's groin and got a few seconds' reprieve as the grip loosened.

Blood dripped from the enforcer's gaping head wound, making its slow course into his left eye, blurring his vision. He struggled to focus on Blaine, who was approaching with alarming force, maniacal glint lighting up his eyes. The enforcer was a career killer, but the feral look in Blaine's eyes left a numbing chill in his bones. It mirrored an unhinged soul set free from its leash. Struggling to his feet, he tried to shield the impact of the incoming blow. Spots of multi-color light clouded his vision as Blaine pounded him with more uncanny strength than he could withstand.

Groggily, he went down on one knee, his strength dissipating with each punch dished out by the young blond man. *This could not be happening*, thought the enforcer, fighting back fruitlessly before he passed out.

Two policemen had intervened just in time, afraid that the enforcer was already dead. It would not look good if he died in police custody. Where was the justice in that? He had a date with Judge Hutchinson, and Blaine was not going to change that. Dragging away the reluctant blond-haired man, they locked him up in the next cell, where he could cool off.

The second policeman eyed Blaine with trepidation. This was a natural killer: cool, calculated, and vicious under the veneer of calm. *A very dangerous man indeed*, he thought to himself as he walked away, feeling the heat from Blaine's feral stare as he left the lock up area. There would be no dozing off tonight. This was a man who, if given the opportunity, would gladly slit his throat. A cold shudder worked its way down the policeman's spine, despite the warmth in the stuffy cell block.

Chapter 57

Senator Lee woke up from his gruesome nightmare. The huge Russian with the broken nose was chasing him and firing his gun. He could see himself falling off the bridge in freestyle, clutching the picture of his wife and son in his hands, frantically holding it close to him as he fell. He feels the thud as his body convulses in pain. Frost was watching on and quickly rose from his seat to assist the Senator.

Totally disoriented, Senator Lee forced himself into an upright position looking wildly around the room, trying to understand where he was. A look of confusion replaced the blank stare as he locked eyes on Frost. He gawped down at his arm where the intravenous tube snaking out of his right arm seemed to take on a life of its own. He felt the pulsation of the fluid making its way through his veins, giving him life, life he was not quite sure he wanted. His mouth opened to speak, but words did not come out. Instead, a hoarse, garbled sound erupted from his throat.

Puzzled, he regarded Frost, perhaps waiting for an explanation. The last three days were a blur because of what had transpired. Reassuringly, Frost placed a hand on the Senator, compelling him to fall back into the softness of the pillow, while Frost's eyes twinkled with joy and relief. He ventured a tired smile; after all, it had been more than a few dark, harrowing days wondering if the Senator would make it. It had been touch and go.

Smiling broadly, Frost said, "I'm glad, sir, that you pulled through. You had me worried. I was dreading the thought of having to relay your death to your sister in Colorado." Senator laid back; eyes fixated on Frost as he spoke. He opened his mouth again, slowly forming the words he so desperately wanted Frost to understand. The words came out with a raspy quality that jarred Frost. It was to be expected.

"Where is my wife?" he demanded. Frost stood up and moved away from the bed, trying to conceal the wave of emotions running through his body at that precise moment. Sadness engulfed him in a way that he could not express. Even when he was in the army, he had always shirked the duty of notifying other servicemen's families of bereaving news. How was he going to do it now? The pain would be unbearable. You see, Frost had loved Mrs. Lee just as much as the Senator. How was the Senator going to bear the loss? Pushing these thoughts to the back of his mind, he paused, trying to formulate the right words in his head. Nothing came to him. There was no way to butter it up. *Maybe honesty would be the best option*, Frost thought to himself. Senator Lee already knew the answer to his question, even if it was embedded somewhere deep in his subconscious.

Senator Lee asked again, more forcefully, "Frost, what is going on? Where is she?" Frost turned to face the Senator; his answer stuck in his throat.

Licking his lips, he started to say "Senator…" but went no further. The Senator's face blanched as his subconscious released the answer. Flashing images broke their barriers and his mind flooded with images of him sitting in the car with his phone to his ears while Frost was driving. He remembered hearing the explosion of bullets and the ear-splitting screams of his wife and son punctuating the morning air. Tears rolled down his cheek unchecked, wracking his ravaged body; trading physical pain for mental anguish. Frost could not help him; silently he retreated from the room. It was best to let the Senator grieve with dignity alone. Anyhow, Frost needed a walk to shrug off the depression that had washed over him. He also needed supplies. *Now was as good a time as any*, he thought as he slipped away from their hideaway.

He would not be gone long. When he got back, he would have to discuss the issue of money and a plan.

Chapter 58

Meanwhile, Kudirat's contact told her that the Russian bear, Alexei, had failed to kill Senator Lee on the bridge. They had lost sight of Senator Lee, who had probably gone underground or had died from the injuries he sustained. Either way, she had to find out. Frost had been a Godsend to Lee, saving him in the nick of time. Admiringly, she watched the news footage of Frost expertly transferring Lee into a vehicle and driving off. The news report said that the damaged car had been abandoned and another car was stolen from an unsuspecting civilian.

Last sighting was on the way to Jersey, and the usual dribble to the public about not approaching them but rather advising them to call 555 4231623 immediately was broadcasted. Kudirat decided to tune into the official police radio band to keep abreast with any spotting of the elusive pair. Stopping by a gas station, she topped up her tank, bought some snacks—tortillas and two bottles of water to staunch her thirst—and stopped at the check-out to pay for the goods. Carrying her brown bag of goodies, she exited the shop and made her way down the steps, colliding accidentally with a six-foot three man dressed casually in loafers, a denim jacket, and trousers. His face was shielded by a Lakers cap pulled down at an angle. He quickly apologized, helped her pick up the fallen items, and went into the gas station store without looking backwards. The hair on Kudirat's neck bristled; there was something vaguely familiar about him.

Depositing the items she purchased in the back seat, she went around and started up the ignition, throwing a second glance at the store as she did so. Through the window, she could see the man in the Lakers cap rummaging through the aisles. Starting up her car, she pulled out of the gas station, driving under 20 m/h, waiting for the tall stranger to join the highway. Seconds later, his hand full with two brown paper bags, the tall stranger re-joined the freeway. A chill ran down her spine as he passed her by. Providence had dealt her a wild card. Frost was driving off with his precious cargo. Spurring into action, she leaned down for her purse, grabbed her Glock semi-automatic pistol, and commenced firing straight at the back windscreen of the dark green Dodge in front of her.

She was rewarded with the shattering of glass as the car swerved to avoid the fusillade of bullets raining down on the Dodge. In response, Frost released a stream of bullets in retaliation. Three slugs coming perilously close to her head as she ducked to evade contact. The other shots flew past and hit the back seat and the roof. One of the slugs seemed to have hit her tire, because she felt her car jerk and veer off the road. With her feet still on the accelerator, she jerked the car over the curb and sent it sailing through the barrier. In the distance, she heard the screeching of the Dodge's tires as it picked up speed and sped away. She seethed inwardly; as she knew that the target had escaped again.

Her thoughts did not linger for long on her failure because her car went hurtling down the side of the road at lightning speed; but she did not panic, waiting instead for the inflatable airbag to blow up. Mercifully, her car came to a crashing halt, slamming into a withering bay tree whose twisted roots appeared to be looking up to the heavens. Groggily opening the car door, she retrieved her gun, backpack, and purse and hurriedly abandoned the car. She could see someone calling in the accident. She needed to get away before the police and ambulance arrived. Weaving her way through the thicket, she changed her blood splattered shirt, cleaned up her face— stemming the gash on her head from when her face impacted with the inflatable cushion that had probably saved her life—and stuffed the shirt into her backpack.

Looking slightly disheveled, she trudged up to the shoulder of the highway and was able to hitchhike a ride to Red Hook. Minutes later, she heard the siren and saw a police car, a black Chevrolet Malibu, and an ambulance heading towards the scene of the accident. Kudirat quickly put her bag in the back seat, in an attempt to minimize the chance of being recognized by any police personnel looking into the car.

Her ride dropped her off on the outskirts of Red Hook, and she made her way to her friend's hideaway home tucked away in the woods. She could not afford another brush with fate. She had already had two close calls, all in one day. Turning up with scratches and bruises would only increase suspicion and probably get her killed.

No, the best thing right now was holing up at her friend's place.

Walking the short distance, she retrieved the key from the flowerpot and entered the little cabin.
Tomorrow would be a busy day, and she needed her strength. Guzzling down some painkillers and downing the rest of her military style meal, she crashed on the sofa and was soon out like a light.

Chapter 59

Kolinsky sat in his armchair fuming at the discovery. His accountant Patrick Hale had been siphoning money to the Caymans. The books were not balancing. Hale had been skimming from the profit for years, and it had gone unnoticed until now. Hale was relieved that he had eluded his employer. But the thought of not being able to rejoin his family filled Hale with regret. Unfortunately, that could not be helped.

Carting his valise, hat, and overcoat, Hale flagged down a cab outside his flat. He knew his life hung in the balance. Within minutes, Kolinsky and his goons could track him down and kill him. Dropping a $100 note on the cab seat, he told the driver to step on the accelerator, silently hoping to get as far away as possible by the time Kolinsky's killer squad went looking for him.

Arriving with ten minutes to spare, he checked in and boarded a Swiss Air flight from New York to Geneva, business class. He was now a fugitive on the run. He did not need baggage, flirting with the attendant was an unnecessary distraction and could have devastating consequences. Sinking further into his seat, he decided to sleep for the rest of the trip and bury the mounting anxiety threatening to engulf him.

Hours later, he woke slightly refreshed, but still edgy. Looking out of the airplane window, he watched the graceful and gradual descent of the plane as it came to rest on the tarmac. Making sure that he was constantly in the midst of people, he made his way to the checkout point. He passed customs, retrieved his suitcase, and made his way through the terminal to the main entrance of the terminal building, continuously looking back to see if there was anybody following him. It seemed ok; he was nearly at the entrance, nearly home, almost home free. Strong hands gripped him from behind. Shock made him go limp. His pudgy hands struggling ineffectually to beat off the hands that held him in a vice-like grip. Sweat began reeking from every orifice as a policeman and airport security surrounded him.

His heart sank like stone. He was in deep trouble. Three feet away, standing by one of the stalls, stood Krivov, one of Kolinsky's loyal cohorts. He had not been as clever as he had thought. He had been followed all the way from America. His situation was hopeless. He had heard of the Americans' torture methods, and knew that, before the night was over, he would be singing like a canary. Why go through the torment? All he had to do was make a deal. He had already burned all his bridges with Kolinsky. The only price of disloyalty was death. Well, he still had a chance. He could get protective custody as part of the deal. Yes, he would testify against Kolinsky. It would not be easy coming face to face with his ex-employer, friend, and benefactor. But what choice did he have? Keeping his head down, surrounded by the airport security and the man with the badge, he was led away to a detention cell.

Krivov kicked himself silently. He had let Hale live, which meant that Hale posed a further risk to his boss. He turned around, looking for a quiet spot to make the call. Kolinsky had to know. Pulling out his cell phone, he made the call. It was now out of his hands.

Chapter 60

The turning of the key in the lock and the clanging of the cell door opening woke Blaine from his fitful sleep. Streaks of daylight shimmered through the fortified bars of the cell that was tucked away at the back of the precinct. The poorly lit corridor was shrouded in cascading shadows of the two police escorts assigned to take him to his temporary home. He knew that with the bombing at the hotel, nobody was interested in a locked-up killer at the moment. The authorities were probably relieved that they had one less criminal to worry about. Nobody liked a terrorist running loose in their neighborhood. Even he felt uncomfortable at the thought. His case could take weeks before it saw the light of day. He just had to be patient. The state lawyer assigned to the case was a greenhorn, and Blaine was under no illusions about whether his lawyer had ever seen the inside of a law court before.

Blaine really did not care; after all, he was a visitor of the state. He knew he was guilty. But did the state have enough evidence to put him away? Anyway, that was the least of his problems. He definitely was not going to make it easy for the state. Propelling him to his feet, the police men dragged him unceremoniously down the corridor, through the squad room, to the waiting transfer bus taking him to Blue County Prison. The prison was situated 15 miles outside Blue County Central. A forsaken piece of land originally allocated for burying the dead. How ironic, it now housed the worst criminals in the state. The main prisoners were killers from New Mexico and parts of Colorado.

Blaine got on the bus and was shackled down by the two officers. He was wedged in between two other passengers destined for the same fate. Both men stared into space, oblivious of his arrival. Neither acknowledged his presence, nor tried to make eye contact. *What a friendly bunch*, Blaine thought to himself. He could do solitude. After all, he had been on his own since he was sixteen.

He was ready to spend the rest of his life behind bars, incarcerated for his sins; but he had one more score he needed to settle. Blaine was looking forward to meeting the nefarious warden, Collin Farrow. Yes, Blue County Prison would be the last act in his macabre play. His blood stewed in anticipation. The final curtain was near. He smiled eerily. His promise to his dying mother would be fulfilled. With that final thought, he sat back to enjoy the bumpy ride; destination: Blue County Prison, where else?

Chapter 61

Induction day had arrived. It was just like a scene from the movie *Training Day*. Blaine had no illusions as to the comfort and heartfelt greeting he was going to receive at Blue County Prison. The only difference was that he knew why he was there. *Yes*, he thought to himself as he caught sight of his new home. The prison was in the heart of sparse land that was spread over many acres. Clear visibility extended for miles. The chance of escaping was slim. The old prison was primed with reinforcements, meshed walls, and steel fortified gates, which left little to the imagination. What else for but to keep the prisoners in?

Bracing himself for what was to follow, he disembarked with the others and their group was shuttled like a herd of sheep through the side gate inviting them into their new hell. Trading the outside world for a stay at Blue County Ritz, Blaine chuckled silently to himself. That was a joke and a half. He must have laughed out loud, because moments later, a truncheon landed squarely on his back, bringing him down from cloud nine. Herded through the narrow gate, they were ushered into a long, winding corridor that led to the booking office. The role call was taken of all incoming prisoners, and the dispatch officer was relieved of his command.

Hastily, he left the unruly bunch as the new inmates were told to strip. Blaine cringed, but he had no choice. He did not want to be prompted again. He was stripped and given a military style physical. A toothless warden grabbed his butt cheeks and he coughed as instructed while an intrusive cavity check was undertaken.

After several minutes of invasive touching, he was pushed into the row of shower stalls. What were these people thinking? There were enough vermin and disease within these walls to kill the prisoners. Why bother about what germs from the outside could do? It was a wonder that there were still prisoners alive within these walls, given the current state of the prison. Maybe that was why he was shipped off here. If he died, it would save the taxpayers a lot of money that would have been wasted on the trial.

Another sharp knock brought him to his knees. He really needed to stop daydreaming, or these guards would have a field day bashing him. He gave the prison guard a baleful glare and got up, his feet moving quickly in the prison train to the mound of clothes neatly stacked with prison soles. Well, he did not need to worry about what to wear; his wardrobe was sorted for as long as it took him to take care of Farrow. The guy behind gave him a hungry look. Disgusted, Blaine wasted no time; he hurriedly dressed up, conscious of the scavenger eyes boring into his back. He was nobody's playmate, and he would make sure of that.

A whistle sounded, and a set of feet walking in unison made their way down the corridor that shone from the gleaming polish on the floor. Blaine imagined that that must have been the hard work of the prisoners, he could not see the guards, with their bulging waists, doing any sort of manual work. Their feet made a belching, swishing sound as they approached. A flurry of activities ensued. The guards stood to attention while a few of the prisoners grappled to put the rest of their clothes or shoes on, unaware of what was going on. Blaine was ready, and he stood up defiantly strong, fully aware that this was a moment of reckoning. Would Farrow recognize him after all these years?

The prisoners all stood in some semblance of a line on a parade ground, awaiting inspection from the warden. Farrow scoured the faces of the new inmates, assessing their body movements, faces, and mannerisms. He stopped short in front of Blaine for a second or two, looking into eyes, scrutinizing the face as if he was etching it into his mind. Blaine looked at him boldly, boring into his eyes, the rage and hate smoldering briefly behind the cool façade. Disconcertedly, Farrow stepped away. Looking down at the rest of the men in the line, he singled out Blaine, the guy behind him, and two other guys from the pack and told the guards to send the rest to A Block. Blaine guessed that that was easy row. By merely looking at the four inmates Farrow chose, you could sense that all these men had history. These would be potential stirrers. By pointing them out, he was silently acknowledging that these men were conceivably his pressure points. Farrow had to manage them; there could not be more than one captain aboard his ship.

166

Thoughtfully stopping in front of each of the prisoners, pausing before passing judgment, he re-assigned the other three prisoners to different cell blocks. As the three men were led away, he drew closer to Blaine and whispered into his ears, "We meet at last. Welcome to my domain. Although I admire your work, I'll make it clear that if you step out of line on my turf, I will ensure that my guards will make your stay here as uncomfortable as possible. Is that understood?"

Without waiting for a response, the warden turned away and spoke to the prick who had hit him in the shower stalls. "Take him to D Block and make him as comfortable as possible," he said.

Blaine looked at the warden's retreating back, knowing that he had to be careful. Farrow remembered who he was. Getting to him would not be easy, but it was still possible. He would find Farrow's Achilles' heel. He had failed the first time. He was younger then, and not so smart. He had learnt from his mistakes. Now he was stronger, fitter, and better at the art of war. Bring it on Farrow, *he thought to himself.*

But before embarking on making Farrow suffer, Blaine had to find a way out of this hellhole, so that he could leave the desperation, degradation, and depravity behind when the time came.

Focusing on the task at hand, he followed foul-face to D Block, where his unsuspecting cellmates were about to make room for another unwilling guest.

Chapter 62

The filtered cries of the inmates being abused by other cellmates (or by the wardens?) permeated the night air. He couldn't tell which. Either way, it sent a cold sliver of fear down his spine. He shivered involuntarily, not in reaction to the cold infiltrating his flimsy jumpsuit, but to the unexpected, unfolding, and unforeseen scenarios lurking in the dank, dark, and rancid dungeon he was about to call home.

All around him, he could feel the palpable sense of fear and depression encasing the prisoners in an embrace bordering on desperation. He felt himself free falling, the sensation of despondency infusing him like a physical vice, caressing his fluttering heart momentarily. He needed to break out this place really soon, or his mental state would plummet into oblivion.

With renewed resolve, he swore to himself that he wouldn't let that happen. He needed help, but who could he trust? And who possessed the information crucial to the success of his task? Another nudge from the toothless warden brought him back from his thoughts. Shuffling out of sync with the other prisoners, he tried to make a mental note of the cell infrastructure, although there was a lot distracting him along the way. Even though the cell block seemed smaller in comparison to other prisons, it did not detract from the fact that escaping this place would be an insurmountable task. But escape he must, if he was to pull off his final assignment and disappear.

Blue County Prison was situated miles away from civilization; anyway, that was what it looked like. It was miles away from anywhere, in a deserted location, and he had no transportation. Topping it all was the fact that he didn't know the area. Escaping from this hellhole was virtually impossible unless he acquired the right help soon. Otherwise, he would be a sitting duck. Shirking off these thoughts, he focused on where he was going. The line had stopped. He had arrived. The door of his cell opened noisily on hinges, screaming for oiling, and he peered inside.

Tentatively, eyeing the existing occupants, he cautiously stepped into the cell and tried quickly to adjust to the smell of rotting rubbish, feces, and rank body odor that hung heavily in the air. Unflinching, he surveyed the denizens and dived for a spot out of harm's way, for the moment. He needed his wits about him if he was going to survive. He had no intention of being an inhabitant of a violent, desensitized pit hole for long.

Crawling into the corner with his back against the wall, he settled down, waiting to know who he was in bed with. He kept his eyes trained on his cellmates for as long as he could before the lights went out.

Chapter 63

Days rolled from mornings into nights. Blaine was surprised that he had spent three weeks here already and, apart from his midnight induction, his time behind bars had been uneventful. But things were going to change sooner than he had thought. A new set of inmates were being shipped in to boost the swelling population. What was a few more people? The prison was already at full capacity and bursting at the seams. It only meant more money for the chief warden and less rations for the inmates. Who really cared about them?

No, today was definitely different. There was an unusual spike of unrest within the prison as the arrival of one of the new prisoners was announced. The prison grapevine was buzzing. Brad Conklin was joining the motley crew. His reputation preceded him. He was revered in the criminal world as a hit man for the Deroni clan, a man whose carnage of dead bodies spanned fifteen years. The wardens were restless, probably wondering what indeed was going on. They handled short term criminals. They left big time criminals for Miami PD to take charge of. Delivery of this notorious mastermind of the underworld left an unhealthy electric current of dread on the part of the wardens, while a delicious sense of anticipation filled the hearts of the inmates. Nonetheless, troubling was brewing, and everybody was on high alert.

With little to do on this scorching day, Blaine loitered around the primal courtyard, staying clear of the prison gangs. He leaned against a wooden bench screwed into the ground, taking up a position from where he could observe the arrival of the prison bus. He was not disappointed. Shortly after three, he caught sight of the bus as it came to a halt outside the imposing gates. The squishing sound of hydraulic brakes stopping abruptly brought other prison-mates to his side. The air was laden with energy as the inmates huddled together, eagerly waiting for the alighting of the phenomenal killing machine.

Peering forward, the wait was rewarded by a 6 ft. 9 barrel of a man manacled with a heavy chain securing his arms and feet get out of the bus. He was wedged between two policemen, one who was guiding the prisoner nicknamed Butch Kid and the other holding onto the tip of his gun, ready to use it at the sniff of trouble. The six other passengers alighted afterwards, flanked by a sheriff in a ridiculous, outdated cowboy hat, like something out of the 1950s.

Blaine's senses tingled, a feeling of dread or was it anticipation? instinctively gripping him.

Chapter 64

The capture of Patrick Hale had pushed things into motion earlier than expected. But it did not matter. Seated on the deckchair by his pool in a casual Hawaiian shirt, shorts, and beach shoes, sipping on a glass of Gusset champagne reserved for such an occasion, Kolinsky cleared his mind, preparing himself for the inevitable offensive on the villa and his imminent arrest. An old friend in America had told him that Interpol and the FBI agent McClaren had been dispatched to take him into custody.

He had sent most of his men away, except for two, whom he trusted would defend him to the end. He had provided generously for both their families in light of their permanent retirement after this incursion. The warmth of the sun beat down mercilessly, but Kolinsky waited patiently under the beach umbrella for the expected sounds of gunfire. Soon enough, the villa was overrun by operatives. It was over before it had begun. The villa had fallen into the hands of a platoon of security personnel armed to the teeth. They must have been disappointed at the feeble resistance they were graced with. The agents must have been relieved that there were no casualties on their part, despite the fact that both his men had been killed.

Running up the garden stairs leading to the pool, guns drawn, McClaren and two other shooters carrying and swinging their .416 Barrett sniper rifles came to a stop in front of Kolinsky. In return, he simply smiled and said, "To what do I have the pleasure of this invasion into my home, Agent McClaren?"

Agent Dickings replied, "Simeon Dmitri Kolinsky, you are hereby under arrest for terrorist acts against the United States of America. You have the right to remain silent. Anything you say can and will be used against you in the court of law. You have the right to an attorney. If you cannot afford an attorney, one will be appointed to you. Do you understand these rights as they have been given to you?"

"Clearly, you don't have to be so melodramatic," Kolinsky replied. "Let's get it over with." Placing his hands behind his back, he waited for the handcuffs to be fastened securely before being taken into custody. McClaren stood watching Kolinsky, wondering who had tipped him off. Who knew that McClaren was here to make the arrest? Only a handful of people had that information. It would also explain the reason why there were only two men watching over Kolinsky when they arrived. Ticking it off in his head, there was the FBI Director, his friend, who had arranged the bust, and himself. Who else knew? Perplexed, but not surprised, he followed behind making mental notes to find out the source of the leak. He would find that out when he got back to America, if they got back there without any hiccups. Well, that remained to be seen.

Chapter 65

Simeon Kolinsky, known as the Russian Baron, had been caught. All the leading newspapers dedicated the front page to narrating the intricate operational precision of the CIA in conjunction with Interpol in apprehending one of the most notorious criminals of all time. He was to be tried in America, of all places. It had created a media hype that was unprecedented. Foreign journalists flocked in droves like people on pilgrimage to Mecca. The buzz was intoxicating. CNN, FOX, and other major players were following the stories and relaying every intricate detail as breaking news.

No wonder why the Governor of New York was nervous. With every infamous baron, there were risks. The scavengers were assembling for a major kill. Those who were sympathetic and bore allegiance to Simeon would release their own bag of tricks. Simeon was powerful enough to wield power in the corridors of government. His cronies were everywhere. A man of such immeasurable wealth had connections. Rumor had it that he had connections with the Deroni family right here in New York. After the last attempt to wipe out the Deroni clan, the Godfather had gone underground and smuggled in a few assassins from abroad. One was supposed to be of Russian descent. Could he be from Simeon's arsenal? The Governor wondered.

Either way, the Governor had been assured by the CIA and his old friend, the President of the United States, that adequate protection for him, his family, and the people of New York was to be put in place before January 6th, when Kolinsky, the Russian Baron, would have his day in court. Meanwhile, all he needed to do was to ignore the media circus building up in his city and do his job. Maybe stepping up his protection detail around the house and being super vigilant would not go amiss till things settled down, he mused. Pressing his intercom, the Governor summoned his faithful secretary of 17 years into his office. After dictating a letter, he wanted her to prepare for the congressional meeting on Tuesday, he also asked her to bring in his chief of security for an update on security detail.

Ten minutes later, the real Russian mastermind in the US government known as Mark Jenkins stepped into his boss's office, and closed the door softly behind him, and stood at attention, waiting to be addressed. The Governor admired the silvery fox's humility, the sleek looking security chief who had been by his side for the last six years. He knew the man would lay down his life for him if the situation arose. But he needed to go over the final security arrangements, especially after what had happened to Senator Lee and his family despite all the security provisions that were in place at the time. Jenkins had recruited a special squad to oversee the protection of his family for the duration of the case. Jenkins would accompany the Governor to court the next day to make his guest appearance, before proceeding to the House to read his congressional address. Satisfied that every possible scenario had been exhaustively explored and his backup plan to counteract the situation was researched, he dismissed Jenkins for the night. Moments later, Jenkins's deputy came in to take over protection detail.

It was time to head off home. Tonight, would probably be the last time the Governor would be able to see his wife and children for a while. Early the next day, his family would be whisked off to an undisclosed location for the duration of the case. Gathering what he needed, the Governor left his office with his security detail trailing close behind. Meanwhile, Jenkins watched as his boss was driven off home in his black Accolade, his mind in momentary turmoil, knowing fully well that things were going to change. The governor was about to know who he really was.

Loyalty to an old friend was more important than spouting faithfulness to his boss. His friendship to Simeon was like wine, getting better and stronger with age. Simeon was about to call in his old chip. Jenkins needed to sleep and prepare for tomorrow. He had a date with destiny.

Chapter 66

Kolinsky was seated in what could only be described as economy class, something he was not accustomed to. Well, he did not really expect first-class privileges to be paid by the US government or Interpol. It was quite confusing as to who would be picking up the bill for the flight; otherwise he could have protested at the shoddy and non-existent cabin service. Oh, that's right; it was, after all, a private charter. He should have advised them to use his Gulfstream jet instead.

His first view of America on arrival was a blur. He was whisked through security and transferred to a dark security vehicle with black-tinted windows and driven off to an undisclosed destination. Due to the special circumstances surrounding the case, the government had no intention delaying his ticket to appear in court. The fast-track process had been instituted, barring all jurisdictional rules, and there was pressure to keep Kolinsky under wraps till his court date; an interview was arranged for him with the District Attorney and Turner.

Kolinsky clammed up, waiting for his counsel to appear. He was taken to a local criminal court for arraignment, where the charges levied against him were read out. Kolinsky was wondering whether this was a special court for the proceedings or a 24-hour court. Either way, he did not care. He was then informed about his right to a counsel, and if he could not afford one, the court would be happy to assign one to him. Kolinsky laughed out loud. Looking behind, he could see old veteran and greenhorn lawyers desperately waiting to nab a case. As if on cue, Levinson strolled in announcing that he was representing Kolinsky, who smiled. This was more like it, a bit of controversy and glamor for such a high-profile case was in order. Exchanging handshakes indicating his approval, Kolinsky was then asked if he wanted to plead guilty or not guilty. Levinson answered on behalf, "My client enters a plea of not guilty."

Satisfied that the first part was done and over with, Kolinsky was released back into the charge of government personnel and lead out of court.

Chapter 67

Mark Jenkins knew that the day of reckoning had arrived. Timing was everything. It was a favor to his old friend. Perhaps the last sacrifice he would ever have to make. A sense of foreboding filled his gut. A wave of purpose, dedication, and love washed over him too, mottling the evil thoughts of fear and impending death. Walking into court would be his final act of heroism. A niggling thought in the back of his head screamed suicide. Either way, it would be the closing act to his 32 years of bloodshed. His reign was nearing its end, and he felt no guilt. Rather, a feeling of relief replaced his doubts. *Yes*, he thought to himself, *I am too old and too tired to keep up*. It was a wonder that he had lasted this long. He looked at his hand, the jutting scar a reminder of how close he came to death 25 years ago. If it were not for Simeon, he would be dead, or languishing in a revolting jail cell in the dankest part of Russia. He shuddered involuntarily, shaking his head to dismiss the notion of what his life could have been.

Simeon had given him a new life, a chance to start over in America. He was given a new identity and money to start his own business, if he had wanted to. He had the choice to be free from the vicissitude of crime, death, and cruelty. He had lived a life of luxury. Working in government security circles had its perks. It gave him the opportunity to eliminate people who could have recognized him and impinged on his freedom throughout the years. He did not need a family. He was a loner. His wife and daughter were in his past, and were well looked after by Simeon. They were oblivious of the fact that he was still alive. It was better that way.

He had kept a low profile for the past twenty years waiting for this day. As a government official, he also had access to a wealth of information. Using his prepaid cell phones, he updated the crew on where Simeon was hidden, the route to the court, and escape routes that would be used. He had set in motion what could only be described as a war on America. Things would never be the same again.

Sighing out loud, he packed his revolver, concealed his knife, and headed for the door. Today seemed like a good day to die. Besides, Simeon was expecting him to make a very valuable appearance in court, and he did not want to disappoint him, did he? Taking one final look at his surroundings, content that he had left nothing behind, he closed the hotel door with a slam of finality. There would be no tomorrow for him, that he knew for sure.

Chapter 68

Sixty -three years had passed, and Simeon had grown old outwardly, but still had his fiery temper, nimbleness, and ruthlessness hidden behind the extra pounds he put on to give the semblance of a middle -aged man. He was wired, not from coffee or anxiety, but from the rush of adrenaline that flowed through his veins. A flush of tingling anticipation ran up and down his spine. The thought of going to court was exhilarating. He had been hiding in the shadows for too long. Now it was time to step into the limelight.

For years, he was a wanted man accused of murder, coups, and acts of terrorism. None of them proven, of course; he had been thorough, and every willing witness had met a quick, decisive death, killed by mercenaries or assassins unconnected to him, until now. So why should he worry about the media circus unfolding before his eyes? He was only curious to see if Agent McClaren would come to the proceedings. He had a special gift waiting for him. Yes, indeed, there was some unfinished business he needed to conclude; like who had betrayed him and given McClaren his undisclosed location. The idea that there was a traitor within his ranks irked him deeply.

First things first, being arraigned for terrorism needed all his attention. So many civilians in New York, Blue County, Illinois, and Memphis had died from the chemical bomb explosion that imploded the Blue County Conference. His lawyer, Jonathan Levinson, was a fixer. He handled high profile cases only. His name had been associated with the most powerful men of the underworld. He represented the greatest crime lords of organized crime, men like Johnny Faccini—the Boston Godfather, known in the underworld as The Weeping Exterminator. Simeon had his team of lawyers flown in to support Levinson, no expense spared. After all, it was a high-profile case, and money was no object. Besides, he was not leaving his fate to an American. He always had a plan B.

The Americans would not know what hit them when the time came.

Chapter 69

The science facility buzzed with excitement as the dedicated crop of leading scientists buried their heads in the task of deciphering the components of the chemical bomb that had exploded at the Blue County Hotel. The clock was ticking, and the stuck-up advisor from the White House was all over them like a sore rash. His boring eyes made Professor Khan uncomfortable. It was like he was questioning his loyalty. *Was it because I am Asian, or am I just paranoid?* Professor Khan thought to himself.

Anyway, his loyalty did lie somewhere else. How long would it take these people to figure it out? Pretending to be useful, he shadowed Dr. Heinz, asking questions and moving chemicals around to distract the good doctor. If there were anybody who was going to crack the composition, it would be Dr. Heinz. Leeching on to him from the start would not raise suspicion, and would give him the opportunity to sabotage his efforts while he was at it.

He knew that his colleagues were close to decrypting the chemical cocktail, because shortly after 12 p.m., Dr. Klein rushed to Dr. Heinz's side excitedly. He had found one of the components. Traces of BZ Agent 15 and VX had been extrapolated from the sample he was working on. All the other scientists milled around Dr. Klein's worktable as he confidently gave a presentation of his findings. Hamilton felt giddy. This was a time to prove himself to the President. The result could be the difference between a colossal failure, with him being relegated with ignominy, and a place in the corridors of power with his name associated to successfully limiting the exposure of the chemical bomb and inventing its antidote. Right now, it looked like he was part of the solution rather than the problem. Thing seemed to be looking up. He rushed off to make a very important call, one that would put him in good stead with the President.

Moments later, Dr. Schneider and Dr. Heinz began to raise their own hypothesis, which did not sit well with Dr. Klein, and an educated argument ensued. Professor Khan excused himself, asking for permission to go to the toilet while the rest debated on what other substances constituted the lethal chemical combination. Making his way into the toilets, he checked out the other toilet stalls before making the call to his handler. Speaking hurriedly into the phone, he gave his handler an update on what was going on. With clear instructions on what he was expected to do, Professor Khan washed his face and hands, dried them, and made his way back to the lab, trepidation clutching at the strings of his heart at what he was expected to do. It was a just war. There were always casualties in war. His only regret was that three of the most qualified minds he had ever met would be dead in a matter of minutes. What choice did he have? There was no point in being sentimental. After all, when the American soldiers carried out the incursion in his village and killed his mother, sister, and his loved ones, they had been regarded as casualties of war in an American victory. Well, now it was his turn. He wanted the Americans to feel the wrath of his vengeance and share the burden of his loss. It was time, and he was the catalyst who was going to make it happen.

Circling around the worktop, he re-joined his colleagues, throwing in a few ideas of his own that his colleagues pondered on before pursuing other notions. All the scientists were animated, feverishly working against the clock for the other elements in the puzzle, lost in the furor of the moment, oblivious of Professor Khan's intention. As if by accident, he casually hit two vials, spilling the contents of Epichlorohydrin and Propane onto the worktable. In an instant, the other scientists stared in horror as the chemicals intermingled, triggering an explosion. A cacophony of sounds erupted with the boom. A warning message voice reverberated out of the sound system advising everybody to leave the building.

Sirens blared louder, and the eruption of the second blast occurred, releasing an envelope of smoke as the whirling of the sprinklers started up. Shards of glass and other objects went hurtling in the air, crushing Dr. Heinz instantly. Dr. Barnes and Dr. Schneider scrambled to get through the door as visibility in the lab became non-existent. The lights went out, and the cool lab turned into a boiling furnace disbursing a firework of chemicals like sparks on the 4th of July.

Professor Khan could hear the sounds of people scrambling about desperately looking for the exit. The emergency lighting kicked in and beacon lights lined the way out. Pumped up with adrenaline coursing through his veins, he clambered up to the landing looking for the electrical box, recklessly ignoring the billowing smoke engulfing the upper landing. Coughing and with his eyes watering, he managed to find a circuit box that housed a multitude of wires. He tugged at the wires fiercely, trying to dislodge the tangled wires, without any success. Spinning around, he caught sight of a fire box that held the fire-hose and mini axe. Leaning down in the debris, he picked up fragments of a table, the steel cold to the touch, and rammed it into the glass protecting the fire box. Seconds later, he had secured the fire axe that he used to pry the wires loose, plunging the lab complex into a second spate of darkness.

He could feel the fear of the employees fleeing the lab complex. It was palpable. Joyously praising Allah for the victory, he stumbled through the smog searching for the stairs. A rumble from below stopped him temporarily in his tracks. A sudden burst of energy released a great ball of fire that leapt upwards, caroming into the upper level. Professor Khan was blown off his feet, and in those final moments, he knew that although he had successfully disrupted the revelatory exposition of the chemical bomb's antidote and killed as many infidels as possible, he would not be there to finish the mission. *I guess that was the price of martyrdom*, he thought. With total submission to the will of Allah, he succumbed to the vagaries of death.

Chapter 70

The clarion call was clear. Avery looked at the encrypted message flashing in his inbox one more time to re-affirm it. Satisfied, he pressed the delete button and shut down his laptop. The time had come. It was time to revisit New York, his boss needed him, and he was not about to disappoint him, was he?

After all, he was sure that the party would not be fun without him. *Would it not be nice for the people to finally meet the Associate?* He thought. With his reputation preceding him, it would certainly amplify the importance of his appearance at Kolinsky's court case.

He reached under the bed, keyed in the security code to his floor safe, and scoured through the contents, arranging what he needed for the journey in a small pile. Content that he had assembled what he required for this delicate and complicated mission, he retrieved his passport and $10,000 and placed the contents in his duffel bag, grimly shutting it with an air of finality. Minutes later, having secured his flat by setting a wall alarm and activating his specially installed motion sensor equipment, he left his apartment and flagged down a taxi; destination: Honolulu airport.

Meanwhile, in Singapore, 4 a.m. was as good a time as any to enjoy a relaxing break in the luxuriant suite Medusa had bought under a pseudonym. She had narrowly been killed on her last mission and was seriously contemplating leaving her line of work. But what else was there for her to do? She just could not sit around in Singapore indulging in luxury. That would not be right. The inactivity alone would kill her, which was if one of the relatives of the people she had killed did not track her down and end her.

No, she thought to herself, the best thing would be to limit the number of jobs she took, otherwise, how was she going to keep up this expensive lifestyle? Sighing contentedly after having tested the water for the tenth time, she slinked into the Jacuzzi, reveling in the warm water and the scents she had put in the bath earlier. She immersed her body in the aromatic spices for twenty minutes and it left her rejuvenated. She got out, dried herself, threw on a pair of tracksuit bottoms and a Velcro top supported by a sports bra, and headed outdoors to her Maserati parked in the garage.

Firing up the beast, she revved the engine, appreciating the engine power under her control as she maneuvered the car out of the garage and onto the road, making sure that she drove at a rate a tad lower than the maximum speed limit for that stretch of the road. She made her way down the Nicholl Highway, crossed over the Ophir Flyover, and cruised through Sungei Road and made her way to the Broadway Hotel, where she was to meet her contact.

Self-conscious, she decided to park the car and walk the last three hundred yards. Stashing the car in her friend's car lot, she made the rest of the trip on foot, spending a few minutes to change her clothes and put on her auburn wig, brown tinted sunglasses, and a dash of lipsticks to accentuate her lips. Calm, she arrived at the foyer and headed for the breakfast room for guests. Her party was ready and waiting, sitting at a table close to a large balcony window with a view to the early morning sun rising in the sky.

While looking directly at her contact seated at the table, she took in her surroundings in one glance. The breakfast room was literally empty. Except for a couple seated two tables away and a waiter holding the menu, there was nobody else in the room. Sliding into the chair, she gave him a perfunctory kiss on the cheek and eyed up her connection, quickly assessing the situation. Was her contact uncomfortable and did his sweating hands and furtive look betray his intentions? Had she been sold out? Her brain buzzed with a million unanswered questions within the seven seconds she took to evaluate her position. The clammy hands and constant shifting in his seat made her sensory radar move into overdrive. With a feeling of foreboding, she re-adjusted her skirt and placed her .22 safely in between her legs as she sat down. Better to be ready if anything was going down.

The contact's Adam's apple bobbed up and down as he tried to clear his throat. *This could not be good*, Medusa thought, trying to read his expression. Silently he pushed over the morning edition of the *New York Times* and flipped it over to the tabloid's head line article. *UNDERGROUND RUSSIAN WARLORD CAPTURED.* Numb, she read on:

186

Simeon Kolinsky, Head of the Russian Cartel, a prolific murderer, terrorist, and owner of the largest sex ring in the world was arrested at his villa in Barbados yesterday. An elusive criminal who had evaded the grasp of Interpol for over 27 years was betrayed by his second in command, Sergei Ivanov, and accountant, Patrick Hale, who are currently assisting Interpol in their investigations.

Meanwhile, Simeon Kolinsky has been extradited to the United States to answer for his involvement in the Blue County incident that claimed over 22 lives and had widespread implications. The US government, in conjunction with the Belgium, British, and Swiss governments, has set up a joint task force to gather evidence on the largest criminal case the world has ever known…

Sick to her stomach, Medusa could not bring herself to continue. The illusion of putting her past life behind her now seemed like a tall order. Deep down, she knew there really was no getting out of it, was there? But Sergei turning state evidence jeopardized her chances and that of others like her of leading normal lives. Spending time behind bars was not what she really had in mind either. There was only one solution. Sergei had to be stopped and the Godfather freed.

Well, here goes nothing, she said to herself. She had better pack. This was totally different, a new ball game that would end with her death or the Godfather released. Either way, it was inevitable that she would go to America. She needed back up to carry out this task. It was going to be tricky. With the current involvement of Sergei, the rest of the pack would have gone underground, waiting to formulate a plan. It was a case of self-preservation. Who would help her in this suicide mission?

Tossing a few bills on the table, without a second look at her informant, she left the table and made her way out of the hotel. She needed to go home and pack. But her situation demanded that she exercise more caution. Retrieving her car from behind her friend's car lot, she headed for the bus station terminus to access her locker.

Relief flooded the man's body as he watched Medusa leave the balcony. He picked up his phone and dialed the number he was given. Speaking softly into the phone, he said, "She's on her way." Terminating the call, he removed the SIM card and destroyed it, grabbed the bills on the table and left. His work here was done. The recruitment drive had begun.

Chapter 71

The American Airline plane touched down on the tarmac, bringing Avery Johnson out of his reverie. It had been 3 months since he'd been in New York, and he was last here to kill a drug lord from Miami, Alberto Perez, who had come up for a meeting with the Dons of Chicago and New York. He was a prolific gambler known to have his sticky fingers in every pie. He was a shady gangster who failed to make his regular returns to Kolinsky and the New York Don—The Weeping Exterminator. He had shown great contempt and disrespect to both heads, and that's why he had been marked for death.

Alighting from the plane, he made his way along the terminal of the La Guardia Airport, passed through the immigration point and out into the busy airport lounge. He marveled at the hustle and bustle of activity swarming around him, stopping temporarily to admire a mother softly berating her child to pick up his toys and hurry if they were to catch their plane. He could see people caught up in the doldrums of their dreary lives and he felt a sudden alienation, disenfranchisement, and detachment from reality. Fleetingly, a feeling of weightlessness encompassed him, and it seemed like a bit of his humanity was splintering like fragments of broken glass shattering all around him.

The flurry of activities in a boring, mundane life might have been a better option in another life. The thought plunged him into an aching state of perpetual loneliness, inflicting a sharp, throbbing pain of despair as his mind reluctantly acknowledged the illusive chance of normalcy.

You would think that a serial killer or the Gentleman Assassin, as he was known in the Underworld, would feel remorse at the trail of blood that he had left over the years. Well, in fact the ghosts were there, haunting him in his dreams, making him sweat at night, many faces rolled into one, acting as judge, jury, and executioner. Now

189

was not the time to dredge up pangs of conscience. Perhaps in another life things may have been different. However, today his mission and primary focus was to secure the freedom of Kolinsky. After all, one million dollars was riding on this. Everybody he had killed deserved it. His victims had all had records of criminal dealings or had killed other undeserving individuals. *Maybe I sold my soul to the devil years ago*, he thought, *it did not matter*. Like I said, that was in another life. Killing a few more made no difference. Sadistic, you'd say, but I would prefer to call it business. There was no room for misgivings especially now, when there were bound to be casualties of war.

Purposefully, with his wits about him, he got into a waiting cab and gave the driver an address just off Madison Avenue. Relaxing tentatively in the backseat of the cab, the Gentleman Assassin focused on formulating a plan while the driver took off, tapping his meter to start billing his fare.

Chapter 72

Senator Lee sat there in a meditative state with swirling thoughts conjuring macabre images of horror. Icy fingers massaged his heart, while contorted pictures grappled for a place in his stream of imageries, pointing him in a direction he did not want to go towards but was powerless to resist. It was like looking in from the opaque window of his mind, trying to make sense of what he was seeing. How long had these hallucinations been imbedded in his subconscious? The flashbacks were vivid. The loss of his wife and son had exacerbated the visual illusions, racking up unsavory images that his convoluted mind refused to accept.

Yes, it was becoming glaringly clear that the lone figure lying lifeless like a discarded doll on his carpet was someone he knew. Snippets of fragmented pieces of the puzzle solidified into a gruesome picture of Anne Marie posed like a broken mannequin that disturbed him. Memories of his fight with Anne Marie came flooding back, breaking through his memory bank. He remembered the blood splatters all over the carpet as he held on to her crying and pleading for forgiveness, watching helplessly as the light of life drained out of her fragile body.

It was all a mistake. Why did she have to pry into things that did not concern her? After all, he was ultimately doing it for her. He wanted to take her away from this life and make her his queen, eventually. Although, he could see that she was becoming quite frustrated of being a mistress, seeing him only after meetings rather than on her own terms. He would then slink off to his wife and son, feeling guilty that he had betrayed his wife, but intoxicated by the vivaciousness of Anne Marie. She made him feel alive.

Coming back to the memory of catching Anne Marie rummaging through his desk, why did she do that? If she had found out what he was up to, it would mean prison time and public humiliation. He could not risk it. Oh, the irony. He was now on the run from the very people he had jumped into bed with. That was the price of failure. He had given them the clearance, brought in the chemicals, yet they were unable to execute the job. Whose fault was that?

His only consolation was that he still had Frost. Frost had always been by his side to help him through the mess. First of all, by clearing up the crime scene and disposing of Anne Marie's body. If that was not enough, he had saved his life twice. Luckily, before the bedlam, he had squirreled away $4 million away for Frost. He hoped that it would be enough. What he could not understand was who had attacked his brother in law? They did not sound like mobsters or assassins, or they would have killed the good doctor and his family.

There really was nothing he could do to help the doctor now. It was imperative that Senator Lee escape from the USA and lay low for a while. He was fit for travel, and Frost had purchased a razor and shaved off his hair, military style. With some contact lenses to change the color of his pupils to blue and make-up to create a false scar on his cheek, his appearance had been altered enough to match photo from the fake passports he had just obtained.

The plan was to drive over the border to Canada and settle at his cabin on the edge of Quebec near the border of Vermont, purchased under an alias until things blew over. Well, that was the plan. What else could he do in the present circumstances?

Chapter 73

Kolinsky had hidden behind his mask for so long. How would it feel to let people really see him for who he was? I mean, really know who he was; no longer hiding under the weight of anonymity. A mask changes you; You could be anybody you wanted. Powerful in the knowledge that nobody knew who or what you were capable of. Interesting, don't you think? That after all these years, going through all the aliases, hiding in plain sight, using different inflections, accents, clothes, poses, and makeup, of course, nobody had caught on. Perhaps it was the plastic surgery that had shrouded his secret for so long? Kolinsky admired Dr. Sinclair's work in the mirror. Yes, amazing what a little silicon to the mouth and cheeks could do. The augmentations and implants to project the chin and blepharoplasty to alter the eyelids rendered his metamorphosis complete. A miraculous transformation, he grinned to his reflection; totally remarkable.

Now the time had come to reveal the face behind the mask and unleash the demon behind the façade. Yes, he was ready. He felt a twinge of sadness, and yet was exhilarated that he would no longer die in obscurity. A floating sensation seized him, like an actor stepping onto stage into bright spotlights while the spectators looked on with bated breaths in anticipation of the final act.

He was led out of his cell; he too had waited for the scene to play itself out. Only fate would write the final conclusion to the scene. Looking right and left, flanked by two burly secret agents, he walked in tandem with them, matching them step for step as they proceeded up the stairs to the court building, into the cavalcade of reporters waiting expectantly to get a glimpse of Kolinsky. Yes, it was exciting to finally be free.

Relishing the thought, he walked through the barrage of reporters and was herded into an elevator to the tenth floor, where his audience awaited. He laughed. Let the spectacle begin.

Chapter 74

Medusa did not believe that she would ever find herself once again in New York, but the stakes were just too high. She had to save her father. She owed him that much. There was only one place she considered safe, and that was underground. Years ago, she had created a safe haven away from boring eyes and inquisitive feet, ready for the unexpected, like now. It was the most unlikely hideout on earth, imbedded in a discontinued train tunnel not recorded on any train map or blueprint held by the state. The opening was obscured by the rotting parts of a discarded train set in a vast space with secret doors and passages leading to the sewage system.

Within the abyss lay a cavernous room etched from stone with solidified walls and protected by a state-of-the-art security system wired to the central grid that was supported with trigger points laden with C4 explosives set to detonate on intrusion. The walls were insulated to keep the room warm and stave off the smell of rotting objects lying outside the secured area. The room was sparsely furnished with the bare essentials, but it served its purpose, housing an arsenal that would put the army of a small country to shame. There was also a month's stock of food and water, if there was a need to lay low.

All she needed to do was wait and act on instruction. Another piece of the puzzle would fall into place by tonight. The e-mail asked her to come online by 9 p.m. She did not know who was pulling the strings, but that was immaterial. The attack on the courthouse had to be definitive and accurate. There were bound to be casualties, but she had no intention of being one, a statistical number who met her fate while trying to save her father. She had a back-up plan, after all. But she felt tired, totally jet lagged. The best thing to do now was to get a few hours' sleep and then think up an exit plan. She certainly wasn't going to be caught holding the bag.

No! No! She said to herself as she dropped off into an exhausted sleep.

Waking up six hours later, feeling fully refreshed, she made a large of cup of Nespresso. She scrounged about in her backpack, extracted a pack from her survival kit, and nibbled on a morsel from her military style dinner. Moments later, she heard the ping of an email dropping in. Foraging through the encrypted message, she assembled the tools of her trade and set off, locking the door to her hideout securely. You never know, she thought to herself, whether she would need to come back to it again. Camouflaging the doorway with the dirty, ragged curtain and run-down shopping trolley, she made her way through the sewer tunnels to Penn Station.

Forty-five minutes later, donned in the maintenance suit of Manny Construction, heavy duty boots, and work helmet, she walked out on to the platform, head lowered to avoid the cameras, and made her way to the door marked Employees Only. Extracting her passkey, she opened the door and made her way to the locker where she had stashed the rest of her arsenal. Quickly slipping out of her work clothes, she dressed up in a black leather jumpsuit, a matching pair of Lowa Renegade GTX boots, and a blonde wig cut short with a boyish fringe.

Mounting her Ducati Testastretta NCR, she drove to a lock up and stashed the bike, changed her boots for a pair of high heel shoes, and made the rest of her trip on foot to the Peninsular Hotel. She checked in under the name Amanda Brown and went to her room to pass the time. The clock was ticking, and the drama was about to unfurl. Patiently, she settled in; waiting for the last piece in the jigsaw picture to emerge and fall into place.

Chapter 75

Kudirat had been ahead of the game. She had been chosen during the jury selection. Now, she was Mabel Kingfisher from New Jersey. A housewife with two kids, called in, unfortunately, to take part in this high-profile case. She had studied her prey well. The file had a full dossier and DVD that spoke of the banal existence of the woman she was impersonating. With heavy make-up, thick tortoise shell glasses, and a blonde wig, she bore a spitting resemblance to the prosaic woman. She mastered her inflections and the tone and speed of her speech, making her disguise complete.

Filing in with the other eleven jurors, she sat down with her hands clasped between her knees, faking the feeling of raw nerves; masterfully playing the role of a timid housewife with little exposure to city life. She sat wedged in between a woman and an annoying pervert who called himself a retired schoolteacher. A lecher, whose roving eyes were focused on the curves of all the women in the court, he was openly gawking at the boobs of the co-chair District Attorney, for starters. His eyes were everywhere, except on the male lawyers. The woman on her other side was a sweet looking Latino housekeeper, named Maria Gonzales, who was struggling to understand the oath she was asked to recite. Her warped mind was struggling to comprehend how she was chosen to sit for jury trial. She had only gotten her green card two years ago. Was this a cruel joke? Or was it a deliberate attempt by the government to turn the case into a fiasco? Either way, Maria tried hard to hide her consternation.

Kudirat, on the other hand, was prepared, she knew her involvement was crucial and had committed her part to heart. All the escape routes were covered. She had been able to repossess her gun from the lady's toilet just before she went into court. Her Glock 19 was tucked neatly in her waistband, ready for use at a moment's notice. All she needed to do was to wait for the cue. Her eyes scanned the incoming crowd milling into the confined space that was to house the large number of spectators of the highly celebrated case. She knew an associate of hers had mingled in with the mob clamoring for the rights to be seated in the crammed court room and was also waiting for the right time. It was all a question of timing.

Amidst the strident chatter dominating the court, the prosecution team made their entrance. Moments later, the two lawyers representing the defendant strolled in, confidently making their way to the table assigned to them. Placing their briefcases on the table, they hazarded a look at the jury line-up and, for an instant, held Kudirat's stare, before moving on to re-assess the other members on the panel. The fleeting stares were enough to convey their meaning. Kudirat shifted ever so slightly in her seat, giving herself room to reposition her Glock without attracting attention.

The noise rose to a deafening crescendo as the accused made his appearance, cameras clicking in tandem with the flashes that lit up the already illuminated space. The buzz heightened as Kolinsky turned around to give the cameras an impressive shot of his features before taking his seat; confidence oozing out of every pore.

The frenzied sounds came to a crashing halt and a sudden hush fell on the room when the court clerk announced: "In the case of the State of New York v. Simeon Kolinsky, we announce the arrival of the venerable Judge James Barrymore presiding. All rise."

Chapter 76

Today was the beginning of his day in court. *Amazing,* Kolinsky thought, *the media was out in full blast.* He even felt like royalty. Ironic, don't you think, that he could muster such media attention? He was here to face a panel of worthless working-class people who had no concept of who he was and what he had achieved over the years. They thought they had the power to convict him of treason.

Who had ever convicted the CIA for all the atrocities it had perpetrated all over the world? Well, that story was for another day. Today, perhaps, he would come face to face with his accusers. He laughed to himself. He would watch one of the traitor's squirm in his seat. Justice will be served this day under the watchful eyes of the Secret Service. He heard that the stooge was being transported from an undisclosed location close to the Pentagon and was expected to arrive at 9.15 a.m., shortly before proceedings started.

He still had his sources, despite the lockdown. There were always capable men who would serve his cause willingly or unwillingly, whatever the case may be. A surge of inner strength rose within him. Regrettably, he had not had a dose of his customized cocktail, an intoxicating elixir made from aloe vera and herbs specially procured from the Far East, but he could feel a burst of adrenalin coursing through his veins in anticipation of the drama that was about to unfold. Walking in between the two federal agents, he paused to admire his reflection in a glowing window, which was reflecting a piercing light from the refracted rays of sunlight that ran through the building.

At sixty-three, outwardly, he seemed a little dowdy, although his arms and shoulders still bulged, belying a hidden strength unbeknown to his captors. His raven-black hair was tinged with grey at the sides, giving him an aristocratic look, and his eyes held a captivating stare that grasped attention. He might be getting old, but his reflexes were still sharp and his features still produced an alluring effect on the opposite gender.

Heads turned and cameras clicked in acknowledgment of his presence. The twelve jurors had been brought into the courtroom through one of the adjoining doors earlier. They kept their eyes averted as they sat uncomfortably waiting for the judge to make his appearance. However, a young, pasty looking lady, juror 11, looked at him knowingly for a fraction of a second, her look laden with unspoken meaning as she squirmed in her allocated seat. Pondering on who the girl was, Kolinsky smiled when the court alarm went off and the lights went out. In the darkness, he felt the strong arms of a FBI agent pushing him through a swinging door, out of sight, away from the mayhem.

Chapter 77

The corridor lights flickered and sputtered three times before going out completely, plunging the north side of the courthouse into darkness. The busy courthouse froze in time, catching people unprepared for the temporary blackout. The battery back-up housed in the lower-level electronic room had not responded yet to the interrupted power supply. Maybe that was because someone had conveniently disabled the batteries, causing the system to malfunction.

The lapse disarmed the CCTV camera and gave access through the side door and window to Avery and his associate, who deftly climbed in and mingled with the flow of moving people waiting for the massive generator to swing into action. Ten seconds later, the security and electrical supply had been restored. Security agents scanned the corridor and waited till things had returned to normal. A second sweep of the floor did not reveal anything ominous. The judge was then whisked into his chambers and three security men were assigned outside his door and along the corridor to protect him. This was after all, a high-profile case, and the President of the United States had an invested interest in the outcome. The security detail could not afford for things to go wrong.

The judge was a close friend of the President and he could not refuse the lawsuit being held in his court. The judge's unease lay elsewhere; it laid in the fact that this case could unravel his secret and put him in grave danger in more ways than one. In his twenty years of being called to the bench, he had handled several important court cases that had landed him the accolade 'The Patriarchal Lawyer'. No, the answer lay deep down in the bottomless pit he called his conscience.

The day of reckoning had come, the past had come unstuck, and he did not know what to do. Perhaps there was a way out. He just had to find it in the next twenty minutes, or his professional life would be as good as over. Resignedly, he donned his wig and gown, counting down the minutes, waiting for the bailiff to summon him to his doom.

Chapter 78

Hamilton sat in the corridor outside the Oval Office waiting to be summoned. What he thought would be the making of his career had turned awry. Furtive looks from passersby said it all. It was the confirmation of his doom. His fate had been sealed.

A sense of foreboding gripped him in his lower gut, he knew fully well that he might as well pick up his bags and leave; after all, his professional life was over, right? The explosion at the lab and the destruction of the only tangible traces of the chemical solution used at the Blue County Hotel had gone up in smoke, smothering any future aspirations of political elevation.

He felt claustrophobic, as if the walls were crashing down around him. His feet took on a restless tap that he struggled to control. Even with his back rigidly placed in the plush Bedouin chair, he felt no comfort. Rather, his composure was on the brink of crumbling. Suddenly, a dark shadow crossed his view, and he could see the figure of the Under Secretary of Defense approaching. Swallowing hard he got up to face him. In response, the Under Secretary of Defense silently pointed, directing him into the Oval office, and quietly closed the door behind him. Hamilton froze in motion like a deer caught in the headlights of an approaching car. His mind whirred in fear and he wrestled with the fusillade of thoughts threatening to crush the already tattered shreds of his self-confidence. All he wanted to do was run and escape the conspiratorial, scowling faces of the occupants in the room.

The cabinet sat at attention. The President, dressed in a smart Armani blue suit, sat still looking at him, his body reflecting the tiredness, tenseness, and tension enveloping the room. All of that was besides the fact that the weight of the decision he was about to deliver bore heavily on him. Words got stuck in Hamilton's throat and a raw feeling of acid burned his esophagus. He shifted on his laurels, trying hard to disguise how uncomfortable he felt; waiting to be berated for the shambolic way he had handled the matter. His voice mirrored the pain he felt as he tried to salvage what was left of his dignity and professional integrity. Frame by frame, in a slow monotone, he related what had happened, from his perspective. Starting with his observations, he gave an in-depth account of the findings of the scientists. He had left the lab complex to make a call to his superior to tell him of the breakthrough. He had barely left the facility, when he heard the rumble of an explosion and the frantic panic of the employees. The sudden burst of flames, followed by an eruption, had sent him flying into space. He had blacked out and was resuscitated with the aid of a paramedic.

If Hamilton was looking for sympathy at that juncture, he certainly was not getting a reaction. The stony stares looked back at him, goading him to finish off his report. There really was not anything else he could add, so he stood numb, stifled by a feeling of abject inadequacy, like a schoolboy caught napping in class. He bit his lip, knowing full well that he had not called his superior as he had stated earlier. He had come outside to light a cigarette and figure out what he would do next. The deafening sound of the alarm blaring loudly along the corridor and the scared faces of people evacuating the multiplex were impossibly clear in his memory. He remembered everything: the smell of burnt bodies, the billowing smoke darkening the skies above, and the agonizing screams that filled his ears. The macabre images were imprinted in his mind, leaving a sickening, hollow feeling in his stomach. He could have been recorded amongst the dead too, but he was lucky. He was nearly a victim. Ironic, wasn't it? Doctors say that smoking kills. In this instance, it was his saving grace. Whatever punishment they meted out to him today, he would gladly take it. After all, where were the scientists from the facility and security details assigned to protect them? All of them were dead, and that was saying a lot.

Frostily, the President relieved him of his post and advised him to go home and refrain from discussing the matter with anybody, and he was dismissed from his presence. Two overzealous, burly agents escorted him outside the White House grounds and watched him as he made his way to his car. Depressed, confused, and uncertain of what to do, he made his way home. Where else could he go? Starting up his old Taurus, he made his way through traffic on his way to his apartment while resonating thoughts whirled around in his head. What came next? He needed to come up with a plan—that was certain. His life depended on it.

Chapter 79

It was only 4.30 a.m., but the small office was packed with representatives from Homeland Security, the police department, court security, and the FBI of course. The collaboration of all the agencies was imperative for the success of the New York v. Kolinsky court case.

All the operatives were on full alert, conscious of the importance of the assignment and how it would impact their individual and joint careers. Total co-operation was expected. No lone ranger antics would be tolerated, the Commander in Chief of the nation had expressed this in no uncertain terms through his mouthpiece for this operation, the grizzly FBI Director, whose cadence, candor, and commanding personality demanded their undivided attention.

"Gentlemen, this is one of the largest security operations ever to be conducted on American soil. The alliance of all those gathered here is imperative. You have each been specially chosen for this assignment because of your years of experience, expertise, and recommendations from your bosses. You will be the elite squad entrusted with the supreme task of protecting the people of New York against every threat that presents itself during the trial. In front of you are dossiers defining your respective roles. The blueprints of the courthouse and surrounding buildings are included, where they are relevant to your part in this undertaking. McClaren from the FBI, Bill Chambers from Homeland, Mike Dutton from Anti-terrorism, and Balletto from Court protection will be team leaders for your respective organizations, and you will report directly to them with updates and any issues that you may encounter. I'm confident that you will execute your tasks with the diligence and exemplary standards that you all possess. Thank you for your service. Good luck," said the Director as he addressed them all.

With the meeting over, the operatives streamed out of the compact office, pre-occupied with what they needed to do. Meanwhile, the team leaders went over key areas that each agency was covering and the backup arrangements. Radio frequencies and distress triggers were also discussed. Forty-five minutes later, after dispensing with the fine print, they dispersed with the aim of having one last meeting before things went down.

McClaren had read Kolinsky's file twice over and met the man, it was not pleasant reading. Deep down in the pit of his stomach, a feeling of unease rose and enclosed his heart. He would be extra vigilant. Kolinsky had allies both here and abroad, and this was as good a time as any to mobilize friends and pull in markers. This operation could not afford to go wrong. The implications would be catastrophic, to say the least.

He'd make a final sweep of the plan before setting off for the courthouse. There were too many variables. Anything could go wrong. All he had to do was make it as difficult as he possibly could for Kolinsky's empathizers. What else could he do in the circumstances?

Chapter 80

Simeon's accountant, Patrick Hale, quivered internally. *What had I done?* He thought in horror. He was not safe. Simeon's men were everywhere. The FBI had herded him from one destination to another at a moment's notice. All ties with his family had been severed. He had not spoken to his wife in days. How would his wife feel knowing that he was herded around by three taciturn agents to a series of safe houses all over Manhattan, Boston, and Detroit? So close to her, but not able to communicate how much he missed and loved her.

Getting to the courthouse was distressing enough. They had to change their vehicle twice. He was smuggled through a back door and made to walk ten flights of stairs. His body could not take the physical abuse. He had been used to a life of leisure for too long. The only exercise he did was walk to the elevator and into a waiting car.

Looking down at his striped Caraceni suit, he marveled at how loose it looked.

What his wife could not get him to do in ten years had been achieved by Kolinsky and the damned FBI. He liked his weight, his wide girth, and the impression of wealth he exuded. Why do you think the young girls were inclined to be with him? What he lacked in charm and beauty, he made up in money and expensive gifts. He was generous to a fault, especially if the girls pleased him. Extravagant, perhaps, in terms of presents, but when it came to information, he was the opposite, economical in every sense of the word. After all, it came with the territory, didn't it?

How did he end up in this mess? What a silly question. He had put himself in this muddle. He had been careless, skimming off Kolinsky's business accounts for years. It had all started when he had set up an account in the Caymans. Five years later, it had a nifty balance of 45 million dollars. Did he really think that Kolinsky would not find out? His greed and desire for opulence had exposed him to unimaginable danger. Now it was too late.

He felt trapped, the claws of claustrophobia slowly grappling at his throat. The suffocating heat in the stuffy stairways made his dilemma even more oppressive. In seconds, he was swaying on the verge of hysteria as the steps were plunged into sudden darkness. He heard agitated footsteps and disoriented movements all around him, and his mind whirled into overdrive. Panic seized his stricken brain. Sweat dropped in giant blobs, leaving large and dark stains on his immaculate Hermes shirt. His heart pulsated at an alarming rate, threatening to explode within his rib cage. His hand flew to his chest while his body teetered on wobbly legs, just as firm hands latched on to him, gripping him tightly in a gentle vice. The FBI agent expertly pushed him through the exit door into a room in three fluid movements, barricading the door with a desk and some chairs immediately afterwards. Instinctively, Hale sank into an available seat, sucking up as much oxygen as he could muster; reeling from the encounter.

Moments later, the air conditioner swung into action, announcing that the generator was up and running. Maybe, Hale thought, this would've been the time to run too, if he wasn't boxed in with the Feds. Testifying looked even less appealing now as he sat miserably looking down at his huge, ugly hands, his mind fraught with infinite possibilities of death and untold risks. He had opened a can of worms, and there was no going back. All he could now was embrace whatever would come his way, so long as his family remained safe and got the life they deserved, even if it was from the proceeds of crime. They would be none the wiser. That's how it had to stay.

This was not the time to nurture regrets. He was doing it for them. Pulling himself together, he took a deep breath, looked expectantly at the FBI agent, signaling that he was ready to proceed to the tenth floor. Nothing would deter him from testifying. He had come too far. Resignedly, he followed the agents up the last three flights of stairs. It was time to face his boss or meet his creator; only time would tell.

Chapter 81

Simeon was on high alert. Anything was possible. Things were unfolding and unfurling quickly. He stood close to the window, admiring the picturesque view through the state-of-the-art ordnance proof glass, wondering if it was time. The thickened window portrayed distorted, convoluted images, shielding him and the others inside from potential threats. He glanced outside defiantly and with confidence, daring any sniper to take him out. He was ready. If they wanted him dead, they would not have orchestrated this media circus. But that did not mean they could not try.

He had dispensed with fear a long time ago. Something held him back. He was not afraid to die and he had no remorse for what he had done over the years. Looking down at his chest, he checked for the tell-tale signs of a red dot from a sniper's scope. You never know, with technological advancement, what type of sniper rifle could be used to penetrate thick glass meant to inhibit the killing of a high-profile scum like him. Anyway, that did not look like it was happening anytime soon from the looks of it. The FBI agents assigned to him were on full alert too, jittery—exuding static bursts of nervous energy—while vigilantly monitoring movements just outside the door behind which he had been barricaded.

Something was definitely going down, and these poor sods had no clue what it was. Breathing easily, he waited for the unexpected, with the stealth of a panther, his ears pricked to pick up any unusual sounds and react instantaneously. It was just a matter of time. *Interesting, though*, he thought to himself, *would it unfold today?* Either way, he was ready.

Chapter 82

Today was Kolinsky's day in court. He was led back to court after the power was restored. He watched the jurors guardedly as they filed in, observing their averted gazes, heads bowed down, and the way they sat in uncomfortable silence, fidgeting in their seats, avoiding Kolinsky's intense look of curiosity.

Kolinsky, on the other hand, relishing their discomfort, held his head up high, gloating at his ability to instill repressive fear in the jury members. His reputation seems to have preceded him. That, and the fact that he had attracted such a large group of spectators, made him feel gratified that his moment in court would blow the minds of the spectators, viewers, and the world. It was like watching a tightrope act in a circus, waiting for the main act without knowing what to expect. The ageing court was filled to the brim with inquisitive bystanders, media men, and armed agents. The room felt airless, the ten-year-old air conditioner ineffectual at cooling the court room.

The palpable excitement in the room and an infectious flow of low-key chatter bolstered the sensationalism of the case being held on American soil. Seated stoically in his seat, Kolinsky's mind wandered back in time. Thirty years to be exact, in another time and another place. He remembered it all, grisly thoughts came rushing back in torrents, flooding the banks of his locked memories. The catastrophic devastation of the factories, schools, and rivers around his hometown situated near the Chechnya border haunted him, even after all these years. The rivers had been polluted with ammonia, nitric acid, and BHZ, extensively destroying the fishing trade and crops that the locals depended on for their livelihood.

The sea was deluged with abominable organisms that had metamorphosed into ungodly creatures like those from a scene in Mary Shelley's Frankenstein film. Young children died from contamination and complications resulting from the toxic substances in the water and in the air. Nobody took responsibility; not the American company responsible for the spillage or the government that turned a blind eye. All the government officials were interested in was lining their pockets with American dollars, living the American dream.

Bunnytox Pharmaceuticals created jobs and the hope of a better tomorrow. In innocence, the locals embraced the hard-working life, poor sanitary conditions, long work hours, and poor wages; ignorant of the adverse human and economic impact the company would have on the community and its environs. Bunnytox Pharmaceuticals was a privately registered cosmetic company owned by Jeremy Bunnytox and Stephen Barrymore. They promised economic freedom, skill development, and recreational facilities for the youth and children living in the area. Nobody bargained for the noxious escape of chemicals that desecrated the area and reduced it to an uninhabitable hovel like Bhopal in 1984.

Yes, he remembered quite clearly the obliteration of his hometown. A place he, his father, mother, and two sisters left behind thirty years ago. Raking old wounds wouldn't assuage the pain and anger that he had carried all these years. Someone had to be held accountable for all the deaths that were unreported and buried in the annals of time. He had dealt unscrupulously with Jeremy Bunnytox and the management team responsible for the spillage. The arm of retribution was yet to fall on Stephen Barrymore's family. Judge James Barrymore, was Stephen Barrymore's only son, the only person who had escaped his wrath until now.

He hurriedly suppressed the most painful memory of all. The CIA leaving his father to die at the hands of the KGB and the persecution and torturing that followed afterwards. In many ways, it made him who he was: a cold-blooded killer, tycoon and godfather—КРЕСТНЫЙ; КРЕСТНЫЙ ОТЕЦ.

The trial of the century was about to take place in this special court of public opinion. He was not only the one who was going to stand trial. By the time he unleashed his arsenal of fireworks, justice would truly have been served.

Sitting back in anticipation, he waited until he heard those famous words. All rise for the honorable judge, James Barrymore.

Chapter 83

Hamilton had locked himself away since his dismissal from the White House. The phone had rung incessantly for the last two weeks, but he did not feel like talking to anyone. Sitting on the long settee in the lounge, he stared hard at his phone, compelling it to ring and break the eerie silence pervading the flat. But nothing happened. Maybe they had finally got the hint.

Depression threatened to grab hold of him. Within a year, he had successfully managed to screw up his marriage, lose his daughter, and now his job.

He gave up his social circle, or should he say his ex-wife's circle of friends. He never really had time to socialize because of work. Her friends found him pompous and withdrawn. Well, that's what you expect when you marry the daughter of a multimillionaire. She believed in the rich life, and poured all her efforts in philanthropic events, dinners, charities, school, and church functions. Deep down, he felt inadequate when he was around her. She wanted nothing from him. Rarely asked anything from him, except sex, and that had become non-existent six months prior to the end of their eight-year relationship. Maybe it was his fault; he did not try hard enough, because of career and all.

Now, what did he have? His career was in tatters and his ex-wife was probably gloating over his failure to hold down the job she had helped him secure. She was probably writing it up as another abysmal chapter in the autobiography of his life. His best friend was dead, and he did not have a close social relationship with any of his colleagues. A sudden rush of loneliness swept over him, and he felt overwhelmed.

For the umpteenth time he stared at the summons. He was to appear at a special meeting at a federal court house. Coincidentally, it was going to be the same day the case of that affluent Russian v. USA was due to start. The court house would be covered by the press, which was itching for a chance to publicize his humiliation. News had already spread that he was on administrative leave pending investigations into the explosion at the private facility. What could be more embarrassing than to walk through the bedlam and face a pack of media vultures? Meanwhile, his rival, Brandon Sucht, had taken over his position and probably hammered the last nail into his coffin. It was not enough that he had taken his ex-wife, his home, and the life he could have had if he had not been so stupid. Hamilton had lost everything. How unfair was life? He had already committed career suicide; how low could he go? In New York, he was now officially a pariah, a social leper, an outcast, to name a few, when he was spurned from Capitol Hill.

Well, looking on the bright side, his appearance at the courthouse would probably garner some comments that would either help him or destroy whatever was left of his shattered existence. There simply was no other option, all he could do was dress up and face the music squarely on the chin; what else could he do? Scouring through his wardrobe, he settled on his grey Armani suit, which, incidentally, he still looked good in. Reviewing his reflection in the mirror, he could see the dour face of a man beaten, but not defeated, looking back at him; a defiant streak twinkling in his eyes, reminding him of who he really was. He admired his frame. At 38, he still held his own. His short, wavy, chestnut-brown hair looked handsome, his hazel eyes still held a glint of steel, curiosity, intelligence, and depth. His face was clear pink and accentuated with fine spidery lines around the eyes, defining them with the maturity and the wisdom they possessed.

Content with what he had seen, he grabbed his car keys, did a final sweep of his apartment, shut the doors and windows securely, and ventured out to the parking lot to retrieve his Roush Mustang 420RE Convertible. This was the only toy his wife had let him keep. After all, it was his 37th birthday present. It, unexpectedly, opened a flood gate of memories Hamilton wanted to forget but nostalgia, despondency and melancholy, threatened to break his resolve at this crucial juncture when he needed to keep it together.

Starting up the car, he warmed the engine, engaged the gear, and listened to the gentle purr of the engine coming to life. He then made his way to the Federal Courthouse to make an unprecedented arrival.

214

Chapter 84

Krivov finally landed on American soil, for the second time in two weeks, exhausted and cranky. The journey was turbulent, fraught with danger, and uncomfortable. Six days of crisscrossing from country to country; his body ached as a result. Yet he knew that this was his last chance to redeem himself in the eyes of his boss, mentor, and friend. This was a call of loyalty, which went far beyond the call of duty. This would be his final declaration of love, and probably his last act of devotion, to a dear friend; an ultimate act of valor that had to trump over fear and the need to protect his life and future existence.

The lone figure waited on the brink of Hudson River Park under a guise of darkness that suited Avery fine. Every minute was crucial to the success of his mission. Avery threw out his hand to help Krivov balance as he got out of the small boat. Within seconds, he had alighted and the paid rower disappeared under the remaining shadows of night. Moving quickly, Krivov grabbed his rucksack and followed Avery through the park to the black Chrysler. Climbing in, they made their way to the rendezvous point.

Huddled in a motel in Red Hook, he met two other lieutenants committed to the cause, both itching to take part in the finale. They both showed unconstrained bouts of energy, taking turns to pace the small space, much to the irritation of Krivov. Avery slipped out to get groceries and run some errands; making his entrance four hours later, hands laden with three grocery bags and a hold all. Nobody cared to ask what was in the hold all.

Krivov felt it better to take a walk to clear his head and prepare himself for the task at hand. Everyone's watches would be synchronized to 0600 hours, which gave him approximately four and a half hours to shake off the throbbing ache in his muscles, get some rest, and commit his part of the plan to memory. He decided to take a run to unwind, pushing his body harder, compelling both body and brain to respond in tandem to the punishment he was intentionally inflicting on them. After forty minutes of invigorated running, he returned to the motel, showered, and had some sleep; setting his watch for 5.30. In seconds, he was asleep, oblivious to the ceaseless pacing of the stocky Serbian.

At 5.30 a.m., Krivov woke up and joined his co-conspirators at the table. Avery ran through the highlights once more and gave them each a set of car keys and a map. His discourse was concluded with a parting handshake of finality; allegiance, friendship, as well as a sense of purpose all rolled into one, if that was possible in such a short time. Nobody looked back, each now focused on the task at hand. Krivov made his way to a Ram 2500 Power Wagon, unlocked the door, and slid open the compartment under the driver's seat. Retrieving a case, he set it down on the passenger seat and placed the bag he carried on the floor. Scanning the map once more, he started up the truck and disabled the GPS. Where he was going, he did not want to leave a trail.

Deep down, Krivov knew he was doing it for the money; it was simply a contract, no more no less. He had dispensed with the notion that it was out of obligation, loyalty, and devotion to a taskmaster who had ruled his criminal empire with an iron fist. D-Day had arrived, and he also wanted to be remembered in the annals of history as part of the assassination team that had rescued the worst Russian criminal in the chronicle of man's existence.

Chapter 85

Driving through traffic, taking in the sights, as if visiting New York for the first time, Hamilton compartmentalized his problem and focused on how he would defend himself. He was an American who had served his country faithfully, loyally, and devotedly, and all for what? He had renounced anything that could compromise his conviction to uphold the law and detract from patriotism. He regarded himself a true patriot, one who had served his country with his blood. That had to count for something, didn't it?

Perhaps an adviser would be assigned to sit in with him in the preliminary hearing. No matter what was going to be discussed behind doors, ultimately, the final decision fell to the President, who would be watching from a distance. He neither cared about who would be there nor what was said, just that a fair outcome should be reached. Bracing himself for the torrent of questions that would follow just as he sighted the throng of reporters waiting in front of the court, he narrowly missed a pedestrian as he made the final curve, bringing the car to a stop in a spot reserved for him to park in. Patting down his hair blown askew by the breeze, he alighted from his car, locked it, and walked towards the throng of gadflies blocking the barrier placed before the stairs leading up to the federal courthouse.

He watched the horde of reporters make a bee-line straight for him, inundating him with questions, which he brushed off. Content that he, at least, still had his game face on, he made his way through the maze of people, stopping momentarily in front of the courthouse, goading the vultures to take a parting shot with their cameras, before disappearing into the foyer of the courthouse, away from the circling newshounds clamoring for coverage inside the courthouse.

Passing through the security checks and receiving courteous acknowledgments from other security officers, he was escorted to a chamber where he was to wait till the proceedings started and his fate was decided.

Game up, it was time to face the music. Drums roll as disgraced Director Hamilton reported for emasculation.

Chapter 86

The prosecution team was eager to intricately catalogue Kolinsky's atrocities during his reign of terror, all the while reveling in the media coverage. They also expected to obtain positive feedback in the court of public opinion and increase the possibility of political accolade. Both sides were expected to complete their discovery exchange no later than 30 days before the start of the trial. This had to be done in compliance with the rules of evidence. They had to appear fair, transparent, and willing to co-operate with the defense counsel. Non-compliance would lead to a trial delay, giving the obnoxious defense lawyers more time to destroy their case and put them in bad stead with the judge. Judge Barrymore was a man not to be messed with, even though he was a federal employee. He was described as a loose cannon, totally unpredictable. The leading counsel was not about to slip up and hand the defense counsel his victory before they even had a chance to argue it out in court.

The three prosecution lawyers huddled around their table after a truckload of files had been carted in, stealing glances at Kolinsky and his legion of legal representatives, who were in a heated discussion about who would second chair the venerable Patrick Levinson. Having made their decision, Camilla Ramirez fluffed her hair and moved her bag and stack of files next to Levinson, fully asserting her second chair position for the remainder of the trial.

The jammed-packed court was crammed with washed out public defenders, government officials, media hounds, slick cartel reps, and enthused members of the public clamoring for justice. The lead prosecution counsel, Mark Turner, was ready. They were leaving no stone unturned and pulling out all the stops to put away this illusive murderer, tycoon, and glorified gangster behind bars, permanently. Yes, they were bent on getting sweet victory for all the people who had died in the Blue County fiasco by obtaining a returned verdict of guilty. It might provide closure for the families, but most importantly, the US government would have made a shining example of Kolinsky. The US did not submit to terrorist attacks. It was time that people like Kolinsky realized how resilient the American people were. Turner's team had streamlined their case, choreographed and prepped their witnesses, carried out mock witness examinations, and reproduced visual clips that were gory, descriptive, and damning.

They had also tried to play fair by providing the defense team with copies of most of the materials they intended to present to the court. This did nothing to assuage the feelings that Levinson and his team nursed. They were sure that they were being sandbagged. Niggling thoughts about full disclosure rattled about in Levinson's head. Although he harbored this notion, he knew that his client was unscrupulous and had his own game plan. He also had a plan of his own that he would unburden on the court at the appropriate time. His lead investigator had uncovered a sealed document from the Pentagon that told him that the honorable James Barrymore was not all that he appeared to be.

The files on discovery were stacked high on both tables, each individual file bulging with substantiated details of crimes purportedly perpetrated by Kolinsky or linked to him, as far as intelligence reports went. Kolinsky looked relaxed; unperturbed by the choking pile of documentation the prosecution was wading through. It would all be for nothing. It did not matter. The case would not be heard. It would not see the light of day. It would be shut down before it started. Smiling and totally composed, he sat back in his chair as Turner made his dramatic opening statement.

In a sleek navy-blue three-piece suit, starched white shirt, and immaculate black shoes, he made his debut appearance before the jury like a movie star. The display of confidence, wealth, and sophistication commanded the attention of the whole court. His calm, resonant baritone filtered to the darkest recesses of the room. Clearing his throat theatrically, he began his opening statement.

"Your Honor, ladies and gentlemen of the jury, good morning. I am Mark Turner, and I represent the prosecution in the matter of *The State of New York v. Kolinsky*. I will set out to expose this felonious businessman by providing the court with a telephone conversation between the defendant and other individuals involved in the unsavory act of the chemical bombing in Blue County.

Further evidence corroborating his involvement in this dastardly deed will show Kolinsky's explicit role in this sordid crime.

I will start by describing to you the events that transformed a beautiful summer day, the 7th of July 2012, in Blue County into a massacre. The carnage killed five internationally renowned scientists, a ten-month-old baby, 49 other civilians and casualties who are still receiving medical treatment. These scientists were on the verge of a groundbreaking scientific breakthrough that would have revolutionized the study of stem cell research in the world."

"At approximately 10.30 a.m. on the day in question, a telephone conversation was intercepted through the hotel telephone exchange that confirms the go-ahead from Kolinsky to kill innocent civilians. Our second witness, Kolinsky's accountant Patrick Hale, corroborates this evidence, and we shall present the taped conversation along with photographs and the testimonies of Samuel Briggs and his mother, both of whom survived the blast, which has been provided by the police. Interpol has also submitted date-marked photographs proving Kolinsky's involvement in the despicable act. Further deeds were undertaken to eliminate other key players who had failed to execute the second bomb that was set to explode in Times Square that same night. The man who committed this act is sitting in this courtroom behind me, and he's the one who committed those murders. By the end of this trial, I will have presented to the court, beyond all reasonable doubt, that Kolinsky was responsible for the killing of at least 50 people and injuring over 200 in the Blue County explosion. In plain, simple language, it was an act of terror and violence intended to serve his selfish political agenda."

Turner pausing momentarily, as if in thought, but really making sure that he had the full attention of everyone present, and continued: "The defense will try to distort the truth by providing reasons as to why an international businessman would not engage in acts of terrorism on US soil. They will attempt to destroy the integrity of the three witnesses that will testify. They will also make further attempts to discredit the sources through which these pieces of information were obtained. But these are mere distractions designed to obscure the truth. At the conclusion of this case, you will have irrefutable proof of Kolinsky's guilt in this grisly affair, and he should not be shown pity. The only acceptable outcome will be to pronounce him guilty. Thank you."

Holding their attention once more, he made his way back to his seat and sat down. Barrymore set his eyes on Levinson, who was on his feet in an instant. Smoothing down his Armani pin-striped dark blue suit, Levinson sauntered elegantly to the center of the court. All eyes were fixed on him, the $1000 haircut and the $25000 made-to-measure suit clinging provocatively yet aptly worn for the occasion, illustrated his success. This was no second-grade lawyer. Even his shoes seemed to have been specially made for the court appearance. The court's stenographer seemed to stop typing to lap up this spectacular Adonis on center stage.

Making his way over to the jury stand, Levinson began, "Good morning ladies and gentlemen of the jury, my name is Patrick Levinson and I represent Mr. Simeon Kolinsky in the case before you today. You have heard the prosecution explain what he hopes will be proven, but the prosecution did not tell you all the facts. The prosecution has stated that my client is the architect of the Blue County terror campaign, but the defense intends to prove that the prosecution's supposed eye-witness is a man who has held a personal grudge against my client for a long time. He has made many inconsistent statements about the case and has been given a great deal for his testimony. We will also prove that the telephone conversation that was submitted by the prosecution was illegally obtained and tampered with to frame my client. The burden of proof lies with the prosecution, and as we present our compelling evidence, we will unwittingly prove that the prosecution has failed to meet the onus of proof and has only circumstantial information that is tainted and constructed with the sole purpose of implicating my client."

Pausing again in front of the jury box for effect, he said, "For that reason, I will limit my opening statement to the matters that I know can be proven through deposition, testimony, documents, or photographs. I will never go out on a limb to include pieces of evidence that, for one reason or another, may not actually see the light of day. So, we would ask you to keep an open mind, listen to all the evidence, and return a verdict of not guilty. Thank you."

He stopped moving to capture the looks of the jury and the crowd. Pleased with what he could see, he made five easy strides back to his seat and looked expectantly at Barrymore. Taking his cue, the judge announced that the proceedings would commence at 9 a.m. the next day, Barrymore admonished the jury, advising them

222

against listening to the media, reading the daily newspapers, or having any contact with either counsels and left the courtroom, bringing Day 1 in court to a close.

Chapter 87

The nightmares were less frequent, but were still a source of concern. Senator Lee had lost the edge that Frost admired and respected. Frost did not sign up for being a psychologist or a nursemaid at best. He was a combat soldier reporting for active duty and possessed the prowess and uncanny skillset of any member of the prestigious elite SEAL army, waiting impatiently for reassignment of the task at hand.

Focused on driving the Mercedes GLZ and navigating through small pit stops and obscure towns, Frost made sure they avoided city centers and areas that were communally occupied by indigents and tourists. He silently wondered about who in his right mind would live in such primitive, defunct surroundings, apart from the natives of course.

Frost slept in short shifts while Senator Lee manned the GLZ. Frost needed to be alert. His body was aching from the tortuous hours at the wheel, but there would be no respite or comfort until they crossed the border and earned some reprieve from their pursuers.

Three weeks on the run had changed both of them. Senator Lee had lost 20 lbs, his face now housed a jagged scar on his right cheek, a permanent reminder of the highway accident, and that was not the only memento he carried. On the left side of his right leg, a deep laceration that demanded medical attention constantly stained Lee trousers. Frost did the best he could, buying medical supplies in small quantities to avoid detection and suspicion, he was no field medic, but he managed a light field dressing.

Frost, on the other hand, had developed a twitch in the small of his back; maybe due to being subjected to long hours behind the wheel. A cooling gel helped alleviate the pain. It was nothing in comparison to Senator Lee's injuries, because he was more or less unscathed. He got away with just a few cuts and bruises that had indistinct scars that would heal over time.

After driving for another three hours, they noticed that the volume in road activity had increased. For years, the thin border separating Derby Vermont and Stanstead had always been blurred; it was now complicated by the fact that Derby Line and Stanstead share a number of streets. The wretched gates separating the two towns had riled the residents, who had enjoyed the quirky vacations and neighborliness in the past. Border Patrol and Homeland Security had been fighting a losing battle against human trafficking and illegal drugs into the US for years, despite the increasing number of personnel and cameras installed.

Senator Lee and Frost both knew that the border would be swarming with Homeland Security and Border control personnel, but they had no choice. This was the risk they had to take. The little cabin Senator Lee owned was west of Vermont. The cabin had belonged to his grandmother, but was sold to a family friend. Senator Lee had bought the property back five years ago to honor his mother's memory. The deeds were still in the name of the original purchaser, so it would be difficult to trace it back to him. Passing through security with their impeccable forgeries was the next test, a test that would spell death or freedom for both of them.

Drawing up behind a red Shelby Mustang, they mentally prepared themselves for what might unfold. Frost looked critically at Senator Lee. Would he pass the scrutiny? He wondered. Senator Lee would, he surmised. The scar on his face, the auburn hair now tinged with grey, the brown eyes, and, did I mention, the beard, totally altered Lee's former look. Frost, on the other hand, quickly surveyed his features in the front view mirror looking for recognizable signs. The tanning lotion he applied earlier made him look Mediterranean and the false implant in his cheek made his face look bloated. He had inserted contact lenses, altering his eye color to a darker shade of blue. To further enhance his overweight appearance, he wore a padded jumper that inflated his body, giving him the semblance of a paunchy middle-age man. *Not bad*, he thought to himself, even his mother would not recognize him if she passed him on the street.

The driver in the Chevrolet Camaro behind him honked impatiently for Frost to move up, or was it to get the security officer's attention? Either way, it worked. Minutes later, they were quickly passed through without thorough scrutiny. The young voluptuous woman in the Chevrolet Camaro had front stage, all eyes were on her. Not surprisingly, the officials were holding onto her details longer than they needed to, enthralled by her beauty. She seemed to melt; no longer in a hurry to go wherever it was she was supposed to be going to. That was fine with Frost; the mystery lady had inadvertently provided a clean break for them. There was no longer anybody curious enough to look at their number plate or crosscheck their passport. Right now, Frost's attention was focused on getting to the cabin before dark, getting some rest, and thereafter plan for his future. He was done with babysitting Senator Lee.

Chapter 88

The meeting went well, better than he expected, and Hamilton was optimistic that he would be re-assigned soon. He still had a chance to redeem himself, which was good. Three hours of grueling questions and answers had taken their toll on him. He just wanted to get out of the court building, head home, and soak in a refreshingly hot bath. That was probably what his body needed. After all, whatever was left of his social life had fizzled away with his marriage. But that would not deter him from making a stop at his local bar to celebrate. He felt like being in the company of people, even if it was just for one night.

Taking the steps rather than the elevator, he made his way down two sets of stairs, before he heard the static burst of gunfire. He could see people running around like headless chicken, scampering to safety. The outpouring crowd from Court room 302 and blast of returning fire alerted him of where the gunman was firing from.

Crouching down quickly, he saw a bullet where his head had been a moment ago. Seconds later, he saw a blast of bullets hit the court officer and a FBI agent simultaneously, and they went down hard. Rushing to the FBI officer's side, Hamilton knew he was dead. Luckily, the court officer had been shot in the arm. Moving him out of the way, he took the dead FBI agent's gun and drew nearer to the doorway, carefully examining the number of bodies splayed there. Three other agents ran down the hall towards him, but he did not wait.

Instinctively, he fired and waited for responding fire. On cue, the shooter released another round of bullets. Re-positioning himself, he crouched lower in a shooter's stance and aimed. The staccato of gunshots stopped and the sound of something dropping confirmed that he had hit his mark. He let the gun slip out of hands and placed his hands in the air. He did not want to take a bullet for the wrong reason just as the first agent arrived at the scene. The respondent took away the gun and told him to lie down, which he complied with readily enough. The other two agents went in to secure the area. A few more shots were fired, and then there was silence.

A whole fleet of policemen, FBI, Homeland, and court guards swarmed around in the confusion, taking pictures, statements, and assessing the damage done. Medical personnel had cleared away the injured and the medical examiner and his crew were on the way to take the bodies. Everybody was baffled by how the stocky European lying lifeless on the floor had been able to smuggle his weapon into the courthouse. Tough questions were going to be asked, and some of the security personnel were going to take the heat for the security breach. Damage control was another issue. The media hounds lurking outside started interviewing the escapees before they could shut them down. The news had already hit prime time TV, and there was nothing they could do to stop it. Hamilton was taken down to the court's interrogating room and interviewed. They took his statement and commended him for his divine intervention and for saving the life of the security guard, who recounted what had happened. Three cups of coffee and five hours later, he was let go and forbidden from discussing anything with the press while it was being investigated.

Hamilton had no intention of engaging the press. He was going to give that cold Grolsch beer a miss as well. All he wanted to do was walk off the tension. He wanted to leave his car in the car lot and pick it up tomorrow, but decided against it. After the attack at the courthouse, security would be ratcheted up tightly. Passing security clearance, he made his way to the car lot and retrieved his car. A long drive would ease the strain of the last few hours. *Amazing*, he thought to himself. His first day outside his apartment had been qualified with uncertainty, endangerment, and the thrill of being alive.

It had been a great day.

Chapter 89

Jenkins arrived at the designated place on time. He sent his driver away and told him to take the day off, because he would accompany the Under Secretary of Defense home and did not need the car for the day. The driver was to report at 8.45 a.m. the next day at Jenkins' residence for duty. Pleased that he had been given the day off, the driver left. He relished the chance to spend more time with his family: his wife and four-month-old son. He did not find it unusual that he had been given time off six times within just the last month; he just chalked it up to an understanding boss. If only he knew the truth.

Jenkins scanned the car lot, making sure that he was not in the vision of the security cameras. Satisfied, he made his way to another official car similar to his own, drove it to his car spot, and parked. He left the keys in the ignition and alighted from the car. He made his way to the Hamilton hearing being conducted in the Federal Courthouse, of all places. This was Hamilton's chance to redeem himself. Everybody made mistakes, it was simply human, but how far would the panel go to vilify a man who had selflessly fought for his country? Was there no reward for faithful service? He had done all that and more, but, at the end of the day, did it really count? Jenkins could still see a lot of servicemen and women who the government and society had failed. They were treated like pariahs, misfits, and outsiders by the very people who had trained them to kill.

Apparently, dedication to duty meant nothing. However, loyalty meant everything to him. His last altruistic act for his old friend would prove this. Settling down for the hearing, he cleared his mind of any distractions or thoughts about what he needed to do in the next five hours and listened attentively to Hamilton's testimonial. After three hours of vigorous questioning and answering, it was over. Hamilton left, and after forty-five minutes in the brainstorming session, reviewing the facts and answers, the panel concluded that he was not negligent and should be recalled to duty.

Inwardly relieved that Hamilton was being given a second chance, Jenkins made his way to the rendezvous point. Looking at his watch, he could see that he had eight minutes to spare. Taking a detour, he passed by Court Room 302, his passing coinciding with Judge Barrymore's closing statement. He slipped into the toilet room, did his business, washed his hands, and waited. Minutes later, the door swung open.

Chapter 90

Jenkins was bent over the sink pretending to wash his hands, which were actually a few centimeters away from his gun holder, when two FBI agents walked in with guns drawn. Recognizing Jenkins, who was still in his military uniform, they greeted him and carried out a sweep of the toilet stalls. Satisfied, they stepped outside and let Kolinsky enter.

Kolinsky's eyes softened as he embraced Jenkins, each knowing that this would be last time they would ever see each other again in this lifetime. Within forty-five seconds both had shed what they wearing, revealing matching clothes underneath that mirrored what the other man wore before each walked into the toilets. As expected, as Kolinsky was putting on the mask, the agents burst through the door. Instinctively, Jenkins cut them down with his silenced pistol and dragged their bodies into the toilet stalls. The two FBI agents were replaced by Avery and Krivov who were each dressed in the same dapple, grey government suits as the guards they were replacing.

Moving quickly and with deft hands, they completed the transformation and waited for the signal. Within seconds, shots were fired, and Kolinsky made his exit from the toilets, down the corridor, to the fire exit door, and out of sight.

Avery and Krivov, on the other hand, went in the opposite direction and got into an elevator. The elevator was intercepted one floor down and Jenkins—dressed as Kolinsky—and the agents were escorted out of the building under the supervision of McClaren's men. Chaperoned by two other government issued vehicles, one in front and the other at the back, they drove off to a secret location.

Meanwhile, the other security officials scrambled about trying to pacify the panicked crowd spilling out of the building and looking out for suspicious individuals. They had all received copies of the identities of known associates sympathetic to Kolinsky's cause and were told to eliminate them on sight. Take no prisoners was the rule, which was fine by them. Kolinsky's sympathizers were cold blooded killers and mercenaries that would not surrender anyways.

Cocked and alert, they vetted as best they could. High above, observing from one of the high- rise buildings, was the tacit gunman who had been at the Red Hook Motel. Through his shooter's scope, he took in the sights and wind gauge. Moving a few inches to the left, he re-gauged the shot that he needed to take, if necessary.

Chapter 91

Panic had set in, and an explosion of activity was rapidly overturning sanity and plunging the crime scene into disorder. The gunshots had set everybody clamoring for the door. In the confusion, nobody stopped to watch Kudirat swing open the fire exit door and make her escape. The smoke bomb Kudirat had detonated created a smoke screen to mask detection.

Following the route outlined by the Old Russian Fox, Kolinsky and Medusa made their way through the tunnel into the car park where Jenkins's official car was parked. In the back seat, there was a change of clothes. He inserted the voice box, and adjusted the mask of his old friend Jenkin. Changing quickly and discarding the prop that made him look larger than he actually was, he assumed his position in the back of the government sedan. Medusa looked into the rearview mirror and marveled at the transformation. Content with the makeover, Medusa dressed in a standard military suit and cap, that had been lowered to partially shield her face; put the car into gear.

She drove the car up the ramp and fell behind the stream of government cars speedily trying to get away from the scene. Security passes and clearances were being rechecked. Security was buttoned up tight. Three agents were crosschecking the number plates and speaking into their radios to reconfirm if these vehicles were assigned to that side of the car lot. A full-scale operation was underway. Ten minutes later, they were at the front of the queue. Rolling down the window, Medusa handed over two security passes. One of the security men looked into the car to check who was sitting in the backseat. Throwing a salute in Jenkins' direction and tapping on the side of the car, he waved them through.

Sighing inaudibly, Medusa moved the car and placed her gun within easy reach. She also gave Kolinsky, disguised as Jenkins a semi-automatic rifle from underneath the front seat. Moments later, back in the court house, the bodies of the two FBI agents had been discovered. McClaren rushed up to the fourth floor, exasperated and out of breath. Realization hit him immediately, and he snatched the radio away from the agent and yelled hurriedly into it. Above the static, he heard that Jenkins's car had already passed through the checkpoint. Seething inwardly, he radioed through to dispatch and ordered the urgent apprehension of Jenkins and his driver.

The sounds of blaring sirens of approaching squad cars put them on alert, and Medusa removed the safety catch on her modified 15 round .357 SIG in readiness. Kolinsky disguised as Jenkins smiled and said, "Now, we shall test the prowess of the American security force and see if it holds up to its reputation."

They heard screeching tires and the onslaught of several bullets simultaneously hitting the back-window screen, roof, and side door. Another set of bullets ripped into the boot of the car and made its way, miraculously, clear of Medusa's head. Lowering the window slightly and positioning his gun in a firing position, Kolinsky let rip his Beretta ARX. Kolinsky returned fire while Medusa accelerated and swerved the car expertly, masterfully dodging the incoming bullets that were threatening to pierce the impregnable steel panels used to reinforce the car. It was incredible that Jenkins had the foresight to install a specially modified set of bulletproof tires.

Her fleeting reprieve ended when she saw the barricade right ahead. Her heart rate accelerated in anticipation of what was about to happen. Unperturbed at the challenge, her adrenaline levels peaked in expectation. Reducing pressure on the accelerator, she waited for her window of opportunity. True to form, Avery Johnson and the other Serbian from the Red Hook Motel fired their rocket launchers from their separate hidden locations. The sudden impact of the rockets shattered the barricade and flung the cars midway into the air before they landed bottom side up, crushing some of the security personnel.

Medusa saw her opening and raced through the gap, not giving the agents time to recoup. Looking into the rearview mirror, she saw the flames engulf one of the agents. Up above, she could hear the whirring sound of a chopper with heavier artillery shooting down on the battered vehicle they were in. Visibility was poor, because of the spiraling columns of smoke from the carnage caused by the rockets, and the chopper was clearly missing its mark, much to the relief of

Kolinsky and Medusa. A second launcher assault hit the rotor blade of the chopper, forcing the pilot to make an emergency landing.

Medusa knew they had barely three or four minutes before another chopper arrived to continue the assault. They were close to the drop point, but would they make it on time? Throwing caution to the wind, she stepped on the pedal. They got to the garage with seconds to spare. Seconds later, Sergei and Vadim drove off in the mangled car while Kolinsky and Medusa shed their jackets and made their way to the roof where their ride was waiting. Within minutes, they were airborne in a City Medicare helicopter.

Avery Johnson watched as Medusa made a clean getaway and mobilized himself into action. He knew that he was on the verge of being caught. He disposed of the rocket launcher in a waste pipe running alongside the building and made a mad dash for his backpack. Extracting his climbing gear, he made his descent from the back of the roof into an open window three floors down. Rolling up his climbing gear into his bag, he changed into a pair of overalls and stashed his backup gun and clothes into a crevice he had created when he did a reconnaissance of the building earlier. Completing his make-up and a wearing a grey wig, he made his way out of the apartment—down the stairs and out the back alley—limping with a bucket and cleaning utensils in tow. It was a narrow escape, almost too close for comfort, because, within minutes, the building was besieged by a team of shooters after his hide.

Chapter 92

This could not be happening. Not again. It seemed like a surreal experience with catastrophe written boldly in flashing colors. The unsavory comprehension of what had truly occurred left McClaren ephemerally shaken. Shaking off the anxiety worming its way through his gut, he gripped his radio tightly, speaking urgently into the walkie-talkie, ordering a lock-down and tracking down of Kolinsky and the two agents assigned to take him to the safe house.

A window of opportunity had presented itself to Kolinsky and his crew, and they had used it. McClaren felt that he and his team had been played. The explosive getaway showed that whoever had staged the great escape had ingenuity, resources, and the skill to elude the formidable security forces recruited to execute protection detail at the courthouse. Losing agents was another touchy subject he would be accountable for. He had screwed up, big time. But that was the least of his problems right now. From the static reports filtering through, they were still pursuing the get-away vehicle, which was heading for the Henry Hudson Bridge. Stopping the car was imperative.

Seconds later, the reverberating sounds of gunshot were followed by the screeching of tires and a loud crash as the car smashed into an embankment. Blaring horns and shouts from bystanders drifted over the radio. With one element of surprise now decommissioned, McClaren decided to focus on the second piece of his puzzle. Calling through to Kolinsky's escorts to confirm that things were all right, he got their stats and asked them to proceed to the hideout at Montclair. Delegating the clean-up exercise to Agent Raines, McClaren drove out to meet Kolinsky and the escorts. He needed to interview them at the safe house and get a better understanding of what had actually happened.

Arriving later with back up, McClaren posted two agents at the start of the road, two at the end of the driveway, and got Agent

Raines to accompany him into the safe house. The two men guarding Kolinsky stepped outside and left McClaren and Raines to interrogate him.

The crash pad was sparsely furnished with a very minimalistic design. The rooms were in pristine condition. The chairs were untouched, and there was a coffee table, open-plan kitchen and a small cabinet that was empty. In the back, there were two bedrooms, en-suites without windows. Nobody was getting in or out except through the front door.

McClaren was satisfied with the arrangement. He did not want the defendant to go AWOL. One bungling fiasco was enough. Five minutes into interrogation, he got a call that one of the men in the get-away car was being transported to the Bronx- Lebanon Hospital Centre,alive.

Instructing his men to stand guard, McClaren departed, leaving Jenkins dressed as Kolinsky staring after them, wondering how long Vinnie would hold out at the hospital. Could he buy them the time they needed to conclude their master plan? All he could do was wait and hope.

Chapter 93

The Gentleman Assassin laughed inwardly; everything had gone according to plan. Kolinsky had disappeared, and the American security forces didn't have a clue. He, on the other hand, had one more job to do before he left the country. In his ten years of killing, he had never failed, no matter the assignment. He was not about to mess up this last hit.

$10 million was riding on this last contract, enough money for him to retire. Now that needed a little rephrasing, 37 years was a bit too early to retire. Perhaps starting his own business in a warm country, maybe Paraguay or Indonesia, would be ideal. He enjoyed the women the last time he was there.

Meanwhile, planning the death of Judge James Barrymore would be his final challenge for a while. The courthouse would be a fortress the second time around. All the other cases had been deferred for the day. Kolinsky's case had sole attention at the court house. Sniffer dogs were checking and re-checking. The embarrassing revelation that a hand gun and explosives had been smuggled and used in the first escapade was depressingly indicting. There would be no second chance. Who else was left for this monumental task?

For seven years, he had hidden behind the façade, a chameleon hiding in plain sight, a master of disguises, a professional killer recruited by the US government. He was a man without a past or recognizable future. He did not exist; a ghost, known only in the underworld as Mr. Smith, aka Gentleman Assassin, whichever you prefer. In short, he was a licensed murderer.

This hit had great appeal. The $10 million incentive would bring any assassin running to do the job, but the satisfaction of revenge was the icing on the cake. It was literally killing two birds with one stone. The opportunity had come none too soon. He would be Barrymore's Nemesis. Corporal Rudely Moore had metamorphosed into Avery Johnson after the devastating changes that had catapulted him from a soldier deployed in Basra into a nomadic, avenging angel exacting judgment at a price. Colonel Barrymore's poor decision had cost the lives of his best friend Jonas and two other members of his platoon. He, on the other hand, was left for dead; a scarred, dejected corporal who was captured by the Taliban forces.

Barrymore was about to get his comeuppance from a ghost of Christmas past.

Chapter 94

The President was furious. It was inconceivable that the security forces had got it so wrong. The politicians, the media, and the public were all clamoring for blood. Their reaction was not surprising in view of the carnage; the killing of innocent civilians and the damning spectacle arising from the breakdown and infiltration by a group of killers. The Mayor of New York tried to pacify his constituents by drafting in a special SWAT squad to protect the three courts that were selected for further court hearings. But the efforts were considered ineffectual.

New York City was crawling with policemen, soldiers, agents, and the like, bringing the commercial hub to a standstill. A curfew had been imposed on the disgruntled New Yorkers, who just wanted the case to be over. Respecting their wishes, Daniel Patrick Moynihan US Courthouse, Theodore Roosevelt Courthouse, and the Federal Courthouse buildings were being guarded by multitudes of personnel as if their lives depended on them. The next trial date was set for the following day, and nothing was being left to chance. The canine patrols were drafted in to sniff out bombs, drugs, and any other foreign substances. The courthouses were buttoned up tight. Only the security crews were given access to the buildings, 200 meters perimeters were set up, and stone barricades were erected. The workers were also sent home with strict instructions. Nothing was being left to chance. Not this time.

Soon enough, Judge Barrymore was delivered to the courthouse and escorted by a fresh set of agents upstairs to the chambers he would be using for the day. Tense and uncertain, he drifted along, anxious of what drama would unfold in court. He sighed, involuntarily, when they got to the third floor. All he could think about was so far so good. He had made it safely to his chambers. He stood outside while his bodyguards did a quick sweep of his chambers. They returned moments later, which meant that it was safe for him to enter. Lingering, at the end of the corridor, Judge Barrymore noticed a lone figure standing sentry, observing him warily. The face seemed familiar, buried somewhere in the archives of his memory, but he could not place him at that moment. Jittery, he dashed into the chambers and hung up his jacket, sweat pouring out of every orifice in his body.

He needed a drink. Opening the drawer, he sloshed a generous amount of Jack Daniels into a glass and downed it in one go. His hands trembled and his mouth felt dry. He felt stiffness in his arms and his legs threatened to buckle. Droplets of sweat plopped on the oak table as he gripped it and lowered his weight into an inviting chair. His body shook in spasms and his heartbeat danced to an unsteady tempo.

He was due in court in seven minutes, and he needed to keep his feelings under control. Raging thoughts gripped him, ominously rearing their ugly heads and sending him into a panic. His body was wracked with indecision, or was there something in the drink? His brain seemed cloudy, as if it was taking it longer to process his thoughts. How could things get any worse? He knew Kolinsky was out to destroy him, but he could not cope with anymore ghosts from his past. Not now, not ever.

Suddenly, he felt lightheaded. Maybe making an appearance in court was not such a good idea. He'd tell the agent. A sharp shooting pain travelled up his arm. Was he having a heart attack? The door opened and he signaled for the agent to draw closer. Avery, aka security guard, entered the confined office and closed the door firmly behind him. Speechless and at a loss for words, Barrymore swallowed hard as his brain whirred into action, struggling to come up with an escape plan. A bitter taste rolled over his tongue, and he looked hard at the glass he held in his hand.

Recognition lit up his eyes as Avery walked straight up to Barrymore and took the glass from him and set it down on the table, a devilish gleam in his eyes. "Hello, Colonel Barrymore, Soldier 453728 reporting for duty," Avery said mockingly.

Barrymore's voice quavered as he said, "What do you want?"

Tersely, Avery replied, "Judgment day, Your Honor. After all, it's never too late to sentence you for poor judgment. Maybe you will be awarded a Gold star too," he concluded sarcastically.

Barrymore sat rigidly in his seat, all sense of feeling leaving his body. In a whining tone, he replied, "I can't believe that you've allowed what's happened in the past to define your future. People change. I've changed. I've turned my life around. I'm President of the Youth Generation program in the Bronx and the Chairman of the Church Committee," he added, desperately searching Avery's face for mercy.

Avery's sardonic grin struck a chord within him, and a chilly feeling froze his fingers. Barrymore saw stars in his eyes as a wave of nausea took hold of him.

"Look at me," demanded Avery. "Perceptions can change, did you say? How can you justify what you've done? People died because of you. Well, here's a little peepshow for you to remember. Perhaps you can carry this image to your grave."

In one swift motion, Avery yanked off his mask to reveal scarred flesh; the remnants of the face that had once been his. Aghast, Barrymore swayed in his seat, shock paralyzing him from the waist upwards. His throat constricted and his eyes clouded over. Words rattled within his throat, struggling in vain to take form while the clear light of comprehension took shape.

Avery bore down on him, his voice sounding like gravel falling, "What redemption were you expecting? You are the catalyst of my destruction, the thunderbolt that catapulted my life to the abyss of hell. You sealed my fate in Basra and defined my future. So how can you change that? Tell me, Mr. Judge."

Rivulets of spit drooled down the side of Barrymore's face and his eyes watered. Frantically, he blinked his eyes trying to focus on what Avery was saying. He had one last chance to reach out and call for help before the concoction took over. He sat there helplessly in the opulently furnished office, willing his hand to move, helplessly fighting for life.

Barrymore fell deeper into his seat, the crippling effect of the drug that had been laced in the Jack Daniel whisky bottle coursed through his veins, aggressively rupturing his aorta and releasing a stream of blood out of his nose and eyes. Avery watched as Barrymore's heart cart wheeled jerkily as his lungs contracted, feebly searching for oxygen, convulsing uncontrollably in the final throes of death. Satisfied that the judge was dead, Avery removed his face mask and replaced it with another, before disappearing through the ventilation shaft.

Mission accomplished. *How gratifying*, he thought. Justice and $10 million all rolled into one, it was totally worth it.

Chapter 95

The Bronx-Lebanon Hospital Centre was bustling with its usual range of activity, people swarming around waiting for treatment, being interviewed by hospital personnel and searching for friends and relatives receiving medical help. It seemed like just another typical day for the Bronx-Lebanon Hospital Centre to the casual eye. McClaren was not taking any chances; he arrived with an entourage of agents prepared for anything. He sealed off the floor where the injured hostage was being detained, and planted two ferocious looking men at the door. The attending physician looked on disapprovingly, but was unable to stop the antics employed by McClaren's men to extract the information they needed. It was a matter of national security. The hostile witness was not forthcoming, and time was of the essence. McClaren was bent on stopping any potential threat that could endanger the lives of over 19 million New Yorkers.

The squat olive-skinned man lay helplessly on the hospital bed with his left leg bound in a fat wad of bandages and elevated in a metal sling, resigned to the fact that there was nowhere to run. He knew he looked a sorry sight with his face mottled with bruises, scathed by scratches, and with most of his body covered in all sorts of dressings. But it did not matter; defiantly, he peered at the authorities through puffy eyelids laced with venom, determined to hold out as long as he could. He had sacrificed himself for his family. He could die today safe in the thought that his family would be provided for. These American thugs could torture him. Indeed, there was nothing to reveal, he was just one piece of the puzzle, confined to just driving the decoy car. The only person he knew about was the one who had brought him in on the deal, and that man was probably long gone, disappeared like a ghost, probably never to be seen again.

McClaren's men showed no restraint, constrained by time and driven by the need to unravel the plot, they pressed hard for any piece of information they could source from the olive-skinned man. Three hours of intense interrogation yielded little to appease the frustrated agents.

Deciding to abandon the current line of questioning, McClaren drove back to the city office with the hope that he could work out who the other players in the sordid plot were. Settling down with a disgusting pot of office coffee, he began the search for the truth, meticulously screening the video footage from the courthouse frame by frame looking for answers.

All his men were putting in overtime. McClaren's biggest worry was that they were racing against the clock. Would they be able to unravel the conspiracy in time? The price of failure was catastrophic. Failure was not an option. The result would be an undesirable pill that would undoubtedly impact their operation, life, and careers, if not hundreds of innocents. The resonant effect would be unimaginable for the veteran agents. They were not about to give up. Feverishly, he reviewed the video footages recovered from the various TV reporters covering the mayhem, searching for clues.

Two hours and a second pot of coffee later, staring at the video screen for the umpteenth time, McClaren found part of the answer. The question was, could he stop it in time? The court session had to be stopped before any more lives were lost. Grabbing his car keys and signaling Agent Raines to follow, he made a dash for his car, hoping that he would be able to obstruct the devastating re-enactment of yesterday.

Kolinsky was the key. Why didn't he see it before? Agitatedly, he put the car in full throttle and pushed his car to the maximum. This last stab at intervention could end with irreprehensible consequences that would stay with him for the rest of his life. The only thing he could do was try, after all, what was the alternative?

Chapter 96

The court dates had been set, and the court appointed lawyer reeled off a list of things Blaine was expected to do during the court appearance. For all he cared, his fate was sealed. Blaine knew that it was just a formality dragging him into court to waste tax dollars that could have been used elsewhere. Ah! What did he care, anyway? He was resigned to the fact that there was no justice. Not really. He may have done so many despicable things in the past, but at least he had owned up to it all when asked. Why were the government officials who were embezzling money on stupid projects that still left the masses vulnerable, neglected, and irretrievably poorer not being held accountable for their actions? He wondered.

What chance in hell did he have with this two-bit, greenhorn, wet behind the ears lawyer, who had probably graduated from University totally unprepared for a real court proceeding? Disgusted, he looked at the young man; his dark charcoal suit looked like it was stolen from the local charity shop. The shirt was rumpled and the cuffed shoes worn and in desperate need of a shine. Even his hair looked disheveled and in desperate need of a comb. Blaine was proud; he had been incarcerated for three months and it looked like he had fared better than his lawyer in his shirt, tie, and complimentary wash. Indeed, his lawyer's bloodshot eyes and loopy grin convinced Blaine that the state was really out to put the nails on his coffin. He was going to be sent down quickly and without a fight, or so they thought.

Well, they would have to wait and see. Funnily enough, Butch Kid was being transported to the same court venue as his to stand trial for the murder of a local businessman, Luis Fernandez, who had obdurately refused to pay his protection money to Deroni. The way Butch Kid kept smirking and looking at the security guards gave Blaine the feeling that something was going down. *Staying close to him might be a good idea this time around*, he thought. If the Butch Kid was getting ready to escape, he had to be ready to tag along for the ride. He enjoyed killing people, and murdering a few security men to be free would not make a difference. After all, he already knew that he would be sentenced to life imprisonment. In the county bus there were seven other prisoners being transported to the courthouse. Two wardens and the driver completed the ensemble. Shackled face to face with the Butch Kid, Blaine relaxed, calmly waiting for the right moment to strike.

Butch Kid sat back, flexing his shackled hands from time to time, making sure that the blood was flowing freely through his arms; a sharp glint accentuated the menacing power his eyes wielded if you looked at him for too long. Uncomfortably, the two escorts shifted uneasily in their seats upon the clinking of chains. If it was Butch Kid's intention to unnerve the guards, he was certainly doing a good job. The oppressive heat and the insidious movements of Butch Kid and Marlboro Malone were enough to set anybody's teeth on edge. The journey to the courthouse seemed to last hours, when, in fact, it was only a twenty-five-minute journey.

The high-profile case on the news was about a Russian guy being tried on American soil in the same courthouse. There was bound to be an invasion of security men everywhere. The only chance they had of escaping was before arriving at the courthouse. Disappointedly, nothing happened, and within twenty-seven minutes they were outside the court house. With all the barriers, they had to go in through the back entrance and were in the process of being handed over to official looking men in dark suits when the first blast shook the building. In three fluid motions, Butch Kid hammered the prison guard, capitalizing on the element of surprise, and extricated the keys from the guard's belt. Marlboro Malone took out the second guard, who was out like a light. The third guard, who was the driver, pulled out his gun and posed to fire when Blaine gave an upper-cut blow to the man's chin, and he went down like a sack of potatoes. Four prisoners followed up with blows while the Butch Kid took off his cuffs and tossed the keys to Marlboro, who undid his restraints and passed the key to Blaine. In seconds, he was right behind the Butch Kid, who was furtively making his way upstairs. Temporarily confused, Blaine watched them go. Suddenly, it dawned on him. It had all been staged. Butch Kid was here for a different reason; he was here to kill somebody.

Patrick Hale, Kolinsky's accountant, on the other hand, could not shake off the feeling of foreboding that made his body tingle all over. Unexpectedly, he felt the effect of the first blast and then heard the sounds of gunshots in the hallway. Filled with dread, he instinctively ducked, trying to fit his massive frame under the table, to no avail. Hyperventilating, he waited for the forceful entry into the office and the fateful bullet that would rip him away from this world to the afterlife. It never came. Within minutes, the gun exchange was over, and the stampede of feet and shouts were all around him, but he was transfixed, paralyzed by fear, unable to move. Cowering behind the desk, he shook uncontrollably and almost screamed when the secret service agent clamped down on his hands and pulled him up, urging him to be quiet and directing him, urgently, towards the door to the fire escape. Impatiently, the agent pushed Hale to reinforce the dilemma they were in. He exhaled loudly, knowing that he was in no shape to run. He was out of breath, gasping laboriously like he had already run a marathon, wheezing noisily as he was frenetically shoved through the fire exit. The soft whoosh of the door closing firmly behind him amplified the fact that danger was lurking nearby, and he had to getaway. His life depended on it.

Inwardly, he shuddered at the thought that Kolinsky would never let him testify. Even with all the agents surrounding him, he was as good as dead. But he could try, couldn't he? Lumbering down the stairs as fast he could, he stumbled just as he heard a crack from a semi-automatic gun. Turning in free fall, he felt the bullet imbed itself in his head, and his body jerked in spasms. He was dead before he hit the stairs. Bewildered, the two agents fired shots in response. Frustrated, they looked down at the gaping head wound and glazed eyes of Hale and knew, instinctively, that Hale was gone. One agent bent to reconfirm the verdict while the second sprinted up the stairs looking for the perpetrator.

At the top of the stairs, he found a discarded set of handcuffs. Jerking open the fire exit door and taking the precaution of avoiding any stray bullets, he surveyed the corridor. The passageway was almost empty, except for the three security personnel with guns intently sweeping the other courtrooms looking for civilians. Retreating the way, he came; he re-joined his colleague, who had radioed for an ambulance. Meanwhile, Butch Kid, Marlboro, and

Blaine stashed their guns in a bin in the toilet and exited the rest room wearing business suits.

Moving at a steady pace, so as not to attract attention, they made their way to a dark blue Chrysler and drove off. With Marlboro driving, Butch Kid opened the cell phone left under the car seat and dialed the number he had committed to heart. After four clicks, a voice asked, "Is it done?"

Laughing, Butch replied, "Elvis has left the building."

Terminating the call, they drove to the 'Used car' Scrap yard to dispose of the Chrysler, change clothes, and transfer to the waiting vehicle. All in a day's work marveled Blaine. It was truly unbelievable; he was free.

Chapter 97

Mark Turner was determined to make a name for himself as the Assistant District Attorney. He was like a dog after a bone, determined to secure a glowing victory in this prolific case. He was not swayed by the events of yesterday. It actually helped to solidify his resolve. He was taking Kolinsky down at all costs. With the blessing of the American government behind him, how could he fail? The only problem looming on the horizon was the incriminating evidence that was delivered to his office around 9 o'clock last night. The mind-boggling file kept him awake all night, while he deliberated on what he should do. The damning records lead him to the only conclusion possible; Judge Barrymore had to be removed from the proceedings while the accusations levied against him were fully investigated.

He had a few buried skeletons of his own. Judge Barrymore was a reasonable man, and would be compelled to step down, somewhat reluctantly. But it had to be done in the interest of self-preservation. He could not have it both ways. His decision would be the difference between criminal prosecution for negligence and the deaths of innocent civilians or a failed case. The government would take every precaution to ensure that they were not culpable, so as not to stir up an international stink storm. He had to call it in, but first he would give the judge a heads up.

Driving to the new location, he was directed to where he was supposed to park. Shutting off the engine, he locked his car and made his way up the elevator, after passing security checks, and headed for Barrymore's chambers. He saw a young agent dressed in a dark blue suit come out of Barrymore's office, pass him by, and enter the elevator. Thinking nothing of it, lost in his own string of thoughts, he strolled up to the door and rapped loudly. Waiting for a few seconds, he tentatively knocked again. Listening carefully for

249

some indication that Barrymore was in his chambers, he placed his hand on the doorknob and called out Judge Barrymore's name.

The door swung open and Mark Turner shouted out in shock. The court bailiff and two agents came running at the same time. Stepping into the room, Turner, followed by the two agents, saw the slumped body of the judge sprawled across the desk, an upturned glass lying at the foot of the table, and a note boldly displayed on the table where Barrymore's head lay.

Holding tightly onto the file in his hand, Turner drew nearer to read the note. His heart nose-dived and a sudden chill invaded his ocular senses as the two agents tried unsuccessfully to revive the judge. The admirable penmanship of the judge read:

For the past twenty-seven years, I have diligently and reverently upheld every oath expected from an Officer of the Law. However, in life, there have always been ways in which we have failed the good people of our country, whether at home or on foreign soil. I regret the pain I have caused to certain families during my life journey and sincerely apologize for the irreversible harm caused by not speaking up earlier in the events that transpired when I was working for Bunnytox Pharmaceuticals and am responsible for what happened in Basra. I ask for their forgiveness, and hope that justice in this case will finally provide solace to the grieving families I leave behind.

To my family, I hope that they can find it in their hearts to understand that I love them deeply, and that I did this because it was the right thing to do.

Signed Judge James Barrymore III

Tears trickled down the prosecutor's face as he stood there, bewildered. There was no way the case was going to be heard today. Another bitter triumph for Kolinsky, mused Turner. Collecting his thoughts, he trudged out of the room, the file burning an imaginary hole in his hand as he gripped it firmly—confusion partially clouding his judgment. What was he going to do with the file now? He had to find the District Attorney and offload this keg of dynamite threatening to explode. He could not count on the discretion of the two agents, and putting it off for later could be dangerous. Summoning up his courage, he dialed the DA's number. Picking up almost immediately, he recounted what happened. The

DA instructed him to leave the vicinity and make his way back to their Manhattan office, where he would meet him.

Visibly shaken, with fear constricting his throat, he made his way to the elevator and out of the courthouse, knowing subconsciously that he had probably bitten more than he could chew. Things like these did not happen in real life. You only heard about them or saw them in films. It could not be happening to him, the Assistant District Attorney being a witness to a crime and in danger of being snuffed out, all in one breath. Faltering for a second to catch his breath and survey the car park, he practically ran for the safety of his car, panic and paranoia spurring him on. Looking around the empty car lot, warily searching for any signs of danger, ears prickling for the slightest sound out of place, he activated the key fob, heard the soft whoosh of the door clicking open, and literally jumped in. Starting up the car, he put it in gear and headed up to the parking lot exit. A figure appeared out of nowhere and stood just a few feet shy of the exit, sending Turner into a flustered frenzy. Petrified, Turner tried to avoid the solitary figure blocking out the exit leading on to the street. Slowing down for a fraction of a second, he could see the face of the man, his towering frame looming eerily close to the windscreen. Winding down the glass a little bit, he mustered the strength to ask, "What do you think you're doing? Get out of my way."

The man in the dark suit crouched down, leaning into the car, speaking softly but ominously, "Give me the file, counsellor." In that fleeting second before the gun appeared in the killer's hand, Turner knew that he had seen the same man coming out of Barrymore's chambers just minutes before. This was a man who was no stranger to murder. Terror seized him, and he struggled to get the seat belt off, subconsciously aware of what was about to happen. Frantically, he fumbled with the belt, oblivious of the incoming bullet that ripped through his cerebral cortex and embedded itself securely in the right side of his brain.

Leaning into the car, Avery Johnson retrieved the file and disappeared like a summer's breeze.

251

Chapter 98

McClaren and Raines must have broken every rule in the Highway Code manual racing through town to the courthouse. The bright neon police light flashed off the roof of the unmarked FBI car as they tore across the city, hoping to avert another calamitous chapter from being written in this saga. Screeching tires and burning rubber announced their unceremonious arrival, much to the disdain of fellow agents and to the curiosity of the milling crowd of spectators, watching eagerly for the drama that was about to unfurl. Taking the stairs three steps at a time with a surge of men at his heels, McClaren shouted out orders and headed for the elevator. The agents dispersed like a trail of ants, sealing off the designated areas, while Raines and McClaren proceeded to the fourth floor.

The elevator door opened, and McClaren picked up radio action when an agent mouthed into the receiver, "Judge Barrymore is down, get a trolley up here quickly." Racing down the corridor, McClaren knew he was too late to save the good judge, but maybe, just maybe, he could curb the impending media hype that would erupt if Kolinsky were to escape. Sending out further instructions, he asked the agent if Kolinsky was still in the building. Indicating that Kolinsky was being housed two doors down, the agent returned to preserve the room, unsure if it was a crime scene or not. McClaren made his way to the office where Kolinsky was being kept, and opened the door. The man in the seat turned at the intrusion; a sly grin plastered all over his face, evidently, enjoying another debacle on the part of the US government. Sitting comfortably in his seat like a relaxed cat, he stared up at McClaren with an imperious look, waiting for a reaction. Steamed up and bursting with rage, McClaren advanced threateningly, struggling to keep his temper in check. He wanted desperately to wipe the smug look off Kolinsky's face. He had broken so many rules in this case;

perhaps one more would not matter. It seemed that everywhere he turned in this case he was confronted with disaster.

He understood that there were bound to be leaks in the overall dynamics, but the intelligence so far had been impeccable. It could only be someone higher up in the organization structure. After all, only a handful of people were privy to the change in the case's location. Apart from him, Raines, the President, his boss, and two others, nobody was supposed to know. In hindsight, McClaren realized that the operation was doomed from the start. It was all orchestrated to allow Kolinsky enter the United States through the front door. Bringing Kolinsky to the United States was a terrorist act in itself. The Blue County calamity was merely a ploy, which culminated in the plot to overthrow the government and expose the ineptitude of the existing government officials. Or was it something more? McClaren's epiphany sent hot flushes coursing through his body. Taking stock of what had transpired over the last four days, an instant clarity pierced his mind's eye, replacing the anger nestled in the pit of his stomach with an analytical calm.

Circling the room while he processed these thoughts, he stared intently at Kolinsky, really hard, for the first time since Kolinsky had got here. Buzzing in his head were warning lights, something was off, but he could not put his finger on it. Pausing imperceptibly, using his FBI training, he scrutinized the subject. Conjuring the memory of Kolinsky's face before the arrest and reconstructing Kolinsky's mannerisms while onboard the plane during his extradition to the United States, a sudden bout of acid lodged itself in his throat. Not wanting to believe, but sick in the realization that they had been had, he set about to find out who exactly they had in custody.

Positioning himself boldly in front of the fraud, blocking the sunlight into the room, McClaren waited for a reaction. Whoever was seated in the chair seemed unruffled; a professional accustomed to waiting out the storm? His eyes reflected a glint of coldness with unwavering alertness. This was a man who would not give up what he knew easily.

McClaren could see the signs. He was not going to break him without extensive 'persuasion'. That could not be done in the court block. The interrogation would have to be conducted in a more secure facility. Meanwhile, the troubling enigma of deciphering when the switch was done continued to plague McClaren. Was it

253

here at the court complex? Or was it while they had him in custody? He needed answers. Kolinsky was definitely in the wind. But the question was, how much of a head-start did Kolinsky have and who was helping him?

It was all down to time, yet again. But did he have time? McClaren thought to himself as he whisked the imposter to a private facility known only to one other person besides himself. Incidentally, that person was already dead, so there was no further fear of a leak or being ambushed.

Chapter 99

News of Barrymore's death had already reached the ears of the people within the court building. The news vultures were running around looking for any available space to set up their camera and relate breaking news live. There was simply no stopping them. The jury was in a state of stupor. The jurors were huddled into an airless cubicle of a room and left to their own devices. For the time being, they were being sequestered. No contact with the media hype spilling around outside the door to where they were being held. "Marvelous," shouted the Mexican house help. The other stunned jurors were beyond shocked. Upset by their confinement, but relieved that they were not in the immediate line of fire, they were each consciously aware that their lives were at risk and the best thing was to stay together. There was safety in numbers. This explosive case had already upturned the apple cart. They were now prisoners of the court, deprived of a social life and any media or commercial connections. It was like living in the early 1930s.

The announcement of James Barrymore's death terrified them. If a top member of the court, one who had protection, could be killed, what chance did they have? Nobody would believe that he suddenly died of a heart attack. Conspiracy theories were running rife in that tiny room, each juror expounding his or her version of events. What other distractions did they have to pass the time until their fate was decided?

It was obvious that they would be under lock and key for a while. The state had to decide who was going to replace Barrymore. The godforsaken process could take weeks. What were they supposed to be doing between now and then? None of them wanted to contemplate or debate that thought. Getting to know each other was the best they could do in the meantime.

Chapter 100

Months had passed, and Senator Lee was now acclimatizing to his new home. The nostalgia of his real home trickled in once in a while to disrupt his idyllic existence. He knew that he could never go back there again. He had wanted to take Anne Marie Cummings away from it all and rebuild a new life with her. Why did she betray him? He loved his son. His wife was another story. They had slowly grown apart, although thinking about it now; he still cared for her in a brotherly way. Maybe things could have been different. That was a luxury he would never find out.

That was a lifetime ago. Now, he had a new lover and was starting all over again under a new name: Patrice Lawrence. He kept a low profile away from the prying eyes of the locals. He hired a housekeeper who did the runs to town for groceries and essentials. He had parted ways with Frost. He owed him that much. Cutting him loose was the hardest thing he had ever had to do, but what choice did he have. It would be unfair to resign Frost to a life of isolation and imprisonment for a crime that he, Senator Lee, had committed. Incarceration was ascribed to him alone. He had perpetrated the crime, and he would do the time; quietly serve the sentence as gallantly as possible in this remote place.

He spent regular hours honing his shooting skills. Now that he had time on his hands, he exercised, used the firing range he had set up close to home and explored the area, familiarizing himself with his environment. You never know when it would be relevant. The tranquility of this quaint little area in Canada silenced any thoughts of going back. The only downside was that news was always received days later, being so far away from the city center. Maybe that was a good thing.

Looking out of the window, he saw his housekeeper, Maria, drive up and park. Placing his Remington rifle in its gun case, he ran out to help Maria offload her shopping from the boot into the house.

Nimbly extricating the first set of brown bags from Maria, he carried them in and placed them on the kitchen worktop. Maria, singing and smiling, brought in the last three bags using her little cart and set about offloading the treats she had bought. Maria was a godsend. She cleaned like she had OCD and cooked like she had a master's degree in culinary skills, which was simply delicious. Senator Lee knew it was good fortune that had brought her into his life. Holding onto that thought, he grabbed the local news rag and settled down to read while Maria churned up a sumptuous meal. The aromatic smell wafting from the kitchen was making him salivate, and his stomach rumbled, demanding to be appeased. Unfolding the newspaper, he eased back into his chair and scanned the front-page articles. On page three, the article of an unidentified male found in an alleyway in Claremont, Virginia caught his attention:

The police in Virginia were shaken by a horrific and apparently random attack on an unidentified victim whose final moments were captured in a chilling recording on his cellphone as he was being attacked and, ultimately, shot by his alleged killer. The only description of the attacker was of a white Caucasian between the ages of 30–40 and about 6 feet 4 tall. The body was savagely beaten, stabbed and shot. The man's wallet holds no clues to his identity except for the army tag 15467890. The body of the unknown victim was discovered by an off-duty police officer on his way home on Saturday night. This shocking revelation has left the small community reeling. One eyewitness saw two men dressed in dark garbs making a get-away in a blue Chevy with no distinct features.

The off-duty officer confirmed the fact that he had seen a blue Chevy with Arizona plates flee the scene. He, instinctively, knew that something was wrong when he saw the battered form of a man collapse at the entrance of the alley. He immediately called for an ambulance and rushed to assist. He heard sounds of the regurgitation of blood and a noise known as the death rattle escape the dying man's throat. His intervention was timely, but too late, as the man died in his arms. The policeman has described it in his own words as, "...gruesome and maniacal,"—the worst he had ever seen in his 13 years on the police force. The officer, whose name cannot be disclosed at this stage of the investigation, is currently assisting the Virginia Homicide unit with their enquiry.

The authorities are looking diligently for the perpetrators of the crime, and in the meantime urge the general public to exercise extreme caution. These perpetrators are armed and exceptionally dangerous. The police are also appealing to witnesses to come forward and are requesting that the locals be vigilant and report any suspicious movements in the area...

Stunned, with his hands trembling, Senator Lee let the paper rustle to the floor. Rooted to his seat, jolts of inconsolable pain shook his innards, leaving him lightheaded. It could not be. The army tag 15467890 was his parting gift to Frost. Who had killed him? Was it the CIA, Kolinsky, or the guys who had chased them to his brother-in-law's place? Another worrying thought started nagging him, replacing the shocking revelation of Frost's death. Were they already coming for him? Did Frost give away his final destination?

There was no time to dither. Agitated, but on full alert, he pushed Maria out of the house and told her not to come back for a few days. He would contact her when he needed her. Surprised, and a lit upset at how rudely and aggressive he had shoved her out of the house, she puffed and fumed as she made her way to her car, reeling off a roll of expletives under her breath and silently admonishing herself for ever coming to work with this recluse. Driving off, she did not look back, still angry at her employer.

Senator Lee, on the other hand, swiftly turned off the stove and recovered his Remington rifle, a lot of bullets, and his AK rifle. He loaded his rifles and set up his position. If it came down to this, it would be his last stand. Would he be the last man standing? He wondered. Well, he was about to find out.

Chapter 101

Ralph and Matthew sat in a seedy motel room trying to figure out where Senator Lee had disappeared to. He had the wherewithal to flee to any country of his choosing. Maybe he was in Cuba, which has no extradition treaty with the United States. The brothers, on the other hand, had little resources and were seriously low on cash as Ralph had not got round to paying in his cheque yet.

Months had passed, and their contacts had been unable to uncover any information about Senator Lee's current location. To raise cash, Ralph and Matthew took on menial chores—painting, decorating and construction work—to pay for food, petrol, and hotel bills. The yearning to exact vengeance was strong, but there was nothing they could do until their source at the Boston Police Department found out where Senator Lee was hiding.

It was just a matter of time. All they could do now was wait.

Chapter 102

Jenkins knew that he would not withstand prolonged torture. At some point, he would have to give up some information. The irony being that he had no idea where Kolinsky was really going. That was the agreement. He had not pressed his friend. It was irrelevant. His fate had indeed been written. It had only taken 27 years to repay his debt; that was all. He had lived a fulfilling life in America. He had no regrets, except for one. He never got to say goodbye to his childhood sweetheart. His first wife, Belinda, who never re-married. He guessed that she still carried the torch for him, as did he. Reminiscing on the past was pointless, he mused, trying to clear his head.

They were in a nondescript part of town, an unsavory place by all accounts. Raines and McClaren had parked behind an abandoned industrial estate that had succumbed willingly to the rust, depravation, and hopelessness of its surroundings. Jenkins wondered what else was lurking in the overgrown shrubbery enveloping the decaying industrial development complex. Steeling himself in preparation of the onslaught of pain that was to come, he dutifully followed Raines and McClaren into the building with a sense of foreboding lingering close at hand, whispering his last prayers.

Waging through the debris and refuse from collapsed ceilings, discarded machinery, and tools, which had all discolored over time, McClaren took them through to a disused office, extracted a key from his key ring, and inserted it into a door hidden behind a dilapidated cabinet. With a click, the door swung open, and they stepped into an elevator that had only one button pointing downwards. Safely inside, they were transported down to an open-plan office with state-of-the-art furnishing. Steel plate reinforcements lined the wall, with video feed of video cameras spaced every five yards. The bright strident lights effused brilliance that detracted the feeling of being underground. This facility was definitely off the grid, and Jenkins knew that nobody would come looking for him here. This was confirmation of his destiny. Looking around, he viewed his final resting place with cynicism, while inwardly mustering every ounce of bravado that he would need to face the grueling interrogation that was to follow, if the plan was to work.

Chapter 103

The first two hours of persistent questioning had yielded little, leaving McClaren irascible, frustrated, and exasperated. The clock was ticking, and he was aware that time was not on his side. Well, to hell with protocol and the fact that Jenkins was an American meant that he wasn't supposed to, technically speaking, be tortured on American soil. But what choice did he have? Giving him a dose of a truth serum would cause further delay. Every second that passed was a second lost in recovering Kolinsky. Fury overtook him, dulling all sense of caution, recrimination, and accountability. Even Agent Raines was unable to restrain the demon unleashed as McClaren pumped and battered Jenkins. Even when the prosthetic mask was torn into shreds, revealing the man behind the disguise; He just stood there tongue tied, shocked, and unable to move, repressing the urge to run out and vomit.

The interrogation then turned, regrettably, bloody beyond imagination. The walls were streaked with splatters of blood, the blood work gave a surreal feel of contemporary art against the clinical backdrop of the spotless facility. McClaren's insatiable rage was fueled by taciturn Jenkins; spiking an indescribable urge to pummel, pound, and punch the squirming, banged up officer. What was the price of treason these days? McClaren was merely doing what he needed to do.

Justifiably, his superiors would not approve of his methods, but, right now, that was the least of his problems. Jenkins was undeniably a terrorist, an enemy from within, and he was being treated like the rest of the scums that meant harm to the American population McClaren had so determinedly declared to protect. Where was the loyalty in that? McClaren fumed as he pummeled harder into the flesh of the sagging Jenkins, who had slumped forward, struggling to recover from the assault inflicted to every part of his body. The cocky smile long replaced by a distorted shape of pain.

Two hours later, Jenkins finally gave him the name of the court clerk who had helped them smuggle guns into the court house a day before the trial. The other snippet of information was that Krivov was supposed to meet him at the W Hotel on Washington Street at 18.45 hours.

A little bit of misinformation would not go amiss, but it would buy him the few crucial minutes he needed, Jenkins thought. Looking down at his watch through inflamed bloodshot eyes, he saw that it was 18.05. Instinctively, he knew it was time. It was time to draw down the final curtain and end the charade. Thinking of all the other martyrs who had died for the same cause, he concluded that this was as good a place as any to die. What was important to him was that the news of his last heroic act would reach Kolinsky, of that he was sure. In one swift movement, his tongue ran along the ridge of his tooth to where the fatal pill was lodged. Smoothly biting and crushing the cyanide capsule encased in his back tooth, he briskly swallowed its contents before his captors understood what was happening. His body shook spasmodically in the seat, writhing uncontrollably until the spasms subsided, and then he was still. He had, after all, been a faithful foot soldier right up to the end; his last and final act of loyalty to a dear friend.

Turning away from Jenkins in disgust, McClaren called through to headquarters requesting that agents be dispatched to the hotel and to the county clerk's house while they waited for the outcome. 15 minutes later, Agent Ramos called back to tell him that the county clerk had been killed in his apartment, but a flash drive from his computer had been recovered.

Another line of enquiry had just been opened, and McClaren was certainly going to be there to find out what had been uncovered. Leaving the interrogation room without a backward glance at the crumpled form of Jenkins, he instructed that the body be transferred to a cell within the facility, pending the decision from above. He did not care about what happened to Jenkins's corpse; he was of no use to him now.

Departing from the facility, he made his way to headquarters; no stone would be left unturned in apprehending the culprits. He had been awake for thirty-six hours, driving on adrenalin and coffee, but sleep was not on the agenda. Tired, wired, and edgy, McClaren drove speedily back to HQ with Agent Raines in tow, searching for answers.

The disheartening news that Krivov never made it to the rendezvous did not dampen his resolve. McClaren hoped that the recovered flash drive would give him the major breakthrough he was looking for. A lot was definitely riding on it. Either way, it was bound to be informative. They would probably know more than they knew yesterday, and that was saying a lot, wasn't it?

Chapter 104

Avery Johnson sat at a bistro drinking his vanilla cappuccino infused with a trace of nutmeg, wondering what to do next. The deed had been done, but yet he felt no satisfaction. Deep down lurked a gaping hole threatening to entrench him in despair. What a bitter victory, deserving yet unfulfilling. Barrymore was dead, but where was the satisfaction in that. Evidently, the throes of revenge were not as sweet as he had expected. Rather, it left him bereft of emotions, a hollow feeling sweltered within him, creating an impassable chasm and darkening his sour mood. The culmination of seven years of meticulous planning in the execution of his revenge did not assuage the void or the emptiness engulfing his deepest thoughts. The fact that he was also being paid to take out Barrymore was not lost on him. Men like Barrymore always had a barn full of enemies.

He, too, probably had a legion of adversaries seeking vengeance of some sort. After all, for the last thirteen years, he had killed—savoring each killing like a conqueror in battle—gathering power, dominance, and perfection with each kill. He was a gun for hire who never entertained remorse or pangs of conscience. It was misguided baggage in his line of work in any case. The sense of retribution spurred him on to excellence, coupled with fueling an insatiable rage within him, challenging him to perfect the art of death, goading him on, preparing him for the final act. Now that it was done, ghosts of misgivings were waging war within his desolate heart, rendering him barren.

He lacked the feeling he so desperately wanted to feel. He had compartmentalized every kill in the past. Perhaps that had helped him remain unscathed, that is until now. The vagaries of his life and his experiences with death had caused an irreversible mutation: from dedicated veteran to cold blooded killer. No matter what the intentions of the other players in the saga were, for him, it was personal.

His job in New York was done. He had checked his account, and the agreed sum had been transferred. There was just one more thing to do before he left. Punching in the numbers in his burner phone, he made the call. The Vice President had to know that the files had been destroyed and all traces leading back to him were eradicated. The VP was safe, for now, his secrets burnt to smithereens.

Chapter 105

Avery Johnson's call was music to the Vice President's ears. The VP wondered what had possessed him to partake in the killing of the Afghan civilians all those years ago. He despised Barrymore for compromising their mission, which had inadvertently killed members of his company and exposed his company to a shooting frenzy in that remote village.

Ten years on, he still had nightmares that endless hours of private psychiatric consultation could not erase. Maybe with Barrymore out of the picture, he might sleep easier. The Kolinsky case had presented itself with an opportunity that was too good to miss. It was killing two birds with one stone. Cross purposes served on one plate. *Convenient, efficient, and less expensive*, he thought with glee. Just one problem remained: The President's ratings were still high. The court of public opinion was still in President Kinnock's corner. Simply stating the obvious, the Kolinsky case did not fully address the presidential problem.

Yes, the media took the President to task, but that was it. The Communications Director had done a good job in deflecting the blame of the shambolic attack on civilians at Blue County Hotel on the bumbling incompetence of the FBI and of the courthouse fiasco on Homeland Security. New Yorkers had taken all of it in their stride and had gone back to focusing on their busy lives; merely filing the events of the last few days to the annals of history, like they had done with 9/11. It was an experience to learn from and move on.

A feeling of dissatisfaction seized him. Kolinsky had not delivered what he promised. Agreed, he created the confusion and the minor upset that did not topple this government. There had to be a bigger game plan that would do away with President Kinnock. Assassination was out of the equation, but what other option was there?

Picking up his burner cell phone, he made the call to Kolinsky. His forty-five second conversation blew his mind. His cover had been blown. Dropping the phone as if were a piping hot potato, he hurriedly gathered his personal possessions, grabbed his keys, and made for the door to his office. He had to get away, either that or face charges of treason. Opening the door, he came face to face with two severe looking agents who quickly flashed their badges and whisked the terrified VP away in their dark green van to an unknown location.

Chapter 106

The President sat back in the oval room, a deep scowl etching trouble lines into his perfectly chiseled face. His brown hair flecked with the stressed grey that comes with carrying the whole nation on your shoulders; adding about another decade to his soft masculine features.

He had gone through all the emotions of fear, disgust, rage, and disbelief in under a minute. How could this be happening? His brain chose to disbelieve what his eyes had seen. Could it be possible that the Vice President was part of the intricate plot to bring down this government? Why destroy the government that he was already a part of? The logic defied all sense of reasoning. He knew that his VP was ambitious, but never in his wildest dream did he think that he would betray him. Vaughan had some explaining to do, once he was caught.

He was, after all, the people's choice, democratically elected 'The Man of the People'. They worked well together, and he had given him free reign to work as he deemed fit. So why did he feel the need to double cross him? He wondered. Whatever it was, it had to be nipped in the bud. Seated across from him sat his closest friend, Director Pattinson, his hazelnut eyes twinkling with concern and the knowledge that the smoldering fire alight in his friend's eyes could only mean one thing. The enraged president was nursing a burning hatred for their mutual friend. Visibly shaken, Pattinson sat there, hands steepled, face ashen, pondering his friend's next move.

A look of general understanding passed between them, surpassing words they were both reluctant to say. Pushing the folder up close, his friend chose his candidate. Hamilton would be the man for the job.

With relief, the President pressed the intercom and summoned his personal assistant, ordering him to officially invite Hamilton to the White House immediately. Hurrying out of the Oval Office, the personal assistant went to do the President's bidding

The call earlier from the White House had changed everything in an instant; Hamilton's boredom was replaced with uncertainty and anxiety. Fighting down the trepidation he felt, he dressed carefully in a Navy blue Giorgio Armani suit, cut to perfection, with a crisp matching blue Van Heusen shirt and a pair of Jimmy Choo shoes to complete his dazzling outfit. He wanted to look his best in front of the President and portray a feeling of self-assurance and poise he did not possess at the moment. Looking at his image in the mirror, he hoped he was conveying that message without revealing any chinks in his armor. Deep down, his stomach was tied in knots and his legs felt rubbery, but he worked hard to hide his anxiety and prevent his mask of calm from crumbling. Removing his gun from its holster, he touched the cool metallic surface, before putting it down. There really was no need to carry his piece; today. He was a civilian and would not be permitted to take it in anyway. Instead, he locked it away in his floor safe and did a final sweep of his apartment before leaving. Was the verdict in? Was he being called back to active duty? Or was this simply the end of the road for him? Either way, he was about to find out, whether he liked it or not.

Twenty minutes later, with his car parked in a spot arranged for him, he was escorted up the stairs through the service entrance to the waiting President. What was the secrecy all about? Was the president ashamed of him coming through the front door? The stone-faced agents gave nothing away. The poor sods were probably as clueless as he was. Confidently, they hurried him along the corridors, eager to drop their special assignment on the President's doorstep. Hamilton, on the other hand, took slower strides in a bid to delay the inevitable judgment day.

Knocking and announcing his arrival, the agents left Hamilton unaccompanied to face the President of the United States of America. *Here goes nothing*, thought Hamilton to himself as he closed the door firmly behind him.

Chapter 107

Tony looked at the file again, disbelievingly. Suddenly, his head started spinning and a buzzing sound resonated in his ears. The pieces fell into place. Conflicting thoughts waged a merciless war within him as he contemplated about what he would do with the information. Side-tracking his exhausted partner, who was stretched out cold on the lumpy squad divan, he made his way to the back of the squad room where the irate Chief of Police was giving out orders over the phone to the listening officer. Stepping into his glass office the size of a miniscule cubicle, he shut the door quietly behind him. With a flash of PSP and dawning comprehension that there was a breakthrough in the case, Captain Brooks terminated his heated conversation and gave Tony a withering look that could wilt even the healthiest flower in a second, waiting for a response. Excitedly, Tony rattled off his findings, spreading corroborating evidence all over his boss's desk as he spoke animatedly. Brooks listened intently and interjected with a few questions of his own.

Ten minutes later, after Tony's summation, Brooks pressed the intercom button and ordered that Michael report to his office immediately. Three minutes later, groggy and disheveled, Michael—nursing a three-day stubble, with bloodshot eyes and rumpled clothes—stood at attention in his boss's office, wondering what the hell was going on. Giving him a once over, but making no comment, Brooks gave them their instructions under strict confidence that they would only disclose what they uncovered to him alone and nobody else. Dismissing them, he made an important call; he had better do damage control before the fan hit the roof. Pondering for a second after he made the call, he mused who would get to Senator Lee first. Things were going to get quite ugly for Senator Lee if the Cummings brothers, Mathew and Ralph, caught up with him, which was likely, considering that they probably had a head start on Tony and Michael. The only difference was that, being officers of the law, Michael and Tony had access to privileged information that someone resembling Senator Lee had crossed the Canadian border three weeks ago. How about that for a stroke of luck? Would it be enough to get to Senator Lee in time, though?

It was definitely a race against time. All he could do now was take a step back and let Tony and Michael get on with it. On the other hand, should he mobilize someone local to deal with the problem? Weighing what was at stake, hesitating for a split second; he picked up his phone for the second time within as many minutes and made the call. Struggling to allay the nagging thoughts of a possible train crash that he had set in motion, he focused his attention on another case file that was clamoring for closure. All he could do now was sit back and see where the dominoes would fall. Either way, the President, Mayor, and Commissioner were clear on this: no publicity and as much damage control as possible. Brook wished things would be that easy.

Chapter 108

The long-expected telephone call came in at 3.40 a.m. Ralph jumped up in bed and nudged Matthew. Things were looking up. Matthew waited until Ralph had finished his conversation with their source before asking, "Where the hell is Senator Lee?" Their source had told him that Frost's body had been recovered and that Senator Lee had been sighted in Canada.

The brothers agreed to leave for Canada in two days' time, which would give them enough time to buy what they needed for the journey and collect their pay from their part time job. A feeling of anticipation gradually took over them as they completed their last shift. They would soon be crossing the Canadian border to Vancouver, where they would receive directions to Senator Lee's hideaway. The information would be left in a locker at the train station.

It was payback time, and Ralph and Matthew were looking forward to killing Senator Lee.

Chapter 109

Hamilton went through the folder. If you were going to catch a tough opponent; you needed to know as much as possible about his mannerisms, tastes, habits, and connections. Brewing a fresh pot of coffee, he sat down to read the contents of the file, committing the salient points to memory.

Vaughan was married, with two children. He majored in international politics and had a master's degree in economics. He taught at MIT and was drafted to somewhere in Chechnya for three months. The other places were classified and redacted. He had a colorful career upon his return to the US: having represented Michigan in the mayoral election and, after seven years, he worked his way up to the Senate from the Democratic Party. There was a one-page summation of every achievement, medal of commendation, and awards given out to him over the last twenty years. The resume was quite impressive, even by Hamilton's standards, and a pang of envy surged through him. This Vaughan was magnificent, so why did the president want him dead? Right before he would kill him, he was going to find out.

Forty-five minutes later, with his holdall that was designed to camouflage his cache of weapons; he set off to the designated airstrip, where a private Gulfstream plane was waiting to transport him to the rendezvous. Sitting back in the small plane, he imagined what it felt like to be a spy in a clandestine operation financed by the government with the rule of deniability riding on his shoulders.

He hummed the national anthem, the words:

And where is that band who boastfully swore
That the havoc of war and the battle's confusion
A home and a country should leave us no more?
Their blood has washed out their foul footsteps'
pollution!

No refuge could save the hireling and slave
From the terror of flight, or the gloom of the grave:
And the star-spangled banner in triumph doth wave
O'er the land of the free and the home of the brave…

Mesmerized by these words, a poignant instinct returned with vigor, choking him, in reaction to the idea and enormity of his mission. Fifteen years ago, things were different. He was young, nimble, and fresh out of training, willing to prove himself. His zeal and physical and mental capacity far outclassed his peers. He was simply a killing machine, sculpted to carry out every top-secret assignment with the skill and stealth of a predator or executioner. He also had the support of his superiors and a network of spies willing to help, if he got into a jam. He was ready then, but was he totally ready now?

There was so much more at stake. He was still a father, regardless of the fact that his ex-wife had made sure that he had no further contact with his kids except for the alimony and maintenance checks he sent dutifully in the post on the 22nd of each month, like clockwork. How much more of a hit could his reputation take? He would like to think that, whatever happened, his children would remember him as a great dad and a national hero. Well, that last part was yet to be seen.

Flashing lights glimmered, bringing him out of his reverie. Reassembling his equipment and synchronizing his watch, he jumped out of the airplane door as the plane flew on. It was now or never, success or failure rested solely on him. His mission had begun.

Chapter 110

Trapped in a secluded place, imprisoned and confined in a picturesque setting and watched daily by an army of personal bodyguards, this was not Vaughn's idea of fun. He pondered his situation.

There was a reason why Kolinsky had not killed him yet, which meant that he was still valuable in some way, right? Whatever the reason, he was glad that was he was still alive. The girls here were easy on the eye, the service outstanding, and the food delicious. "All to die for, excuse my pun," Vaughan muttered to himself. There was nothing he could do but wait. *Meanwhile, another Margarita would not go amiss*, he thought as he reclined on a pool chair on the edge of the swimming pool, admiring the clear blue pool set in the center of his delectable prison.

With the right sort of entertainment, his life was fulfilled. The only worry clouding his idyllic stay in this imposed paradise was how long he could live with the monotony and what his life's expediency was. *Quite worrying indeed*, he thought again to himself, readjusting his position in the pool chair looking for a strategic pose to take and view oncoming traffic. After all, he did not want to be taken totally unaware now did he?

Settling down to lap up the sunshine, his mind drifted off and he fell asleep. Disconcertedly, his eyes fluttered open moments later when a dark shadow flitted across his face, blotting out the sunshine. He sensed a light wind suddenly hit him, jerking him awake from his unscheduled nap. From the look on the messenger's face, it was clear that time was running out for him. He had been summoned.

On shaky legs, trying to maintain a shred of dignity, Vaughn mustered a garment of courage, bracing himself for what came next. Either way, he had had a good life before it had gone awry. Seething inwardly, the name Kolinsky pounded loudly in his ears, rattling around his brain like a ping pong ball. Vaughan's brain writhed in agony trying to pronounce the name in monosyllables, reeling off each letter as if his tongue was enveloped in iron; all the while, another part of him wrestled with self-incrimination, cursing himself for his greed. Did Kolinsky symbolize the Avenging Angel? Was he about to wreak his version of punishment on the world for treason? Well, re-phrasing the last part. Was judgment time upon Vaughn for his part in the sedition against his homeland? After all, that was what he was guilty of, wasn't it?

Whatever the case, his meeting with Kolinsky would straighten things out, right?

Chapter 111

Avery checked in at Union Station, grabbed his ticket, and boarded a train, readying himself for the long trip to Seattle, where he was expected to make the last leg of the journey in an unmarked government car that would take him over the border to Vancouver. He would have preferred air miles, but that was not the government way. Maybe it was Avery's sardonic joke on himself; either way, he could not care less. He sat back in the comfortable First-class seat staring despondently out of the window, his body moving in tune with the rocking cadence of the 200 miles per hour train galloping through cities, passing towns and bright lights in a blur of flashing objects.

The Three course meal and wine set before Avery did nothing for his modest palate, the attentive waiter hovering outside his carriage door—expectantly waiting for a nod of approval at the succulent meal laid out before him—only added to his irritation of being cooped up in the boxed area for the insufferable journey. Avery could not fathom why he was not being flown in by air. Perhaps the lavish meal was to compensate for the tacky mode of transportation he was being subjected to. He was sent to do a job that was supposed to be urgent, yet he was destined to arrive two days later than he otherwise should have. The only reason he was probably travelling First- class was because economy class was full. The irony was not lost on him.

He hurriedly ate his meal and the floating attendant professionally dispensed with the plate, glass, and untouched wine, carefully closing the carriage door firmly behind him, leaving the unimpressed Avery to focus on cleaning his small array of weapons. He relished the polishing, cleaning, and checking of his arsenal; it made the time speed by and channeled his mind to focus on the job at hand. He replaced his guns after oiling the springs, stopping briefly to examine the final product. Remarkable, he said to himself, he still had the ability to reassemble a gun in ten seconds flat. He hoped his shooting skills were still as good. There was no room for rusty shooting where he was going. "Prepare for the unexpected," his drill sergeant always said. Well, only time would tell whether he was ready or not. With that thought, he put his little toys away and dropped off into a light, troubled sleep.

Three carriages down, unbeknown to Avery, sat a thickset Latvian and a reedy, diminutive looking Chinese who both had similar plans to take out Senator Lee. They were there to tie up loose ends on the instructions of Deroni, as a favor to Kolinsky. Both men were trained in different martial arts: Aikido, Jiu-Jitsu, Krav Maga, and mixed martial arts. They were also proficient marksmen—ruthless mercenaries for hire. Their skills were to be supplemented with the supply of guns and knives that would be provided to them when they got to Vancouver. For the time being, they were two straggly passengers travelling to Montreal with a stopover at Vancouver. Their clothes were casual—loose fitted and tailored to conceal a couple of knives as a precautionary measure. They took turns to sleep, watchful for any unusual activity onboard the train. They kept to themselves, eating the snacks they boarded with, keeping away from the restaurant, and limiting human contact, except for when they took unavoidable toilet breaks and had to travel past the narrow corridor to the toilets. These were men used to anonymity, caution, and inconspicuousness. They did not want to be recognized under any circumstances and intended to keep a low profile for as long as possible.

How wrong could they have been?

Chapter 112

The train came to a stop at Seattle, and Avery alighted from the train and fell in line with the stream of other passengers who had disembarked with him. He kept his valise close to his side while his eyes swept the platform searching for his ride. Moments later, his eyes settled on a man who nodded in his direction, and he then moved briskly towards the waiting car and slid into the front seat.

Silently, Avery made his way to the black Accolade and got in. Engaging the gears, he drove off. The three-hour journey, apparently, was to be done in silence. Looking out of the window, Avery decided to occupy his time with observing and memorizing the different districts they drove through—he never knew if he might ever need to travel this way again, Avery surmised.

A few minutes later, the two quirky travelers carrying their wares got into a 1976 Potomac and were driven the same way. They synchronized their watches and reviewed the files showing the layout of the terrain they were going to cover, photographs of Senator Lee, and the architectural plan of the little cabin. They did not want any nasty surprises, did they? Convinced that they were abreast with the assignment and the hit, they returned the file to a dark-skinned man who was accompanying them for the ride. Both men viewed the third occupant with curiosity and waited expectantly for further instructions, none of which were forthcoming. If they were disappointed, they did not let on, but sat back in comfortable silence watching the taciturn passenger with interest and in anticipation of any sudden unwelcome movements in the confined space.

It stayed that way until they arrived at the rendezvous point.

Chapter 113

The snowy Canadian Rockies towered invitingly, welcoming Avery to the wintry hills of Canada. Hamilton had mobilized Avery to carry out the job of killing Senator Lee. The landscape was scenic, like a photo on a Christmas card. This certainly was not Christmas, and the Christmas spirit of giving was far from his mind. The cold biting air cut through his overcoat and he pulled up the collar, gathering the coat closer to his body, hoping to get out of the bitter chilly breeze that was threatening to paralyze his legs, which were already stiff from the arduous journey. Avery would drive up to the cabin, check the terrain, memorize the layout—grid by grid—catch up on sleep, and exercise his tired body before the strike. The drive would be about forty-five minutes, ample time to set his mind into sniper mode.

Avery disembarked from the Accolade and went in search of the hired car inconspicuously tucked away at the furthest part of the parking lot, away from CCTV vision, passersby, and roving eyes. *An isolated a spot as any*, he thought to himself. It served his purpose just fine. This was not a mission that he wanted to be associated with. He checked out the dark blue Corvette, retrieved the keys from the exhaust, and started up the car. The car purred in ready response, and Avery set off to find Senator Lee's secluded cabin surrounded by foliage and perhaps bland secrets that Avery was about to find. Undeterred and determined, he put the car in drive and steered the Corvette out of the parking lot.

Three hours later, exhausted, resolute, and wired, Avery returned to the parking lot and ditched the car in its designated spot. He needed to get some sleep. Avery would be back by 2.30 a.m. to put his plan in motion. Carrying only a small holdall, he made his way to a small, modestly furnished motel situated within a five-mile radius from the car park. The motel was right on the corner of two

roads and had access to the shopping mall a few doors away—
certainly a hit with the tourists who made a stop-over in the town.

Avery made his way to the front desk, paid for three nights, and
turned in time to see the incongruous men from the train moving
slowly towards the counter. His eyes sparked with sudden interest.
This could not be a coincidence; the lumbering duo resurfacing in
the small town he happened to be in. Were they following him? Or
was there a more sinister twist to the saga that was yet to unfold?
Casually retrieving his holdall, he grabbed his keys and made his
way to the narrow staircase, all the while speculatively watching the
men for any action or reaction. Apart from the initial glare he got
from the stocky European as he passed them by, nothing transpired,
no flash of recollection, but some curiosity or caginess was
apparent. Avery instinctively knew that they were not there for him,
but why were they there? He would to have to keep an eye out for
these guys. They smelled like trouble. The kind of trouble he did not
have time for. Turning his mind back to the task at hand, he let
himself into his room and made best use of the four hours he had to
rendezvous time by dropping off into a light, fitful sleep.

Chapter 114

Simeon Kolinsky sat on a pool chair admiring the sun gently arising from the east. The warm orange glow giving him the boost he needed. Leaning back on his chair, he watched his daughter, Kudirat, applying the finishing touch of sunscreen lotion to her lithe, tanned body. She stretched out like a sleek cat, basking in the early rays of the warm Dominican sun shining down from the cloudless skies.

Deep down, Simeon Kolinsky smiled at his accomplishment. Justice had finally been served. The American President had been disgraced, convicted, and disrobed of all he had held dear. His marriage, reputation, pride, and freedom had also gone up in smoke. How gratifying was that? Revenge was sweet, but had its own price tag. He had lost a few of his loyal stalwarts. The most painful loss was that of his childhood friend, who had taken his place and died for him. That selfless act had given Kolinsky a second chance to live, escape, and be free. It was an opportunity to rebuild his life, a new identity, a new home, and, at last, get a stab at being with his family. His retirement plan was coming to fruition, and all at his retirement home. All the planning and success had boiled down to the brilliant execution and parts played by the key players. His plan had been near perfect. There were always casualties in war, and this was no exception. A twinge of regret pricked his conscience momentarily. There was no point in dwelling on the past. The fatalities were minimal, considering the size of the mission. Kolinsky had sent out eye-watering cheques to the families of his fallen comrades in atonement and in appeasement. They had been fully compensated, and that was the end of the matter. What was important was making sure that nothing went wrong from this point onwards.

Kudirat had a sister she never knew she had. What a surprise. How would she react when they met face to face? There was no way

283

he could have left Medusa behind. The risk was too great. McClaren had found out the true identity of Medusa. It would have been just a matter of time before he would have used that knowledge against Kolinsky, and he could not risk that, could he? Did he say that word again, risk? He was becoming soft in old age, his paternal instincts clearly getting the better of him and pushing his mind into overdrive. It was probably time to facilitate the return of all his children. Summoning his childhood friend, closest confidant, and head of his personal security team, he gave the order to recall his children from the field for an impromptu meeting with the boss, benefactor, and father all rolled into one. It was about time they really knew who they worked for. He could not wait to land this bombshell. It could not have come at a better time. The stunned look on their faces would be priceless.

Chapter 115

Hamilton was not afraid of the consequences if he got caught. He had spun his web delicately, masterfully, fooling even the closest people involved in the case, the biggest one being the leader of the free world. The President would be fuming with rage at this recent discovery. Yes, he was the mastermind, not the incompetent, bungling Aide to the Vice President who had shown his hand so early in the game. Simeon Kolinsky was the puppeteer, the Pied Piper, as it were, but he was the puppet master pulling the strings, the main man behind the screen, intricately unravelling and strategically destabilizing the US government from within its strongholds. Flying below the radar, destructively reaping from the confusion, smearing the present administration with subtle negative media coverage, and using Twitter, Facebook, and Instagram to expose the government for the fraud it was. Ironically, he was destroying a government he was an integral part of. It did not matter; his reward was already waiting for him.

He had to get away, though. It was just a matter of time before he would be brought in for questioning. The President wanted answers, and wanted them yesterday. It wasn't a stretch to think that the President would misconstrue his actions as being politically motivated, a chance at the White House. How far away from the truth could he be? Another spin could be that he was motivated by the Benjamins. All these suppositions could not be further from the truth. For Hamilton, it was all about immeasurable power and the persuasive argument of Kolinsky's representative. His decision was swayed and sealed by the knowledge that Kolinsky was his biological father. Kolinsky, on the other hand, was unaware that Hamilton knew his real identity, suffice to say, the financial remuneration was staggering. The chance to be the next VP of the United States of America was the clinching motivating factor in propelling him to treason. So, apart from greed, power, and riches, did loyalty to an absentee father trump allegiance to his country? The question was, could he technically call himself an American?

It did not matter; his father was ready to unleash a torrent of funds to influence the populace through the media. He was ready to lobby politicians and rig elections in different states to get the desired result, efforts that would culminate in his installation as Vice President. Could you imagine the son of an immigrant rising to such an esteemed position?

Apparently, that was not going to happen any time soon because the intel he received from a reliable source left him feeling cold. The cat was out of the bag. Hamilton knew that failure and the exposure of his part in this act of subversion would not go down well with the American public or his father. It would only lead to his death. The government would concoct a convenient story; a convincing, elaborate, and believable tale that would explain away the reason for his death. An unexpected illness, an accident, in the line of fire during an assignment, a mugging gone wrong, or, the classic example, of a home invasion gone awry. Take your pick. The government was a master at subterfuge. His death would be another statistic filed away in the minds of Americans—unverified, not investigated or corroborated, simply a distant memory.

A sense of self-preservation galvanized him into action. He needed a getaway plan. A suicide attempt could be verified. No, he had to be mysterious, obliterating any trail that would leave traces that he was alive. He had to die, with compelling evidence persuading the public, government, and anyone willing to look into that fact that he was actually very dead. How interesting it would be to plan his death by creating a plausible, believable demise. The idea would take a masterstroke of creativity to pull off, and he knew the man for the job. Pulling out his disposable prepaid cell phone, he made the call.

The voice on the other side listened for a minute as Hamilton told him what needed to be done and disconnected the line. All Hamilton needed to do now was to let things fall into place.

Chapter 116

Hamilton had been quick after he made the call. He had to get out of his motel room immediately. He only had time to grab the few possessions he could carry, along with his passport and money from the safe. He did not want to be left high and dry. He really did not expect Kolinsky to shoulder all the expenses. Well, that was a lie. He was going first-class on a private jet for a start. Having his own money was wise in case he had to get away from Kolinsky. He knew that it would not be easy, but what else could he do? He was now formally a fugitive. It was now up to Jenkins to complete the assignment. However, he needed to kill Senator Lee and bury the true extent of his involvement. VP Vaughan also needed to be killed. Avery would carry out the executions.

Arrangements had been made to get a double who would drive his car and incidentally have a fatal accident. The DNA and dental records had already been doctored. There would be no doubt as to who died in the car. Money could buy you a lot of things, including someone willing to die in your place for the right price and buy you time to escape. But that left one thing undone. It was something he could not overlook. He had to sever all ties to his past if he was going to have a chance at a future. Before he left, he had one more stop to make. Regrettably, it would be a tragically painful break up that would leave him remorseful. He had no choice. He could not take his girlfriend Jenny with him; it would compromise his safety. In situations like these, you had to look out for number one. Besides, he did not need the extra baggage. His father would not approve of it, too. Knowing Jenny had brought with it a bag of exclusive fringe benefits, benefits that had apparently now reached their expiry date.

Jenny was the President's Personal Aide, as well as Hamilton's lover and confidant. She was under the illusion that he was in love with her, which worked in his favor. Her infatuation made her

287

pliable. She was susceptible to giving him tidbits of valuable information that he had used to find out Kolinsky's whereabouts when he was in captivity. Logistics for the deployment of Kolinsky's transportation was another crumb made available to him. She had definitely proven to be an important piece of the extraction process, and for that he would be eternally gratefully; but that was as far as he was willing to go. Ironically, though, he did have feelings for her, but not as a future Mrs. Hamilton.

Hamilton certainly had commitment issues that he did not want to dwell on. Maybe by virtue of the type of job he held or the realization that loving someone that deeply would derail him from his ulterior motive of achieving his burning ambition. He needed to keep his heart under lock and key, for the moment. Overthrowing, the existent president and becoming a potential heir to the Kolinsky empire was foremost on his mind, and there was no room for distraction. What a price to pay for wealth? he sighed to himself.

He barely had time to get to Jenny's apartment and get to the airstrip. He knew he was cutting it fine, but this was a task he was not willing to assign to anybody else. It was, after all, his final goodbye; he had to make it count. He wanted to look into her beautiful green eyes one more time before she died. Instructing the driver on the fastest way to get to her apartment, he prepared his mind for what he had to do.

Chapter 117

The President sat back in his chair in the Oval Office, a file lay open with papers scattered all over his desk to where he had flung the file in anger. He sputtered, barely trying to rein his temper while his red, mottled face revealed his disbelief and shock. He grabbed the report once more, gripping the sheet tightly as he read the words a second time. No, it could not be happening. What had the secret service been doing? Now his personal aide was also dead. He knew that she was having an affair with Hamilton, but what other information had Hamilton got out of her?

Perplexed, he wondered when Hamilton had sold him out. Hamilton had been privy to all the meetings and actions he had taken during his tenure in office—not only on the Blue County incident or the Kolinsky debacle, but also the report on the blown-up laboratory. With trembling fingers, the President lifted the half-filled glass of Johnny Walker, its ice cubes clinking loudly in his glass, and slurped down the contents in one deft move. He stared absentmindedly at his Special Adviser, daring him to speak. The rivalry between Pearson and Hamilton was an open secret in the White House. He could not bear to see the smug look Pearson was struggling to suppress. His eyes clearly saying, I told you so.

Sanctioning another kill was inevitable. He did not want the news of Hamilton's treachery to be heard. The whiff would destroy what was left of his crumbling administration. The Kolinsky scandal had already created irreparable damage. His approval rating had plummeted from 80% to a precarious 45%. The back benchers were already murmuring about an early election. He supposed Pearson would be in favor of that, too. But first, the distasteful matter of disposing off Hamilton had to be dealt with pronto. Giving the authorization, Pearson gleefully left the Oval Office, excited and eager to carry out the President's instructions to the letter.

Meanwhile, a pensive, distraught, President sat in his presidential seat despondent, apprehensive of what it all meant. Would his secret finally be revealed? The bitter taste of the Johnny Walker and Jack Daniels whiskey running down his throat was doing nothing to quell the uneasy, nauseous feeling stirring in the pit of his stomach. His political career was on the brink of extinction, if he did not nip this matter in the bud.

Hamilton knew too much about him, especially about the prostitute he had killed in that mousey hotel during his gubernatorial election campaign. Hamilton had brought the girl, after all. What happened was a mistake, just another one of his indiscretions. Otherwise, why would he compensate Hamilton so handsomely? Hamilton was paid to keep his mouth shut. The Catherine Baxter incident never saw the light of day, because Hamilton made it so. He had been discreet, handling all the minor details. Now, President Kinnock wondered if Hamilton had disposed of her or paid her off. The matter was never discussed, he guessed, for good measure. But what if old coals were raked over again? President Kinnock knew that he would lose credibility. He had committed murder and raped an intern during his election campaign. Who would want a murderer or rapist as the face of their government?

What he had done was despicable; President Kinnock was not denying that fact. When you had money and power, things tend to swing your way. The problem was, for how long? Who could he confide in? Would it be better to resign? Who would he leave the country to? The Vice President was out of the equation, and Kinnock did not trust the next in line. What to do was the question? Taking another drag on his cigar, Kinnock sat back to formulate a plan that could help him possibly salvage what was left of his political career. After all, the American people would not want their President to go to jail, no matter how hideous his crime might have been. But it was an issue of moral dilemma. What exactly was the right thing to do?

Sullenly, Kinnock sat in his presidential chair as dusk cast a deep glow over the room, heralding the dark shadows of night time, chagrined at the thought that the alternative was far worse than he could possibly imagine.

Chapter 118

Hamilton had walked along the corridor of power for years, obscure, unappreciated, and without power. The discovery of his birth father had changed everything; creating a burning desire to break away from the conundrum he called life. The hunger to meet and acquire part of this remarkable man's dynasty burned fervently within, compelling him to discreetly research Kolinsky. He came away impressed with Kolinsky's achievements and substantial wealth. He wanted a piece of it. It was his birth right, right? It was, after all, his God given right.

He always wondered why Kolinsky never married. Perhaps the saying that 'a rolling stone gathered no moss' was appropriate in this case. It would have been a big deterrent to the man; perhaps it would be instrumental to his capture. His illusiveness was only rivalled by the fictitious character Jason Bourne's from the Bourne Trilogy. The more he read about his father, the more his admiration for the tycoon grew. Kolinsky was a cautious, clever man, devoid of any routine or conceivable pattern. He had a yacht, planes, cars, and a submarine at his disposal. This was a man who could not be found unless he wanted to be found. That was why Kolinsky's arrest bothered and intrigued him. Kolinsky was a legend, a man of great resources—very spontaneous and extremely unpredictable. Efforts to penetrate and corrupt his empire had been met with fierce resistance and countless bouts of failure. It seemed that his people were incorruptible or taken out of the equation before Interpol or the US government got their claws into them. That was why when Kolinsky's representative made contact with him, Hamilton welcomed it. It was a chance to play with the big boys and finally have the opportunity to make a connection with the icon that was his biological father.

Common sense overrode Hamilton's zeal for power. He had to remind himself that even though Kolinsky was his father, he was a man to be feared. He unscrupulously disposed of competitors and people who threatened to betray him. He had sanctioned more than 200 deaths, if the information in his secret dossier was anything to go by. Kolinsky kept a close rein on his affairs, especially those pertaining to his personal security. Nobody knew his itinerary. There was never any conceivable timetable that was followed. That was probably what kept Kolinsky alive. Being one step ahead of the different enforcement agencies had put him in good stead, until now.

Well, that being said, it was time for Hamilton to meet the man. What better way to travel than in his father's private jet? Could it get any better? He was about to find out.

Chapter 119

Medusa's real name was Samantha Perkins. But it seemed such a long time ago since anybody had called her by that name. She had evolved into so many people over the last ten years, that she had lost track of who she really was. She enjoyed the roles, the thrill, and the excitement at not being caught. Maybe she was a born killer, and the killing instinct was imbedded in the genes. Well, she could not figure that out because she did not know who her father was. Her mother had died when she was five, and her Aunt Bess took care of her until she was old enough to leave home and fend for herself.

Reflecting on her past stirred good and bad memories, some of which she wanted to forget forever. Eradicating the catalyst of her transformation was something her subconscious mind was not willing to do. It had changed her, metamorphosing her into the dispassionate predator she had become. Her survival skills had been sharpened by the missions and the precarious circumstances she had been subjected to. She became the real-life Catwoman. She loved what she did. What other job could boast such an unpredictability factor? She enjoyed the feeling of power to wield death over a human life, the chase, adrenalin, imagination, and creativity that she took to every assignment. What could ever replace the financial rewards and travel benefits that came with the job? There was never a dull day, unless you included the waiting time taken to survey the prey before it was killed. The satisfaction in the kill and compensation made up for the lull.

From the coded e-mail she received, it seemed that things were about to change. She had got orders to meet with her employer face to face. This was an unusual request. But, safe to say, she had come out of temporary retirement to play a fundamental part in his extraction from the United States of America. She had already been adequately remunerated. Her bank balance had shot up a few zeros, a full $2 million healthier. What else could a girl ask for?

The plane journey was less than three hours away, but she was not ecstatic about making the trip. The only problem was that no one turned down an invite from the boss. She wanted to make a good impression, but would have to approach this meeting with caution. Instinctively, she knew that if he wanted her dead, she would have been swimming with the fishes by now. That was why she could not understand what the meeting was about. Her assignments had always been delivered to her mail drop under the pseudonym Martha Fielding's and never face to face. Yes, it was highly unusual; nonetheless, there was no point in dithering. It was about time she found out what the boss wanted. Grabbing her overnight case, she made her way to the private airport where one of Kolinsky's Cessna planes was idling, ready to transfer its precious cargo to the dispatcher.

Chapter 120

Kolinsky looked at his reflection in the mirror and he felt good. He had exacted his judgment on Barrymore, brought confusion within the corridors of power, weakened American domination, and tied up the ends of his fractured life. The puppet master was writing the last scene in the theatrical production that had complemented his fiendish purpose. Kolinsky had committed a large amount of his wealth to this project, and the projected return was nothing in comparison to the actual realization of his investments. Wall Street was tizzy from the blow, as stock prices took a nose dive, tumbling like the 2008 fiasco when the global markets crashed into oblivion. The Japanese, British, and Chinese Stock Exchanges responding convulsively, like a patient with an epileptic fit, forcing the stock prices up while the world tried to cope with the incredulous knock-on effect the crash had generated. All he had to do was buy up as much gold and diamonds as he could manage earlier and then sell them off at a ludicrous price. It was totally worth it. His net worth spiraled from $3 billion to a staggering $17.8 billion in under a year. It had always been about the money; vengeance was just an added bonus. What better time than now to sit back and enjoy his wealth and kids.

His four children were well cared and trained in their respective roles. No expense was spared in their education, training, and life experiences. A fulfilling life accompanied by opulence, opportunity, and danger. As a precaution, he had them enrolled in a variety of survival courses appropriate to their circumstances, without being overly obvious. This was designed to prepare them for their recruitment into his organization. It was certainly interesting reading their impressive dossiers, reading of their exploits and the exemplary skills they had each exhibited on different assignments. Their achievements left him feeling like a proud father. That was, if he allowed such a mundane sentiment to penetrate the formidable wall surrounding his heart. His major achievement, so far, was carefully planning their lives behind the scenes up to this point, in a bid that these factors would culminate and coincide with his master plan.

The pieces were falling into place, and the grand finale was in sight. His heart pounded loudly in his chest and a euphoric sensation seized him, a rush of anticipation swelling within him. Where was the fun in building an empire and leaving it to strangers? Retirement was on the cards for him, but perhaps one last game would not hurt. He had to know who was worthy of handling and owning a large conglomerate of companies he had acquired through blood, sweat, the proceeds of crime, and the impeccable power of negotiations, otherwise known as hostile takeovers.

An ethereal sense of accomplishment washed over him, suppressing the nagging, disquieting vibe taking hold in the pit of his stomach, forcibly banishing the previous notion to the darkest recesses of his brain. Any unforeseen circumstance could destabilize the grand design he had worked so hard towards. That was why he had tried to keep one step ahead, but he was getting tired of looking over his shoulder all the time. He was aware that all it would take to bring his world crashing down was just one unpredictable factor. All it needed to unravel and destroy his financial kingdom was one loose thread.

Watching his children through the video feed linked to his office, he fought down the uneasy thought: what if his children were more perverse than their father? Viewing up front their individual mannerisms, he struggled to suppress the sharp pangs of uncertainty stirring conflicting emotions within his subconscious. Was he really ready to surrender his business to these strangers tied to him by blood only? Was retirement really on the cards for him?

Whatever he was thinking had to be put on hold. Hamilton was due to arrive at any moment now. Focusing solely on the task at hand, putting on his inscrutable mask, he left his fortified office to complete the final introductions with the hope that the meeting of the siblings would not turn out cataclysmic. Five trained assassins, four of which were assembled in one room, could be dangerous; linked to him not only by employment, but by blood too. His last son had not been invited in case things went downhill. How would they react to that piece of information? Well, he was about to find out.

Chapter 121

The Gulfstream plane landed softly onto the tarmac and taxied to a stop. The flight attendant appeared by the door and opened it with a radiant smile plastered all over her face. The pretty blonde's blue eyes twinkled invitingly, and her body movements insinuated the desire to know him more. At another time and in another place, he might have been interested, but not today. He was here to meet Kolinsky, his biological father. He took in a full view of the smooth, milky skin of the diminutive blonde, her robust bosom, and curvaceous features and breathed an inaudible sigh of approval. Regrettably, he would not be plucking this cherry tonight. He had other more important and pressing matters to contend with instead.

For years, he had tried to uncover who his father was. His mother was an academician, devoted to her career and married to her work. Well, that was what he remembered about her. He'd been told he was born from her romantic tryst with some lover boy who had sired him. Years later, he felt that she had kept him in the dark to protect him. His chance encounter convinced him that his mother had done the right thing. But that did not stop him from ruminating on what he could have been if his father was a regular Joe.

His eyes caught sight of a well-dressed chauffeur holding his name boldly written on an A4 sheet, and sauntered towards him. The driver relieved Hamilton of his bags and placed them into the open trunk of the smoking hot Rolls Royce, then opened the back door for Hamilton to get in. Within minutes, they had arrived at the massive villa where Kolinsky and his guests were eagerly waiting to meet him. The villa was set apart—sited on the outskirts of town—with an orchard of trees obscuring full view of the palatial backdrop of the estate; it was encased behind steel-clad corrugated gates and complemented with four guard checkpoints situated at the cardinal points of the property. Hamilton surmised that there were motion sensors, booby traps, and extensive CCTV coverage completing the security measures in place.

There was no one to open the gates; they swung open of their accord, letting them through the entrance way and up the three-mile driveway to the house. The opulent setting was breath-taking, and Hamilton paused fleetingly to admire the view, before being lead into the magnificent building. The stairwell was adorned with a marble frame. In the center of the foyer, an impressive diamond-studded chandelier dangled and glistened provocatively, while delicate porcelain vases set on expensive pedestals lined each side of the corridor, highlighting the trendy paintings that gave credence to the room's lavish furnishings.

Hamilton was shown into the pool area, where there were four other people, relaxing on pool chairs, and a man he instinctively knew was Kolinsky were waiting. Pushing his apprehension aside, he walked directly towards the silver-haired fox whose captivating eyes held him mesmerized. Kolinsky, in-turn, looked expectantly at the four other people with a smile on his face and made his mind-blowing announcement in a voice filled with pride, "I would like you all to meet your brother, David Hamilton, Special Adviser to the President of the United States of America, the final beneficiary of my estate," to the shock and amazement of the others.

Chapter 122

Ralph and Matthew had made good time in crossing the Canadian border. With winter setting in, border control was a little slack, perhaps because it was Christmas week and everybody seemed happy and eager to get out of the cold to celebrate the Christmas holidays. The checks had been perfunctory, which suited Ralph and Matthew just fine.

Most of the hotels were already pre-booked and full, but by a stroke of luck, they were able to find a quaint little room in one of the boarding houses they were directed to. Worn out from the journey, they stole a couple of bites of a lush Canadian special sandwich from a diner and settled down for the night. Tomorrow was going to be a big day for both of them.

The noise of human traffic woke them early the next morning. Leaving the boarding house with the map Deroni's men had provided them, and armed with their guns tucked under their winter coats, they set off to find their sister's killer. They wanted to do a reconnaissance of the area. They would rather be late to execute the deed than become the late. Discarding their dressing boots, they changed to steel-studded boots that were more practical in the present circumstances and locked the car, out of sight, under a thicket of trees. The light blanket of snow lay undisturbed as they followed the trail drawn on the map, stopping about 300 yards away from the cabin.

An inviting wisp of smoke snaked its way out of the mini chimney, where they imagined an unsuspecting Senator Lee was nestled close to a burning hearth, unaware of their arrival and the price he was about to pay. Mapping out areas and articulating their plan of attack, they retreated under the cloak of darkness. Meanwhile, Senator Lee observed the two men from his bunkered quarters through the motion sensor cameras, wondering who the heck these men were who had proceeded to case the area with as much professionalism as new recruits on the first day of boot camp.

These men were not government operatives and did not look like trained assassins. No, these two were a different breed that he would have to contend with at some point. Intrigued, yet baffled by the new set of players, he continued to prepare against the oncoming assault with renewed vigor, focusing on surviving the attack that was going to be launched at him. Somberly wondering who and what was coming next, he did his best to steady his nerves.

Chapter 123

Ralph and Matthew sneaked out of the boarding house in the middle of the night, using the back entrance. The street was empty and the still, cold winter night was punctuated by a wailing dog seeking solace from the wafting cold breeze settling down on the sleeping community.

They made their way to the black sedan they had hired earlier that was stashed near the central park, wedged between five other cars that seemed to have been parked there for a while. Slipping into the car, Matthew started up the engine and left it idling for a few minutes while they went over the ground plan. Satisfied, Matthew set the gear in motion, convinced that Anne Marie's death was finally going to be avenged.

Parking the car at the spot they had parked in during the day, they did not bother covering the car, in case they needed to make a speedy escape. One never knew in such situations, planning for a quick get-away was always in order. The area was remote and the chances of other cars driving by were slim, close to impossible, but there was no need to take chances, even if Senator Lee did choose a secluded place to be his burial ground. Removing the safety catch off their Remington rifles, they prowled the area searching for any incursions. Nothing triggered their sense for extra caution, so moving furtively under the shadow of darkness in the direction of the cabin, they headed for its backhouse. The lights were out and the cabin looked desolate, undefended, and vulnerable to attack, but they were not fooled. They were expecting some level of resistance; Senator Lee would not live out in the sticks without at least some sort of protection. They did not see any protective detail earlier, so he was definitely alone. Maybe he had some sophisticated gadgets to scare off uninvited visitors, they wondered.

They were nearly at the back door without incident, when Ralph tripped on a pool of thawing ice which inadvertently, changed the course of his life. A bullet accidently discharged from the chamber of his Remington gun, innocuously piercing the still, dark night. Within seconds, a retaliating bullet echoed in the dark, hitting Matthew dead center of his forehead. With a stiff hand encased around his Remington rifle, Matthew crumpled to the ground, eyes wide open, dead before his body reached the slushy forest floor. Ralph stayed down, realizing that he was a sitting duck without any backup, totally unprepared and unskilled to return fire at an undetected target that was certainly out of his firing range. Shifting his body weight and scouring the direction from where the last bullet came from, he calculated his next move. Thinking quickly, he moved to the side as a fusillade of incoming bullets rained down on him.

Finding cover behind the side wall of the cabin, he tried to assess the damage to his person. A bullet had hit him in the shoulder and a splash of blood spurted from under his shirt. Disconcertedly, he placed a hand on the injury, trying to stem the flow of the blood and find the entry point of the bullet. He heard a sudden rustle of feet from behind and turned as quickly as his reflexes could respond bringing him face to face with an Asian man who had appeared as if out of thin air. His cold, beady eyes revealed a smoldering intensity Ralph had never seen before. They betrayed his intent to kill him. In one swift, deft move, before he could react, he was professionally disarmed and incapacitated.

Surreptitiously, moving in tandem, the two passengers from the train, Ludis and Dao, breached the back door and made their way into the cabin, warily listening for sounds that indicated impending danger. In seconds, their eyes acclimatized to the dark interior and they entered the warm enclosure. The bungalow was dissonantly quiet, not even the presence of a miniature grandfather's clock disturbed the tranquil setting. A sudden sixth sense of premonition gripped the killers. Something was off. The two men simultaneously felt that they had somehow been compromised and were sitting ducks. The indistinct sound of a safety catch being released from a gun spurred them into action. Both men instinctively dived down as the first volley of bullets bounced around the small room. In rapid succession, both men offloaded their chamber of bullets and retreated behind the sofa while they reloaded their guns, waiting to pinpoint which direction the firing was coming from. With a nod, Ludis moved away from the couch, trying to draw fire, whilst Dao focused on pinning the shooter. Instead, they heard the sound of running steps retreating to somewhere at the back of the cabin, followed by the loud clanging of a door being closed. The movement propelled them to their feet. Guardedly, they ran in pursuit of the runner, determined to catch the shooter and finish the job they were sent to do.

Bursting through the rest of the practically furnished lodgings, they came up short at the front of the cabin and sneakily peered out of the window in search of the escapee. Footsteps in the snow showed the footprints of size 10 shoes freshly imprinted on the ground, but there was nobody outside.

Warily retreating further into the cabin, using fingers to indicate to each other their next line of action, they moved back towards the front of the log cabin, raking the perimeter as they went. In less than two hours, it would be daylight, and they would be more vulnerable to attack. They had to use the last snippets of darkness to get away, after they killed Senator Lee of course. But where the hell was he hiding? Putting on a pair of heat-vision binoculars to his eyes, Dao spanned the area for potential hot spots. The art of subterfuge lay in surprising the prey. Dao did not like the fact that Senator Lee had been waiting for them, removing the advantage and that he had to take out two people as well.

Suddenly, Dao was hit by an explosion; the air knocked out of him as he lay sprawled out on the wooden floor. Ludis struggled to re-orient himself. The impact of the blast had thrown him against the bookshelf, dislodging it from its setting and landed on top of him. Groggily, he pushed a section of the bookshelf away and wriggled out from underneath, careful not to fall into the massive opening in the floor that lay like a giant abyss waiting to engulf him. With his body lying close to the ground, on hands and knees he shuffled over to Dao's body and checked for vital signs. Dao was alive, but a patch of blood was pooling around the middle of his jacket and his breathing was coming out in ragged gasps. Ludis skillfully lifted up the top part of the jacket and assessed the damage. First, he needed to find his gun and then get Dao some medical help. A few meters away, Dao's AK lay within easy reach. Crawling over by sliding onto his stomach, he retrieved the gun, checked the chamber, and checked the area.

A plume of smoke had considerably reduced visibility inside the cabin, which worked both ways. The smoke temporarily acted as a shield for them, but it was also forcing them out because of the fumes as the fire spread within the brittle wooden structure. They had to get out quickly. What was waiting outside the entrance of the cabin was anybody's guess. Carrying Dao's body would impede his escape, but leaving him there was not an option, even though it was very likely that Dao could possibly die from his injuries. It was a no brainer; Dao had already done the same for him once. Gagging briefly from the rising smoke, Ludis lugged Dao to the far north wall and propped him up using the lower part of the window to shield his partner's body, then resumed his check for possible routes of escape.

There only seemed to be one logical path, but it would leave them vulnerable as they approached the car. But there was no other choice. Balancing Dao in such a way that would enable him to fire off some shots, he emerged from the cabin, carefully surveying the terrain as he went. So far so good, the coast seemed clear. Sweat clung to his clothes as he lumbered with Dao down the slope towards where they parked their car. The car was in his sights; he was nearly there. Ludis was so focused on reaching the car in one piece, that he did not hear the incoming soft whoosh of the bullet from a high-powered rifle penetrating his frontal lobe. His body dropped, dragging Dao down with him. The semi-conscious Dao lay there, helpless, sprawled out on the cold mountain floor, unaware that his partner laid just a few feet away, dead. The shooter released a second shot that nicked Dao's aorta and a fresh spurt of blood appeared on the thawing snow. Dao succumbed to death in seconds.

Chapter 124

Senator Lee had not envisaged that there would be two sets of operatives sent to kill him. The first pair was easy picking. What were they thinking approaching the house like that? Even more worrying was the thought that whoever had sent these men would be waiting for confirmation of his death, and when that did not happen, would probably send another batch of killers. He was sure that the President would dispatch another set of men quickly from his arsenal of homicidal maniacs already at his disposal, men who did not ask questions. Either way, he was in terrible danger. The cabin had been compromised; he had to move on to his second pad. He did not know how long his anonymity would last, but at least it would buy him time to figure out what to do next.

Regrettably, he had to erase the cabin. Blowing it up had taken him a lot of willpower. It was the last link to his past life. Memories of the last Christmas with his wife and child lay buried among the embers of the razed cabin. The cabin had also served to flush out the burly man and his associate. Now that it was done, all he needed to do was pack up before the local sheriff and fire brigade turned up.

Packing up his expensive surveillance equipment and military tool box, he loaded the rest of his stash, money, driving licenses, passports, and safe deposit keys and headed over to where he had discreetly concealed his Range Rover in plain sight. He went over the place with a fine-tooth comb, expunging anything that would lead back to him, and set a timer in the bunker to go off in t+10 minutes. Enough time for him to get clean away.

Shutting the door with a sense of finality, Senator Lee walked around to driver's side of the Range Rover, but never made it. From nowhere, Avery stepped out from his hiding place and plunged a camping knife into his sternum. A look of incredulity marked Lee's face as he half turned to face his attacker. Where had this fifth assassin come from? He held on to his assailant and fumbled weakly to withdraw his Sig Sauer pistol from his pocket. He was not going down without a fight. Although, he felt his life ebbing out of him, he fought like a wounded lion, trapping the pain in the darkest recess of his brain as he clung on to life. He wanted to live. He was not prepared to die. Not just yet.

Avery was stronger, younger, and nimbler on his feet, but Senator Lee's indescribable will to live was overwhelming. Forcibly brushing away the Sig Sauer from the Senator Lee's hand, he levelled two powerful blows to the Senator's head. Slightly dazed, Senator Lee let go of his attacker, struggling to clear his head. Blood flowed out of his wound, but he did not care. He was determined to hold on to life with as much desperation as possible, as if he was losing the most precious thing he owned. He had to defend himself. Side stepping Senator Lee's right jab, Avery returned a forceful whack to Senator Lee's stomach. Lee's hands flew to his midriff as the air was sucked out of his lungs. Doubling over, he tried to avert the incoming punch aimed at his head. Stumbling back, he made contact with a jagged rock that he curled up in his hand and compelled his body to adjust to the grueling punishment it was being subjected to. Summoning the strength Lee needed to strike back; he clutched the rock and made contact. He was rewarded with an involuntary grunt as the rock hit its mark.

The rumble of sirens pierced the air, mobilizing Avery into action. The sheriff and fire brigade were closing in. He had barely more than a minute to disappear, or be arrested for the killings. In a split second, he unstrapped his Colt pistol and fired. The bullet struck Senator Lee right in the middle of his forehead, rendering him impotent.

Avery turned him over to confirm that Lee was dead. A set of blue, vacuous, still eyes stared back at him. Feeling Senator Lee's pulse to reaffirm that he was dead; Avery slunk away before the wailing sirens came to a hasty stop.

Chapter 125

The only palatable news he had heard all week was the death of Senator Lee. Hamilton had completed the task. He had dispensed with the details. All that mattered was that Lee was dead, and that his secrets died with him. But killing Lee posed another problem. Could he trust Hamilton to keep silent even with his betrayal? Or would there be another skeleton rattling in his wardrobe of sins? The President was now in a quandary over what to do with Hamilton. Who could he trust? This was a dilemma that he was not willing to face just yet. The extradition of Kolinsky to the USA was the beginning of doom for his presidency. The catastrophic lapse in security and subsequent incompetence made him shudder within. How had the FBI taken over the investigation when it should have been Homeland Security's jurisdiction? Would Homeland Security have done a better job if they had the first stab at protecting the citizenry?

These disturbing questions added to his agitated state. He could not comprehend what went wrong. What had happened to inter-agency participation? A lot of things were not adding up, and he felt a numb sensation spread all over him. Cleaning up the colossal mess that had rocked his government weighed heavily on him. The hope of recapturing Kolinsky was a pipe dream, but he would discreetly find those who would be willing to do the deed at the right price and off the books.

Meanwhile, there was a crisis evolving on the Syrian front, and he had to focus his attention on averting an international unrest that could only lead to a humanitarian disaster. Straightening himself to his full 6 ft. 4 height, he made his way to the crisis room where the rest of his personnel were anxiously waiting for the President of the USA to make an appearance.

Chapter 126

Life as the President of the USA had its perks, but there were other mundane tasks that came with the job that were ethical dilemmas, tasks that would leave any sane man in an ocean of moral quagmire. This President had engaged in a list of unsavory activities that had ensured the safety of the American people, but had left him morally derelict. The sleepless nights, worry of discovery, and the unabated guilt affected him deeply. Spidery lines marked the smooth chiseled face, etching its visible story of pain, anguish, and uncertainty under his passive demeanor.

He was holding on, but barely functioning under an illusion of calm. Nothing could prepare one for the job's pressure and difficult decisions, bartering one's conscience for the safety of others. It was the right thing to do; the only way out. There were always going to be sacrifices, no matter how painful or costly it might be. There was no other way. If threatening the Syrian President with a potential strike would grab international attention but force him to the negotiating table, then so be it. Chemical warfare was abhorrent, and the killing of women and children intolerable. It simply had to stop; any reprieve was welcome. He also had other pressing national matters to contend with that needed his undivided attention.

The peace talks and interjection of Russia's representative would speed up the process. Glad that he had finally made headway, tired and distracted, the President left the crisis room longing for a hot bath and some sleep. God knew he needed it. A lone figure stood by the door, conspicuously trying to get the President's attention. Two agents from the President's security detail moved in to block the bleary-eyed man, but the President dismissively signaled for his men to stop. Curiously, he walked up to the man and stared at him, searching for an answer in the tense, pensive stance of the agent whom he recognized by sight. McClaren had had his stint of publicity, and had appeared in *Time* magazine for his courageous thwarting of a terrorist attack on the previous Vice President in 2004. Another cold finger of fear crawled up and down his spine, instinctively telling him that something was drastically wrong.

McClaren was not known for social visits, although his political connections were deep-seated within his government. Strangely enough, the level of face-to-face interactions were strictly limited to Level 1 threats and were meant only for his ears only; which made McClaren's visit all the more ominous for him. Today, of all days, and without forewarning was disarming. A bitter acidic taste ran along his throat and he did well to contain himself, walking slowly while trying to gather his thoughts. It would not leave a good impression on the others seated in the room if he appeared unnerved by McClaren's intrusion into state matters. *What was one more crisis to deal with?* he thought as he walked with feigned dignity on the lush red carpet.

With a resigned sigh, dismissing his earlier thought of a shower and nap, he summoned McClaren into his office and asked the two secret agents to wait outside, knowing that the meeting would hold unpalatable connotations. The fewer that heard what McClaren had to say, the better. Seated behind his desk, the president listened as the agent gave an in-depth analysis of the security blunders; Kolinsky's escape; Senator Lee's role in the murder of Anne Marie Cummings; and the capture of one of Kolinsky's stalwarts and a possible location of the absconded fugitive.

A wave of relief flooded the President's heart, realizing that although McClaren had stumbled on vital information that would further damage his government's credibility and political ratings, he had discreetly decided to share this knowledge with him first. It didn't matter. McClaren was unaware of his complicit role in the whole saga. Probably even more damaging than that of the other players put together, but his involvement would not be revealed just yet. Judgment day seemed to be looming ever closer. Pondering over what McClaren had told him, he asked who else knew about the plot and killings. Apart from his partner, nobody else knew, but McClaren had no intention of putting his partner and friend of six years in jeopardy. He eyeballed the President, looking directly into his eyes as he glibly lied, stating that only the President knew the full story.

The answer seemed to please the President who swore McClaren to secrecy and called in his aide. Briefly introducing McClaren to Pearson, who was part of an elite squad, President Kinnock officially assigned McClaren to the squad tasked with the capture and extraction of Kolinsky from Barbados. He did not want to know the details, all he wanted was the results.

It was out of his hands. He had provided the logistics and had every intention of distancing himself enough to create a shroud of deniability, in case anything went wrong. He did not want to be associated with another botched attempt at bringing Kolinsky to justice. Now, it was down to Pearson and McClaren to invade Barbados, but it was Pearson's singular mission to eliminate Kolinsky. There was no way the President could risk Kolinsky being transported back to the United States to stand trial. It would be a waste of tax payers' dollars and it would open a can of worms that the CIA had fervently suppressed so far. Which American would like to hear that Kolinsky's vengeance on America was because of the CIA's failure to protect Dr. Kolinsky and his family; knowing that Dr. Kolinsky had been an active agent for the US? He had been turned into spy against his homeland, and was promised protection for him and his family. The abandonment of an American spy on Russian soil was unheard of. Coupled with the untold hardship and suffering the family had endured under the KGB, it was no wonder why Kolinsky's attack on the US was in order. The only downside was that Kolinsky had decided to wreak his vengeance on the American public during his tenure.

He hoped that McClaren's intel was right. He needed to exorcize one more demon from his cubbyhole of sins. Although, within the recesses of his mind, he knew that he would never be rid of the nagging voice of conscience or would ever truly know peace again. No one could ever completely recover from that level of turpitude, no matter how stone-hearted that person was.

Chapter 127

McClaren fully appreciated the fact that this undercover operation could not go wrong. The margin of failure had to be less than 1%. Pearson was a slimy bastard, and McClaren discerned that although their missions were interlocked, Pearson had another agenda. The directive handed down to him straight from the President left McClaren on edge. He only hoped that he would not be among the expendables after the killing expedition.

Pearson was a classic example of a pathological killer. His eyes bore an unnatural glint that associated him with other psychopaths in the annals of FBI history. It was totally inconceivable that there was such a being hiding in plain sight; as high security clearance is normally restricted to the privileged few. Or was it just McClaren's training kicking in as an adept profiler? It also made him wonder what other secrets the good President was hiding. Either way, he had to be attentive to Pearson's mood and actions if he was going to survive the excursion.

They were set to fly out at 0000 hours with a small team of trained men recruited from different agencies. The poor suckers were not fully read into the operation. McClaren guessed that it was strictly on a need-to-know basis anyway. The men were merely sacrificial lambs being led to the slaughter. But that was not the point. Nobody wanted to fail twice apprehending the same suspect. His impeccable record at apprehending criminals and executing justice had been shot out of the water with the court debacle. He needed to repair the chinks in his armor and salvage his career. A clear road to redemption was what he needed, and this was it. He had another chance at capturing the most notorious criminal who was wanted all over the world. His itch for Kolinsky had risen to the top of his list. It was like a rash that had to be scratched, with or without Pearson. This brought him back to the same perplexing question that had been taunting him since the beginning of his new partnership: could he trust Pearson when it came down to it?

That was highly unlikely. A clanging warning bell ricocheted ceaselessly in his brain, reminding him of why he became an FBI agent in the first place. Discarding the rambling thoughts inundating his mind, he focused on ways to protect himself from Pearson's tricks and any plans that he might have in store for him. There was no comeback from calculated mistakes that could prove fatal. The only thing he could do was avoid becoming a target or standing in Pearson's crosshairs. In war, it was just as easy to be killed by friendly fire as it was by enemy attack. Nonetheless, he had every intention of becoming the victor and not the victim in this scenario, regardless of how honorable or dishonorable Pearson's aspirations might seem to be.

McClaren made a crucial call to his partner, specifically requesting certain items that would be invaluable to his survival. His shopping list was to be delivered to his confidant, the new Under Secretary of Defense. Meanwhile, he would take a nap, run a few miles, and report to the rendezvous point in eight hours' time, refreshed and prepared in every way possible.

Chapter 128

The introduction had gone remarkably well, Kolinsky thought. He felt lightheaded with joy, glowing in fatherly pride. His special treat was seeing their shocked faces when they opened the envelopes they were given at the end of the meeting. Each child had been given a token check of $ 1.7 billion, the funds of which had already been credited to their respective accounts. His will took care of the other beneficiaries of his estate. There simply was no room for probate or letter of administration from where he came from.

The different governments would happily pounce on the funds left, which were in excess of $6.8 billion. The monies remained undisbursed in four proxy accounts, after being carefully siphoned through 16 different banks that acted as tax havens, around the world. Now that the family reunion was over, it was time for the children to move on with their lives. They were a potential threat to each other and in greater danger by staying with him.

Tomorrow morning, he would send each of them on their respective ways. Perhaps this would be the last time he would ever see them. He was determined to make an impressionable leaving party in their honor before they left, emphasizing the importance of being a child of the great Simeon Kolinsky. Nostalgically, he remembered his childhood friend, one who had taken his place and had died for him. That was something he knew his children would never do for him. He had trained them well. They were as ruthless and sharp minded as he was when he was their age. They also possessed incredible reflexes, beauty, and wealth beyond their wildest dreams. It should make up for all the fatherly love they had lost along the way. Kolinsky was certainly not making excuses. Love was a feeling he rarely lingered on.

He had no allegiance to any country, family, or lover. He had severed any sentimental attachment that could compromise his continued existence. With both parents, his sister, and closest friend dead, there was little to ponder over. His brother was in the wind. His children were merely strangers sharing the last shards of family camaraderie that he cared to indulge in. Why spoil the moment? Today was all about sending the children off. Summoning his chef, he outlined what he had in mind for the evening banquet, and retired to his quarters. Tomorrow was pregnant with promise, uncertainty, and finality. Nothing had changed, because that was how he had always lived.

A part of him cherished the fleeting opportunity that fate had given him to spend with his children. Tomorrow would define not just his children's lives, but his as well. He had decided that he would never come back to this place again. It was time to set down roots in a place he had always wanted to live in, free from the shackles and encumbering shadows of his past. That was, after he had taken care of a few minor details. Sitting down in front of his iMac, he started to erase the last breadcrumbs of a life he once knew.

Yes, it was time for new beginnings.

Chapter 129

Miles away, the small array of commandos enlisted for the task of capturing Kolinsky were seated, combat ready, in the military cargo plane, briefed, and eager to execute their mission. Their resolute faces said it all. They looked fully alert, adrenaline coursing through their young veins. It reminded him of one of his missions to Vietnam to extract POW's. He wondered if he had known then what he knew now, would he have willingly signed up for the extraction. Anyway, it was too late to rake over old coals. He needed to focus. They would be at rendezvous point in less than five hours, and his survival and the success of this operation depended on the professionalism of these men. Building a rapport was essential. There was nobody from the Bureau with similar training or demeanor to watch out for him here. Not that he was degrading the training techniques of the other agencies.

Pearson watched from a distance, clad in dark military camouflages, totally looking the part of a serial killer on the loose, content enough to listen to the banter without interjecting. While he watched McClaren intently through dark, smoldering eyes and whet his military knife until it gleaned and sparkled as if it were brand new. The other commandos knew that the quiet giant was ex-SEAL and had an impressive military record with medals acquired for exemplary service to his nation. The gossip had it that he did not tolerate failure, and was specifically assigned to head this taskforce because he got results, no matter how unethical his methods were. If that was not enough, his aloofness, detachment, and supercilious behavior left little to the imagination. This was a man in a dark place where nobody onboard was willing to go to. Everybody steered clear of him for the remainder of the journey, sharing nervous glances amongst themselves at the uncanny, standoffish manner of their newly assigned commander.

Four and half hours later, a red light flashed intensely, indicating that they were in the drop zone. Tightening their parachutes and assembling their gear, they made their way to the door and waited. Moments later, Pearson opened the door, and it was time to fly. The next thirty minutes was the most crucial time, it spelt the beginning or failure of their military maneuver. Synchronizing his watch, McClaren made the jump.

Chapter 130

While the evening meal was a complete actualization of Kolinsky's vision of what he wanted the last supper with his children to be, the unexpected arrival of the eight man command team that had landed on the beach without incident and on time would create an unexpected twist to the night entertainment. Rolling up their parachutes and hiding them from sight, they met their point man, who transported them to the RVP in his beat-up truck and drove away under the guise of night. Perusing the schematics of Kolinsky's estate to ensure that the blueprints matched with what they were given at camp, they stealthily made their way through dense thickets to a safe distance outside Kolinsky's property.

Blending in with the shadows of darkness with their dark fatigues, they crawled on their stomach to within 100 yards of the high-towered gates that shielded Kolinsky's residence from public scrutiny. The three outpost guards were relaxed, so distracted by their conversation and the quietness surrounding them that they did not bother to keep an eye on the CCTV in front of them. Two of the guards were jesting heartily in their native tongue while the third was taking a leak, a cigarette dangling precariously from his fat lower lip. He puffed vigorously on the cigarette and zipped up his trousers. Backing away from the wall where he had urinated, the smoke trail from his cigarette clearly visible in the warm, night skies revealed his exact position, thereby making him the first and easiest target of all. Positioning his gun, the sniper took him out with the silencer and he dropped like a stone.

Within seconds, the mirthful couple was on their feet, they cut off their bantering conversation, instantly sensing that something was wrong, but unable to determine what was happening in this quiet fortress. Kolinsky's residence was prided as being exclusively enforced with the most expensive security equipment money could buy—in consequence, an impregnable bastion. Both sentinels, swallowing hard, contemplated how a breach into their safe haven was possible and the repercussions if the intruders were allowed to get past the gates and spurred into action. The second guard called out to the third guard, Jacques, who did not respond. Swinging his gun from off his shoulders in one fluid motion, he released the safety catch and peered through the sniper binoculars he was equipped with, poised for the impending assault. He was not going down without a fight. He had already seen first-hand what Kolinsky did to those who failed. The first guard, on the other hand, was a new recruit and fumbled with the controls on the CCTV, frantically looking for clues. His hands visibly shaking as he realized that the cushy job was turning into his judgement day, his own private hell. Panicking and undecided on what to do, an incoming bullet zinged by, hitting him squarely in the chest, and he folded like a set of cards, dead before he hit the floor.

In response, the other sentry fired a round of shots, but was cut down by another sniper. An incredulous look marked his features as he looked down at the jagging hole in his midriff where blood was gushing out of the orifice like water cascading down a waterfall. His arm seemed heavy, unable to lift the rifle to take aim, all he could do was wait, his gaze focused on one of the approaching commandos who was moving in for the kill, he was vulnerable, powerless to resist, and ready to face the inevitable.

The soldiers were pleased that the front gate had been penetrated with little resistance, but proceeding to the house and replicating the same offence there was another matter. They knew that the incursion of the main house would be a major challenge. The house was fully armored with titanium plates and secured by a small army of mercenaries recruited from all over the world. They were seriously outnumbered, but the elite squad had some fancy toys that they were going to unleash on the poor suckers, starting with the special chemical package they would use to infiltrate the front gate. Laying charges at the lower part of the gate and retreating a few feet, they set off the explosives, ripping the impenetrable gate wide open—littering its pieces all over the place in an undistinguishable pile of corrugated iron—indirectly announcing their arrival.

Chapter 131

Kolinsky's eyes fluttered open, and with the agility of a panther he slunk off the bed onto the floor, his trained ears listening for any immediate threat within the confines of his room, before moving towards his closet. In seconds, he was dressed all in black and armed with his custom-made UZI pistol and a Beretta PX4. Grabbing a security box key and a set of passports, he slipped through his secret partition, firmly closing the door behind him. He had to get to his children. His legacy would not go down with him, come what may. Weaving his way through the maze of tunnels—sweating and anxious for their safety, but assured of their individual competencies—he made his way to the new extension, hoping that he would be able to get to them in time.

In the annex, his children Kudirat, Hamilton, and Medusa had also heard the blast and had gathered together in Kudirat's room trying to figure a way out. This was no mission where they knew the target, exits, or the other dynamics in the game. They were totally blindsided, and this was new to them. Undeterred by their apparent inadequacies, equipped with the guns they came with, they prepared for the onslaught. A soldier was always battle ready. You were not a trained assassin with a prolific history of success if you did not think fast or improvise. Their consolation lay in the fact that they were all formidable killers with no compunction to kill. Knowing Kolinsky, they also knew that he would not leave them there to die. They were his progenies and future lifelines, unless he was injured or dead, and that was something they were not willing to contemplate.

True to word, Hamilton peered out of the window and saw three of Kolinsky's bodyguards moving towards them, acting as a human shield, barricading them from a frontal attack. *How endearing*, he thought to himself. Kolinsky's men were loyal to the end, no matter the cost. He pondered for a second on who Kolinsky really was if his men were prepared to die to protect his children without any regard of their own lives. He concluded that he must have a special effect on them.

They were a fair distance away from their father's quarters, but they could hear the reign of bullets loudly in the night air. It was a matter of minutes before the battle got to their front door. There had to be another way out. Medusa was already scrutinizing the walls, feeling for a false door. Kolinsky was a man who valued his security highly. Each room had to have an escape route. She started searching methodically for any inconsistencies in the wall, feeling for panels along the smooth surfaces under the paintings hanging on the walls while Hamilton and Kudirat stood poised to shoot, covering the door and window from possible invasion.

The stridency of sounds grew louder and louder as the attack drew closer. Sweat lined their faces as they stood their ground, calmly waiting in the cool interior of the luxuriant surroundings they were trapped in. Suddenly, they were rewarded with the impact of a bullet slamming into one of the bodyguards, hurtling him from his position straight into the bedroom door—the momentum of the crash deafeningly loud on contact. Instinctively, Hamilton killed the lights and crouched down in a shooter's stance. From across the room, Medusa whispered, "Come on. I've found it." Pressing her fingers on the corner of the frame of a replica painting of Rembrandt's *The Night Watch*, a door sprung open. Kudirat ran through the door while Hamilton held up the rear until he was certain that the girls were safe, and then he made a dash for the opening. Seconds later, the thud of a grenade ripped the door off its hinges.

Needing no further motivation, they ran along the tunnel, moving as fast as they could within the narrow passage, listening for footsteps behind them. At the juncture of the second pathway, they stopped to determine which route to take. Quickly agreeing to take the first turning, they filed through, and were suddenly confronted by a shadow just out of their peripheral vision and shooting range. Kudirat, who was in front, lifted her gun to fire, when they heard their father's voice saying, "Hurry, follow me," in a controlled, concise, and urgent tone. Like they had suspected, Kolinsky had come back to enact the great escape.

Chapter 132

McClaren and Pearson had expertly disposed of the human barricade blocking the entrance to the room where the three dedicated defenders had so valiantly protected Kolinsky's guests, whoever they were. The men had been neatly dispatched to the afterlife, but Pearson, venting out his frustration, gave the last man a sharp kick in the head, clearly exhibiting his displeasure at the amount of time wasted by their obstruction. McClaren observing Pearson's irritation ignored him. He side stepped the body and did a sweep of the room; doing a swift reconnoiter of the enclosure to fathom the identity of the elusive occupants, forcefully compelling his analytical and investigative nature to take over. Within minutes, he found a round of spent casings from a Taurus pistol and bagged them. Seething, Pearson stomped around the room looking for tell-tale signs of how they escaped. A wine glass smudged with lipstick and a tie on the dresser gave the illusion of a tryst interrupted by their arrival.

Turning his attention to the walls, McClaren expeditiously inspected both sides of the room; his quick assessment led him straight to Rembrandt's *The Night Watch*. Fiddling around for about a minute, the secret side door swung open, revealing a stairwell leading down into a well-lit tunnel. McClaren squeezed through the opening and tore through the tunnel searching for the escapees. Pearson was trailing closely behind. Arresting the guests could provide valuable clues to wherever Kolinsky was hiding. Besides, information from Kolinsky's associates could potentially lead back to the main man. The breadcrumbs were a start; the only issue now was determining which tunnel they had fled through. The complex multiple routes snaking out of the maze produced another dilemma. He did not have the manpower to search each channel, nor did he have the luxury of time. Speaking into his headpiece, McClaren urgently gave instructions to cover the exit routes outlined in the blueprint of Kolinsky's estate, what else could he do? If there were other outlets, then the two men would be in great peril. Returning his attention to catching the elusive fugitives, McClaren let his gut instinct lead him as he looked for obvious clues like clothes snagged or footprints in the disused corridors.

The immaculately maintained passageway they had taken led out to an open courtyard that bordered on a massive garden, perfectly manicured with Cattleya skinneri, Poinsettias, Cabeza grande, and Lycaste skinneri var alba in full bloom, showing off a beautiful display of vibrant arrays of colors. Viewing the tantalizing scenery for a brief second, they resumed their search of the layout. Speaking rapidly into his microphone and making radio contact with the third commando posted close to the hangar that housed Kolinsky's Challenger 604, McClaren re-confirmed that there was no sign of Kolinsky. Fervently, they continued to scour the west side of the palatial estate, aware that the longer it took to find Kolinsky; the chance of actually apprehending him would become slimmer.

The war-ravaged building exhibited the dead bodies that were littered everywhere as they passed by. The lifeless carcasses, felled like trees, were spread out like broken dolls from a toy set. It looked like a macabre scene for some ghoulish mural. Observing from a short distance amidst the shrubbery, Hamilton, Kolinsky, Medusa, and Kudirat waited for the unsuspecting pair to pass within shooting distance before unleashing their joint fire power. The two men dressed in fatigues were clearly visible in the first rays of morning. Hamilton and Medusa killed them instantly.

Moments later, Pearson and McClaren surfaced from the tunnel to see two of the elite team lying dead in the courtyard. The incursion had taken longer than expected. Both agents were more determined than ever to capture Kolinsky and his followers. They had not come this far to meet failure. Kolinsky was accompanying them back to the States, dead or alive. Either way, it did not matter. It had to be mission accomplished, full and final stop. That is, if they had anything to say about it.

Chapter 133

The four surviving commandoes fanned out in a military formation, moving stealthily through the garden using the pillars and garden chairs as lines of obstruction from enemy fire—knowing that Kolinsky was both rich and powerful enough to buy sophisticated ammunition that could easily puncture their Kevlar vests and protective armor.

Hamilton laid low, crouched in a shooting stance, poised and ready for the attack. His sniper's scope trained on any movement within his perimeter. A boost of adrenalin ran through his body as he focused on a necessary kill. His sisters were interspersed in the shrubs near him, providing him with additional cover and back up. A luxury he rarely had in the field, and, for a moment, he felt a warm glow of pride and reassurance swell within him.

His father, on the other hand, held a modified Beretta Px4 with a look of sheer determination, listening attentively to the frontal assault of the commandoes as they furtively searched for their prey. He had a few surprises up his sleeve that could prove useful in their dire situation. All it needed to work was for the attackers to breach the terrazzo patio area where a small case of C4 was embedded underneath. To the north of that were automatic guns imbedded in the walls in strategic positions that were just a remote control switch away from activation. Yes, quite a surprise.

They could bring it on, he thought to himself. Either way, their assailants were heavily outgunned; only wit and luck could save them now. Pearson and McClaren held the back flank while the two fellow combatants edged forward to the patio area in a sweeping motion. Sighting through his sniper lens that the men were close to the mapped -out space, Hamilton parted the shrubbery and signaled to his father to trigger the explosives. In seconds, a thunderous explosion ripped through the courtyard, totally wiping out the two young men, obliterating them into oblivion. Debris rained down everywhere, and a light veil of smoke settled over the garden. The force of the detonation threw Pearson and McClaren high and wide, stunning them momentarily. They sat up afflicted with minor cuts and bruises and quickly assessed their positioning. Thankfully, there had been enough distance between them and the explosion for them to escape relatively unscathed.

The swift, fluid movements up ahead indicated that Kolinsky and his crew were on the move. Jumping up, the surviving men gave chase, fixated on catching them before Kolinsky's crew made off in any mode of transport Kolinsky had secretly stashed away for such a situation. Both men, recharged by the possibility of imminent failure and the regret of the death of so many worthy men—fully aware that their window of opportunity for catching Kolinsky was precariously closing—threw caution to the wind, breaking cover. They had to stop Kolinsky, whatever the cost.

Chapter 134

Ripples from the explosion had littered rubble everywhere. An incoming fragment hit Kudirat in the face and a streak of blood ran down her face, into her eye, and down the front of her shirt. She was a survivor. Briskly cleaning the blood with her shirt, she made the run with her family, the escape from Sobibór playing vividly in her mind. The sound of a plane rumbling up ahead; beckoning them invitingly to liberty spurred her on. Nothing was going to stop them from eluding these government assassins sent to wipe them out, or worse, capture them. There was no way they would surrender, ever. Proudly, she watched her sister, father, and brother zigzag in a retreat formation, each aware that their lives depended on luck and the ability and agility of the others to protect them from the imminent danger moving in from behind. She could hear the shallow breathing of her father as he nursed his injured leg, blood flowing freely as he ran, his face resolute with purpose, clearly defining his will to live. The determination and drive encouraging her to go on, despite the throbbing pain threatening to blind her and derail her from her current objective, which was merely to survive. She faltered, and for second, was spellbound in an interlude of giddiness as her body swayed out of tune, her legs ominously intent on buckling before she got to the plane.

Hamilton looked back to see Kudirat frozen in her steps, a distressed stare plastered on her face. Coming fast and furious behind them were the two men in military fatigue with their long-range rifle in front, struggling to make the few yards that would put them within firing range to cut down their targets. Kolinsky and Medusa were well within the area of safety and both of them were climbing the steps to the plane. He had no choice but to go back for Kudirat. Gauging the distance before he was target practice, he raced towards Kudirat, darting from one side to the other till he reached her. Gripping her firmly under her armpit, he impelled his sister into action. Her legs moving in automation, eyes slightly unfocused as blood dripped down her face and blouse. There was no time to focus on the extent of her injuries; he dragged her, shouting out to Medusa for backup. His gun clattered to the ground as he made the short run with his sister in tow.

Moments later, he heard the zing of a bullet as it whizzed past his head and hit the lower part of the plane. Medusa fired a magazine of bullets before stepping out of the way for Kudirat and Hamilton to board while Kolinsky yelled out instructions to the pilot. In seconds, the luxury plane was in motion. The passengers hoping that it would not be shot down before its ascent into the sky and freedom.

Chapter 135

Kolinsky looked down from his Challenger 604 to catch a final glimpse of the dwindling figure of his nemesis: McClaren. He was just a speck amidst the fallen heroes scattered along the Barbados shoreline. His shape receding into nothingness as the plane ascended to the right altitude. Kolinsky took a deep breath, acknowledging silently that he had come too close to death this time. He might not be so lucky next time.

Dismissing the morose thoughts that were threatening to engulf him, he turned his attention to his other passengers, paternal relief flooding his chest as he observed his children, pleased that they were thankfully unscathed, unflustered, and united by the will to stay alive. Kudirat had been hit, but the wounds did not look life threatening. In any case, he was sure that Kudirat was strong enough to withstand the pain until they docked in Algiers, where another of his planes was waiting in a private airfield to transfer them to an exclusive hospital that would render the necessary medical help they sought. His momentary respite was shattered by a dull ache slowly spreading up his leg, seeking to distract him, demanding immediate attention.

Taking a deep breath, he took a look at his left leg that was pulsating in pain, blood trickling down his pants and pooling at the bottom of his seat, serving as another reminder that he had just escaped free entry to the gates of hell. After all, where else do you think his body would be accepted?

Today, he had been lucky. It was another shot at freedom. He had been given another lifeline, a chance to start over, maybe with his children, or maybe not. Either way, it was never too late to start afresh. What he did know was that 'He who fights and runs away lives to fight another day'. For now, he would focus on receiving the best medical care and convalesce and rebuild his life somewhere else.

His vengeance would not be complete until he brought the Unites States of America to its knees and exacted his fury on Agent McClaren and President Kinnock. The fight was not over, not by a long shot. No, in fact, this was just the beginning.

If you enjoyed the first instalment, why not try out *The Phoenix Rises*.

Just turn over the page

The Phoenix Rises

A piercing scream echoed loudly in the dark-filled room as she scampered to flee the executioner. Her lover had been shot multiple times in the chest as she watched helplessly. Instinct and a surge of self-preservation pushing her brain into overdrive as she ran blindly, searching for an escape route, not waiting to find out if the man she had been with was dead. Tearing about in the large house looking for an escape route, she ran blindly through the west wing of the house, frantic, confused, and fully aware that death was knocking on her door. This angel of damnation personified in the sadistic masked man who was in hot pursuit of her. His regulated breathing and running footsteps told her that he was close behind. Panicking, she ran into the kitchen aisle, her breaths coming out in quick ragged burst as she tried to maneuver her way around the worktop. Colliding with the kitchen island brought a quick twinge of pain that ran through her, but before she could react to the throbbing in her leg, the air was knocked out of her as two large hands gripped her throat.

Thrashing about, her flaying hands reached out in desperation for anything that could prove to be a welcoming weapon. The killer was mounting increasing pressure on her gullet, and his intention was clear. He was about to crush her esophagus, ceasing the air flow to her brain. Why did he not finish her off with the gun? she wondered as her hands caught on to a kitchen knife and she jabbed the sharp cleaving knife into her assailant, imbedding it into his upper arm, which went slack for a moment in reaction to the sharp pain that must have hit him. But like a true professional, he grunted and tightened his hold until her body went limp. He checked her pulse to make sure that the spark of life was truly gone before he stemmed the blood flowing from his arm.

Meticulously, he scrubbed the entire floor, erasing any blood trace of his visit to the Smith mansion. He did not want to make it easier for the police to catch him. In his line of work, there certainly was no room for error if you wanted to retain your reputation or get future clientele. He then quickly set about cleaning down everything he might have touched, before leaving silently into the night.

Printed in Great Britain
by Amazon

71769567R00182